Secrets of The Sun

Reveal Mystery of Death

Secrets of The Sun

Reveal Mystery of Death

Book 2 of the Kopaz Series

Dale Groutage

Copyright Material

Dedicated to the Travelers of Life

To my lovely wife, Nancy, and my three exceptional children, Phil,
DaleAnn, and Lane—thank you for your love and support.
We travel our worldly journeys together.
To my Desert Pirate friend, Robbie—thanks! Our adventures in a coal
camp in the 1950s made us who we are today.
We travel on—our journeys are not yet complete.
Two very special people—who gave me life and sent me on the road to
search for hope—are no longer with us. They sit on their lofty thrones
above and smile—their earthly journeys are complete. My father, Fred,
spent twenty-five years in a coal mine. He taught me to never give up.
My mother, Katharine, made our little abode in the desert and our
lives in the ever-present shadow of a bleak existence just a little piece of
heaven.
For all of us who travel on, our journey not yet complete,
there is an old Navy saying:

Fair winds and following seas!

Table of Contents

CHAPTER 1

The Daily Headline

Torrents of water dumped from the sky as thickening black clouds swirled over Danny's head. Stopping briefly, he used his hand to wipe away the water on the window of the newspaper dispenser. He read the headline: "Crazy Man Kills Miner's Widow." It gripped his soul with anger. Not having a quarter to drop in the slot to release the lock, his fist pounded on the metal top as he stared at the picture of LeRoy, grinning as if cackling at the readers who were searching for an answer to a single question: Why? Stepping back, he raised his clenched fists and looked to the heavens as rivers of tears streamed down his face, mixing with the downpour. And to the rhythm of the falling rain pounding on the nearby street, he screamed, *"You bastard!"*

On the far side of the road, Jeannie LoneTree sat helpless in the front seat of Danny's '55 Chevy pickup, watching him deal with a pain in his heart that was ripping his soul from its foundation. She knew exactly what was going through his mind as she thought about the headline he was reading. *Danny, the authorities said that he has fled the state. I know you want to kill him, but he's gone, and I don't think he'll be back. The police have already raided his filthy house and found nothing.*

For some reason, it never crossed Jeannie's mind that the police report never mentioned a palace.

Although she grasped the harsh sadness that Danny was walking a lonesome highway of pain, she would be by his side no matter where the unknown road of destiny took them. Following his movements caused her mind to search for answers. *Oh, my wonderful Danny, I'll never leave you, and soon, my love, we'll find the pathway to happiness, far away from the miseries of this dreadful coal camp.*

Now soaking wet from the pounding rain, Danny stepped back, turned his head, and looked at Jeannie waiting across the street for him. His heart told him his actions were affecting the one who cared the most for him. He lifted a hand and shouted, "This won't take long, Jeannie. I'm only going to stay for a minute…just long enough to pick up something that Pastor Duncan has for me."

But the raging deluge of muddy water ripping a new bed in Bitter Creek could not distract Danny as he walked along its banks, his old shoes slopping through puddles of brown water. His mind was consumed with thoughts of revenge.

The early spring squalls drifting across White Mountain were busy causing the flash flooding that was descending on Granite Springs. The wave of destruction had already claimed many victims who had challenged Mother Nature by building in the flood plain. The price they paid was far and above the gain they thought they had achieved by building cheap housing in the low-lying areas.

Although the town's volunteers were out in force, filling sandbags and building dykes to stem the flooding that still threatened homes, Danny had another agenda. His consciousness was centered on the act of finding and destroying the deranged crazy man who had taken his mother's life.

Aware of Danny's hatred, his newfound friend, Pastor Duncan, waited in the small house behind the old community church. It was not more than two hundred feet from the roaring gully washer that was eating away at the vertical banks of the town's only streambed.

Catching the movement of the young man in Levi's and a white T-shirt, Pastor Duncan waved as he hollered out his back door, "Hurry, Danny! The rain is picking up, and you are soaked!"

Clever and observant, Duncan waited for Danny to reach his house. His mind reflected on the hatred he'd seen in the young teenager over the past several weeks. *It was not more than three weeks ago that Danny's canker of hate was vented in my direction. Now it's Crazy LeRoy who is in the spotlight of Danny's venom. How nice…he no longer hates me! It must have been the money I gave Darla and Danny the week before she died. I'll just keep it up!*

Danny lengthened his stride and was at the back door in seconds.

Motioning for Danny to step inside, Pastor Duncan said, "Boy, the heavens opened up today. It's more than just a sprinkle from the good Lord—it's a cloudburst! Sit over here, Danny." Duncan motioned with his hand to an old couch that was covered by a threadbare blanket.

Not sure what the pastor wanted, Danny remained silent, waiting to see why he had been asked to drop by.

"I've got a pot of coffee brewing. Danny, would you like a cup?" asked the preacher as he walked through the living room door into the kitchen.

He had no intention of lingering and was quick with his answer. "No, I'm fine."

It was only a moment before Pastor Duncan reemerged. He not only had a cup of coffee in one hand but also an envelope in the other. "This will only take a minute," he said, looking out the window. "I see that Jeannie is waiting in your truck."

There was a long thirty seconds of silence. Danny looked at the window and thought, *What was that comment about?* Then quickly, Danny blurted out, "She didn't want to get wet. You know girls and their hair."

"Oh, I see," responded the pastor. "Well, that's OK. It's you I want to talk to."

Pastor Duncan took a seat next to Danny. He placed the envelope and his cup on the coffee table.

The brilliant flash of light that streaked across the rain-spattered window, followed by the loud crack of thunder—*kaboom*—as the cloudburst intensified, lit up not only the room but also the pastor's face.

The pastor's ringless fingers curved over the knobby piece of flesh where his ear should be. Danny wondered why he was covering his facial defect. Trying not to stare, Danny asked, "Are you OK?"

Quickly, the preacher dropped his hand and grabbed the envelope that was on the coffee table. He turned to face Danny, who was sitting next to him. "I really don't have much, Danny, but your situation is much more desperate than mine." Danny thought he detected a tear rolling down Pastor Duncan's cheek. He waited, and the preacher continued. "So I decided to give you five hundred dollars," he said, stretching out his arm with the money. "It is not church money, but my own."

Breathing deeply, Danny clutched the gift. "This is very special to me. You know, Pastor Duncan, I've had to leave my house. The old CPC, our lovely guardians, the CoalVille Progressive Company, wasted no time. They've moved another family in."

Duncan watched Danny choke up and broke into the conversation. "I know that, Danny. That's why I personally decided to step in and help out again, even though it will set me back financially." He stopped briefly, searching Danny's face for a reaction, and then continued. "I know you have moved in with the Lopez family, Tony and his mother, Rose. They're wonderful people and—"

Danny cut the preacher off. Fiddling with the envelope in his fingers, feeling Duncan's stare, Danny stiffened and struggled to put on a serious look. Uneasily, he thought, *God, I hope Duncan didn't put himself in a financial bind*, as he said in an effort to change subjects, "It's fortunate that the Lopez house has three bedrooms, so we each have our own. I was concerned that I might have to sleep on a rollaway in the living room, but that is not the case." The grandfather clock filled the dimly lit room with an eerie ticktock, ticktock. Even though his new residence was more than he could ever ask for, it was not home. His face serious, he managed to hold back a tear that was threatening to come.

At that moment, the clock signaled the five o'clock hour with a loud *bong bong bong bong bong*.

In a hushed voice, Danny said, "I think I had better go. I don't want to drive to CoalVille in the rain after dark."

He had no sooner finished his comment than Pastor Duncan stood up, patted Danny on his back, and said, "You're a good son, and your parents are on their lofty thrones smiling down on you. Say hi to Jeannie." The blast of rain dampened the floor as the preacher stood holding the door open. He held out his other hand to shake Danny's and said, "Keep safe!"

Watching Danny race across the street in the monsoon-like rain, Jeannie's heart pounded. Her cutoffs had left her growing cold, and she was happy to see him. He flung the truck door open and said, "Let's get out of here. I hate this miserable weather. I…I…wa…wa…"

Her keen awareness of the struggles Danny was facing was foremost on her mind. "Danny, what's the problem? What happened in there?" Jeannie's thoughts were running wild, and his expression of pain sent up red flags.

Danny had also come to realize that his emotions had a profound effect on her and tried to convey clearly what was troubling him. "Oh, Jeannie. I'm sad. God, I miss my mom and dad. Why? Why? Why me? And then this awful weather. What's next for us?"

Scooting close to him as he put the truck in gear and started their journey to CoalVille, she sweetly said, "Danny, I'm your bridge over troubled waters. We'll get through this."

"Yeah, Jeannie, we will. I couldn't do it without you." He turned quickly, gave her a smile, and added, "I've been out of school for a week, and our big basketball game is tomorrow night. I'm going to be there for my school and teammates."

Jeannie gazed up at his face as he held the steering wheel tightly with his left hand. Navigating through potholes filled with water, Danny had to concentrate on the treacherous road ahead. His eyes focused on bright flashes from the headlights dancing on the wet pavement.

His truck's windshield wipers flopped back and forth, smearing the torrential downpour as Danny and Jeannie made their way home on the old highway between Granite Springs and CoalVille.

He moved his free hand from his lap, found her cold bare leg, and touched it softly. "But most of all, Jeannie," he stammered, a lump gathering in his throat, "you're my priceless treasure. And yes, you are my bridge over troubled waters!"

CHAPTER 2

Zanzee Comforts
and Pirates Play

Early Friday morning, Jeannie lay on top of her bed with only a skimpy nightshirt on. She had a lot on her mind. Locking eyes with hers, Zanzee snuggled next to her and purred loudly. He used his paw to pat her hand. She responded to him by playing with his right ear—rubbing it gently between her fingers.

She was excited about the upcoming basketball game her friends would be playing that evening. She was excited about Danny. She wondered about their future and where it would take them. A new chapter in her life with Danny was starting. She thought of raising a family with him— little green-eyed boys and blue-eyed girls. That got her thinking about her blue-eyed cat.

She was also excited about the role her cat was playing. *Zanzee is fulfilling the role my mother said he would—he's navigating the way for me, the Chosen One, to redeem Kashom's honor. I don't know how it will end, but for sure, we are on an adventure.* She looked at him and was grateful he was so unconditionally committed to protecting her. She talked to Zanzee as if he were a person.

"You are special, Zanzee—you once lived with royalty in Egypt. I've always known your main purpose—to comfort me in times of sadness and protect me from the dark side. Oh, Zanzee, I just love you!"

Her slender white fingers stroked his soft black fur. Never doubting his powers and what a true friend he was to her, she picked him up and nuzzled him with her face.

"Zanzee, Danny, Tony, and I could be very close to where Kashom is leading us—three times you have guided us when we were stymied. Yes, Zanzee, you're special! You are navigating the path for Kashom to return to Kopaz with honor!"

His eyes followed her hands, and he gently wrapped his paws around her fingers. His claws extended and softly touched her soft white skin. He was careful not to alarm her in any way.

"Zanzee, Danny is very special to me. We have always been good friends, but now our relationship is way beyond just being friends—I'm falling in love with him. What do you think of that?"

He stopped his playful fondling of her fingers with his paws and said, "Meow! Meow!"

"That's a good kitty. Thank you, Zanzee!" Almost ready to get up, she remembered the most important question she had for him. "Tonight, Danny will need help from both of us. That bad man, Crazy LeRoy, made him an orphan. He's been really sad, so I will be his cheerleader. You be a good kitty and use your powers to help Danny win the game tonight! Will you help him?"

Without hesitation, he said, "Meoooow! Meoooooow!"

She giggled and patted him tenderly. "Good kitty!"

It was not just Jeannie who had a lot on her mind. The line of light streaking across the dark kitchen floor in the Lopez house came through Danny's bedroom door. He was up before the sun and rustling around, going over the notes that Coach Bollas had given him on basketball plays.

Tapping his pencil on the set of notes charged his mind with the thought of winning. Electrified by the very real possibility of his team becoming the state champs, his skin rippled with goose bumps. He was bound by the driving spirit that propelled him to give every ounce of effort and move one game closer to reach that goal.

His thumping around caused Rose to stir and waken, but that was not a concern to her. She reached and flicked the nightstand light on. *I had better get up and make Tony and Danny breakfast. They have a big day and will need my support.*

The sun now peeked over the horizon, and the line of light that had come through Danny's bedroom door had faded. As Rose entered the kitchen, she was greeted by the pink rays of the sun shimmering on the plaster of the old walls. Danny was already in the bathroom, running cold water into the sink to wash his face, knowing it would not turn hot with no fire blazing in the water-jacket stove.

Brushing his teeth, he listened contentedly to the bustling in the other room as Tony's mother prepared breakfast. And for the first time in what seemed like an eternity, the young man in the old oval mirror stared back at him, a smile emerging around the handle of the brush. Despite the cracks in the mirror's silver backing, his reflection offered him an expression of confidence, brushing his teeth along with Danny.

He rested his foot on the toilet seat to tie his shoelace, and the old, worn-out leather he was touching seemed so distant from the images of treasure racing around in his mind. Caught between poverty and riches, Danny could only dream once more, knowing the paramount danger of letting their secret of treasure escape.

In a small coal camp of less than one hundred and fifty people, there aren't many secrets. This week, however, Danny was less concerned about protecting his secret. Something else was dominating his mind, as well as the minds of all the townsfolk. On basketball night, the focus was the game, and the force was the community spirit.

The bustling stopped. Tony's mother called out, "Danny, are you finished in the bathroom? Tony has been up for a while and is ready for breakfast."

"Be right there, Mrs. Lopez...just finishing getting dressed."

Sitting with him at the breakfast table, Rose sensed his anxiety. His eyes reflected the early morning sunlight bouncing off the orange-juice glass in front of him. He took one last drink, stood, and looked for his school bag. Looking fondly at his new mom, he reached across the table and grabbed it from the back of the chair next to her. She touched his arm and gave him a wink. "You boys will be the school's heroes tonight," she said, reaching for his hand to give him her support. "But most of all," she added while reaching to touch Tony's hand, "I have two sons now! And I love you both the same!"

The three of them shared a quiet moment. Then Tony stood, turned, and motioned for Danny to follow.

"We won't be home after school, so I'll see you at the game" were Tony's parting words to his mom as he and Danny dashed out of the back door and flew down the steps four at a time. Rose's cheerleading sendoff had buoyed their spirits.

Tony lived a quarter mile from the CoalVille high school and made the trek from his house to the school every weekday. Even though this was game day, today's walk to school was no different from any other.

The same events that take place on most game days were about to take place one more time at the Calhoun house. As Danny and Tony were walking down Main Street, Mrs. Calhoun parted her window blind and peered at the handsome, tall, blond boy walking up the street next to his best buddy. *That Danny Roberts is always getting a break. My son Eddie should be the one playing on the varsity team. I don't understand why the school officials let that gangly boy play varsity basketball. Eddie should be on the varsity team and not just the junior varsity flunkies. I just don't know why Coach Bollas made an exception for Darla's boy. My boy is better than hers.*

Poking Tony in the side, Danny said, "Watch this. I'm going to have some fun with old lady Calhoun!"

Tony chuckled and just nodded his head.

Her eyes watched them though the crack in the blinds. Danny and Tony intentionally walked with a stride they knew would push her buttons. Danny was sure of himself. He kicked a rock on the road with his next step. It flew through the air like a football. It bounced ahead of him—up the slight incline he was treading. With his head looking straight ahead, he tracked her actions out the corner of his eyes. His mind was on target. *Those curtains will swing shut as she pulls her long nose out from between them.* He was getting ready. Right on time, Danny flipped his head and looked right at the front window of the Calhoun house. He lifted his hand and waved. *Sure enough! There go the curtains swinging back and forth—the old witch nose lady just pulled her face from the gap in the curtains. Her bitching to Coach Bollas will not make her son a better player. She will just never get it through her thick skull that Eddie is a horrible basketball player. Coach Bollas wants CoalVille to be state champions this year. Besides, I'm six foot three, and he's a five-foot-six-inch runt!*

"Danny," said Tony, "you got the old lady pulling her Gretchen-witch nose back through the curtains so fast it reminded me a sewing-machine needle flying through a piece of cloth!"

Danny laughed. However, Danny's main concern was not old lady Calhoun but winning. He had his work cut out. *The game this evening against the Superior Grizzlies will be a tough one. They have a tall center and quick guards. I'll be glad when this school day is over and I can suit up.*

They walked through the school door and immediately heard the hubbub of excitement—laughter, loud talking, and footsteps walking down the halls. Danny's mind raced. *The entire school is sky high in anticipation of tonight's game.*

The school day seemed as if it would drag on forever, but finally, the last class of the day finished.

"See you tonight at the game," Danny said to Jeannie as they walked out of American History class. "Tony and I have to run. Coach Bollas wants the team to get together right after classes. He has a lot to go over with us."

"Good luck tonight, guys. I know you'll be great," Jeannie said to them as they started walking backward. They stopped momentarily. She blew them a kiss and added, "The Pirate cheerleaders will be cheering our hearts out for you guys."

Danny nodded, looking at her affectionately. He threw an arm into the air and reached as if catching her airborne kiss. "The Pirate cheerleaders are the spirit of the school, and you guys make such a difference. The team appreciates your efforts to involve the crowd. I'll be watching you as we race up and down the court—see ya later." He blew her a kiss.

Instantly, she mimicked his actions, reaching to catch an emotion that caused her heart to thump. She grabbed KateLynn's hand, as she'd been standing next to her. They turned and together started skipping down the hallway.

Danny and his teammates did not go home after class. Following a special meal in the school's cafeteria, Coach Bollas met with them for two hours, going over every detail of every play they had been practicing. He drilled them constantly with questions about the weak points of the Grizzlies. He grilled them about team sprit and working together. He wanted to know how they would turn the tide from losing to winning if they found themselves behind.

"It's now seven and game time in CoalVille." Danny heard the announcer over the loudspeaker system.

His mind was on one thing and one thing only. *We're going to win this game tonight. Superior is big and fast, but we have the determination to win—we will blow them off the basketball court. Wow, the pep club and band are making lots of noise. The crowd is really into it. There must be at least three hundred people—the gym only seats two hundred fifty—it's standing room only for this last regular-season game.*

Coach Bollas called a team huddle to give the Pirates a pep talk just before the starting buzzer.

"OK, team, we have to win tonight. We're well on our way to capturing the state championship. Superior is the toughest team we've faced this season. When we beat them tonight, it's on to LaRayme for the state tournament. Superior has a fast, aggressive, well-coached team. They're disciplined, but their weak point is their center. He's clumsy, so Danny, while Robbie has the ball on the left side of the court under the basket, you hang out on the right side near the out-of-bounds line. Then at Robbie's signal, you start your move toward the basket. Jerry, the center for the Superior Grizzlies will always step in front of you. When he does, you do a quick right-hand pivot to the center of the floor. Jerry's too slow to follow a fast pivot. At this point, Robbie, bounce pass to Danny. Then, Danny, you lay it up for two. Got it? Danny, one more thing. I've told you this before. You can't wear that gold chain with your ring on it when you play basketball. I know you like that emerald ring, but you know the rules."

"We got it, Coach Bollas," Danny and Robbie said at the same time.

"Sorry about the ring, Coach," Danny added. "Will you keep it until the end of the game?"

Coach Bollas looked at the large emerald ring Danny had just handed him. *Wow! I wonder where Danny got this ring. This emerald is huge—it must be worth a fortune!*

Two minutes before game time, the cheerleaders ran out on the floor to get the crowd revved up. Jeannie led the cheering squad while the band played the school song, "On CoalVille Pirates." The pep squad started the crowd singing.

> On CoalVille, on CoalVille,
> On to victory!
> We're the Pirates of CoalVille,
> We're for our school
> Loyal we will be, rah, rah, rah
> We'll stand by you,
> While you're fighting
> For our high-school fame,
> So fight, Pirates, fight, fight, fight!
> We'll win this game!

Then the band played the national anthem. When finished, the game got underway. The Pirates scored first. But the Grizzlies were relentless, and the lead went back and forth during the first half of the game.

The half-time buzzer sounded, and the teams exited the gym floor to their locker rooms.

"You guys are doing great. We're only down by two points—thirty-three to thirty-one. Danny, that center is catching on to the pivot move that you're using to get away from him. In this next half, pivot to the right and then to the left. He won't figure out what you're doing until it's too late."

Danny was concentrating on what Coach Bollas was telling him, but trying to shut out all of the noise was impossible. *I need to try harder. Coach Bollas and the team are counting on me. I have to prove to them that they made a good choice letting me play varsity ball. I'm going to make them proud. Dad, this one's for you!*

Danny heard Jeannie cheering her lungs out as he walked through the doorway onto the gymnasium floor. The crowd, the band, the pep club, and the cheerleaders were all standing and clapping to the rhythm of "On CoalVille Pirates" to cheer on the team as they entered the gymnasium and took their positions on the basketball court.

Danny watched his opponents take their places. *Last year, the Grizzlies beat us fifty-nine to fifty-eight. That hurt! That ain't going to happen this year! This year CoalVille is going to the state tournament as the number-one ball club in Wyoming! The crowd is doing their job tonight—if an excited crowd could manufacture electricity, there would be enough electricity coming from this crowd to light up New York City!*

With only nine seconds left in the game, the Grizzlies had a one-point lead—fifty-four to fifty-three. Danny was inbounding the ball and standing next to the CoalVille cheerleaders. He tossed it to Robbie.

Over the noise and excitement of the crowd—and the band and pep club—Danny heard a small, sweet voice. "You can do it, my love! Tonight you're going to be the school's hero. I'm so proud of you!"

Robbie tossed the ball to Tony, who was at center court. Danny knew this play well. Jerry, the center for the Grizzlies, moved into place at the free-throw line. Danny was right in front of Jerry, and Tony threw him the ball. The ball didn't make it to Danny's hands—Jerry moved in front of Danny and deflected the ball down the court.

Damn, now what? I've got to get the ball before it gets out of bounds. He raced down the court chasing the ball, and he grabbed it just before it went out of bounds under the Pirate's basket. *I made it! I got it!* Danny took a quick glance at the scoreboard. *Damn! Only four seconds left, and I'm as far away from our basket as possible. What do I do?* He was concentrating so hard that he didn't hear a sound. He had locked out all the noise, and it was as if he were in a noiseless chamber. But outside his mind, the crowd, the cheerleaders, the pep club, and the band were making a thundering noise that would practically deafen any living soul.

Jeannie was watching, horrifying emotions racing through her being. *Danny, you can do it. I know you can. You have superhuman powers. I know it, and so do you! Jump high and throw the ball—it will fly through the air and split the net. You have the power to do it, Danny. Just do it!*

Coach Bollas watched the final events of the game. *My golly! My hell! We're going to lose again by one point. I can't believe the stinking luck we're having!*

With only one second left, Danny put every ounce of energy into his final effort. He leaped high into the air at midcourt and threw the ball with all his might.

Time stood still for Jeannie, Tony, and the entire crowd as they watched the final moments of the game. Their minds were silent, shutting out everything just as Danny's had shut out the roar of the crowd in the CoalVille High School gym, all watching the last home game on a Friday evening in 1958.

Jeannie's heart was pounding. *He's going to do it! Yes! He looks like a Roman god standing in midair, four feet off the gym floor, hurling the ball half the length of the court at the basket.*

Over the roar and excitement of the crowd stamping their feet in the bleacher stands, Danny heard the sweet sound of *swisssssh* as the ball split the net. *We did it!* He landed on one foot with no time remaining on the scoreboard.

The crowd erupted, and the roar was deafening. Danny was mobbed by his teammates. They picked him up, put him on their shoulders, and raced around the gym floor with the band playing "Pirates Romp," the spirit song for CoalVille High School.

The Pirates beat the Grizzlies with a final score of fifty-five to fifty-four.

Waving at Jeannie as his teammates raced past the cheerleaders with him on their shoulders, Danny shouted, "*I love you!* State tournament, here we come!"

CHAPTER 3
Back-Alley Meeting

After the excitement of seeing their team win the regional championship in the final regular-season basketball game—a win that propelled the team one step closer to the ultimate glory of state champions—the crowd's energy subsided. The bright lights that had flooded the basketball court were turned off. The spectators filed out of the gymnasium—their individual energy levels dropping in the wake of a phenomenal win, thanks to a yellow-haired, green-eyed boy. Janitors walked up and down the basketball court with giant dust mops, cleaning the floor in preparation for the next event.

Two shadowy figures skulked under the bleachers—they watched the events taking place among four kids in the moments before all the lights were turned off and the gymnasium doors were closed and locked. Four eyes peered through the cracks between the bleacher stands. Eddie and Terry were curious. They monitored the activity on the other side of the basketball court from their dark vantage point.

Moving a little closer, Eddie leaned his forehead on the board of the bleacher stand to see through the stair-step opening. It was a perfect place to watch and not be seen.

"What's going on?" whispered Terry. "Can you make out what they are saying?"

"No! I can't hear anything that makes sense—just jumbled sounds that

I can't understand," muttered Eddie.

Danny had just captured the hearts of the crowd, but now he had to tell his love he couldn't take her on the date he'd promised.

"Jeannie, I'm sorry, but I have to do this," he said in a sullen voice. "This coach I am meeting with is from Chapel Hill. I believe his name is Coach Smith. I'm hoping that our discussion this evening will be the opportunity that leads to something big and gets us out of CoalVille."

"Oh, Danny, I completely understand. This is what we've been waiting for. Do you know this could be an answer to our dream—an answer that would secure our future?" Jeannie grabbed his hand and squeezed. "My love, you did it tonight. I'm so proud of you!"

His hand came from his pocket, holding his keys. Danny turned to his right and said, "Tony, here. Take my truck. You and KateLynn go as planned. You guys will have fun in Granite Springs. Have an extra hamburger and milkshake at TerryZ's Burgers for Jeannie and me. You can return my keys tomorrow."

Tony reached for the truck keys, but Danny grabbed his hand instead. He winked, paused, and said, "Keep it cool on Lovers' Lane, Tony! I know you and KateLynn are three months older that Jeannie and me—already seventeen—but that does not give you guys license to you know what!" He handed Tony his keys as a grin engulfed Danny's face.

Eddie stepped on a paper cup, making a popping sound, but the janitor opening the custodial closet diverted the foursome's attention from the bleachers.

"Danny just gave Tony his keys," Eddie rasped. "Maybe Tony and his fancy-pants girl are going to go someplace. That KateLynn thinks she's hot stuff when she trots up and down the court and does her cheerleader thing with Jeannie. She's just a little, redheaded, freckle-face showoff. She's only five foot six inches tall. Someday, someone will cut her down to size—she'll be a lot smaller than five foot six."

A tall man in a gray, pinstriped suit waited patiently. He stood next to Coach Bollas at the end of the court, next to the exit door.

Terry's squinting eyes turned to Eddie. "Who is that guy standing next to the coach?" Terry panted.

"How should I know?" Eddie snapped in a raspy whisper. "It looks like they're waiting for Danny. He's heading over to them now."

Danny stopped and turned around. "See ya tomorrow, Jeannie. Call me."

A smile crossed his face as he looked at his friend Tony. He thought, *KateLynn is cute hanging on to Tony's arm. Yep, they're headed to Lovers' Lane at the base of White Mountain...I just know it!*

"You guys have fun! Enjoy my red racer." He laughed, gave Tony a high five, turned, and started walking again in the direction of Coach Bollas.

Turning to face him, Eddie grabbed Terry's coat sleeve. His foot accidently kicked a popcorn bag. It quietly rolled along the concrete floor, stopping at another piece of garbage as it hit the pile of debris discarded under the bleachers.

"Hey, Tony and KateLynn left," Eddie whispered as he poked Terry in the side. "Danny just walked out the door with Coach Bollas and that other character. Jeannie is all by herself. She's the last one in the gym! Let's wait until she goes out the door and then follow her. There's no moon tonight. It's black as hell out there. She won't know we're following her."

The door slammed behind Jeannie. The head janitor turned the lights off. He used his flashlight to locate the exit door. The CoalVille gymnasium was pitch-black, except for a small beam of light coming from beneath the bleachers.

"Let's get out of here. Shine your flashlight over here so I don't trip," Eddie snapped at Terry. "Hurry up! She's getting away!"

Terry's hand pushed the bar on the exit door. It opened with its familiar grinding sound. Leaving the dark gymnasium, they spotted Coach Bollas and the tall man walking with Danny. Eddie grabbed Terry's coat and threw his finger up to his mouth. "Shhhh!" He motioned Terry to stop as they watched the three walk toward the high school.

They heard sounds of conversation coming from the direction of the two men and Danny. They had no idea what the meeting in the high school would be about. They didn't care. They had an alternative agenda. Eddie grabbed Terry's arm, pointed, and then they hustled down a back alley.

"Danny, this is Coach Daryl Smith. He's the head basketball coach for the University of North Carolina at Chapel Hill. He heard about you and wanted to get a firsthand look at your athletic skills in action. He came all the way from North Carolina to see you play this evening. We'll go to my office and talk."

The concrete stairs leading to the main door of the high school were slowly being eroded by the elements of nature. Scorching heat in the summer and freezing cold in the winter were carving out large chunks of crumbling masonry from each stair, the frost chiseling away a little more with each passing season.

"Watch your step, Coach Smith. These damn stairs are treacherous at night. Never know when you're going to step on a piece of loose cement and take a tumble down them."

At the top of the stairs, Coach Bollas fumbled for his key under the faint light of the door lamp. He found the right one. He opened the main door of the high school and pointed to the staircase.

"My office is on the third floor. Let me find the light switch, and we'll head on up."

While the two coaches and Danny walked up the stairs, headed for a late-night meeting, Jeannie headed home in the dark. She was deep in thought about what could be a bright future for her and the boy who'd just energized the entire town of CoalVille. *I wonder where Chapel Hill is. Danny didn't tell me. I know it has to be a neat town...I love the name—Chapel Hill. Oh, that would be just too neat to have Danny playing basketball for a big-time college school. It would be so fun to start a family in a neat town.*

In CoalVille, there were two rows of houses on each side of the main street. The rows were identical. The houses were separated by an alleyway, the backyard of each house facing the alley. Jeannie's house was located on the back row. Most residents had built backyard picket fences.

Leaving the gymnasium, Jeannie elected to take the shortcut home down the lightless alley, planning to enter her house through the back door.

Undetectable in the dark shadows, Eddie and Terry stood stealthily against the fence of the house three doors up from Jeannie's. The moonless night provided a perfect cover for them.

While a meeting was taking place on the third floor of the CoalVille High School, another meeting was about to take place in a back alley of CoalVille.

"There she is," whispered Eddie. "She doesn't see us. This is sweet! This back alley is perfect for our chance to trap Jeannie. We'll have fun with her!"

When she walked by, Eddie jumped out of the shadows and grabbed her. He flung her backward, stepping in front of her, and held her arm in a tight, pinching grip.

"Hi there, cutie!" Eddie muttered as he stood in front of Jeannie, blocking her path. His flashlight shone brightly into her eyes.

Her eyes flew open. Her heart dropped like a rock descending to a bottomless pit. "My God! Who are you?" she screamed. Blinded by the light, she couldn't see his face.

His free hand touched her face. "Pretty white skin...my daffodil...oh, so soft and sweet. I'll bet it smells luscious and soooooo soft to the touch!" Eddie rasped in a slow, singsong voice.

His black, shadowy figure was featureless, but his voice was a dead giveaway. "It's you! *Eddie!* You bastard! Get away from me! What do you want?"

His hand brushed over her lips. "You know what I want! I want my little daffodil! Eddie won't hurt you. We'll have some fun! Won't we?" Eddie muttered as he reached to grab her.

Jeannie's hand swung from her side and grabbed his, pinching it with all her might. "You son of a bitch! Get your filthy hands off me," she screamed.

Terry grabbed the bottom of Eddie's dirty plaid coat and yanked on it. "Eddie, leave her alone!" Terry snapped.

Eddie turned slightly and kicked at Terry. His hand never released its tight hold on Jeannie's arm. Terry's fingers slipped from Eddie's coat. "Shut up, Terry! This is between Jeannie and me!" Eddie shouted in Terry's face. Swinging around quickly and grabbing Jeannie with both hands, Eddie snapped, "What did you guys find? We've been following you guys." He loosed one hand and slid it alongside her head, burying his fingers in her hair. "You think you are hot stuff with your boyfriend, Danny!" Eddie jeered.

Jeannie's heart was pounding. She pulled to get away, but his free hand came from her hair and grabbed her arm again. "What are you talking about? Eddie, you're a dipshit. Get away from me! Leave me alone. Danny is going to kick your ass over the moon!" Jeannie screeched at him.

Both hands clutching her arms, Eddie growled, "He'll kick nobody's ass. Just tell me what you guys found."

One hand released its grip, and Eddie slapped her leg, making a pop. Jeannie jumped. She started trembling. She was scared.

"If...if w...we found anything, we sure wouldn't let y...you know where it's buried! You're a slime bucket!" she stuttered.

"Well, if you won't tell me, how about a date, cutie? Eddie would love to date you!"

His remark infuriated her. Her body no longer shook. She was mad, standing tall and erect. "*You ass, Eddie!* I wouldn't go out with you if you were the last boy on earth!"

"You get a slap for that, cutie. When I'm through with you, you'll be a wilted daffodil!" Eddie rasped as he slapped at her.

Jeannie dodged his swinging arm.

"Leave her alone, Eddie. This is enough! Let's get out of here!" Terry shouted.

"Zip it, Terry. You keep your mouth closed. This is my thing—not yours! This is between Jeannie and me!"

That momentary diversion of attention to Terry was all that she needed. Jeannie lunged backward and spun with a huge jerk. Eddie lost his grip.

Not being slow, Eddie jumped in front of her and was ready to grab her again as he said, "Eddie wants a good-night kiss. I want to taste your sweet lips. Come on, honey!" Eddie stared at her. "I know you guys found something. If you don't give me a kiss, I'll tell LeRoy you've been snooping in his house. He won't like it!"

"I hate you, Eddie! And guess what? LeRoy is gone!" Jeannie yelled in response to Eddie's threat.

Eddie reached to grab Jeannie, but she was quicker. She was already in full swing, her school bag in motion. It found its mark—the side of Eddie's face.

"You little bitch!" Eddie howled as he felt the impact of Jeannie's canvas bag, heavy with all her schoolbooks, smack him upside his head. He dropped to the ground.

"Danny is going to kick your ass, you bastard!" she screamed as she ran for dear life toward her house.

Racing into the stillness of the misty fog that drifted between the backyard fences of the alleyway, her footing was sure. Absolute darkness settled around her as she disappeared into the foggy night.

Her hand was grabbing the latch of the fence gate even before she thought it possible. Leaping across the stone pathway with the speed of a deer evading a predator, she found the back door waiting to let her in. Her heart pounded as the eerie silence behind her continued, feeling comfort when she turned the doorknob. She opened the door to safety and shut it quickly behind her.

CHAPTER 4

A Trip Down Lover's Lane

T he moonless night left the Milky Way sparkling with an expansive
pathway of stars in the black Wyoming sky. It was the perfect back-
drop, with desert hoot owls providing the serenading music for young lovers on a heart-throbbing trip down Lovers' Lane. The beckoning hand of
temptation led them into a forbidden and uncharted territory. Although
cautious, Tony and KateLynn were anxious to experience the most intimate pleasures of young love.

Danny's pickup truck sped along, with a young, redheaded girl on the
seat next to a six-foot-two-inch tall, black-haired Latino boy. They were
headed for Granite Springs. As the truck bounced through the potholes
and frost heaves along the highway, KateLynn's left arm was around Tony's
waist, and her right hand was on his lap, under the steering wheel. Their
first stop at TerryZ's Burgers would be just the beginning of their night's
planned adventure.

KateLynn felt a leap of joy, and she said in an extra sweet voice, "Tony,
you were really good tonight. I had so much fun…can't wait to go to
LaRayme next week. The state tournament will be a blast. Jeannie and I
have talked about it for weeks—we've been making plans. Wow, and now
it's going to happen! We will have so much fun in the big city. Danny and
Jeannie, and you and me—we'll do the town and see the sights!"

She reflected on her home as she talked about spending a few days in a big city—far away from CoalVille. "Tony, I wish we didn't have to live in CoalVille. I hate living with my grandmother. I wish my parents were still here. It has been a year now since they were killed in that awful accident. They didn't even see the bus that hit them head on. Yeah, we'll have fun in LaRayme—and we'll get out of CoalVille for a few days."

Tony's heart sank listening to the agony in her words. His mind took in the sadness of it all. *I know how she misses her parents. I never met them, but she sure has said some nice things about them.*

The image of an old lady railing at a young girl day in, day out pressed heavily on Tony. "I don't care for your grandmother either," he said, thinking about a young girl in pain living with a crotchety old grandmother. "She's rude every time I call you." There was a moment of silence followed by a sudden anger in his voice. "I don't want to offend you, but she is just not nice to me on the phone. She calls me the 'coal-camp Mexican'!"

She sensed his anguish. Her left arm squeezed his waist tightly. "Tony, don't worry about her. As I said, we only have two more years here, and then we can go someplace and start our own lives."

Her right hand lifted to his face, and he felt the sweet sensation of her touch, her fingers moving across his cheeks. Her voice carried a ring of happiness as she said, "Can you just see the little brown-eyed babies with freckles?" She giggled and thought about a brighter future with the boy sitting next to her.

"Yeah, I think about that too, KateLynn. Let's have fun tonight. Too bad Jeannie and Danny couldn't come. Oh well. We'll have some time by ourselves to park on Lovers' Lane after we get our burgers and shakes at TerryZ's. It's too bad for Danny and Jeannie—for them, the game is over. Their fun ended when the game ended! Ours is just starting!"

Tony reached to find KateLynn's hand, and he squeezed it. "You sure are cute, KateLynn. I love your blue eyes, red hair, and freckles! You are just too cute for words!"

Holding the steering wheel tightly with his left hand, he slid his right arm behind her back and around her waist. He gently pulled her as close to him as he could and said, "KateLynn, you're a super cheerleader. I just love watching you do your thing on the basketball court. I don't think the team would win if it weren't for you girls getting the crowd revved up!"

He took his hand from behind her back and laid his forearm along her leg. Lifting his elbow slightly, he put his hand on her knee. His fingers, with a feathery touch, slid up her thigh, stopping at the edge of her short cheerleading skirt. She giggled as he said, "You look so cute in your maroon-and-white cheerleading outfit. KateLynn, I think my heart is telling me, 'Watch out, Tony! You're falling in love with the neatest girl around!'"

Tony gently continued to rub her leg with his hand as he said, "I wish we didn't have to go home tonight. We'd have a blast in the front seat of Danny's red racer!"

"Tony, don't worry! Our fun is just starting. I'd kiss you, but you have to keep both hands on the wheel. Oh well, you won't need both hands on the wheel when we get to Lovers' Lane. Fun! Fun! Fun!" She put her fingers in his black hair and let them slide down his neck. "You have such nice, shiny, soft hair. You're so handsome! This night is very special to me. Tony, you're the first boy that I have had these special feelings for. You make my heart skip! Sometimes I wish we were a few years older."

Tony gunned Danny's truck as they rounded the last curve in the highway leading into Granite Springs. He had both hands on the wheel as he watched the two bright lights of the car coming in his direction. The car passed them, and in his rearview mirror, he watched its red taillights get dimmer and dimmer and then disappear.

The road was now free of oncoming cars, so he slowed down and gave her a quick glance. "KateLynn, it's good that we're young. We'll be older before we know it! Let's just enjoy the moment. This night is special to me too. Someday we'll look back with fondness on this evening and tell our kids about a joy ride in a 1955 red Chevy truck!"

Tony and KateLynn pulled Danny's truck into the parking lot of TerryZ's Burgers. He spotted a single slot between two cars—the last one, as there were at least thirty cars in the lot. Carefully pulling between them, he eased his foot from the accelerator and hit the brake pedal. He turned the key, shut the engine off, and opened his door gingerly. The car next to his door—a 1956 yellow-and-white Ford Crown Victoria with a chrome continental kit on its rear—instantly caught his eye. *God, that's a cool car,* thought Tony. *I sure wish I had it.*

Walking around the back of the truck to get to the passenger side, his eyes were caught by another gorgeous car. The red-and-white 1957 Chevy convertible with its top down further got his mind racing. *I can't believe the money these kids in Granite Springs have.* A twinge of sadness swept through his mind as he thought, *I wish that were my car. KateLynn would just love it!*

Elvis Presley's smash hit "Jailhouse Rock" was blaring from the speakers attached to the light poles in the parking lot. It was TerryZ's that had started the parking-lot Dance-A-Rama, knowing that magnet would draw every teenage kid around into his place of business. At least forty kids were dancing under the lights to the rhythm of rock 'n' roll. They were swinging, jumping, and shuffling with every beat of the music.

His eye caught a short kid with rolled-up Levi's standing next to a blond girl with a full skirt. She was ignoring him, but he kept trying to get her to dance.

Tommy Huntsaker stepped in front of MaryJane Hamilton. Her long blond hair swirled under the parking-lot light in the slight breeze. She tried to move away from Tommy, but he grabbed her hand and pointed to his yellow-and-white '56 Crown Vic. She shook her head and yanked her hand from his. She turned and ran to three of her girlfriends standing twenty feet away.

Tony opened the door and helped KateLynn out. No sooner had her foot touched the ground than he heard a loud voice coming from Tommy's direction. "Get the hell away from my car, you coal-camp rats!"

He looked and saw that short, ugly kid now moving away from the blond girl and her friends. Tommy walked to his friend Billy Sartwick and said something to him. He then raised his fist and shook it at Tony.

Tony's hand tightened on KateLynn's arm. "Let's go inside. There are a couple of jackasses out here that think they are better than we are. Just 'cause they live in Granite Springs and their dads have businesses, they think they're hot sh—" He stopped in the middle of his sentence.

Tony wanted to say what was on his mind, but he held his tongue and just smiled at KateLynn. He pulled her close to him as he whispered into her ear, "They are not worth cussing at. We'll have more fun tonight than they'll have in their lifetimes!"

He laughed, and she giggled.

His mind was not idle, and Tony thought, *That ass Tommy Huntsaker is trying to impress MaryJane. Shit, she wouldn't give him the time of day. He thinks he can schmooze her with his '56 Crown Victoria. That ass is uglier than a pile of rat shit. He wouldn't have anything if it weren't for his ugly old man's money. MaryJane told me she can't stand Tommy.*

Pointing his finger at the kid making the rude remarks, Tony said, "If you care to come to CoalVille, you ass, you'll find out what coal-camp life is all about. I'll kick your ass over the moon!"

KateLynn laughed more briskly. "Tony, you're so big and strong, you would kick both Tommy and Billy over the moon. You have more muscles in your little finger than they have in their two ugly bodies."

At that moment, Elvis's voice blasted out of the parking-lot speakers. "If you can't find a partner, grab a wooden chair." The song had at least forty Granite Springs teenagers having fun rocking and rolling under the parking-lot lights on a moonless night.

She paused and grinned at Tony. "Tommy is not just a jerk…he's so ugly, he must be the one Elvis is talking about!"

Tony laughed freely. "Yeah, I don't think that jailbird could even find a wooden chair that would want to dance with him!" He sighed briefly. "I have to admit, I would like to have his car, but oh well…I guess that's all they have to brag about."

Tony pointed to the entrance of TerryZ's. On either side of the door were large picture windows with bright red-and-blue neon signs spelling out "TerryZ's Burgers Is the Place for You." His eyes blinked with the signs. "Come on, KateLynn. We're going to have fun tonight. Let's get started."

Teenagers were talking, walking, and having fun with each other as they entered and left TerryZ's. In similar fashion, KateLynn and Tony carried on making their way to the doorway with playful teenage gestures. He squeezed her hand briskly. "They are not all jerks. I know most of the kids in Granite Springs. Larry Martin and his girl, Donna Comét, are really neat. They might be already inside. Let's go see."

Strolling next to Tony, she looked at him with fondness. Her head was slightly turned, her eyes peeking upward at his face. Her red hair shimmered in the light. She gleefully grabbed at his arm and put her hand on his chest.

Walking through the door, he didn't see either Larry or Donna. He pointed to a booth on the back wall. "Is that good? They are not here, so I guess we'll just enjoy each other tonight."

An instant beam of joy raced through her body. *I don't have to share the evening with Larry, Donna, or anyone else—I have Tony all to myself.* "Yeah, we're going to have fun tonight, Tony," KateLynn said as they walked up to the counter and placed their order.

TerryZ's had been in business over thirty years, and the order counter, floors, walls, and booths revealed their age. They were marked with gouges, dings, scratches, and carved names, displaying the acts of teenagers having fun over the years.

The music played on. TerryZ's had the inside speakers' volumes set to the same level as the outside ones.

Their faces were locked in a lover's stare. They could almost touch—their lips just inches apart—as they leaned on bent elbows across the tiny table in the booth. Occasionally one would take a bite of a french fry held by the other's hand stretching across the small table.

Then it happened. The song by the Polar Bears, "I Know Him and I Love Him," filled the airways of TerryZ's establishment. KateLynn watched Tony's smile light up his face. She touched her wet tongue and then reached and gently touched his lips as the song played on:

> I'll be good to him, and I'll bring love to him
> Whenever I'm near him, he makes my heart smile.
> He brings me a happiness that is more than joy
> I'll make love to him, 'cause he's my golden boy.
>
> I know, know, know him, and I'll love, love, love him.
> Just to see him smile, makes it all worthwhile.
> I know, know, know him, and I'll love, love, love him,
> And I will!

Listening to the words of the song, a jangle of joy raced through her body as if someone had just plugged her into an electrical outlet. In her sweet little voice, she said, "Tony, you make my life worthwhile." A tear came to her eye as she let her fingers slide across his cheek. Her soft, sweet voice competed with the loud music from the speaker overhead as she said, "To know you is to love you, and I do! Tonight I'll be good to you. I'll bring love to you!"

His hand squeezed hers tightly. "KateLynn, this is our night. Yeah, it's just the beginning of a long, wonderful journey we'll have together." His finger brushed away the tears trickling down her face.

She was anxious to get their next adventure underway. "Are you ready? I can't wait any longer," KateLynn said as she stood and motioned Tony to follow.

KateLynn was five foot six, and her maroon cheerleading miniskirt barely covered her upper thighs. Her white top tightly stretched across her small breasts. She looked up at his face, grabbed his hand, and softly gave it a tug.

Tony, taller than six feet, reached down, took her in his arms, picked her up effortlessly, spun around, and gently set her down facing the doorway.

The night manager waved goodnight as Tony and KateLynn walked out the door.

Danny's pickup was the lone vehicle on the dirt road leading from Granite Springs to a vacant field at the base of White Mountain. The stillness of the dark night fell upon them as Tony turned the key off and pushed the light switch. They rolled the windows down, letting the faint sounds of the desert creatures drift through and fill the night air inside the truck.

KateLynn moved closer to Tony and pulled his body next to hers. With no words spoken, their arms locked in an embrace, and their lips met in passionate kisses. The tranquility of the night pressed on, the Milky Way streaming across the night sky. Its bright twinkling stars peeked through the windshield at two young lovers lying on the front seat of a 1955 red Chevy, locked in each other's arms.

An old pair of Levi's with patched knees, a red plaid shirt, and a cheerleading suit with a white top and a maroon-colored miniskirt were draped over the steering wheel. They swayed peacefully back and forth, the movement caused by the gentle, rolling motion of the parked truck. The only sounds that broke the quiet stillness of the night were the serenading hoots of great horned owls. They were calling for their lovers to come and mate with them for the springtime ritual of bringing new life to the Scarlet Desert.

CHAPTER 5

A Ballplayer's Dream

s the private courtship of two young lovers venturing for the first
time onto Lovers' Lane was underway, a different kind of meeting in Coach Bollas's office on the third floor of CoalVille High School continued. Danny's dream of leaving CoalVille was being fueled by the discussion he was having with one of the nation's leading college basketball coaches. His mind shot to a joyful height just thinking about the possibility of an impossible dream come true—a full-ride athletic scholarship to one of the nation's most prominent universities. *Could it be that Jeannie and I won't have to worry about how we will pay for my college education? My God, could this be real?*

"Coach Bollas tells me you're interested in becoming a doctor. You know, Danny, we have a great medical school at Chapel Hill. We've been successful in getting many of our players into our med school," Coach Smith said.

The questions by Coach Smith were intense, but Danny was up to the challenge. Finally, the meeting wound down, but not with a conclusive ending—at least in Danny's mind.

Coach Smith grabbed Danny's right arm with his left hand. He smacked his right hand into Danny's and shook it vigorously. "Danny, it sure was great talking to you. You're one hell of a ballplayer. Who knows? UNC could use a player like you. At this stage of your development, your game is the best we've seen. We'll keep an eye on your progress. You have one more year—we'll keep in touch," Daryl Smith said as he tightened his grip on Danny's hand, giving it one final shake.

Then Coach Bollas stepped in front of Danny. He reached and grabbed Danny's arm. Danny looked from Coach Smith to Coach Bollas.

"Danny, I almost forgot. Here's your ring," he interjected as he handed it to Danny with his other hand.

"Thanks, Coach," Danny replied, looking directly into the coach's eyes.

Their eyes remained locked, and Coach Bollas continued holding his arm. A strange look spread over Danny's face. *Why is he still holding on to me?*

"Oh, Danny, something puzzled me when you made that phenomenal winning shot. I swear that your ring was glowing with a green light. What was that all about?"

"Oh! Nothing!" said Danny, startled by the question.

Coach Bollas had still not released Danny's arm. Looking at his coach, Danny stepped back several feet so as to force the release. For a moment, Danny merely looked vague. The uneasiness of Coach Bollas's stare weighed on Danny's mind as he searched for an answer. "It was probably the bright gymnasium lights reflecting off it. It does that," Danny said with a smile.

"Yeah, that must have been what it was. That's one large stone! Is it real or a chunk of glass?" Coach Bollas asked. "Whatever it is, it catches a lot of light!" There was a brief moment of silence as the coach was thinking.

"Where did you get this, Danny? It has to…" Coach Bollas was asking when Danny cut him off and offered the pat answer that he had rehearsed for occasions like this.

"It's a fake gemstone and fake gold. My dad, bless his soul, gave it to me, and he even had my name engraved on it! The chain is also fake gold."

With no further questions, the coach nodded and said, "Anyway, see you Tuesday. We have a holiday on Monday—thanks to you. The entire school is off on Monday because we are going to the state tournament. Tuesday, we'll start getting ready for LaRayme. Have a good weekend, Danny."

The meeting on the third floor of the CoalVille high school broke up, but the back-alley meeting of Jeannie, Eddie, and Terry had long finished.

A young boy dreamed about his future as he started his walk home. Danny was unaware of the back-alley scuffle that had occurred minutes earlier as he walked by his love's house. *I hope I get it. God, it would be neat if I got a full-ride athletic scholarship to UNC at Chapel Hill. Jeannie and I would have our dream—we'd raise a family in a grand mansion with a white picket fence!*

CHAPTER 6
Problems With Bullies

Jeannie had a problem, but it was not just hers. Danny and Tony had no idea what the problem was. Jeannie knew old lady Calhoun was a snoop. Danny had filled her in on the peeping-tom activities of Eddie's mom. Jeannie had laughed at Danny's description of the inside-out peeping tom as opposed to the more conventional outside-in peeping tom. Like mother, like son, but the snooping was no longer a laughing matter.

Zanzee snuggled against Jeannie in her bed during the early hours of that Saturday morning. She had a lot on her mind and somehow knew that Zanzee was trying to comfort her. Her memories of the terrifying events following last night's game caused her to shudder. *I can't believe those perverts. What would they have done to me if I hadn't gotten away? Oh! I can't even think about it. Eddie and Terry are slime birds! Danny is going to beat the crap out of them. They'll be sorry after he finishes with 'em.*

The morning sun beaming through her window announced the beginning of a new day. She put her arm around Zanzee and pulled him close to her. "Zanzee, you have special powers. You got them from the gods. Danny also has special powers. I know that, Zanzee. You do too. Don't you?"

His shiny black body shimmered in the morning sunlight. Jeannie spoke softly to her cat, stroking his sun-warmed black fur as she thought about Danny. *Where does Danny get his supernatural powers? That's what they have to be—how else could he have moved the rock that had trapped Tony? It was three times his weight. How could he react faster than the strike of a scorpion? How can he make those unbelievable basketball shots that are almost impossible for anyone else? That was more than a coincidence last night when he made the game-winning shot. He's the neatest boy in the world, and he and I are falling in love—wow!*

She turned her head to Zanzee and pulled him to her face. He purred. *I could lie here all day thinking about my love, but I had better get up and get going. Eddie and Terry need to be dealt with. I've got to give Danny and Tony a call. We need to meet and discuss the problem and what to do about it. Those bastards—they're a couple of slimy cowards! I can't believe what they tried to do to me last night.*

Saturday in CoalVille was chore day. Most families were up early, doing house cleaning and yard work. The wire-fenced yards were hidden from the street. A strange, entangling vine had been introduced as a floral curtain by an old man who wanted privacy from curious passersby. Its thorny stems and pungent, bright-red berries made it the perfect barrier. With its hardy success in the desert climate, it crept through the town, and one by one, the residents of CoalVille adopted the old man's plant to entwine through their front-yard wire fences. The Lopez family's fence was no exception. Their front yard was hidden from view by an entwinement of vines that wove through the square holes of their wire fence.

Behind the vine-covered fences were struggling wannabe lawns. From the lack of sprinkler systems and, more importantly, a steady supply of water, only slivers of grass survived in lawns made mostly of weeds. The chore the residents of CoalVille faced each Saturday morning was to make their wannabe lawns look like the bowling green of the Pebble Beach Golf Course. That was a challenge of unreachable magnitude.

Danny was up, dressed, and having breakfast with Tony by seven o'clock. Rose Lopez had rolled out of bed an hour before them. She was already busy with house chores, trying to make a dilapidated, fifty-year-old shanty look like a palace—an impossible task.

"Tony, would you mow the front lawn and clean your room before you and Danny head out on your adventure?" she asked.

Danny finished his bowl of Wheaties, stood, and headed to the kitchen sink. Tony asked, "Danny, would you help me with the yard?"

"Sure, best buddy! We'll knock this yard out in no time."

Rose could tell they were in a hurry, as their conversation did not include her. She watched Danny for a few moments as he rinsed his bowl, turned, and started walking toward his bedroom.

She waited for him to close his door. "Tony, what are you guys doing today? You were out kind of late last night. I talked to KateLynn earlier this morning, and she told me you took her to Granite Springs in Danny's truck."

Danny, meanwhile, could not hear what the conversation in the kitchen was about, but he figured it had to do something with chores. He called, "Mrs. Lopez, I've already started on my room and will help Tony with the yard next." He fluffed his pillows and straightened the blankets that hid the lumpy mattress.

"Thanks, Danny," Rose called back. She immediately turned her attention back to her son. "So where did you take Danny's truck? I assume since you were out so late that you parked someplace?"

Filled with uneasiness, he sat at the table gawking at his mother. He was at a loss how to answer. For a few moments, silence took over as mother and son explored a delicate subject. It was Rose who cleared the air, knowing Tony was struggling. "Well, son, I was young once too. Your father and I found love when we were about the same age as you and KateLynn." But then her face grew serious as she added a final word of motherly advice. "Tony, if KateLynn gets pregnant, you cannot break her heart and leave her stranded with your child."

The silence was deafening. With a smile on her face, she added, "Your father never left me stranded in that condition." Now her eyes filled with tears, and she spoke softly. "We had the most wonderful journey together raising you." And then her eyes spilled their tears. "Your father and me, until the day he was killed, had a love for each other like no other. He was the dearest and kindest man I have ever known. Our love was otherworldly!" Wiping her tears with the back of her hand, she finished her parental council. "Tony, I expect no less from you."

Tony's smile was bigger than the rising sun that was peeking through the window over the old porcelain sink. "Mom, if you have any worries, they should not be in that area. Believe you me, KateLynn and I are going to share the same wonderful journey that you and Dad did." With a little chuckle, he said, "And who knows? Your dream of having a grandbaby will be a joy to not only KateLynn and me. You can put that whole subject to rest, Mom!"

The phone rang. Her fingers slipped around the heavy black plastic receiver as the phone's second ring screamed the announcement of someone on the other end of the line.

"Swell, Tony. I still want to know what you are up to today," Rose said while putting the phone to her lips. Her mind was still wandering as she thought of her son and of her love, Jack. *Young love. It's what makes the world go around. They are a cute couple—Jack would be very proud of him.*

A quiet voice on the other end said, "Hello."

Rose smiled instantly, recognizing who was on the phone. "Oh, Jeannie! Hi! How are you? Good to hear from you."

Jeannie spoke in the sweet voice of a young girl anxious to talk to her love. "Hi, Mrs. Lopez. It's nice to talk to you also. I'm fine." There was a long pause, and then Jeannie asked, "Is Danny up?"

Although Rose's awareness was heightened by the sparse conversation, at first she was not all that concerned.

"Sure, I'll get him. Danny, the phone is for you—it's Jeannie," Rose hollered. From where she stood in the living room, she could see straight through the kitchen to his partly opened bedroom door.

He ran from his room and took the receiver from Rose's hand. "What's up, Jeannie? You're up early! I thought you'd take it easy this morning—especially after all the excitement at the game last night."

Dead silence pressed for a moment, and then she said, "Danny, we've got big problems! I need to talk to you and Tony about something that happened last night after the game. After I left the gym, while I was on my way home, Terry and Eddie cornered me."

He heard concern and something less easily definable in Jeannie's voice. It gripped his soul. "Jeannie! What did they do to you? Are you OK?"

There was more silence. He lowered his voice to a whisper, repeating himself. "Are you OK?"

"Danny, I can't talk now—my mother just came into the house. Talk to Tony and suggest that we rendezvous sometime today. I'm busy until about one o'clock this afternoon. Can you make it then? Can we take your truck for a ride and get out of town? Let's cruise Main in Granite Springs—I'll fill you in on what happened to me last evening."

Reading between the lines of her reluctance to talk, his voice became fraught with concern. "Sure, Jeannie, but you got me worried. You don't sound good. What did those bastards do to you?"

Not wanting to diminish the severity of the situation, yet sensitive to Danny's concerns, she said, "Danny, I'm OK. I've gotta go. I'll see you guys at one."

Rose had walked into the kitchen to give Danny some privacy, but the acoustics of the old house did not allow for privacy. She heard every word of his conversation and was troubled. *I wonder what's going on!* she thought.

Any trace of Danny's earlier jovial mood had vanished.

Tony had also overheard the gist of the phone call. "Is everything OK with you? I couldn't help but overhear part of your conversation with Jeannie. What's the problem?" His mind immediately felt the severity of whatever was pulling on Danny's composure. *He can't fool me—something is going on.*

Aware of the boys' growing anxiety, Rose grew more troubled, watching their faces tighten to looks of distress. Concerned, she waited for an answer from either Danny or Tony.

"Terry and Eddie bugged her last evening. That's all I know. She's upset and wants to get out for a while. Tony and I are going with Jeannie to Granite Springs—we aren't leaving until one. We should be home by five."

Trying to grasp the full picture, Tony suggested a plan. "Danny and I will have lunch with you, Mom. We can talk about the game as we eat—it will give us some time together. You've been busy with work, and I was really tied up getting ready for last night's game."

Tony stumbled over his words, but Rose picked up on his feeble attempt to divert the conversation and nodded. "Sounds like a plan. You guys get your chores done, and we'll have lunch together!"

Not sharing his thoughts with either Tony or Rose, Danny stared out the window, his mind filled with anger. *What did Eddie and Terry do to Jeannie? I'm going to beat the crap out of both of them. I've had it with them. This is it—they've crossed the line by messing with my girl. They are too cowardly to confront Tony or me, so they pick on Jeannie! They'll be black-and-blue from nose to hind end when I'm done with 'em!*

Knowing his body language so well, Rose had no doubt he was troubled. Her motherly instinct guided her as she sought to get Danny's mind on more productive thoughts. She walked to him and put her hand on his cheek. He turned from the window and listened to Rose's questions.

"Danny, are you OK? Does the yard need to wait?"

He smiled and put his hand on her face. "I'm OK, Rose. I'll get busy with my chores. The lawn is first on Tony's and my list!"

The roar of Briggs and Stratton gasoline engines powering lawnmowers was commonplace in CoalVille on Saturday mornings. Most folks liked to get their weed-patched yards mowed in the morning. Pushing his mower behind hedges of vines budding with tiny spring leaves, Danny had the pattern down pat. He tried to make their sow's ear of a lawn look like a silk purse with a unique mowing pattern. It was impossible, but he tried in spite of that. First, he paralleled the fence line with each pass. Then he made a second pass over its entirety at a diagonal to the first.

Tony had finished picking up the trash that had blown up against the fence and was busy pulling the towering weeds that were anxious to take over the yard. He saw that Danny had finished cutting the grass and hollered out, "Good job, best buddy! The front lawn looks super!"

"I'll put the mower away and help you with the weeds," said Danny as he started wheeling it to the woodshed in the backyard.

As he walked by his Chevy truck, he thought, *That's a good-looking truck. I got that thing as clean as a whistle and shining just like a new penny. Dad would be proud of how I'm keeping it in tip-top shape. OK, that's done—on to the next chore. I hope Jeannie is OK. She really sounded upset when she called.* Danny came out of the woodshed, closed the door, and put the padlock in the hasp. *Farewell lawnmower—have fun in this godforsaken woodshed for another week!*

He raced back to where Tony was kneeling by the wire fence, pulling the entangled weeds from their anchors. He heard Danny race through the yard and come up next to him, so Tony didn't even look up as he said, "I'll finish the yard work…how 'bout if you haul the trash to the dump?"

"Sure," said Danny, already sprinting back across the lawn.

He bolted up the back stairs and hollered, "Rose, Tony is finishing the yard work—I've got to load the burn barrel and take the garbage to the dump. Then I'm going to Sam's to fill the truck up with gas. Do you need anything from his store? Do we have everything we need for lunch?"

"Danny, pick up a loaf of bread, milk, and some lunch meat—get a pound of baloney—and just have Sam charge it."

"OK, Mrs. Lopez, I'll be back in an hour—I should be here by twelve—see ya later."

Looking out of her kitchen window, Rose watched Danny tilt the fifty-five gallon metal can and roll it on its bottom rim. He held it snugly to keep it from falling as he rolled it to his truck. He sat it upright, tilting it just enough to get his hand under it. He put one hand on the top rim and slid the other under the bottom. He lifted it, loaded it into the back of his pickup, and drove off. She pondered. *Hmm. I wonder what's going on. I can sense he's upset. Eddie is such a sneaky boy—I don't trust him. There's something fishy going on.*

He was gone for over an hour. Behind schedule, he ran up the back stairs and bolted through the back door. Not seeing Tony or his mother, he hollered, "Tony, I'm back. I'm running late. I got the truck stuck in the sand at the dump, and it took a while to dig it out. It's twelve thirty, so I won't have a lot of time to spend with you."

He heard no response. He was sure they could hear him, so he continued. "Tony, let's have lunch and talk about our win last night—you know that we will be in LaRayme next week for the state basketball tournament."

Hearing nothing, he added, "Mrs. Lopez, do you think you will come to the state tournament?"

He waited for her familiar voice to come from somewhere. It finally came from behind her bedroom door. "I'll be there in a minute," Rose called from her bedroom. "I think Tony is in his bedroom changing from his work cloths. Go ahead and make us sandwiches—potato chips are in the cupboard. I'll have a Pepsi. Be right there."

There were a long few minutes of silence, and then he heard her footsteps sending the living-room wood floor into a symphony of creaking and cracking. Smiling, she stepped though the living room–kitchen doorway and said, "I would not miss the state tournament for anything! I know Tony helped out, but Danny, you're the school's hero. I wish your father could have seen you. Maybe he was watching from his lofty place on high. Who knows!"

Danny was busy at the counter making sandwiches, so Rose set the table and then sat down. Walking gingerly, balancing three plates in his hand, Danny said, "We're ready. Got lunch prepared, so we're just waiting for Tony." He stumbled but balanced the plates in quick response and chuckled. Recovering from his misstep, he gave Rose a quick glance and said, "Don't get up. I can handle this."

It was only a matter of seconds before Tony appeared on the scene. "I had to change my pants 'cause I ripped a hole on that damn wire fence."

Danny laughed and pointed to the plate of food waiting. As they ate, their talk centered on the basketball game of the evening before. Proud of the two star players, Rose reiterated every game point in full detail, knowing that Danny took great pride in her interest in him. After they finished eating, Danny was the first to leave the table, quickly followed by Tony. Sensitively aware of Danny's eagerness to meet Jeannie, she walked to him standing by the back door and put her arm around him. "Have a fun day!"

Standing next to him, Tony turned and reached for the doorknob. "See ya later, Mom."

He opened it but didn't walk outside. He spun around, looked at her longing eyes, and said, "I guess you have to work the swing shift tonight." Tony swiftly took a step back, turned sidewise, and gave his mom a quick kiss on her cheek. "So I'll see you around midnight when you get home."

Then they were on their way out of the house, but Tony stopped momentarily. "We'll stay up and wait for you. I know you're in a hurry, but you be careful on your drive to work." Then the door slammed shut.

CHAPTER 7
A Plan Emerges

Shortly, Jeannie heard the roar of Danny's truck coming to pick her up. His radio was blaring out the twangy sound of Duane Eddy's "Movin' 'n' Groovin'."

The door flung open, and Tony jumped out. Jeannie hopped in, scooting next to Danny. "Hi, Danny. We've got problems!" she said as Tony held the door. She then motioned for Tony to hurry. He jumped in and closed it. "Let's get going. I'll fill you in on our way to Granite Springs," she said.

They drove out of CoalVille—they had no idea who would follow them. Danny was concerned about his love. Jeannie was concerned about a new diversion plan. Tony just wanted to be there and provide whatever help he could.

Driving down the hill leaving CoalVille, Danny's eyes and mind were not on the road. He was furious. He glanced at her, then back at the road, and then back to her. She put her hand over his, which was gripping the wheel. She had picked up on his agitated state. Softly rubbing her fingers on his in a smooth, circular motion, she said in her sweet, girlish voice, "Danny, it's OK." She lifted her arm and pointed her finger down the road. He picked up on what she was nicely telling him: *Keep your eyes on the road.*

He thought. *You're right, Jeannie. We don't want to tangle with another pronghorn.* His eyes remained on the road ahead, but his agitation was not gone. "Jeannie, what happened last night? I'm going to beat the living crap out of Terry and Eddie. I'm through with those bastards. This is it—I'm going put them in their place." Danny ground his teeth as he spoke.

Stumbling over her words, she spoke softly. "Danny and Tony, last night after we talked, I was the last one to leave the gym. I did, however, spend a few minutes talking to KateLynn before all you guys took off. We…talked. You know, girl talk. About how great you guys are."

With a lump gathering in her throat, she squeezed Danny's fingers again and said, "We were so excited. It was such a great game. Then everyone left. I was the last one to leave, but I didn't think much of it."

Approaching a tight curve on the road, her hand dropped, letting him have full control of the steering wheel.

Once they were on a straight road, she paused and looked at Danny sitting next to her, putting her hand on his arm. Her eyes were shiny with the tears she was desperately trying to hold back. His name just kept tumbling out of her mouth. "Danny and Tony—I really appreciate you guys. Danny, you know what you mean to me. Danny, you're my whole world!"

Although his eyes were fixed on the road, his focus was not. "Jeannie, I know. We share a lot—you're my girl—finish your story—I need to know what happened."

Danny had one thing on his mind. *Someone is messing with Jeannie, and they are going to pay dearly!*

Her fingers tightened on his arm as she thought about what words would best recreate the events of last evening. Now with a bit more composure, she continued. "Well, like I said, I didn't pay attention to the fact that I was the last one, except for the janitor, to leave the gym. I started walking home by myself. I was halfway between my house and the gym when Eddie and Terry came out of the alley and cornered me. First, Eddie tried to grab me, and I told him to keep his filthy mitts away from me. Terry said, 'Leave her alone.' Then Eddie said, 'What did you guys find?' I was flabbergasted."

Jeannie took a long breath. She sighed as she searched for words to tell her story of that late-night, dark-alley meeting. "I didn't say anything at first. Eddie kept needling me about that fact that he and Terry had been following us and knew we had found something of value. Then he got smart with me and asked me for a date."

She stumbled over the next words. "I-I told him that ev-even if he were the last guy on earth, I wouldn't go out with him—no way! That made him mad, and he tried to slap me. I was quicker than him, and he missed. Terry butted in and told Eddie again to leave me alone. My mind was racing all over the place."

Without even thinking, her natural reaction was to embrace her hero, who she knew would go to the ends of the earth to protect her. She wrapped her left arm around his right arm. She swung her right arm across her chest, also grabbing his right arm with her right hand.

Sensing her yearning for comfort and protection, his heart pounded, knowing that he would do anything for the most precious thing in the world to him—a young girl that was wrapping herself around him, a young girl who was at the center of a mystery that he did not fully comprehend.

She squeezed Danny more tightly as she started speaking again. "Then Eddie said that he knew we had found something in the desert and wanted to know what it was. I told him we didn't find anything. I said if we did, he would never know where we buried it. He got nasty at that point and said he would find what we were hiding. If we didn't tell him what we had, he said he would tell Crazy LeRoy that we'd been snooping at his house. That scared me."

She paused and looked up at Danny's distraught look. She breathed deeply and lowered her voice. "Then he said he was going to give me a good-night kiss and reached out to grab me. I had my canvas bag with my books and school stuff, so I swung it as hard as I could—smacking Eddie upside the head, knocking him to the ground. I took off running and screamed at them. I said that you were going to beat the living crap out of both of 'em."

His fiery eyes darted from the road, quickly glancing at her as he said in a low, rough voice, "Jeannie, they are going to pay dearly for what they did to you. When I'm done with them, they'll wish they never came near you! They'll never threaten you again!"

She felt his body harden almost instantly but was not sure why. He said nothing for a moment, and then his face dropped to a look of guilt. She touched the tear leaking from his eye as he started to speak. "I should have known. I'm so sorry, Jeannie. I should have walked you home last night. I wasn't thinking. Oh, I should have been more perceptive." He exchanged hands on the wheel as he reached his right one to hers holding his arm.

Sensing his disappointment with himself, she said, "Danny, it isn't your fault."

He didn't buy it. "No. I do take responsibility. I should have had you wait outside Coach Bollas's office until I finished talking with Coach Smith. Damn those bastards. I'm so sorry, Jeannie!"

She was reluctant. "Danny, you didn't know."

Danny charged forward, getting what he wanted to say off his chest. "No, Jeannie, I should have known. Yesterday at school, Terry came up behind me. I didn't even hear him approach me. Then he said, 'Where did you hide it?' I thought he was bugging me to rattle me before the game. He said, 'You guys have been up to something at LeRoy's house. Eddie and I'll figure what BS you thugs are up to. We're watching you. We'll find where you, Jeannie, and Tony have hidden it.'"

He paused momentarily and said, "I just didn't connect the dots. Those bastards know something."

His mind filled with thoughts of revenge. *I'm going to kick the shit out of both of those asses! They crossed the line when they messed with my girl. That's it! They're going to answer to me! By the time I'm through with 'em, they won't ever threaten another girl as long as they live.*

Tony had been content to remain quiet for the time being and let Danny and Jeannie release their tensions and get a load off their minds. That time had passed.

"OK, what do we do?" Tony asked. He had been listening and knew they needed to do something to get Terry and Eddie off their backs and get the treasure hidden in a place so no one could find it. "I just hope they don't already know what we've found. It worries me."

Tony's intervention was exactly what was needed. Jeannie had had time to think of a strategy. Now it was time to reveal it. "Don't worry, Tony. I've been thinking about a plan. Actually, I hope they follow us!"

And like Jeannie, the best thing for Danny was for him to get focused on something else, like the diversion plan that Jeannie had formulated and was now taking charge to implement. But he hadn't got up to speed yet, and he shot a puzzled look at Jeannie. "You want them to follow us? Why?" Danny blurted. "I hope you know what you're doing. I sure don't! I hope somebody has a clue what's going on…I'm clueless!"

The activities they were devising while rolling down the highway in a red pickup were underway. The details of a diversion plan were about ready to be explained. A talented young girl with the innate ability to take control of most situations was ready to set her plan in motion. Meanwhile, back in CoalVille, her plan was not the only plan being concocted.

In a small coal camp, not much happened without someone noticing what went on—a mentally retarded man walked to Granite Springs on Mondays, Thursdays, and Sundays—a jealous mother watched the best ballplayer walk by her house through a peephole in her curtains. These activities were commonplace, so there was nothing to concern those who noticed. When there was a departure from the day-to-day routine, however, those who noticed the unusual activities quickly grew concerned. Such was the case today. Yes, mothers were especially observant when a daily routine changed—such was the case with Rose Lopez.

Rose snipped dead leaves from the geranium on her front windowsill. Her mind was not on geraniums—she was preoccupied with what was going on with her son, Danny, and Jeannie. She stared out the window. *Hmm, that's strange—was that Crazy LeRoy? My God, is he back?*

The driver's face sent a wave of questions tumbling through her mind. *He doesn't own a gray 1950 Chevy truck, does he? I thought his was a green 1948 Ford truck. My God, I hope it wasn't him.*

It's funny how imaginations can run wild, especially when a murderer has fled a small coal camp, leaving those in his trail of misery questioning anything out of the ordinary. *I missed seeing who was at the wheel. It wasn't fifteen minutes ago that I saw old man Calhoun's Dodge truck going down the road with Eddie driving it. Something is going on. Jeannie is upset, and Danny is concerned—hmmmm! Eddie starts driving. Crazy LeRoy kills Darla. Something doesn't seem right!*

Back on the road, Danny spotted something. He bit his teeth and furrowed his brow. "Damn! Can you beat that?" Danny said, looking into his rearview mirror while driving. "There's a 1942 blue Dodge pickup about a half mile behind us. That's old man Calhoun's truck. I know Eddie has been driving it lately, so his old man must have relented and let him take it out. We've got bigger problems than we expected. I didn't think those a-holes had wheels!"

He stopped speaking and looked at her. "Sorry, Jeannie, for my bad language. I'm really pissed! They're going to get a taste of my fists, big time!"

She understood that guys were guys, and their language was part of their makeup. It was their way of expressing tied-up feelings exploding inside them, waiting to escape.

"It's OK, Danny. I've got a plan," said Jeannie. "Here's what we do. We divert their attention tomorrow by getting them off chasing a phantom while we take the treasure out to the Boar's Tusk and bury it."

His expression quickly changed from one of anger to one of puzzlement. "Jeannie, I'm not following you—what do you mean? A phantom!" Danny questioned.

Tony was equally flabbergasted. "I've got the same problem as Danny. What are you talking about, Jeannie?"

It was her moment, and she knew it. She had two young men waiting like two little boys for their mother to give them a lollipop. She loved it.

Her breath increased, a smile quickly spreading across her face. "Just give me a few minutes to explain—hang on. I've got it worked out. OK! We head to Granite Springs. We know they're behind us. That's good! We also know there's that old warehouse on Elk Street that has a bunch of large wooden boxes behind it. You know, they use those boxes for something and have a big pile of them in their back storage yard."

She stopped, first looking at Danny and then at Tony. Both nodded at her reassuringly. She took a few quick short breaths and said, "I knew you guys were familiar with the junkyard and the stash of boxes they keep there."

Electing to have some fun in their conversation, she put her two rolled-up fists to her eyes and made a motion like peering though binoculars. Danny picked up instantly and said, "Terry?"

"Yep!" was her snappy answer, and then the words just came rushing out. "It will be real easy to sneak back there and grab one. I'm sure Eddie and Terry will be watching from a distance. Terry always has his binoculars with him and will be using them to spy on us. So once we get the box, we cruise Main once or twice and then head back to CoalVille. We'll just keep going as if we have no idea they're following us. I'll fill you in on details when we get back home with the wooden box."

She put her hand on the steering wheel over Danny's and stole an upward gaze at his face. "Both you guys will get a kick out of the phantom— we'll fix those buggers!"

The three teenage kids driving to Granite Springs had no idea they were being followed by another onlooker. LeRoy grinned as he sat behind the wheel of his truck, barely going the speed limit.

His hand reached out and touched the gray metal dashboard, and his mind drifted. He felt calm and confident. As he stared over the hood of his pickup, his hand tapped slowly on the warm metal under the windshield. *I don't think anyone saw me leave town. I have my face concealed with my floppy hat and sunglasses. No one suspects a crazy person would drive.*

His hand suddenly stopped tapping the dashboard, and LeRoy changed his train of thought. *Why are those two boys following Neferzul? Something is amiss. But never mind. They cannot outsmart me. I'll have them soon.*

CHAPTER 8

Chasing a Phantom

If her plan had a ghost of a chance of working, Eddie and Terry had to chase after a phantom. *After all*, she thought, *finding a ghost fart is impossible. How do we get them to bird-dog after one? It will be tricky, but it can be done.*

The early morning azure sky quickly changed color with the climbing sun. Clouds sweeping across the horizon above White Mountain rose to new heights, the wind driving them into a circular motion. Their brilliance as they changed to pinks and light-scarlet reds reminded Jeannie of Van Gogh's talented touch on the canvas, a swirling array of colors that emerged as a gripping painting.

With Van Gogh on her mind, the image of his painting *Starry Night* flashed before her. It immediately took her back to the events of last night, another moonless evening. Her heart sank, but then a vision of Tony and KateLynn under the starry night sky gave her a sense of tranquility.

Jeannie put her hand on Tony's and glanced at him. He turned his head and gave her a rather blank look. He was unusually quiet. He had made several comments during their ride to Granite Springs, but for the most part, he had spent the time staring at White Mountain off in the distance. "Is there something the matter, Tony?" she asked.

No sooner had her words tumbled out of her mouth than she realized what was on his mind. She immediately asked him the next question. "Did you and KateLynn have fun last night?" She touched his hand on his lap again.

A funny little expression emerged on his face.

She gently pinched his fingers and said, "I see! You did have fun!"

Danny immediately jerked his head from the road and looked past Jeannie at Tony. "Well, fill us in, Tony!" said Danny with a questioning smirk. "What happened on the front seat of my red racer last evening?"

Tony made no comment. In fact, Tony looked away and continued to stare out the window.

There was no doubt in Danny's mind. *Hmm, Tony and KateLynn frolicking on the front seat of my pickup? My pickup will never be the same again. Could it be first love? Wow!*

Fortunately for Tony, the quickly approaching pothole caught Danny by surprise. His left front wheel hit a foot-deep hole at fifty miles per hour. His truck veered to the right, and he had to crank the wheel to keep it on the road. Any thoughts he might still have had about Tony's activities last night under the Milky Way were far gone.

"Hey, we're coming up to where we turn off," said Danny.

He spotted and then pointed to their destination—a large scrap-metal facility on the outskirts of Granite Springs. It had been established in the early 1900s by the Dome family and had been in operation for three generations. They were the only company that recycled steel, copper, and other metals used in the outlying mining communities.

Approaching the turnoff, he glanced from the corner of his eye at Jeannie's face. He caught her drifting. *She didn't even see me look at her.* "What are you thinking?" he said as he tickled her left side.

"A ghost fart, Danny. Yes! A ghost fart! Our plan is to have two bullies following a ghost fart!"

He laughed. Tony, who was also now on board, laughed joyfully. Danny said. "You got me on that one! I guess you know what's going on. I'm just the driver!"

She laughed and grabbed his hand to stop him tickling her.

They slowly drove into the storage yard of the large warehouse on Elk Street in Granite Springs. On Saturday morning, the large, silent mountains of separated scrap metal waited patiently next to the railroad tracks running through the middle of the property. Unlike the residents of CoalVille, who rarely had the opportunity to travel, the metal's opportunity for travel by rail was guaranteed. It was shipped weekly to metal yards in the east. Behind the warehouse on the north end was a small dirt road that trucks used for pickup and delivery.

As Danny parked his truck in front of the large pile of metal, they were being watched. They walked on toward a large stash of shipping boxes, giggling and laughing about Jeannie's reference to ghost farts. They searched the pile of old wooden boxes looking for the best one—the one that would make their diversion work.

"Damn, these things come in all sizes. What size do we want, Jeannie?" asked Danny.

Pointing to one on the other side of the pile, she said, "That's it. That one is perfect. Come on, Tony. Let's get it."

Jeannie directed Danny and Tony to pick up the large wooden box with rope handles on its sides. They started walking away, but she stopped them. "Hey guys, get the lid for it. It was next to it where you picked it up."

Danny ran back and grabbed the lid while Jeannie scanned the area for someone…or someones. She found them. "Danny and Tony, I want you guys to keep carrying the box to the pickup. As you're carrying it, look in the direction of the service road leading to the warehouse. One block further north is G Street. Check out who is parked on the side of G Street! Be careful not to let them know you're looking in their direction." She giggled.

"They see us! Yes! They see us. We can play their game better than they can. If they think they have one up on the Pirates in the Desert, they need to think again!" Danny said as he helped Tony lift the wooden box with rope handles on each end into the back of his pickup.

Jeannie was ecstatic. "Good, we did it! Yippee! Eddie and Terry are two blocks away in that old Dodge truck, peering at us through Terry's binoculars. They took the bait!" squealed Jeannie in a soft tone.

Danny glanced at Eddie and Terry one more time. This time, however, his eyes wandered and focused on something two blocks farther down G Street that he never expected to see.

"Hey! There's a gray 1950 Chevy truck parked about two blocks up the hill from where Eddie and Terry are. All I can make out is that the driver has a large hat on. I can't see a face. Why would someone be parked there? My God, is that person spying on Eddie and Terry? What's going on?" Danny tensed as he squinted.

She cringed at just the thought of someone stalking teenagers. *Who would it be?* She tried to throw the thought away. "Danny, don't get paranoid. Who knows who it is? We don't know why they would be here. It has to be someone just messing around. Come on. Let's just go," said Jeannie.

Tony slammed the tailgate shut and made sure everything was tied down so nothing would blow out on the highway during their ride back to CoalVille. "OK, Danny, we're good to go! Let's jump in your truck and head back to CoalVille. We did it, Jeannie. We got the box and are ready to go back home," Tony remarked as he listened to Danny and Jeannie. "I hope you know what you're doing, Jeannie. I'm still lost. What do we do with a wooden box?"

The slender, well-manicured fingers of his right hand grasped the brim of his hat. Mochcom moved them to his sunglasses and lifted them slightly to get a better look. "How interesting—two boys—two little lambs watching Neferzul!" Eerie eyes peered from under the large brim of a hat. They rolled back and forth—staring first at a red truck and then at a blue truck. "They have no idea who she is, but I do! That's OK. Soon I'll have them as mine. Their skulls and hearts will be added to my collection."

His heart was pounding with delight as he visualized his next move— getting his hands on Neferzul. As his mind filled with heinous thoughts, he dug his fingernails into the wrapping on his steering wheel. The passing of time had not relieved Mochcom's nervous habit. It was a throwback to the victims he'd delighted in tormenting with his fingernails.

Mochcom's delight went undetected by Danny, Jeannie, and Tony. Eddie and Terry had no idea he was even there.

"Yes! KeeLord's skull and heart will have company." LeRoy smiled as he mumbled. "The two little lambs in their old blue truck are a bonus. I'll use them. I'll follow them so there's less chance of me being spotted following Neferzul. This is so good. What unexpected good luck. They follow Neferzul looking for riches. I follow them. Soon I will have all of them and all the riches of eternity!"

Jeannie's plan was a go. She was not only thinking about diverting Eddie and Terry from further snooping into their business but also thinking about Danny sitting next to her.

"Good work, guys," squealed Jeannie, sitting next to Danny and pawing at his arm. Her emotions were climbing, and the very thought of pulling a con on two bullies who had nabbed her in a dark alley was lifting her sprits.

"What's next?" Danny asked as he put his truck in gear and gunned the engine.

First she looked at Danny and then at Tony, speaking in an upbeat tone of voice. "Just hang on. I'll fill you in on all the details. You'll know what's next! Tony, you'll get a kick out of the wooden box! What time is it, Danny?" Jeannie asked.

He pulled his watch from its pocket and gave it a quick glance so as not to take his eyes from the road longer than necessary. "OK, Jeannie. We're hanging in there with you! It's four thirty, so now what?" Danny replied.

She beamed at the progress of her plan and the careful timing that was critical, knowing all was on track.

"Super! We're right on schedule! We'll be at Rabbit Ears at five thirty, which is perfect," Jeannie said as she laughed and looked out the back window of the truck. "Those idiots took the bait—they're following! Yippee!"

Jeannie was street-smart, something learned by experience. She grew up in CoalVille in the 1950s. Her short seventeen years of being schooled with the horse sense of life were paying off. Early on, she had discovered that diversion had been a tactic used by humanity since the dawn of time.

She giggled to herself as they enjoyed their ride, racing down the highway on their way to pull a con on two bullies chasing them in a 1942 blue Dodge pickup—a con to chase a phantom.

Jeannie sat next to Danny, thinking about the con. She laid her arm on his lap and slid her hand down his thigh. She had time to think about how lucky she was to have Danny as both a sweetheart and a friend. He was ready to defend her and beat the crap out of the two bullies who had threatened her.

He looked down and caught her smiling at him. He said nothing but was happy to see her mood had lifted.

She mused as the miles clicked away. *He's in love with his truck*, she thought. *But I think he is starting to figure out that girls are a lot more fun to love than an old red pickup.*

The ten-mile ride back to CoalVille took less than fifteen minutes. Jeannie was keeping track of time, as time was the most critical element of her plan.

"Hey, we're at my house," said Tony. "So, Jeannie, what is the plan? What's the phantom? We're all ears!"

This was the moment she'd been waiting for. "I was waiting for someone to ask. I'm patient—don't you think?" she said, giggling.

Danny's mouth pulled to the side, and his upper lip wrinkled as he asked, "Jeannie, are you having Terry and Eddie chase Harvey the Rabbit? That is too cool!"

There was a break for Tony to respond. "Come on, Jeannie, who's the phantom?" Tony turned and faced her squarely.

She poked Tony in his side and then pointed her finger at the truck's back window. "He's in the back. Eddie and Terry watched us collect the box from the warehouse, so now they're going to chase after it on a wild search for nothing!" Jeannie said with glee. "It's payback time for those jerks."

Opening his door and jumping out first, Danny hooted, "OK, Jeannie, give us more. You got my curiosity up."

Sliding under the steering wheel and following Danny, she jumped out. Anxious to divulge her complete plan, she inhaled to make sure she could finish. "All right—they know we found something," said Jeannie. "I have no idea how they found out, but they did. We need to make them think it's at my house. We're here at Tony's house, so we get a couple of shovels and a pry bar and throw them in the back of the truck. Then we go to my house and get a big cardboard box—I have it in the garage. You guys will carry it, making like it's real heavy. You'll put it in the back of the truck and rope it down so it's secure…then we head out to Rabbit Ears." She looked at Danny and Tony for comment.

There was another break for Tony to respond again. "So what's next, Jeannie? Where do we go from there?"

Their faces reminded her of two puppy dogs waiting for a treat. Giggling to herself, and with two quick breaths, she was ready to continue. "When we get to Rabbit Ears, it will be dusk but light enough for those jerks to use their binoculars to spy on us. I know that's exactly what they'll be doing. They'll watch us lift the large wooden box out of the truck. You guys will carefully put the cardboard box into the wooden box. We put the lid on it, and Danny nails it shut," said Jeannie. "Danny, do you have a hammer and nails?"

On board with every detail of her plan, Danny slapped the front fender of his pickup. "Gotcha covered," Danny said. "Nary a worry in that department. In fact, I have two hammers in the truck, so both Tony and I can nail 'er up. I've got plenty of nails."

Like clockwork, they loaded the materials, made a quick stop at Jeannie's to get the cardboard box, and then they were ready for their next phase.

With the boxes in the pickup—an empty cardboard box and a wooden box—the diversion was underway. The red racer left CoalVille with three teenage kids, all with grins on their faces.

"Our con is working," said Jeannie as she spotted a 1942 blue Dodge truck on the back road behind the old house where Danny used to live. The two bullies peering through the windshield were watching a phantom drive out of CoalVille.

CHAPTER 9
A Phantom in a Hole

His foot left the accelerator as they turned off the main highway, onto the dirt road. He gave Jeannie's hand a quick squeeze to let her know she didn't have to warn him about running into another pronghorn antelope.

"All right, almost there. Just a few more minutes. Rabbit Ears is only two miles up the cutoff road. Here we are, so hang on tight! We're on a roll…off the pavement and onto the dirt," Danny said as he gave a darting glance at her, gripping the wheel with both hands. "Jeannie, you didn't comment about my speedy turnoff this time." Danny laughed as he made the turn.

Jeannie did not reply to his remarks, but her eyes stared at the sandstone formation that was fast approaching.

Two large sections of a sandstone anticline defined what local folks called Rabbit Ears. On the east and southeast sides of the formation were small sagebrush-covered hills, each approximately a half mile away. Using these hills as a vantage point, one could observe activities only on the east side of Rabbit Ears. The back side was obstructed by the large sandstone formation.

They spoke few words for the last miles of their drive, and Danny parked in silence. Then Tony said, "We're here—and the next phase of the plan begins. Let's jump out and go to work. We've got Jeannie's con to put into motion. Those idiots are out here watching every move we make."

On a hill about a half mile from where Danny had parked his truck at Rabbit Ears, two teenage boys were watching activities unfold. They had driven to the far side of the hill and snuck over it to get to their vantage point.

"What do you think they're up to?" Eddie asked Terry.

Flapping his hand, Terry motioned for Eddie to get lower behind the brush. "Jeannie and Tony are standing next to Danny's crappy truck," said Terry, lying on his belly behind some tall sagebrush, peering through his binoculars. "They have something going on. Danny is about twenty-five feet away, kicking some dirt and messing with the ground. What are they doing at Rabbit Ears? That formation is nothing more than two big sandstone rocks that some idiot thought looked like a set of rabbit ears."

Eddie grabbed Terry's flapping hand and threw it downward. "Give me the glasses," Eddie snapped at Terry. "I want to take a look at those idiots." Terry handed Eddie his binoculars and screwed up his face in a contorted gesture, which let Eddie know that he was also a tough guy and wanted to make Danny miserable.

Crouching on his haunches, Terry looked at Eddie, not necessarily with respect but with a longing to be important also. He listened intently to Eddie.

"That pimple head Danny really thought he was hot stuff last night at the game. He thinks he's the only basketball player on the team. Well, we'll rub his nose in some real smelly stink before we get done with him," rasped Eddie.

There was a long pause with Eddie holding the binoculars, and then he raised them again. "Danny and Tony just jumped into the back of his pickup. They're messing with the boxes."

Terry's patience was waning. "Let me have a look, Eddie. They're my glasses!"

"You'll get the glasses when I'm ready to give them to you," snapped Eddie. "I'll tell you what's going on! You don't have to look!" He breathed heavily, talking to Terry while watching the con unfold. "Terry, Danny and Tony just took the heavy box they got from Jeannie's house out of the back of the pickup. Now, they're taking that wooden box out—the one they got from Granite Springs."

Getting braver, Terry moved closer to Eddie. He shot his hand over the lenses of the binoculars and snapped at Eddie, "Give me my binoculars!" Terry looked for a reaction but got none, so he barked a bit louder. "I want to see what's going on!"

"Cool it, Terry! You can look in a minute. Holy mackerel! They just put the heavy box into the wooden box. What's Danny doing? He's nailing a lid on it, and Tony's helping him. Whoopee! We'll soon have their find in our possession!" Eddie growled in a low voice.

On the southeast hill, another set of eyes—one undetected by all five kids—was observing the activities of everyone at Rabbit Ears. Mochcom had driven to the back side of the hill on an old dirt road. He, like Eddie and Terry, had parked his truck on the back side of the hill. Sneaking like a slithering snake, he made his way through the corridors of sagebrush. He found the vantage point that best suited his needs.

"That box they got from Granite Springs. They just put something into it. Hmm! What's going on?" Mochcom muttered. He rolled a rock behind the largest bush in front of him. He swayed back and forth on the rock, hands folded in his lap. His nervous conditions were not limited to digging his fingernails into whatever they grasped. A constant bobbing and swaying of his upper body was also a nervous habit.

"I'll trap them soon," LeRoy muttered, peering around the large clump of sagebrush that offered him a fine concealment from any viewers at Rabbit Ears or the hill eastward. "They can't escape me. KeeLord already has company—the skull of Nibbles. He was a bad monkey and unlocked the door to my palace. Soon my collection of skulls will grow, but they won't be chimpanzee skulls—they'll be human skulls, my little children's skulls!"

Eddie and Terry were so engrossed in the activities at Rabbit Ears, they had no idea another onlooker was chasing after them as well as a phantom. The furthest thought from their minds was that they were the unsuspecting bait for another con that was occurring as a quirk of fate—a quirk of fate that would pay huge dividends to Danny, Jeannie, and Tony, buying them the time they needed.

"Eddie, what's going on now? Come on, tell me!" Terry whispered.

"Terry, just hold your horses. I'm looking right now, and I'll tell you when I'm done," Eddie mumbled curtly.

When the lid was nailed down firmly, Danny sat his hammer on top of the box and looked up at Jeannie. "OK, Jeannie, we're ready. What's next?" Danny asked curiously.

A faint smile started to emerge as she planned her response. Looking directly at him, she said, "Danny, I'm going to point my finger in a direction. When I point, look very cautiously in exactly the opposite direction, and you'll see a flash of light every once in a while. Don't look directly at it— look at the ground first and sort of take a quick glance in the direction I told you to."

As she stopped briefly to catch her breath, he waited, knowing she wasn't finished. Then she continued. "We don't want them to suspect that we know they are up there. I think they're hiding less than a half mile from here, on a hill east of White Mountain. I see flashes of light out there in the tall sagebrush—it must be sunlight reflecting from the lenses of their binoculars. At least, that's what I think. You can judge for yourself and come up with your own conclusion," Jeannie said, stretching out her arm and pointing it toward White Mountain in the distance.

When he turned to the side, Danny came around enough to see what was going on out the corner of his eye. He smiled and said, "Yeah! Jeannie, you're right! I see the flash of light every once in a while. Those little twerps are up there spying on us. Can you beat that?" Danny said, trying not to show his anger because of what he was seeing. *They haven't seen the last of me. I'm gonna fix them good for what they did to Jeannie.*

Jeannie motioned for the boys to take a seat next to her. She wanted to kill a few minutes to make sure the sun was well on its way to hiding its face behind the western horizon. She let her eyes drop to her note pad and couldn't help but think of the bullies as Danny, Tony, and she sat on a rock for a few moments. She was going through the motions of writing something on her pad of paper, but in reality her mind had drifted. *Eddie is scary! He scared the crap out of me last night. I have no idea what he would have done to me if I hadn't gotten away!*

"Jeannie, what are you thinking about?" Danny blurted, watching her fiddle with her paper. "That funny little expression you get on your face when you're daydreaming is so predictable."

"Danny, I'm not daydreaming! You guys, pick up the wooden box by the rope handles on either end. I'll grab the shovels. We're gonna walk around to the back side of Rabbit Ears. OK! On my command, let's go."

"Eddie, what are they doing now?" Terry showed his frustration. "Come on, Eddie, those are my binoculars, and it's my turn."

"Shut up, Terry. I've got this one covered. They just picked up the wooden box and carried it to the far side of Rabbit Ears. They're out of sight."

"What now, Eddie?" asked Terry, scooting away from Eddie and resting on a small mound of desert sand.

With the sun kissing the horizon at the top of White Mountain, Eddie squinted, trying to keep the evening rays from interfering with his concentration. "We wait until they come back around to the truck. I think they're burying that box on the back side. If they hurry up, we may get a chance to dig it up tonight," said Eddie.

It didn't take long for the sun to hide half of its face behind the western skyline. At that time in the evening, shadows lengthened by the minute, and Terry took notice. "It's getting dark. In fifteen minutes it will be too late to do anything this evening. We'll have to come back in the morning," Terry rasped.

The sun making its way to its night's resting place was of no concern to Eddie. "Terry, don't worry about it getting dark. It's not a problem. We'll come back in the morning if we have to."

Meanwhile, Jeannie, confident in her execution of the unfolding con, was ten feet in front of Danny and Tony. They were carrying the wooden box, each with a hand grabbing a rope handle. She stopped and turned to face them.

"OK, guys. The next phase of the plan goes into effect," Jeannie said, smiling. "We did it, guys! Those jerks fell for it!"

Characteristic of mining operations during the 1950s in Wyoming, open mine shafts were left unattended once no longer in use. Walking through the desert at dusk or in the evening was risky without a precise knowledge of where they were. Falling into an open mine shaft that descended hundreds of feet straight down would be like being swallowed by a whale, but unlike Jonah, you would never return. The location of the open shaft behind Rabbit Ears was something indelible in Jeannie's mind.

Once they made their way to the west side of Rabbit Ears, Jeannie was positive Eddie and Terry couldn't observe their actions anymore. Looking at Danny and Tony holding the box, she pointed and said, "One hundred yards in that direction is an open mine shaft. We carry the box to it and toss it in! Terry and Eddie won't have a clue. They can't see what we're doing—Rabbit Ears is blocking their view."

It was an unusual twist of fate. Little did Jeannie know that her plan to conceal their activities from Eddie and Terry by locating a perfect spot on the west side of Rabbit Ears to carry out her con was also concealing their activities from another set of eyes. Mochcom—hiding on the hill to the southeast—had the same problem that Eddie and Terry had. Because of his lack of vision, he was also being conned.

Her heart was soaring just thinking of masterminding payback for Eddie and Terry. It was working like clockwork. "They'll think we buried it back here and can dig forever to find it if they want. They won't go near the mine shaft—it's five hundred feet straight down. They can search forever. It's a phantom they're chasing!" Jeannie squealed in a barely audible voice. "We don't have to dig back here 'cause it's impossible to detect where any digging took place in this sand."

The lengthening shadows were no more. The sun had hidden its face and only a glow of brilliant orange clouds highlighted the long western horizon of White Mountain. The frustration of two bullies who wanted to get a clear view of what was going on was building. Their problem was that they couldn't do anything about it.

"What's going on now? Have they come back to the truck yet?" Terry continued, his voice clearly showing his elevated state of annoyance. "I want to take my turn, Eddie."

"Shut up, Terry. I don't know what the hell is going on. Are you blind?

We can't see them," snapped Eddie, whose temper was also on the rise.

Jeannie, Danny, and Tony cautiously approached the gaping hole in the ground. Enough twilight remained to reveal the impending danger of the open shaft entrance to the abandoned mine. Jeannie walked in front, Danny and Tony carrying the nailed-up wooden box with an empty cardboard box inside.

Danny lifted his left arm, still holding on to the rope handle of the box with his other, and said, "Jeannie, stop! You are getting way too close to that hole. Let me and Tony go ahead."

She stepped aside and let them move in front of her. Danny was extra cautious as he approached the black mouth of that huge hole. It was a dangerous pit, deadly if you fell into it. Ten feet from the edge of it, he stopped and said, "Tony, this is far enough. We don't want to get any closer."

They put the box down. He looked at Tony and continued. "OK, we pick this thing up and swing it back and forth. On three, we let it fly, and then down the hatch she goes! OK, one…two…three…let 'er fly!"

Danny, Jeannie, and Tony watched the wooden box fly through the air and drop out of sight as it headed for the bottom of the mine shaft. The shaft was so deep they never heard it hit the bottom.

Mochcom held his shovel erect, directly in front of him. He continued to rock back and forth, sitting on the rock, grasping his shovel with both hands. "My little Neferzul is hiding something behind Rabbit Ears. I can't see her now, but I know she has something. That rock formation is hiding her from my view. Maybe, my little lambs, the two little boys who are also watching will help me find what they buried. Hmm—did Kashom show her where the emerald star and five worox stones were hidden?"

His heart pounded as he visualized it finally happening after waiting so long. "Very, very interesting. I'll get more than my little Neferzul as my prize. I'll soon control eternal youth! Yes! And as a bonus, I'll have two little sacrificial lambs. My two little boys—they watch Neferzul, and they have no idea I'm here," LeRoy mumbled in a low, rumbling voice.

"What time is it, Danny?" Jeannie asked, grabbing his upper arm.

"Five on the dot!"

She let out a small squeal of joy. "Super! It's going to be dark in five minutes!"

Tony's hand smacked Danny's, and they entwined fingers in a high-five grip. "We did it, guys! They'll chase after Jeannie's ghost fart until hell freezes over," Tony hooted.

She giggled and flicked Danny's arm with her little finger. "They have no choice but to come back in the morning to look for what they think we buried back here. Hallelujah! We'll know if our con was successful in the morning! Let's go!" Tugging at Danny's hand, Jeannie started walking back to the truck.

As they walked in that direction, she grabbed his arm firmly with both hands and unrolled his T-shirt sleeves. She looked up at him, strolling by his side, a tenderness on her face that echoed the expression Leonardo da Vinci gave his *Mona Lisa*. She was having fun not only with her love but with someone else that soon would chase her phantom.

"There're coming back to the truck. They don't have the wooden box. They buried it," Eddie squealed softly. "We're going to find pay dirt tomorrow morning."

Desperately wanting the respect of Eddie, Terry tried a new tactic by speaking harshly about Danny. "Danny thinks he's a real cool dude with his '55 Red Chevy," Terry said peering through the binoculars. "Someday I'll have a red '57 T-Bird with a round side window that will blow him away and make him take that old piece of bucket-of-bolts truck to the dump where it belongs."

His words fell on deaf ears. "Quit talking about his truck. Let's go. We're out of here," Eddie snapped at Terry.

"Hey guys," yelled Tony as they walked up to Danny's truck. "It's Saturday night, and we have no plans!"

Danny was already opening his truck door but stopped. He knew Tony had something up his sleeve. "What do you have in mind?" he asked.

Now Jeannie was in on the act. "What, Tony?"

"Well, my mom is working late at the hospital and won't be home for at least three or four hours. Let's go to my house, have something for dinner, and mess with the treasure!"

Watching Jeannie nod her head, Danny yelled, "Sounds like a plan...

let's do it!"

CHAPTER 10

More Mysteries Solved

Tony rolled the edges of the paper in his hand. His finger slid over the symbols written on it. *We derived these from the answer to the riddle on the bow. What are they for?*

He suspected they were the combination to open a lock on something. He pinched the paper tightly between his thumb and fingers, thinking of the new problems they were now faced with. One, they didn't know what the lock opened, and two, whatever it opened was not in their possession.

Danny looked at the clock on the wall, which was covered with soot from years of ticking next to the coal-burning stove.

Jeannie noticed, and that got her thinking. *Why is Danny staring at the clock?* She didn't wait but blurted out, "What's up, Danny?"

"Let's take a break. It's dinner time," said Danny. "Pepsi and peanuts only go so far, and boy, am I hungry! Jeannie, will you help me make sandwiches? I went to the store for Rose today, so we have some potato chips, lunch meat, and more Pepsi…that sounds like a plan."

Jumping from her chair, she was already headed in the right direction before Danny finished his comments.

"Sure, Danny, bread is in the cupboard, and lunch meat in the fridge, right?" she said, first opening the cabinet drawer and gazing at the mismatched utensils.

"Yep! You've been here before and know where the food is located."

Listening to Danny and Jeannie's conversation, Tony grinned as he watched Jeannie head for his mother's breadbox.

Her natural instincts took over as she prepared a meal for all of them. She arranged folded paper napkins, old tarnished silverware, plates, and glasses in proper order to set the mood for a relaxing break.

Danny's heart skipped, watching his newfound love making dinner and setting the last detail in place—a large geranium in full bloom she'd lifted from the kitchen countertop—placing it at the center of the table.

"OK, guys. We're ready!"

It was gone in a flash—the thirty minutes they sat talking about clues over their dinner break. They had no idea where their adventures would take them, but staring at the gold treasure on the table was far from routine for the children of coalminers who had only dreamed of being rich.

"Hey, that was great, Danny. That food hit the spot. You're a good host—so now I guess it's back to the search for clues," said Jeannie.

Turning in his chair, he smiled to himself, knowing that there was at least enough food in the kitchen to make a meal. "Hey, you're the one that fixed the meal…not me."

Jeannie took a breath. "Where's the paper with the ten symbols?" She swung around on her chair and reached for it. "Oh, there it is. I'll get it. Tony's been playing basketball and tossed it in the flowerpot."

She giggled. Danny added nothing but just nodded at Jeannie, took it from her hand, straightened it out, and asked, "Where do we go from here?" Paper in hand, Danny gestured with his glass of Pepsi, lifting it in the air. "We don't have a clue what this string of symbols is all about. We might as well be looking at a two-thousand-year-old book written in a foreign language. I don't think it could be any stranger than these symbols."

She laughed and pointed her finger at Tony and said, "You'll figure something out. Isn't that right, Tony?"

Tony threw an arm over the chair back and looked past Danny to her. "Hey Jeannie, don't put all this pressure on me. I don't know if I'll figure out what these symbols are for. I may just agree with Danny and consider it a bunch of gobbledygook, like his two-thousand-year-old book written in a strange language." He rolled his eyes at her. "But I do have a suggestion."

Sitting at the end of the table, Danny first glanced at Jeannie on his right and then to Tony on his left, not necessarily understanding what was up but knowing the hunt was on again.

"Oh yeah? What?" blurted Danny, watching a smile stretch across Tony's face.

Jeannie stood and waved for Danny's help. "Let's clean up the table and let Tony get the treasure ready so he can show us his new revelation."

It didn't take long. Tony had things ready. He flipped a few gold tablets over in their binder and pointed his finger at various drawings on them. "There are a bunch of pages in the gold tablets. We haven't looked at many of them yet. Why don't we start looking to see if they have any clues that might help solve the mystery of what this code of symbols is for?"

"Good idea, Tony," Danny replied. "Let's go!"

For the next hour, they sat around Tony's kitchen table and took turns looking for clues in a set of gold tablets. They wrote things on Jeannie's pad of paper that they thought were important. As they struggled to find a clue, time drifted by.

Standing behind Tony and looking over his shoulder, Danny was looking not only at the drawing but also at Jeannie sitting across the table. Her eyes were reflecting the orange glow from the late afternoon twilight that danced on the tablets of gold, which reminded Danny just what a beautiful treasure he had. He smiled slightly as he thought, *Sunlight dancing on gold is not commonly seen in CoalVille…especially when it's on gold between me and the most gorgeous girl in the world.*

"Wow!" Danny said, pointing to something. "Look at this drawing." Raising his eyebrows, he continued. "This looks like people holding hands in a chain—the first guy is holding on to a green handle on a box with a pink object on it. Look, there are five orbs at the end of the points on the star. What does it mean?"

Tony wasn't looking at the page Danny was focusing on, but the one adjacent to it. He was half listening to Danny and at the same time trying to concentrate on what he was studying.

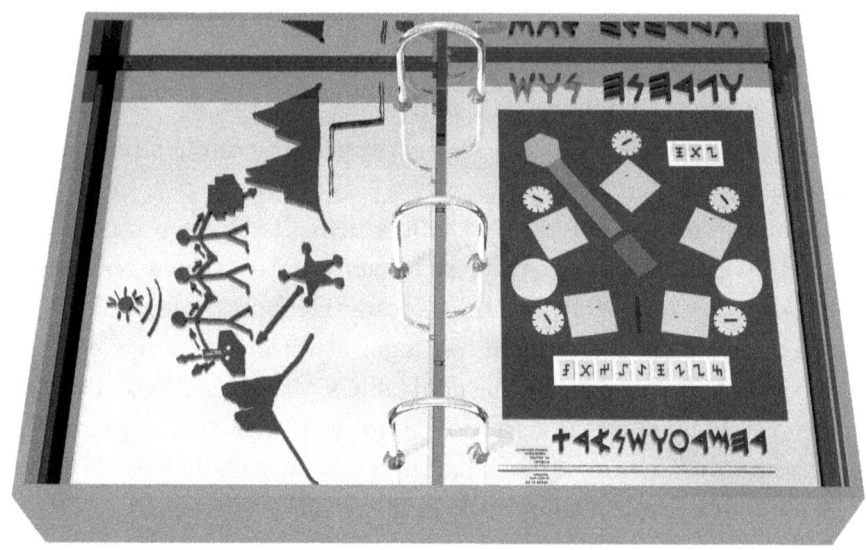

"I don't know, Danny," Tony said in a puzzled voice. "Whoever wrote on these gold tablets used the Phoenician alphabet—but that isn't all they used. There's something that looks like a combination dial on this drawing. Yeah, look at that! Look! Aren't those mirror-image symbols on the combination wheels? Yes! This is the clue we are looking for!"

In a frenzy of excitement, Jeannie jumped to a conclusion. "We're on to something *very big*," squealed Jeannie. "Those symbols on the combination dials represent the answer to the riddle, 'The key dances on the seventh moon for seen far as a distant star,' which we figured out to be Intipraimi. First we translated the ten English letters to ten Phoenician letters, and then we translated the string of ten Phoenician letters using the dial and my medallion to ten mirror-image symbols. Those ten symbols are the combination to open something depicted on this gold tablet. Yes! You know it! We hit pay dirt. We just need to find the object that has the combination on it!"

Despite her sudden excitement, Tony remained calm and let her finish. At the appropriate moment, he shook his head and said, "Not so fast, Miss Jeannie." His voice jumped. "Look closely at that drawing on this gold tablet—what do you see?"

Her jaw dropped while her hand came to the table with a slap. "I have no idea, Tony. It's way too late to play games and be a smarty—just tell us!" Jeannie snapped at him. "Your mother will be home in an hour and a half, so let's not play games. Let's work together."

His face pulled to a frown, not angry but with an expression of concern. "I hate to rain on your parade! But that's life! And I know it's late," Tony said. "Look, there are only nine combination symbols on the drawing. Intipraimi has ten letters, which would be ten mirror-image symbols, so what do you think of that? You jumped the gun. Better slow down, Lone Tree, and be a little more observant!"

That stinks! You did rain on my parade. "Why are you so smart and... observant?" she muttered. "I'm sure glad you are, though," she added.

She stood and walked around the old wooden chair she'd been sitting in. She gazed out the window and slowly slid her fingers along its top. She felt the chips in the layered paint that had redecorated its appearance over its years of service. She drifted into thought. *We have another riddle to solve.*

"*Juventud eterna viene desde dentro la estrella intacta por medio de le cuyos ojos refleja,*" she said with glee in her voice, speaking in Spanish.

Now it was Danny whose jaw dropped. "What in the sam hill are you talking about, Miss Jeannie?" he snorted. "Speak English!"

Her reply to his remarks was swift. "We need to figure out what 'Eternal youth comes from within the intact star by means of him whose eyes it reflects' means. The answer to this riddle must have nine letters associated with it." She watched his every expression to see if he was buying her line of reasoning. "That tells me there's something else we need to find—something that has a combination on it, something that the string of nine mirror-image symbols opens—the object depicted on this Gold

Tablet!" Jeannie said with a polite smile on her face.

He didn't buy it. "Jeannie, you're on a tangent. Look, we're working on finding a clue for the ten symbols, not heading off on a tangent toward another riddle."

She studied the strange little smile that started creeping across his face and knew his mind had taken off someplace.

Pulling a chair from the table, he sat and looked at the tablets in front of them as he thought, *I saw something earlier. Which gold page is that drawing on?* Slowly he continued. "We need to keep focused on one thing at a time and not get derailed. I know you have good intentions, but let's stay on topic," Danny commented politely. "Push those gold pages over here. I have an idea."

She helped Tony slide the red metal box containing the gold tablets across the table to where Danny was seated. She walked around the table to his chair. Then, standing behind him, she looked over his shoulder.

"I want to see if there's anything that might give us some help," said Danny as he studied the gold tablets methodically. Unlike Tony and Jeannie, who flipped through the tablets doing a cursory study, Danny was more observant. He was half listening to what Jeannie and Tony were talking about as they watched him and half concentrating on drawings in the tablets he was leafing through.

Then, suddenly, Danny burst out, "Jeannie! Jeannie! Jeannie, look at this! Look at this drawing. On one side it shows a green star with the rainbow-colored gemstone orbs at the star points." He took a gulp of air and exhaled quickly. Then he rushed on with his theory. "I don't know what that is all about, but look at the adjacent tablet—the one on the opposite page. *There it is!* It's a drawing of a box with a combination lock—a combination lock with ten wheels! Yep! That's right! There are ten symbols! We need to find this box. I'll bet it's got something of real value in it!" Danny said, beaming from ear to ear. "Cool, eh?"

"Good work, Danny!" shouted Jeannie. "That is SWEET!"

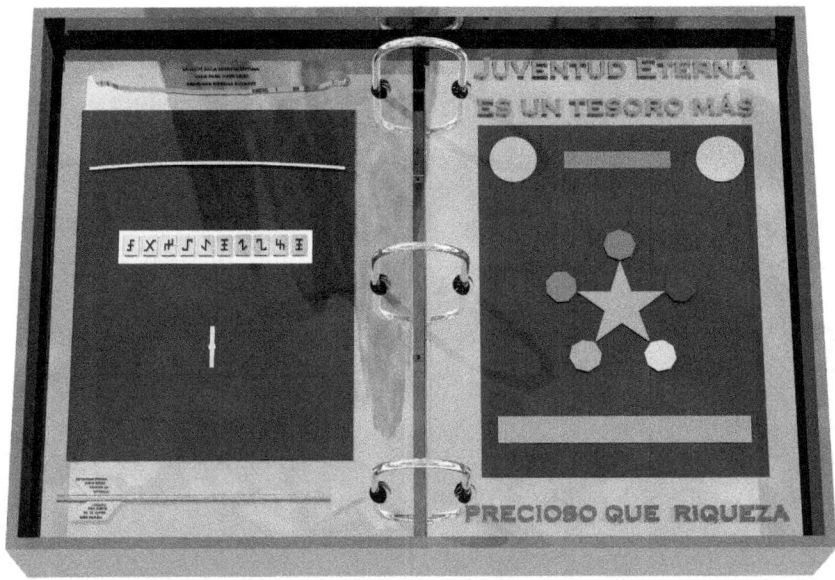

"I'll bet the combination you're looking for has to do with a star. On the other drawing we looked at, the sun is shining on some people holding hands and a star with the five orbs. In this drawing, the star and rainbow-colored orbs show up again."

There was a long pause. His face looked puzzled as he asked, "Do you think the sun and star are connected?"

Like the slap of a killer whale's flipper on her face, his last question jangled her inner soul. She shuddered and answered, "I don't know, Danny." But her mind was already pursuing an answer. *Our legends talk about the keys that open the bottomless pit by the star of the chamber. They also talk about harnessing the power of the sun. Hmm…Danny just hit on something, and he didn't even realize it.*

He waited for more, but as the pause lingered, Danny said, "No daydreaming, Jeannie." Then he hesitated as his eye caught something else. "By the way, what does this mean?" Danny pointed to the Spanish words just above the diagram of the star.

With her hands resting on his shoulders, looking over the back of his head, she studied the drawing. Then, letting her fingers glide upward through his hair and fiddling with his ears, she repeated the Spanish phase that Danny was pointing to. "*Juventud eterna es un tesoro más precioso que riqueza.*" Then she translated it. "Eternal youth is a treasure more beautiful than wealth."

Her head bent down, and she breathed hot breath down the side of his neck and said, "Basically, it's telling you that the treasure is priceless—but can't be spent! Danny, whoever wrote this is talking directly to you! Don't spend the treasure!"

He turned in his chair and looked upward at her. "Well, do you know what I say to that, Miss Jeannie?" Without hesitation, he answered, "Danny Roberts *es un tesoro más precioso*—and I will spend what I please!"

Jeannie burst out laughing. "Good comeback! *You* are a priceless treasure! Danny, you're just too cool! You must have paid some attention to what Miss Black was teaching us in Spanish class last year—but you can't spend the treasure! And oh, by the way, thanks for pointing out the drawing of the box with a combination lock. That's going to be significant! You're a sweetheart!"

CHAPTER 11

Legend of the Boar's Tusk

"Where do you guys think the box is? And what do you think is inside it?" asked Tony. In search of answers, his mind churned, but it was like a blank stare into nowhere. Tony suspected the combination on the paper he kept fiddling with opened something. But that was the mystery. Tapping his fingers on one of the gold tablets gave him a clue. He knew the value of the treasure they'd already found had to be enormous; he suspected that whatever the combination opened must be of incalculable value.

He looked at Danny and Jeannie and waited for them to answer. They didn't. The volume of his voice rose with his next series of questions. "What are you guys doing?" Tony asked. "Why are you guys messing around?"

Standing behind Danny's chair, Jeannie's arm draped around his neck and glided across his chest. For a few moments more, she paid no attention to Tony. But her sense of unease grew as Tony's eyes remained fixed on her. She glanced at him sidewise, her hand moving slowly under the top button of Danny's shirt, and said, "Tony, Danny just scored a big one! And yes, we are just messing around."

Her attention swung back to Danny. Sliding her fingers just barely under his partly opened shirt, they suddenly came to a stop. She gingerly pinched his chest and said, "Tiny muscles."

Perplexed, Danny looked up over his shoulder at her. "What?"

She giggled. "Me, not you! I need to lift weights to catch up with you!"

He didn't answer. He stood up, turned, put one foot on the chair between them, and grabbed the back with both hands. His eyes rolled around, looking at Jeannie's body standing straight as an arrow by his chair. His hand came up and tucked under her arm. Letting his fingers slowly slide down her side, she started giggling as they bounced over her ribs. He waited a moment and then said, "Big ribs!"

She laughed more freely. "Good, Danny!"

About at the end of his rope, Tony looked on, his face drawing into ever more impatient lines by the moment, not angry but wanting to jump headlong into their next adventure. But unfortunately, without Danny and Jeannie, he was stalled.

Bang! The loud sound came from Tony's direction.

Jeannie's arm flew into the air, Danny started, and both of their heads snapped to the direction of the loud noise. Just in time, they saw Tony's hand lift from the table. It was still wobbling from his hard slap.

"What the hell are you doing?" Danny hollered.

Tony gave them many darting looks but said nothing. He gestured to them to sit at the table and get back to business.

Reluctantly, they bobbed their heads. "OK!"

Rearranging the chairs a bit, Tony again put Danny on one side of him and Jeannie on the other. His scribbled notes lay on the table in front of him. "All right, you guys, here's my plan," Tony said as he started to take the leadership. He was sure of his position—captain at the helm of the good ship *Wisdom*. He was ready to sail it to the discovery of a box containing a priceless treasure. In his own mind, he had just appointed himself the captain. His problem was that, without the aid of a navigator, he had no idea where to sail the ship.

Tony's serious look was now directed right at Jeannie. "Jeannie, what do you think this combination opens?" he asked. "I think we were real lucky to find what we have already."

"Tony, luck is not what's leading us to hidden treasure—it's Kashom."

Surprised by her answer, he responded, "Jeannie, I know you have your beliefs. I know you have been brought up in the culture of the Kashome people, but I'm not Kashome, and I think it's Lady Luck."

Quick to jump in and give Tony some support, Danny added, "Jeannie, I think Tony's right. We've had a lot of luck!"

Things started smoothly, but suddenly Danny squirmed in his chair. He gave Tony a puzzled look. Tony said and did nothing. Then it happened again—a firm clawing at his leg. At least, that's what Danny felt. He looked past Tony at Jeannie, who had both hands on the table. He felt it again, but with a more pronounced jolt.

This time, his sudden jerk got Tony's attention. "What's going on with you?"

Noticing Danny squirming, Jeannie had a hunch. She scooted her chair back from the table a bit and snuck a quick, nonchalant glance under the table that neither Tony nor Danny detected.

Two dark blue eyes peered around Danny's leg. She smiled and waited for Tony to finish questioning Danny.

There were no more questions because then it happened again. Danny jumped out of his chair and hollered, "Something is under this table." His words just kept coming. "I think it bit me!"

Jeannie's smile was waiting to explode further.

Tony's eyes followed Danny jumping around behind him.

Danny yanked the chair from the table and dipped his head to look under it. "What the hell is that damned cat doing in Tony's house?" yelled Danny.

Zanzee shook his head, and the old familiar sound of his earrings chiming together came from under the table. *Tinkle, tinkle!*

There was no stuffing his words back in his mouth. Danny's foot was in it, and all he could do was look sheepishly on at Jeannie.

That wasn't good enough for her. "Danny, quit calling my cat 'that damned cat.' I don't like it! I've already told you that Zanzee is a special gift from the gods and that he has special powers. You just made fun of him, but soon you'll realize who he is!"

She reached and picked up Zanzee. Holding him on her lap, she said, "Oh, Zanzee, you're here. I thought you'd come around today. You always show up when I need you the most—appearing out of nowhere!"

He looked at her, twitched his tail, blinked, and said, "Meow, meow."

Nodding her head at Tony, she said, "Right now, we need your help to unscramble a mystery. Tony is stuck. He needs a navigator. Yes, Zanzee—can you help us solve the mystery of where something is hidden that has ten combination wheels on it?"

His head shook up and down, rattling his earrings. His little mouth flew open and he meowed loudly.

She petted him with one hand, and looking at the boys got her laughing out loud as she said, "Thank you, Zanzee!"

Tony's eyes popped. He no longer was fumbling with papers. He'd just lost his position as captain of the good ship *Wisdom*. He was no longer at the helm—Zanzee was.

Zanzee jumped from Jeannie's lap. He dashed across the kitchen floor in three bounding leaps. He landed in the wooden box. Following his moves, Tony blurted out, "Jeannie, look at Zanzee. He's in the box with the treasure stuff. Hey, he's pawing at one of those gold plaques!"

She was on her feet in a flash and at the box in record time. Standing with her head bent, she asked, "What are you trying to show us, Zanzee? Let me look! Yes, you are helping us solve the mystery! We'll show Danny a thing or two, won't we?" Jeannie picked up the thing he was pawing at and said, "This is the plaque we haven't looked at yet."

She spun around and raced back to the table. "Guys, Zanzee is telling us something. He's the real navigator of the ship that Tony is trying to sail." She smiled and said confidently, "I think he's helping us solve the mystery of where the hidden object is. Danny, would you hand me my Biblia Reina-Valera!"

He didn't know what was going on. Holding it in his hand, he said, "Here it is." *Maybe that cat is special—this is just crazy.*

Although she reached to take it, he didn't give it to her. He grabbed her hand instead and said, "Jeannie, I didn't know what was scratching my leg. When I saw the cat, I didn't know it was Zanzee." He paused, his sad, forlorn eyes staring at her. "Forgive me. I'm sorry!" Then he handed her the Reina-Valera.

"Thanks, Danny," she said, as she flashed her eyes at him. "Well, we have references here to four more Reina-Valera verses."

He got her message and nodded, returning her smile.

She took the lead and was on her way. "Here we go. Four more references: Salmos, chapter eighty, verse thirteen; second Samuel, chapter twenty-two, verse three; Ezequiel, chapter forty-two, verse twelve; and Mateo, chapter two, verse ten."

Drawn into the excitement of another hunt, Danny and Tony moved closer to her. "What do they say, Jeannie?" they asked.

Jeannie felt a great rush of affection for Danny as she reached and took his hand before she started to read. "The first one is 'Boar out of the wood doth waste it.' The second one reads, 'The god of the rock… and high tower…saves us from violence.' The third is 'The doors of the chambers…a door…even the way directly before the wall toward the east…one enters into.' And the fourth one is this: 'When they saw the star, they rejoiced with exceeding great joy.'"

"Danny, what do you make of this?" Tony threw his arms in the air as if to signify a state of complete bewilderment.

"Look, Tony," Jeannie chimed in. "This is a simple one. We are about to take a journey that is being directed by the gods—with Kashom and Zanzee showing us the path to travel."

Tony's lips pulled down, and his eyebrows dropped. "Like I said, Jeannie, that's a giant leap of faith—but please go on."

She didn't look at him, knowing full well his facial expression echoed his last sarcastic comment. "I'm sure the first two verses are telling us to search at the Boar's Tusk," she said, clapping her hands. "My people tell the legend of the Boar's Tusk."

Tony added a pout to his frown.

Still not looking directly at him, she rolled her eyes and said, "I will tell you guys the essence of that legend. Oh, by the way, Danny? You have no choice in this matter. You have to listen, and please pay attention! Here we go."

The Legend of the Boar's Tusk

In the faraway land of Kopaz, at a time long ago, Kashom, a young prince, lost his honor and position in line for the throne. His younger sister, Princess Aeraipondes, was murdered by Gorom Mochcom—a very evil man. He was the high priest of the royal court of Kopaz, and he had pulled a con on the royal family that put the blame on Prince Kashom. That young prince had to leave his homeland and somehow came to the Scarlet Desert, but he never dies and has the gift of eternal youth.

Kashom vowed never to be hurt again by lies. In his new life in the desert, he became the father of the Kashome Indian Nation, and the first law of his people was never to tell a lie. The person who first broke the law was Kashom's firstborn son, Yellow Moon. He lied to his father about killing the sacred desert eagle. He left his sister, Moon-Of-Day, alone while hunting for the eagle, and she mysteriously fell into a crevasse and was killed.

The spirit of the wild boar came to Yellow Moon in a dream, enraged at the young warrior because he broke his father's law. The spirit of the wild boar told him he must conquer the beast within himself by killing a wild boar with only a knife. Yellow Moon left his family in disgrace to search for a wild boar. But the wild boar was not to be found in the Scarlet Desert, so Yellow Moon spent the remainder of his life carving a large rock into the shape of a boar's tusk—with only a hatchet. By the time he finished his task, he was an old man.

The old man, who was Yellow Moon, called his father and the Kashome people to gather at the base of the large towers that rose as a high monument from the desert's floor. He climbed to the top of the Boar's Tusk and looked down at the still-young man who was his father, Kashom, and said in a loud voice, "Father, it is finished. The keys unlock the bottomless pit by the star of the chamber!" Then he threw himself from the top of the monument and fell to his death at the feet of his father.

Kashom told his people that his son Yellow Moon no longer had a wild beast within him. He had redeemed himself, and his spirit has befriended the wolf, Yellzor, who reminds us in the stillness of the night when he howls to the moon that the Boar's Tusk stands forever for truth and honor.

Danny paid attention to every word but was figuratively thrown by one of her comments.

"So, Jeannie, what does this legend have to do with these verses in the Reina-Valera? What do these gold tablets and the sundial key have to do with the Boar's Tusk? What is this business about 'The keys unlock the bottomless pit by the star of the chamber'? Your legend doesn't make a bit of sense...and a wolf called Yellzor!" Danny said with a questioning look on his face. "That all sounds like crazy stuff!"

Jeannie was offended by his last comment. *Crazy stuff? You'll find out, Mr. Know-It-All.* But the reality was that she knew she didn't have an answer that would satisfy him. Jeannie elected to move on without any more confrontation, as she had more on her mind than Danny making snarky comments.

"I don't know what the sundial has to do with the Boar's Tusk. I'm not sure what Yellow Moon's final words—the keys unlock the bottomless pit by the star of the chamber—mean. My mother once said it had to do with what the Kashome people call the Pearl of Time, which is eternal youth. Quite frankly, I don't understand it!"

Then it dawned on her, and her face burst into a huge grin. "No, wait! I do have the answers!" she said enthusiastically.

She stepped next to him and quickly, teasingly, pulled his shirt out of his pants before jumping back from his reaching hand. She giggled. "Not fast enough!"

Now with intent interest, she grabbed the old wooden chair, flipped it around, straddled the seat, and sat with her back to the late afternoon sun. Her arms rested on the top, and the front of her body pressed up against its back as she continued. "As far as these verses in the Reina-Valera, let me explain what I think is going on: The first verse—Salmos eighty thirteen—refers to the spirit of the wild boar that came to Yellow Moon to tell him how to regain his honor! But there was no guarantee!"

Putting her finger to her mouth, she paused. "Here's what I think: it says, 'Boar out of the wood doth waste it.' Basically, Yellow Moon would have to fight the wild boar with only a knife, and he might lose and be killed by the boar!"

Dropping her finger from her mouth, she made her point. "The wild boar was not in the desert, so Yellow Moon chose an alternative—to carve the Boar's Tusk with only his hatchet. He did not know if his efforts would be wasted."

She studied their facial language to determine if she had their attention. She did, so she marched on. "This verse and the second one are tied together and are telling us where to search. The second verse—second Samuel twenty-two three—I believe refers to the high towers in the desert—the Boar's Tusk that Yellow Moon carved with only a hatchet. The completion of this task freed him from the violence of the wild beast within him. Basically, it's at the Boar's Tusk where our search continues."

Taking a large breath of air, she looked at Tony. Plainly, he was convinced, knowing it took a special kind of competence to get to where they were today. "Keep going! You're doing great!"

She looked at Danny and asked, "Are you good?" He remained silent. Finally, Jeannie asked stiffly, "Are you OK?"

His smile grew increasingly large in a matter of seconds, and he answered, "Oh, don't mind me. I was just deep in thought. Sorry! And please forgive me, my love, for making fun of the wolf Yellzor…who knows, maybe someday I'll see that wolf in person. Yeah, you have Zanzee. Maybe I'll have Yellzor!"

She waved a high five and said, "Yeah, you just might!" She smiled and went on. "OK, the third and fourth verses tell us where to search at the Boar's Tusk. These are the ones we need to study closely. You both have been to the Boar's Tusk many times."

They nodded. She giggled and pointed to the doorway between the kitchen and living room.

"So the third verse talks about the space between the towers, which it calls a door, and it refers to the east tower. The last one tells us to look for a star. Combining the third and fourth verses tells us to stand in the doorway and look for a star on the east wall."

After all the studying by Tony, it was Zanzee who had opened the door to their next adventure. It was Jeannie who flawlessly interpreted the Reina-Valera references. It was Jeannie who unscrambled the clues. It was

Jeannie who had the ingrained knowledge of a desert people's culture, the centuries-old Kashome culture. Tony was not about to invade that territory.

His only response was "Good work, Zanzee! Good work, Jeannie!"

She stood and motioned for Danny and Tony to stand—Danny on her right and Tony on her left. She put an arm around each one but squeezed her right arm a bit more firmly. "Guys, our next adventure is the Boar's Tusk! There have to be petroglyphs on the east wall of the doorway! We'll look for them because I think that will lead us to our big find!" she said giggling and laughing. "Thank you, Zanzee. You did come through for me! I knew you would."

"Meow, meow." Zanzee looked at Jeannie and twitched his tail.

Tony's frown and pout had evaporated. He took a deep breath as if bracing himself and said, "*Super!*"

With Jeannie still holding the two boys, Tony turned his head slightly and gave her a nervous look, but her playful nodding told him that all was well and that there were no hard feelings.

"I'm glad you and Zanzee can figure this stuff out! God, I try, but—"

Her face thoughtful, no sign of teasing, she cut him off. "Tony, you are essential. Believe me, you are!"

His heart jumped, knowing she was respectful of his role.

She dropped her arms, walked forward a few steps, grabbed her chair, and turned it. She sat and motioned to Zanzee to jump on her lap. Now she was facing Danny and Tony, standing a few feet in front of her. Two sets of blue eyes reflected the afternoon rays of light filtering through the window behind the boys. They sparkled more brilliantly than the stars of the Milky Way in the black Wyoming sky at midnight.

Looking past Tony, Danny's heart grew a little larger, making room for a sleek black cat along with his true love. He blew her a kiss. "I think we had better wrap it up. Rose will be home in half an hour. Tony and I will clean things up and hide the treasure in the box out in the coal shed behind the house. We have a busy week coming up at school, so we won't be able to do anything until next weekend—the Boar's Tusk adventure will just have to wait a week. We have a big basketball game next Friday. Tony and I have a lot of practicing with the team to get ready for the game."

He walked to the chair where Jeannie sat holding her cat and said, "And like Jeannie said, 'Zanzee, *thank you!*'" He reached and scratched Zanzee behind his ear as he thought, *I want to spend an eternity with her! And Zanzee…well, I guess he'll be our cat!*

CHAPTER 12

A View of Terror
From Spider Hill

They were everywhere—crawling and scurrying over the sand and rocks and venturing onto the asphalt road. Their problem was that they weren't fast enough to get out of the way of speeding cars. Stepping over a squished glob of goo on the edge of Main Street, Jeannie was careful not to get her shoe close to it. It was that time of the year, and giant monkey-faced spiders were out in force. Jeannie had no intention of having dead spider guts on her.

She cringed as she walked by the splat of gunk on the road that now had a trail of red ants leading to it. They were having an early morning breakfast, feasting off the entrails oozing out of the hard round shell that had the face of a monkey on it. The legs were no longer stretched out, making it the size of a silver dollar. The spider's dying movements had curled them up under its giant hard-shell bottom.

As she walked on down the street to Tony's house, she had no idea she was being stalked. She had no idea the horror that lived in the mind of her stalker. Jeannie was totally oblivious that a mentally retarded person was not who he was pretending to be.

CoalVille at seven thirty on a crisp Sunday morning in the spring of 1958 was a ghost town. The only movement—other than the myriad monkey-faced spiders crawling in random directions—that caught Jeannie's eye as she walked alongside the road was an old, scraggly black dog chasing an alley cat. The cat managed to jump to the top of a wooden fence. The silhouette of the cat on the fence and the howling dog jumping up and down in a desperate last-ditch effort sent a chill through her. *I hope we're OK. I hope nobody finds our treasure. I hope nobody tries to get it. I hope nobody tries to hurt us!*

The time it took Jeannie to walk down Main Street through Sand Camp gave her the perfect opportunity to get lost in the caverns of her mind. *I saw Eddie drive by my house this morning. He picked up Terry and went the back way. I think they took the bait—can't wait to tell Danny and Tony. Terry and Eddie are mean boys. I hate them. Why do they have to butt into our business? I sure hope they spend two or three hours looking for the phantom. I hope we can get the treasure out to the Boar's Tusk and hidden so no one but Danny, Tony, and I know where it is.*

It was not only Eddie and Terry who consumed her thoughts. The message on the brass arrow was haunting her, and she couldn't stop thinking about it. *Juventud eterna viene desde dentro la estrella intacta por medio de le cuyos ojos refleja. Am I getting the correct translation? Eternal youth comes from within the intact star by means of him whose eyes it reflects. What does that mean?*

Not only was the meaning of the message on the brass arrow haunting Jeannie, not only were the bullies and what they we up to haunting Jeannie, but suddenly a new challenge emerged as well.

Her hand flew to her gaping mouth, covering it with widespread fingers. Her head slowly followed, monitoring the movement of an old Chevy truck that was so well maintained and clean that it looked essentially new. Immediately, her mind envisioned the worst. *Oh my God! There's that gray '50 Chevy truck! Who was driving it? I hope I'm not imagining things! Why is that truck in CoalVille?*

A cold chill swept through her body, causing her to tremble—a chill not from the cold spring drizzle, but rather a chill from suspecting that a stalker was after someone.

Walking the last few hundred feet to Rose's house, she saw Tony. *Oh, there's Tony, sitting on his porch steps. I hope we have a fun day.* But black clouds hanging low in the sky and a drizzling rain spattering on her face sent feelings of depression though her. *I sure hope the sun comes out and this drizzling rain goes someplace else.*

"Hi, Tony," she said, stopping in front of him.

Surprised by the tense look on her face, he answered, "You look like you just lost your last friend."

"Oh, Tony," she said with a sigh. "I started out great when I left my house, but then, as I walked down through Sand Camp, I just started thinking."

"And?" said her friend with a puzzled look.

"Well, Tony, I have a lot of things on my mind."

Her look was blank. She said nothing and stared at him sitting on the bottom step. He waited. "Are you OK?" asked Tony.

She hesitated for a few moments and then continued. "Oh, Tony, where do I start? We have started the most unbelievable journey. I'm excited, but I'm scared."

Perceptive, Tony picked up on her drift. "What are you scared of?"

"LeRoy," she snapped. "I think he's driving that old gray Chevy truck. Why is he?" Tony didn't answer. She stared at him. He remained speechless, so she continued. "I'm scared of Eddie and Terry too, but at least we know who they are. We have no idea who LeRoy is. I think he is a deranged, crazy old man who is unstable. He scares me."

"Jeannie, come on! You're letting your imagination run wild! The authorities said that LeRoy fled the state. They have searched high and low for him, and now they suspect he is in California."

Her face was blank, and he knew his words were flying over her head, but he raced on anyway. "Look, Jeannie, he doesn't own a Chevy. You saw his Ford in his shed. It was impounded by the police. Come on, he isn't around here. The police have roadblocks everywhere searching for him. He's gone!"

He knew she wasn't buying it. Tony wasn't sure what to say. He thought for a minute, trying to formulate something that would console her. "Jeannie, someone once told me that when you climb a high hill, it's lonely at the top. I think that's not true for us. Our adventures are taking us to untold heights. It's not a small hill we're climbing but one large mountain, and when we reach the top—look out, world! Here we come! We're a team, and there's nothing like having friends to pick us up when we're weighed down," Tony said with a smile on his face.

For all his efforts, he might as well have been reading a Shakespeare play. She just shook her head and changed the subject. "Where's Danny?"

"I think he's talking to my mom. He'll be out soon!" answered Tony.

But he picked up on her lingering concern. No matter what he said, he wasn't going to relieve her of her fear of an unstable, crazy old man. There was no fantasy involved. The subject was real. His mind filled with the horror that he had witnessed in LeRoy's palace. *He's an evil old bastard!*

Yet his smile told her he also wanted to change subjects. "Jeannie, thanks again for talking to KateLynn. Boy, did we have fun on Friday night. I owe you a lot. I don't know if she would have noticed me if it weren't for you. She would have probably thought I was some technical geek she didn't want anything to do with."

Jeannie laughed. "Thanks, Tony, and you're not a technical geek." She had a twinkle in her eyes. "That's what friends are for. I know you would like to have her out on adventures. Let's wait a few weeks and see where all this takes us." She grabbed his hand. "We'll have fun today. As soon as we are on our way to the Boar's Tusk, I'll fill you guys in on the latest about our con and how it is going!"

"Can't you tell me now? I'm anxious!" he asked.

"It will only be a minute or two. We'll be on our way shortly," said Jeannie. *Danny, Tony, and I are going to find more treasure—I just know it!*

Just then, Danny came out. "Hi, guys! Top of the morning to you! Let's get the treasure from the shed, load 'er up, and out to the Tusk we go!" Looking at Jeannie and Tony, he thought, *Good friends—Jeannie and Tony—couldn't have better ones! And Jeannie is much more than a friend.*

"Jeannie, do you think our con worked? Do you think they took the bait and are, at this very moment, searching for a phantom?" Danny said with a chuckle.

She walked to his side. "I was just telling Tony that I will fill you guys in on the phantom chase. But let's get going. We'll have time to talk on our ride to the Tusk. We do, however, need to take the back road and make one stop," she said.

He stopped and turned to give her a strange look with drooped eyebrows and turned up lips. "What stop are you talking about, Jeannie? I got the back road covered, but why are we stopping?" asked Danny, not totally frowning but squinting with his green eyes, making them look even more deep set.

She entwined her fingers and put her hands over her face. Speaking behind her hands, she said, "Remember this?" She slowly slid them down her face, exposing a smile.

He laughed. He mimicked her actions and put a smile on his face.

She laughed. "Danny, what we need to do—and this goes for you too, Tony—is to take the back road behind the Robinson's house. Oh, I almost forgot—no loud truck noises today, Danny." She took a breath. "OK! Once we leave CoalVille, we drive to Spider Hill. It's about a mile and a half from Rabbit Ears, but what's neat is that the route hides us from anyone watching from Rabbit Ears." Her voice rose with a hint of humor. "We'll drive halfway up the hill. Then we'll stop and walk the rest of the way to the top. From there, we'll have a clear view of the back of Rabbit Ears. The sun will be behind us, so there will be no reflections in Danny's binoculars as we survey the progress of our con!"

Jeannie gave a joyful squeal and giggled as she watched the expressions on Danny's and Tony's faces.

This time it was Danny who fiddled with Jeannie. He mimicked what she always did to him. He pawed and grabbed at her arms, flicked her clothes and hair. Then he gave a chuckle as he put his fingers on his lips and then on hers. "You're good, LoneTree. You're not only good lookin', but you got one hell of a brain."

For a moment, her only body language was a smile, but then Jeannie giggled. "Let's get going," she said. Then, for no apparent reason, she stopped. For a long thirty seconds, she said nothing as Danny and Tony waited. "You know what?" Jeannie said out of the clear blue. "I've already talked to Tony, but I can't shake this awful feeling I have."

She shook her head. There was a tremor in her voice as she continued in a whisper. "I know I saw that old gray truck sneak down the back road behind my house earlier this morning. It was barely moving and didn't make much noise. Eddie had taken the same route about five minutes before the truck came along. I saw Eddie driving his old man's Dodge truck, but I couldn't see who was driving the gray truck—the driver had a huge hat with a big brim covering his face."

"What?" Danny said, his voice concerned. "I'm puzzled! It's twice now we've seen that gray truck."

She started to shake. "Danny, you're scaring me. Do you think someone is stalking us?" It was definitely real. Someone was stalking someone. The question was who. She blurted, "Danny, do you think someone is after Eddie and Terry?" There was silence, and then she added, "Do you think someone is after us?"

Her questions hung in the air. Murder in a small coal camp was not common, but something was going on. The police could not find a motive for Darla's murder. It had been the senseless act of a crazy man.

The subject of his mother's murder was way too delicate, and Jeannie was well aware that things were digressing, so she changed the subject.

He grabbed her and put his arm tightly around her waist. She looked at him and said, "Come on, Danny, let's go get the treasure from your shed and load it into the pickup—and oh, by the way, do we have lunch?"

Although her words were meant to change the subject, her mind wasn't silent and wasn't about to change subjects. *I did see that truck…I know what I saw.* Her body tensed, imagining what might be—the return of a deranged man stalking someone through the back alleys of CoalVille.

A forced smile was all Tony could manage as he struggled to change the subject. "Got lunch covered, so no worry there. Mom made us kranjska klobasa sandwiches. We've got lots of potato chips—and plenty of Pepsi. I also have several jugs of water, so we're good to go."

The sun was warming up the back of Spider Hill. That brought the army of monkey-faced spiders out searching for their victims in the sand, brush, and rocks. Their pincers ripped out the guts of insects that fell prey to them. Danny's shoe kicked one every other step. He'd laugh as the spider took flight like a soccer ball headed for the goal—prey in mouth and all.

They climbed to the top of Spider Hill, wondering if their con had worked. It didn't take long to get their answer.

"Look at those idiots digging for a phantom. They are such nerds! Let's go. They have no idea what's up." Jeannie poked Danny in his side as she snickered.

Danny didn't move. She looked at where she thought he was looking. She didn't see anything out of the ordinary. She grabbed him and motioned to him to look at her. He did. She cringed at his expression. She was well aware he was about to say something that she didn't want to hear.

"Wait a minute!" snapped Danny. "We've got problems! That truck is parked about a mile from where Eddie and Terry are. Someone is watching them. He can't see my truck behind this hill, but I'm worried. He's up to something. Oh shit! There's that vulture again!"

"God, I hope not! What's going on? Tony remarked, fear written on his face.

Mochcom had the sun to one side—he was undetected by two boys digging for a phantom. He had no idea Danny, Jeannie, and Tony had spotted him.

His focus, at the moment, was on Eddie and Terry. Clutching his upper left arm with his right hand, his fingernails dug deep into his flesh. Crimson red blood oozed from the sides of his buried nails. It slowly rolled down his arm and dripped on his greasy shoe. He nervously wiped his hand over it, creating a smear of red blood and dirt. It flattened down the hairs on his arm.

He mumbled as he watched Eddie and Terry. "Neferzul hid something down there. I'll wait as long as it takes for them to find it. I have all the time in the world. She has the emerald star and five rainbow-colored worox stones. She buried them down there! Hmm. I hope these two little lambs find what I desire! Yes! I enjoy my state in endless time. Time means nothing to me—but without the emerald star and worox stones, I'm stuck in this time. Soon that will change! My little lambs will help me get what I need."

Now she was to the point where she was convinced something was horribly wrong. At first, Jeannie gingerly slapped at Danny, who was staring at the distant hill through his binoculars, knowing he was watching something unusual. His intense focus on the view made her nervous. She pulled at his sleeve, pointed to the truck, and then to the Boar's Tusk. Even though it was five miles up the road, its stature made it seem no more than a rock's throw away.

"Come on, Danny. I want to get out of here. This place is scary. Let's go to the Tusk and find a star."

Taking a huge breath, Danny was able to hold his binoculars steady as he took one last look. He could never have imagined in a million years the view he was witnessing. Although not knowing who it was, the man's actions sent a wave of horrifying thoughts into Danny's mind. *My God, who is that? He's nuts! Why is that old bastard making himself bleed? He's digging his fingernails into his flesh. Holy shit, his arms are covered with blood! Wow, how weird. He's slithering his fingers through the blood on his arm.*

Tightening his fingers around the barrels of his binoculars and staring at the very presence of evil, Danny's heart froze with a thought. *He's stalking Eddie and Terry.*

CHAPTER 13

A Star is Found

It was impossible for her to know. The late-night meeting in the back alley following the sensational win by the Pirates was just a strange twist of fate that was now buying her time. Being stalked by bullies made Jeannie furious, but now Eddie and Terry were being stalked by Lord Mochcom. He was waiting for them to find what he wanted. Had the meeting not happened, Mochcom would be stalking his more sought-after prey— Neferzul—and not waiting for a ghost fart to appear at Rabbit Ears.

Jeannie had no idea how precious little time she had to unravel the secrets of an ancient mystery that would free her, Danny, and Tony from the bonds of death. With the clock ticking, Jeannie suspected her life was in danger, but she was unaware how close Mochcom was to closing the hand of death around her.

She tugged at Danny's sleeve. He was intently looking through his binoculars, watching a crazy old man claw at his skin.

She put her hand over the binocular lenses. "Come on, you guys. You're scaring me. Let's just go! I want to have some fun today. I don't want to think about or talk about Eddie, Terry, or some crazy stalker," Jeannie commented. "Let's change the subject and just have fun."

Sensing her fear, Danny dropped the arm holding his binoculars and put his other arm around her. She peered up at him, her face distressed. There was a feeling of security that immediately swept through her body as his large, strong arms gently pulled her against his body. Looking down at her, he said, "I'm with you, Jeannie. Let's have fun."

Knowing that Jeannie and Tony were concerned, Danny had one final comment, which was to let them know he wasn't afraid of anyone. "Guys, I'm a hell of a lot stronger than some old man that has his eye on teenagers! If he comes near any of us, I'll kill him!"

They walked to Danny's truck and got in. Within moments, he had the engine running and in gear, ready to roll.

"Do you know how to get to the Boar's Tusk?" Tony asked Danny, his arm hanging out the window as the Chevy raced down Spider Hill.

For the sake of lifting the mood and getting Jeannie cheered up, Danny jumped on his infatuation with pirates. He put a joyful twist in his voice as he talked about a make-believe pirate that he labeled Peg Leg Peter.

"Tony, I will say one thing. Does the ghost of Peg Leg Peter roam forever in the hills of the Scarlet Desert?" Danny said, slapping the steering wheel in time to the music of Elvis Presley's "Wear My Ring Around Your Neck."

> Won't you wear my ring around your neck,
> To tell the world I'm yours, by heck,
> Let them know I love you so,
> And let them know by the ring around your neck.

Danny was singing along with the song on the radio, one hand on the wheel and the other searching for Jeannie's hand. "Jeannie, as soon as I get my class ring, it'll be around your neck to let the world know I'm yours, by heck!" He tugged on her hand and said, "But in the meantime, old Peter's ghost will lead me right to the Tusk!"

"I can't wait for the ring!" said Jeannie as she looked at Danny and then at Tony, a grin on her face.

She started tickling Danny's ribs and pointing to the back window. "Danny, yes, Peg Leg Peter is still out here. He's hobbling around on one leg, and he ain't a ghost. He's a living zombie and is looking for his wooden leg, so just be careful, Danny, 'cause he thinks you stole it from him! Soooooooooo, if you hear a thud in the back of your truck, you better duck 'cause old Peter will be pounding on the window, trying to get you!"

Danny laughed freely. His plan was working. Peg Leg Peter might be just a figment of his imagination, but the old pirate was good for something. Danny had lifted her spirits with thoughts of a pirate ghost and got her mind off a crazy old man.

They were joking and having fun, racing through the desert in a shiny red truck—headed for the Boar's Tusk. They used humor and small talk to get their minds off the miserable subject of a crazy man, especially since they had no idea what he was up to.

Finally, they were having fun. "We're on our way! This is my baby!" Danny hooted.

Dirt flew, and a cloud of dust followed Danny's truck as they sped along a two-rut road leading to the Boar's Tusk. Through the windshield, they could see it rising high above the sifting sand of the Scarlet Desert in southwestern Wyoming. It was not more than two miles up the road.

It was a natural wonder, a great curiosity that brought visitors from all over the world. The unusual formation was created by two towering pillars of rock, and there was a space between them that represented a doorway.

His concentration on the towering pillars of rock in front of him was somewhat broken by the arousing activities in the front seat of his truck. *Man alive, Jeannie, you sure know how to get a guy frustrated*, thought Danny as he felt her fingers stroking his inner thigh.

"Hey, we're almost there." Danny's level of excitement was elevated not only by what Jeannie was doing, the Pirates winning, and the thought of being state champs but also by the thought of finding more treasure.

There was no doubt what Danny was thinking. He was convinced. "We're gonna find something, something that is opened with a combination lock, a lock that uses the code of symbols."

Danny drove his Chevy truck to the small hill at the base of the two giant towers and stopped.

"Look at those massive rock towers. Wow—this is way cool!" shouted Tony, jumping out of the truck.

Jeannie gave Danny a teasing look as he popped the door handle and jumped out. Standing at the base of the hill the Tusk sat on, Danny's face went blank. Seeing nothing but dirt and rocks everywhere, except for an occasional scrub, he started to question his visions of treasure. Danny's mind swirled. *Is this like hunting for a needle in a haystack? I don't think so! The Boar's Tusk is over four hundred feet tall. If someone said that a marker—something that sticks out like a sore thumb over four hundred feet tall—pointed to the spot where a treasure is buried, well, the place where the treasure was buried would be obvious, wouldn't it? Yeah, but this is a huge area! Where is it buried?*

Danny's mind was on treasure. There could be no denying that. His eyes wandered up and down the east wall of the doorway. He didn't see a star. Danny wasn't convinced that the treasure they had found at White Face Cliff wasn't actually pirate treasure. *Hell, pirates steal all kinds of stuff,* he thought. *I don't care who they stole if from. We found it. It's ours!*

Not without hesitation, he turned to Jeannie, mulling that thought over in his mind. "Jeannie, what are we doing out here?"

That caught her by surprise. She thought she had him under control. "What are you talking about? We're looking for a star."

He didn't wait for her comeback. "You don't know there's a star out here. Hell, we don't even know what kind of a star we're looking for."

"Danny, our legends tell us, 'The keys open the bottomless pit by the chamber of the star,'" she snapped.

"Ah, but where's the bottomless pit?" he said grinning.

He's playing games, she thought. *I'll fix him.*

"Well, my dear, what have you found?"

Momentarily, she said nothing, but then she added, "Danny, we're looking for a star. I don't know what kind of a star—but a star for sure. Remember last week? We were looking for a hand. And what did we find? We found a rock with the imprint of a hand on it! But we also found much more…so I think it's a star we search for today."

Standing on shaky ground, Danny was well aware of the fact they had found treasure due almost entirely to Jeannie's brilliance. His game plan was to humor her. By choosing to give her some rope to search for her star, he wasn't losing anything. He thought, *Who knows? We may get lucky. We may even find more treasure. But I doubt it.*

With a strange little smile on his face, he looked at her out the corner of his eye, and he saw she was thinking. "Come in, Jeannie, you're drifting again. Where are you? No thinking about legends today…just thinking about treasure and the Pirates beating the Grizzlies," said Danny with an incredulous laugh.

"Come here, Danny."

He walked to her. She took him into her arms and pulled him gently next to her body. She whispered into his ear, "I was thinking about you and me. So, my Danny, what do you think of that?"

"That's cool. Now what?"

She grabbed his T-shirt, pulled it out of his pants, and slid her hand under it. Her fingers searched for the right spot. She found it. She pinched him gently on his belly button. "Danny, my love, we have a star to find. Be patient. It's out here."

She held his head in her hands and gently gave him a quick kiss. Then her eyes caught Tony staring at them. She frowned at him. Tony flinched.

He quickly responded. "OK, guys. Enough lip smacking!"

With her lips still on Danny's, she waved Tony off.

Cleverly, he put a smirk on his face and raised his right shoulder. Then he gave her an imitation of a little girl waving her hand.

Jeannie took his hint. "All right, back to work! First, we need to figure out what 'Eternal youth comes from within the intact star by means of him whose eyes it reflects' is all about. Second, we need to locate something on the east wall of the doorway between the two rock towers."

Not dropping the smirk from his face, Tony answered, "Well, I disagree with you, Miss Jeannie." Tony cupped one hand palm up like a cart and galloped the fingers of his other hand, as if chasing the first. "You have the cart before the horse. First, we search the east wall for something, and then we find out what that brass arrow message is all about."

"Oh, have it your way. We all get the drift," she answered.

It didn't take long for Tony, Danny, and Jeannie to hike to the passageway between the large towering rocks of the Boar's Tusk.

The beautiful Sunday morning sunshine engulfed the two tusks with scarlet rays and got Jeannie thinking. *They look as if they're pillars of fire,* she thought. *Only the sound of a slight breeze is competing with the serenading courtship songs of distant meadowlarks as they lure their mates to join them—to build nests and bring new life to the earth. Maybe that will be Danny and me when he graduates from the University of North Carolina at Chapel Hill. We will start our new family.*

"What do you think these rocks are?" Danny asked his friends as they reached the doorway.

"Danny, I think they're the core of an ancient volcano. It must have erupted eons ago. So that's all I know," answered Tony.

No, Tony—it's more than just an old volcano. It's a monument for truth and honor. It's a monument to Kashom's firstborn daughter, another Chosen One, Moon-of-Day. She lost her life because of her brother's carelessness.

"Jeannie, you're our leader—so, how do we go about finding this star?" Danny said, smiling at her and at the same time looking out the corner of his eye at Tony.

"Look, guys. The clue has to be on the east wall. Let's do exactly what we did last week. Let's examine the side of this big rock cliff by using a grid."

"What do you mean, Jeannie?" Tony chimed in.

"Well, here's what I think. Danny has his binoculars in his truck—right, Danny?" Jeannie looked at Danny for confirmation.

His gesture, his hands rolled up, one on each eye like the barrels of his binoculars, got a chuckle from Tony. "Yeah, Jeannie, I have 'em," Danny reassured her. "Either Tony or I will run to the truck and get them."

The sun was shining on the cliff. The dark black jagged rocks protruding from a patchwork of thorns were absorbing not only the sun's rays but also Tony's attention.

"So what's the plan?" Tony asked jovially. "Do we search the cliff with the binoculars? Jeannie, how do we get past the thorny rocks to find a star? Searching a rose stem for a no-see-um might be easier!"

A few jagged rocks on a cliff were not a deterrent for Jeannie. "Yep, we do, Tony. That's the plan. Let's get going. We have a star to find," Jeannie responded.

Danny took the hint. He wasn't about to start fencing. Tony just ventured into an area of discussion that his best buddy decided to get him out of. "Tony, would you run back to my truck and get the binoculars?"

Tony raised one eyebrow as he thought, *Danny and Jeannie always have me racing around doing something when they want to be alone.* Even though he felt like a gofer, he elected to go. He raced down the hill to where the truck was parked.

Jeannie's agenda was not quite as subtle. She slipped her fingers into the top of Danny's pants and pulled him toward a nice flat rock in the sun. She had a few moments alone. "What did Coach Smith say, Danny? We didn't talk about your meeting with him. Did he tell you that the University of North Carolina would like you to play ball for them?"

The rock was nice. It was warm. He slipped his hand in her pants, grabbing the waistband, and pulled her next to him.

"He didn't say anything for certain, but Coach Bollas talked to me for a few minutes after Coach Smith left. He said that the University of North Carolina couldn't make me an offer yet but that if my athletic skills continued to improve as they projected, I would be playing basketball at UNC in two years. Jeannie, we could get married that summer before I had to start school. What do you think?"

She looked to the sky with tears in her eyes. Her fingers could not wipe away the tears. She looked at him. "Danny, I just love you. Yeah, that would be the perfect future! You and me starting a new adventure together—Mr. and Mrs. Danny Roberts!" she said, holding his hand.

This cliff holds a secret we must find, Tony thought as he opened the truck door. He got Danny's binoculars from the glove compartment and ran back up the hill, showing his excitement to get the search underway.

Tony kicked a small pebble at the reclining couple. It landed next to Danny, but he didn't flinch. Not moving his head away from Jeannie, Danny took his hand from Jeannie's waist. He raised it, high-fived Tony, and said, "OK! Let's get to work. Tony, you have a keen eye. So you have the honors and can search the cliff with my binoculars!" said Danny.

The kids at the base of those two massive rock towers started searching. At the same time, two kids at Rabbit Ears were also searching. All of the kids were poor. They all wanted to find something of value. The kids at

Rabbit Ears were chasing after a phantom—the three kids at the Boar's Tusk were chasing after a priceless treasure.

"What time is it, Danny?" Jeannie asked.

"Oh, it's just about nine," he replied.

"Super! We have time to search but much to do, so let's all roll up our sleeves and get started," she commented as she thought, *Nothing in life is a sure thing, and until we find something concrete, it could be nothing more than a wild-star chase.*

Shining on the face of the cliff—making it light up like a neon sign—the morning sun gave Tony the perfect conditions to search the towers of black rock. *In their lightless condition,* Tony thought, *forget it.* Fortunately, that was not the case.

His eyes were sharp as tacks. They searched with eagle-eye vision. It did not take long. Only five minutes had gone by before he screamed, "*Look!* Look up there!"

"You scared the crap out of us!" Danny and Jeannie said in unison. They hadn't expected his sudden outburst.

"What do you see, Tony? Where are you looking?" yelled Danny.

"This petroglyph is very obscure. You'd have to know what you were looking for to see it. OK, so do you see the small ledge about halfway up the cliff? It's over there," Tony said, not taking the binoculars from his eyes but using his free hand to point in the direction where he was looking.

"I see it! I see it! I see the small ledge!" Danny shouted with the same level of excitement that his friend Tony was displaying.

"OK, so just underneath the ledge there's a crack in the rock that goes up and down." Tony described the view he was seeing through the binoculars.

"I see it. I see it also," Danny remarked.

"Follow the crack down to the smooth piece of rock on the cliff that the sun is shining on. It almost looks like a mirror up there." Tony was trying to be methodical as he explained to Danny and Jeannie where to look.

"We follow you, Tony," both Danny and Jeannie said, staring at the mirror-like rock reflecting the early morning sun's rays.

"On that shiny, smooth rock, a star is etched."

She frowned. "I can't see it," Jeannie muttered.

Danny's eyebrows dropped. He squinted. "Neither can I," Danny added. "You said it, Tony. If that's a petroglyph of a star, that thing is one obscure carving up there. You'd have to have a treasure map to find it!"

"Here, you guys, take a look! Look through the binoculars," Tony said as he handed them to Jeannie.

She let her eyes focus and adjusted the binoculars for perfect vision. "Tony! I see it. Wow, it's really there. I can't believe it…wow…I thought we needed to find a star. And like you said, it's obscure, but it's a carving of a star on the side of this tower. The way it's etched on the rock with the sun shining on it makes it almost impossible to see with the naked eye," Jeannie said, laughing so loudly that the boys stared at each other. Then they lifted their hands and shouted simultaneously, "Give me five."

She pointed with her arm to a spot slightly to the left of a massive thorny rock protruding from the east tower. Danny stood motionless behind her, trying to aim down her pointing arm.

He couldn't see it with his naked eye, so he yelled, "Let me have the binoculars, Jeannie," motioning with his hands between bursts of excited laughter. "I want to see the star!"

He looked through the binoculars. A puckered lip and wrinkled nose created an expression of bewilderment on his face. He gave a long, searching look. "Are you guys sure that's a star? That thing looks pretty weathered, and it just may be a bunch of weathered stains on the side of the cliff. Maybe Jeannie is right. It's not *almost* impossible to see—but *impossible* to see," Danny said over the conversation that Tony and Jeannie were having.

He squinted into the bright sunlight and pointed to some unusual markings. "What about all those markings? They're all over the place. Even right under what you guys are calling a star." Danny retracted his arm. "How do you guys know some ancient elder crawled up this rock tower and carved a star up there?"

Jeannie shook her head and pointed again. Her look was intense. "Danny, there is no doubt in my mind that someone put that figure on this cliff," blurted out Jeannie. "Those are *not*—I repeat, *not*—your so-called stains on a rock!"

There was a sudden shine in Tony's eyes. "Yeah, it may be weathered by the wind and rain, but it's definitely manmade, and it's definitely ancient!" Tony said with authority, supporting Jeannie's views. "And *it's a star!*"

CHAPTER 14

Zanzee Points the Way—Again

*H*oly shit, she's done it again. Danny couldn't imagine his foot getting any larger. Especially given that his mouth was normal size. It just wouldn't fit. His dreams of pirate treasure started to fade. His problem, however, was that he didn't have a clue what was going on.

He stared at the star. *I thought we would wrap up early out here for the lack of not finding a thing. My God, was I wrong. She's always right.*

"How on earth did anyone get up there to carve that star on this rock pillar?" Jeannie said. *I know Danny is wondering the same thing. He made that comment about my people crawling up a cliff. Oh well, that's just Danny. He didn't mean anything bad by his remarks.*

Then she answered her own question. "I think they climbed up the side of the rock to the ledge that is just above the star. If they could get to the ledge, they could lower themselves by rope and voilá—there ya go!"

Danny decided there was only one thing for him to do. There was no need to wait any longer for Danny to get in on the act. He was ready. "OK, guys. We have a star etched on the side of a cliff one hundred feet straight up—now what? We need to get our bodies up and going pronto! Oh, how sweet it is! Come on, you guys," Danny exclaimed, as he tried to be the practical one and figure out what to do next. In reality, he was lost.

Knowing him so well, Jeannie looked at Danny, who nodded enthusiastically. "Well, Danny, just a minute ago you were pooh-poohing the whole idea that a star was up there. Now you're acting like you're the one that got the show going. Pray tell—what's your problem?" Jeannie snickered.

"Lone Tree, zip it," Danny snipped at her.

Tony paid little attention to the conversation Danny was having with Jeannie. He had better things to do. He was scouring the area around the shiny rock, looking for anything that might give them a clue about the star.

"Wait! Wait! There's more!" Tony blurted out in a voice loud enough to make himself heard above Danny and Jeannie's back-and-forth joking.

The interruption was fortunate for Danny. His foot was getting close to his mouth again. The dialogue between Danny and Jeannie came to a screeching halt when they heard Tony's comment.

"What do you see, Tony?" Jeannie squealed with excitement.

"Ah, I think…well, maybe it's something…there are some words. They are also really faint and obscure. I think it's writing…I don't know for sure." Tony was trying to find words that would make sense of what he was looking at. "I can't make them out. Wait…let me see! Danny, all those other markings you saw below the star? I think they're a word."

There was a sudden shining in Jeannie's eyes. "Tony, what are you looking at?" she asked, tapping her finger on his shoulder.

He was about out of air, and his hands were shaking, but he tried to hold on a bit longer. "Jeannie, I'm trying to figure it out…hold your breath. I mean, I need to hold my breath," said Tony. "These darn binoculars are shaking all over the place, and I'm having a heck of a time reading what's up there. Come on, you guys. My hands are shaking—my heart is pounding—and both of you are asking what's up there!"

Thinking it might help his shaking, he took a deep breath. He couldn't hold it. He tried again. Same result. "Danny and Jeannie, be patient—hold on to your pants, and let me figure this out!"

Impatient Danny had had it. Certainly he couldn't fence with Jeannie. Tony was a completely different story.

"Tony, give me my binoculars. I don't have Saint Vitus's dance like you seem have. I can hold those damn glasses steady as a rock. I'll get the job done," Danny snapped as he took over.

Tony's balloon was popped. Danny's needle was sharp—his needle of words. Tony was furious. He had failed to carry through. He had a chance to complete the discovery of the star, but just couldn't get the job finished.

"OK, here you go, smarty-pants. You think you're so smart! Go right ahead and give us the words!" Tony said as he handed Danny his glasses.

Danny was now at the helm, guiding the ship of discovery. He had no idea where he was taking it. "You're right, Tony. If this petroglyph is words, it's more obscure than the star. Wait a minute! Just wait! I've got eagle eyes. *I've got it! Yes! I've got it!*" Danny shouted. "It's another reference. It says: Apocalipsis nine one."

Tony tried to regain control. He had missed the boat. He didn't connect the petroglyph to another reference found in an old book.

"OK, I've heard of the apocalypse. What is it? Are you sure you know what you're looking at? Is it...is it a petroglyph? A petroglyph made of letters?" Tony chimed in.

Danny dropped his hand holding the binoculars, and his expression showed his confidence. "Yes, Tony! I'm absolutely sure. It's very obscure and camouflaged by the cracks and stains around it. It's definitely a petroglyph of letters, and like I said, it says Apocalipsis nine one."

Observant Jeannie picked up on it immediately. "You guys, it's not an apocalypse; it's *Revelations*, chapter nine, verse one. I have my Reina-Valera in my canvas bag—I'll translate it," Jeannie said, as she ran to the spot where she had set her bag on a flat rock.

It took her only a few minutes to grab her book and race back to where the boys were looking at the cliff with the binoculars.

"Tony, would you write this down for me? Here's the English translation: 'I saw a star fall from heaven to earth...and was given the key of the bottomless pit.'"

Without one flaw, Tony wrote on her pad of paper exactly what she had just said. "Jeannie, here it is."

"Thanks, Tony."

Idle his mind was not. Racing to take the lead, he had been waiting for the right moment. It just arrived, and he was ready. "*I have it!*" Tony yelled. "Your question got me thinking!" He pointed to the star etched high on the cliff.

"What have you got?" Jeannie squealed.

Beaming, Tony spun around in excitement. "What we're looking for!"

They stopped. Questions on two faces were met by a smirk on Tony's.

"Yes, I do have it. Danny's question got me thinking."

He pointed to the petroglyph of the star high on the cliff. "You guys, follow my hand." Tony's finger traced a line from the star down the cliff, and he ended pointing at an indentation at the base of the rock tower. "Did you follow it? Let your eyes fall straight down, as if following a rock that was falling from the high point on the cliff. At the bottom of the cliff, your eyes rest on this indentation—a bowl-shaped hole about ten feet in diameter and five feet deep."

He had the lead. He had one on Jeannie, or so he thought. He was positive this was the answer. "Yesssssssssss! What we're looking for is in this bowl-shaped hole! How sweet it is! It's in this pit over here at the base of the cliff. Jeannie, read your verse again."

Tony repeated each word that Jeannie recited from her Reina-Valera.

"You see? It says, 'I saw a star fall from heaven to earth,' and then it says, 'and was given the key of the bottomless pit.' Something is buried in this pit!" he squealed with excitement and raced to the pit to get a closer look. "Let's dig here. It should be easy digging in sandy soil, so it should go fast." He poked his hand into the loose dirt near the edge of the indentation.

His level of excitement was far from waning. He had no idea what was happening, but throwing dirt was Danny's idea of action. "Let's get the show on the road! Get the shovels, guys. We got digging to do!" Danny hooted with excitement. "This time I brought three shovels—we can all dig in."

Jeannie needed to stall for time. Tony thought he'd scored one, but Jeannie didn't buy it. She had no immediate comeback. She needed help. It wasn't far off. Until help arrived, however, she needed time.

"Wait a minute! How do we know there is something buried in that pit? If it were that simple, someone else would have found it. A lot of people come to the Boar's Tusk all the time. They are always digging out here—looking for something. You know it! People are looking for arrowheads, agate, jade, and who knows what," Jeannie commented. "Tony, I don't want to be the one to break your bubble, but we just need to think about what we are doing before we start digging up the desert!"

Before she had to resort to more stalling, Zanzee suddenly appeared. *Tinkle, tinkle.* Jeannie's head snapped around when she heard the familiar sound. "Zanzee," she screamed.

She knew exactly what came next: "Meow, meow."

"I'm so glad you showed up!"

He leaped through the air in long bounding strides, running to the indention at the base of the east wall of the doorway.

"Oh, Zanzee, you did come! You're here! I thought you'd show up and teach Danny a lesson or two!" squealed Jeannie.

The quiet smile she gave Tony shouted with silent one-upmanship as she raced to get closer to her protector.

Danny's pirate dreams were fading quickly, but he held on just in case.

"My golly! Your cat does have special powers!" Danny yelled. "There is no way Zanzee could get here. I'm sorry for making fun of him. He is one special cat. Wow!"

Tony thought Jeannie's cat was helping him. Little did he know that was not the case. "Look! He's pawing in the ground at the edge of the indentation at the base of the tower! Yes, the east wall of the doorway that has the star on it! Whoa! This is just too cool! Zanzee is pointing the way again! Good work, Zanzee," Tony shouted as he laughed and grinned.

For a moment, Jeannie wondered. She'd never doubted him in the past. He'd never let her down. *What's going on?*

"Zanzee, what are you telling us? Is Tony right? Is there something buried there?" Jeannie questioned. *Maybe Tony was right. I jumped the gun and questioned his logic. Oh well! I can't be right all the time.*

Her love pulled her T-shirt from her pants in a teasing gesture. She giggled and glanced at him. He was just happy there was action. He flipped his head.

Jeannie noticed the look on Danny's face. His facial expressions were a sure giveaway when his excitement level grew. *Bright yellow hair reflecting the morning sunlight and flipping around in the breeze is a sight to see—especially when he's treasure hunting.*

"Let's get going. Let's find the buried treasure! I feel it in my bones. This is where the pirates buried the treasure," Danny shouted.

Ah ha, she thought. *Zanzee didn't let me down!*

"I don't know!" Jeannie mumbled. "Zanzee is next to the base of the cliff. He is pawing at the cliff—not the indentation or hole that Tony pointed out."

Jeannie ran to where Zanzee was pawing. "What?" Her mind raced. *I knew he wouldn't mess up*, she thought. *He never has. Thank you, Zanzee!*

Her soft white fingers dug through the dirt, pawing in the same place as Zanzee. "What are you telling us, Zanzee? Why are you pawing at the dirt right at the base of the cliff?" Saying nothing, she watched him first put his paw on the dirt and then on the cliff itself.

"Hmm—this is strange! Why are you pawing at the cliff right here where it meets the ground?"

Zanzee looked at Jeannie, put his paw out, and touched the cliff. He then scraped a little dirt away from it and said, "Meow, meow."

It was time for new orders. She was in charge once more. "Danny, did you bring your small spade? Zanzee is telling us something. He wants us to look at the base of the cliff—on the cliff itself—just under the dirt."

She loved it. He was her love and would do anything for her. Little did she know just how far he would go to save her from impending danger and even death.

"Yeah, I'll run to the truck and get it. Maybe I ought to get all the tools." The keys were emerging! She was sure of herself. "Danny, get the two bronze boxes also. We will need them," said Jeannie.

"Come on, Tony. Help me carry the stuff from the truck."

Both boys took off running in the direction of the red pickup parked at the base of the small hill the Boar's Tusk rose from.

Jeannie was content to let Tony and Danny have their moment of joy. *They think that it is just some buried treasure out here. But Tony didn't pick up on the Apocalipsis reference—"I saw a star fall from heaven to earth...and was given the key of the bottomless pit"—especially the part about the "key of the bottomless pit." Our legends say that the keys open the bottomless pit by the chamber of the star—so our legends are connected to what we're finding. That phrase, "the key of the bottomless pit," is tied to our legends. The only keys I know that are tied to the legend of Kashom are mine and the brass bow and arrow.*

Jeannie thought about what her mother said when she told her the legend of Kashom. The golden key was a special gift from the gods— the supreme god Viracocha and his wife, the goddess Neferdor. They personally gave it to Princess Aerapondes. The key was the means to harness the power of the sun and unlock the Highway of Time, which would endow travelers with eternal youth.

The key to the bottomless pit, but what is the key? Is it my key? Is it the mirror-image symbols derived using my key? Is it the brass bow and arrow? Could it be that these keys open something out here at the Boar's Tusk? What does the "bottomless" part of the phrase mean? Could it be something endless? What's endless? Time is endless! Yes, maybe these keys open the Highway of Time, according to the legend of Kashom. This is more proof that Kashom is tied into all of this. Yes, Zanzee is navigating the way to help Kashom.

Danny and Tony raced back to where Jeannie was next to Zanzee.

"What are you doing?" Danny asked as he looked at her. "Come on, Jeannie. Grab a shovel and start digging."

Time for a lesson, my love, she thought as she flashed her eyes at him. "Not so fast, Danny! Would you hand me the small spade?" she asked.

He was eager. He'd do anything at this point. Soon he would discover that not just at this point, but any point, he'd do anything for her, even save her from the hands of death.

"Sure! Here it is." He was curious. "What do you have in mind?"

She knew exactly what was going on. Soon she would see for herself that all was falling into place. "You'll see! Zanzee is showing us a clue! There's something at the base of this cliff he wants us to know about. Danny, just hold on for a minute!"

Jeannie carefully scraped away the loose dirt at the base of the cliff where Zanzee had been pawing. It was only a few moments before she found it.

"My God! Look at this!" she screamed. "There's a slit carved in the side of the cliff that the bow fits into. Look, there's a hole the arrow tip will go into. The bow and arrow are keys to open something at the base of this rock tower."

CHAPTER 15

A Bottomless Pit in a Secret Chamber

Jeannie discovered something with the help of Zanzee. Danny was ready for action—whatever it was. Tony was curious. Looking at the slit and hole that the bow and arrow would fit into, they all were perplexed. They all shared one thought. *Where does this lead?*

Jeannie carefully cleaned the dirt from the markings. She had no idea what they were about or why they were carved into the base of the east wall of the massive rock tower of the Boar's Tusk.

Danny took charge. He could at least give orders. "Jeannie, put the bow into the slit carved on the side of the cliff," Danny said. "Go ahead! Just do it!" He was anxious to see what would happen.

It didn't take long. As soon as Jeannie put the bow into the slit, an unusual sound filled the air, a rumbling from inside the rock wall.

"Hey! What was that?" hollered Tony.

Jeannie yanked her hand away. She wasn't about to get it trapped. The bow was sticking partway out of the slit.

"I don't know. I just put the bow into the slit. I think something moved in there. Did you hear it, Danny?"

The thought was unanimous. *What is inside this rock?*

"Yeah! I did," said Danny. "It sounded like something moved inside the cliff! What on earth would that be? Go ahead! Put the arrow tip into the other hole."

She was cautious, unsure what would happen. Gingerly, Jeannie put the arrow tip into the hole. She waited for a moment. "I didn't hear anything. Now what?"

Danny had no intention of waiting. Something fascinating was going on, and he was going to get to the bottom of it. At least, that's what he thought. "Turn the damned thing. Just turn it, Jeannie," Danny blurted out.

The massive tower was no longer silent. Unnatural sounds shot forth from the east wall of the doorway at the Boar's Tusk. It startled them all.

Ruuummmmble! Ruuummmmble! Grrrrind!

"What's happening? What's going on?" yelled Jeannie.

More startling even than the sound of a once-silent rock structure was its movement.

"*Oh, my hell! Look at that!*" Tony screamed. "That rock is moving!"

Screeeech! Screeeeech! Screeeech! Crrrraaaack! Ruuummmmble!

"*Oh my God!* That rock just moved and opened up a hole into the tower! There's a doorway into this rock tower. *My lord!*" screamed Jeannie.

"*Holy mother of St. Andrew! Look at that! Holy crap!*" Danny shouted.

"What's in there?" yelled out Tony.

Musty air rushed from the dark and dank chasm on the other side of the rock doorway.

"Danny, do you have a flashlight?" Jeannie muttered.

"Yeah, it's in my canvas bag. It's lying right there on that rock behind you," he said. "This is spooky!"

The screeching and grinding sounds made by the opening of the massive rock door stopped, and there before them was a black void. Things at the Boar's Tusk seemed normal again—the only sounds were those of Mother Nature, except for the distant sound of Black Vulture's whooping wings and howling screams as he circled the Tusk.

Tony looked skyward. At that moment, his attention was not on a rock door but on the presence of a bird stalking them. His mind erupted with a frightening thought. *Oh shit. There's that vulture again! I don't like him! How the hell did he know we were here?*

Her reaction was spontaneous. She immediately grabbed Danny's arm and squeezed for dear life. "Danny, he's here. What do we do?" she screamed. Her eyes flew open as she watched the vulture a thousand feet above preparing his strike of death.

Vulture glided through the air high above the massive rock towers and waited for the right moment. Then he started his dive toward the kids, his eye on Neferzul.

Instantly, Danny grabbed a small round rock and prepared to fling it at the diving bird.

Vulture's innate sense warned him once more of the power of the yellow-haired boy with emerald-green eyes. Raking the air with his wings, he diverted his dive and streaked toward safety in the deep-blue sky that kissed the western horizon of White Mountain.

"He's going," said Danny as his eyes followed the bird's flight pattern. "I have no idea why that bird was flying overhead. He's gone now. We're fine."

Except for the sound of a gentle breeze, silence prevailed at the Tusk. The bird's interruption was but a momentary distraction. A gaping hole into a black chasm at the base of the Boar's Tusk immediately took center stage once more.

Danny stepped next to Jeannie and gently held her. She relaxed in his arms as she looked into his eyes. She turned her head and pointed at the rock door.

"Do we go in there? Damn! That's one black hole! Holy mackerel!" Tony shrieked.

"Let me see your light, Danny," Jeannie asked. "I'm going to look inside." She walked to the hole that had been exposed at the base of the east wall of the rock tower. She pointed Danny's light into the chasm beyond the doorway. "There's a room in here. It looks like a room carved out of the rock," she mumbled.

Then she saw it. Directly in front of her was an open mouth of death at the surface of the ground.

"Holy crap! Whoa! Right on the other side the doorway is a huge big hole in the ground." She picked up a small pebble and tossed it into the hole. "My hell! That is one deep hole! I never heard the rock hit the bottom! It's the bottomless pit!"

Her mind raced. She thought of the legend of the Boar's Tusk. *"Father—it is finished. The keys unlock the bottomless pit by the star of the chamber!" This chamber is what Yellow Moon must have spent his life making!*

It dawned on her. This was where it was hidden. *"You guys! It's in here! The star is in this chamber!"* screamed Jeannie.

"What star? What are you talking about?" yelled Danny.

"The star of our legend! Yes! The keys unlock the bottomless pit by the star of the chamber! We just unlocked the secret chamber with the keys! The star of our legend is in this chamber!"

"Jeannie, when we were working at my house last week, you told us your people's legend about the Boar's Tusk. Tony and I did not understand the statement 'The keys unlock the bottomless pit by the star of the chamber' then, and we don't understand it now!"

In complete agreement with Danny, Tony wasn't buying Jeannie's assertion. "I agree with Danny," said Tony. "That statement is as confusing now as it was a week ago. I don't think we know what's in there. What's this 'by' business? The part that says, 'Keys unlock the bottomless pit *by* the star'? That doesn't make a bit of sense. How could keys use a star to unlock a bottomless pit? That's just goofy!"

Tony's statement made her mad. She bit her lower lip. She flipped her head and rolled her eyes. "Well, don't believe me then, but I'll say this. Something of unbelievable value is in this chamber," Jeannie shot back.

More diplomatic than Tony, Danny had just gotten over foot-in-mouth disease and had no intention of getting it again. He was bound and determined to keep his feet out of his mouth. "I don't know about your star. But holy mackerel! Yeah! I'll say that this is unbelievable! A secret chamber out here in the Scarlet Desert! This is the most unbelievable thing I have ever seen in my life. Who made this thing? There has to be something of value in there. I don't think it's a star. I think it's treasure!" asserted Danny.

Then she spotted him. She hadn't expected this. She didn't think she'd need him again, but there he was. "Zanzee, what are you doing in there?"

Jeannie shouted. Her look of sheer excitement got the attention of Danny and Tony. "Guys, Zanzee got in the chamber. He's pawing at something in the ground at the edge of this big hole. What's he doing in there?"

"Do we go in to see?" Tony asked.

"Yeah, let's go," Danny shouted. "He's showing us where something is hidden. He is one neat cat! Jeannie, I take back everything I said about your cat. I don't understand, but he does have special powers! He's showing us where the treasure is buried."

Three teenage kids at the Boar's Tusk on a beautiful Sunday morning in the spring of 1958 had just discovered a secret hiding place in the Scarlet Desert. They had no idea what the hidden chamber contained—a chamber carved into the base of the east wall of the Boar's Tusk. They had no idea how a mechanism could have moved a giant rock to expose the doorway into the chamber.

"Be careful. We don't want to get close to that big hole. If we fall in there, it will be all over," Jeannie said to Danny and Tony.

They held hands and walked into the chamber. Jeannie led the way. She carefully walked around the edge of the giant hole in the ground. She held Danny's flashlight with one hand and held on to him with the other. Danny extended his arm behind him, holding on to Tony.

"All right, we made it," Jeannie whispered.

Danny gently gave her a tug. "Why are you whispering, Jeannie?" he asked.

She gave him a quick glance over her shoulder. The flashlight provided just enough light to display the sparkle in her eyes. "Because this is spooky!" she whispered even more quietly.

His nod was firm. "You're right, Jeannie. This is damn spooky!" Danny's grip tightened on Tony's hand. "Tony, you carried the shovel, right?" asked Danny.

Tony stepped back and raised the shovels. "Yeah. I carried two of 'em. Now what?"

Zanzee was doing his job. To Danny, he was no longer a "damn cat." "Well, Zanzee is telling us where the treasure is. He's pawing at something." Danny pointed the end of his shovel at the spot Zanzee had pawed. "So let's get it and get the hell out of this dungeon!"

CHAPTER 16

Zanzee Warns the Seekers

Surrounding Danny, Jeannie, and Tony, the dank, dark, and musty chamber invited them to linger as the mouth of the bottomless pit waited silently for its next victim.

Light filtered through the doorway leading into the chamber, allowing the kids to see what Zanzee was pawing at.

"Look! Zanzee is sitting on a piece of polished granite," said Jeannie. Their curiosity was at a peak.

"What is it, Jeannie?" Tony queried.

Neither Danny nor Jeannie smiled. Their faces were totally serious.

"Not the foggiest. What do you think, Danny?" she asked.

Not only serious but also curious, Danny moved cautiously toward it. "Good grief! This is a large, flat piece of polished granite," he muttered.

With his heart pounding, Tony's hand shot straight out like an arrow. "That's a vault. Zanzee is sitting on the lid of a vault." Tony's mind raced. *Wow! Someone went to a lot of trouble. They put a vault in a secret chamber to keep unwanted intruders from its contents.*

Even in the heat of a treasure hunt, Danny had time for Elvis. "Hey, guys! Do you know what Elvis said?"

Elvis was not on Jeannie's mind, but coddling Danny was—at least for the moment. "No. What, Danny? Jeannie answered.

"He said you've got to follow your dreams. Right now, I'm dreaming about treasure in this vault, and I'm following my dreams to find it—wherever they lead me—just like Elvis said. 'I've got to follow that dream wherever that dream may lead! I've got to follow that dream to find the love I need!'" Danny's rendition echoed around the dark chasm and bounced off the walls of the chamber. "And right now, I'm in love with treasure."

Jeannie decided that enough was enough. "All right, Mr. Presley, let's move on! No more dreaming until we get this box opened…and yes, you're right, Danny," Jeannie said. "This is a flat piece of granite."

Tony glanced intently around the vault, his eyes inspecting every detail. "Look, there are two large bronze rings on this thing. We don't have to dig. We just need to lift the lid off this vault!" Tony exclaimed.

Rings or no rings, Danny was in a hurry, and inspecting vaults was not active enough for him. "Let's get it off! Boy, am I impatient! There is something in this vault. We just found pay dirt, and I don't want to dillydally. I want to get it opened," Danny hooted. He waved at Jeannie to step back. "Let Tony and me have the honor of opening this treasure vault," hooted Danny. He was only thinking of treasure, not realizing the danger he was putting her in by telling her to move aside. "Jeannie, you stand there," he said, pointing to a narrow strip between the chamber wall and the ominous black hole. "Tony and I'll try to lift this thing. It sure looks heavy." Danny motioned for Tony to give him a hand in lifting the lid.

As Danny and Tony lifted the lid, their excitement grew to the breaking point. The thought on everybody's mind was the same. *What's in this vault?* Danny's thoughts were more specific. *What if it's gold and jewels and silver and all kinds of neat treasure?*

"There! We got it off. What is this?" Danny questioned.

They all waited patiently for a chance of a lifetime to see something that had been tucked away from everyone's sight for who knew how long.

"Jeannie, shine the light in here. Oh my God! Look at that!" yelled Danny.

Then, suddenly, there was a terrible screeching sound.

"Merrowwww, merrowwww," Zanzee howled.

"What is it, Zanzee? What are you telling us?" Jeannie yelled.

Screeeeeeech! Screeeeeeech! Screeeeeeech! Crrrrrack! Ruuuuuumble!

"*Get out! Get out!*" screamed Jeannie.

"*What's happening?*" hollered Danny.

Her arms were frantically waving.

"*The door is closing! Run! Run!*" Jeannie shouted to her friends as she bolted for the opening. Her voice was elevating by the second. "*Hurry, you guys! Oh my God!* That rock just moved. The door is closing! *My lord!*" Jeannie screamed.

It finally dawned on Danny that their situation was deadly! "*Holy crap! We've got to get out of here!*" Danny shouted. His innate ability to take over in emergencies kicked into high gear. "*Run!*" screamed Danny, "*Run for your life! The doorway! My God, it's almost shut! We're going to get trapped in here.*"

Already balanced precariously on the narrow strip of ground, in the rush to get out, Jeannie tripped and fell. She rolled to the mouth of the bottomless pit.

Scrambling for her life, she grabbed at the edge of a rock with her hands—but not in time. Her body flipped and dangled in the mouth of the pit. Her fingers tightened, holding on to the jagged rock for dear life. The sharp edges cut into her flesh. Bright red blood flowed from her fingers. They slipped. She was losing her grip. Blood dripped down her arms and onto her face. Her fingers were weakening.

"*Help me! Help me!*" she screamed.

His heart sank. Fear shot through him, and his body was encapsulated by terror. "*On no! She's falling into the pit!*" wailed Danny. He screamed at Tony. "Run, Tony! Get out of here! I'll get Jeannie!"

Faster than any human being could possibly move, Danny raced to the edge of the pit. He grabbed her arm. "Let go," he screamed.

Her clutched fingers grasped the jagged rock edge. Fear had gripped her, and her hand was not releasing. The rush of blood was increasing. Danny had no choice. With a huge yank, he pulled her up over the edge—ripping her fingers from the rock. He held her tightly and jumped for the small opening. He flew through the air like a flash of lightning and jettisoned out of the narrow passageway. Danny and Jeannie hit the ground and rolled, locked in each other's arms. An incredible booming sound blasted through the air as the rock door slammed shut.

CHAPTER 17
Gifts From the Gods

She was safe. Her body trembled. Her mind was not still, exploding with questions that begged for answers. She stared at him. "Danny, you saved my life! You must be supernatural! *My God! Who are you?*"

She was so shaken, and he tried to comfort her. "Jeannie, you're trembling. Are you OK? You didn't get hurt when I yanked you out of that hole, did you? Did you get hurt when we tumbled out of the rock doorway?" Danny's voice was full of concern.

She could not stop shaking. Her voice was quavering. "Danny, I'm scared. You saved my life, and I will never forget it! Thank you! I don't understand what's going on."

It was clear he heard the words, but it was not clear that he grasped the meaning behind them. "I'm scared too. What are you scared about? I don't understand what's going on either!"

There was no question in her mind. She made it clear. "The light, Danny…it's scaring me!"

Startled, he had no answer except a flimsy one. "What light?" She didn't seem to want him to comfort her, and that confused him.

"That brilliant, green light coming from your chest. Is it your ring?"

Now he got the point. Steadfast in her quest to understand what was going on, Jeannie's remarks caught him off guard.

He had no choice but to answer in the affirmative. "Yes!" he replied.

His single-word answer was not sufficient. "Tell me about it, Danny. There was almost no sunlight in that chamber, yet that brilliant green light came from you when you pulled me from the pit. We flew through the air on that beam of light, right out the door—before it slammed shut!" Her eyes locked on his, and she looked at him intently. Guarded and cautious, she whispered, "Who are you?"

He held his ground. It was his secret and his alone. "Jeannie, I don't know who I am! All I know is that sometimes things happen I can't explain. I try not to think about it! I'm just grateful we made it through the door in the nick of time."

A lack of understanding was not one of Jeannie's traits. Perception and insight were. "Danny, something very strange is going on here! Tell me who you are."

He didn't budge. He was revealing no information. "Don't ask me. I just don't want to talk about it!"

His defense was not working. Jeannie was relentless. Her voice rose, and her face tightened to an expression of concern. "Danny, I need to know who you are!"

His head dropped, and he stared at the ground. He never expected this encounter with Jeannie.

It was at the base of the Tusk so many years ago that his parents spent their first night together—their wedding night. Danny was standing on the very spot where his parents had been a little more than seventeen years ago. Tightening his fingers, his mind saw the image of the gold note his parents had found at the Boar's Tusk. It was next to them in the morning, lying on their blanket. He tensed as the message on the note flashed through his mind, and he once more remembered the warning. *Reveal the secret to no one until they reveal the source.*

"Jeannie, I don't know! I can't talk about it!"

She had no idea who he was, but she knew his weakness—her. "You have to, Danny. If you value my love, you have to! Tell me about your ring!"

His defense weakened further. He was being forced into a corner. "Jeannie, it's just a crazy story that doesn't make any sense! Please don't make me talk about it! I don't know what's going on!"

"Danny, we must talk about it if—"

Cutting her off, he charged on, and as a last resort, he tried sharpness, knowing that was a dangerous path. "*No! I don't want to!*"

He missed her point. She had made it clearly, but his focus was on defense, not love. This time she made it indelibly clear. "Danny, you must not have understood what I just said! If I don't know who you are, we cannot have a future together!"

Danny tensed. He was on the horns of a dilemma. A tear rolled down his cheek.

Now the situation was where she wanted it. It couldn't have been clearer. It hit him like a ton of bricks. "Jeannie, it's a crazy story that I just don't want to talk about! Please don't make me! I can't!"

She was unyielding. The issue she was dealing with was far beyond her willingness to relent. She could not coddle him now. "Danny, tell me who you are. *Now!*"

He had no choice. "All right. I've always had the emerald ring. Ever since I was a baby, I've had this ring on a gold chain around my neck."

She realized something very special was happening. Jeannie watched Danny struggling for words. She reached out and took him by his hands. Her voice softened. She sensed his anguish. "Danny, it's OK! Trust me— trust me, my love! It's OK!" she pleaded. "I'm sorry I was sharp with you."

She pulled his body next to hers and held him close. She put her cheek on his and spoke in a low, sweet voice. "Danny, this is much bigger than you and I can ever imagine! I don't have the answers, and neither do you. We must put our trust in each other at this point. Tell me where the emerald ring came from!" Before he could respond, she interrupted, saying, "Let me see it please!"

He took it off the gold chain. Holding it with his left hand, he reached into his back pocket with his right hand to extract a piece of black cloth.

She lifted her arm to grab his ring. She missed her mark and hit his hand with hers. Scrambling, she was only able to touch the ring briefly. She could not hold on to it before it fell and hit the rock they stood next too.

"*Oh no!* I'm sorry, Danny! I did not mean to drop it," said Jeannie in an elevated voice as she watched Danny's ring hit the rock that they were next to. "I didn't mean to scratch or dent it!"

His ring bounced off the rock and landed on a small pile of sand.

Danny stooped and picked it up. "Wow, there is a big dent on it now!" he said seriously.

Jeannie winced. She said nothing. Then Danny laughed and said, "Jeannie, a freight train could run over my ring, and it would not even put a scratch on it. It is weird. This thing is impervious to anything!"

"Are you sure? You scared me," she said

He held it in the palm of his hands. She gingerly took it from him and held it tightly.

It was no ordinary ring. The brilliant thirty-five-carat flawless emerald was its main beauty. The setting was massive and demanded to be worn on a finger of extraordinary size. Gold workmanship worthy of being worn on the finger of a god surrounded the gemstone. The brilliant yellow-gold foundation was massive and would have only fitted a finger the size of Danny's. Inlaid into the pure yellow gold were the shapes of celestial bodies fashioned from white gold. The Boar's Tusk was reflected in those silvery orbs. The thirty-five carat emerald was held in place by large, white-gold cylindrical shafts capped with round, faceted spheres. The metal facets sparkled in the sunlight as if directing light into the gemstone.

Trying to find words to describe the ring, Jeannie stammered with excitement, "Danny, this is just incredible. *Oh my!* I've never seen a ring so magnificent. Truly, this ring is a gift from the gods. What else would be impervious to any kind of destruction?"

"Can I have that piece of black cloth? I assume you use that to wipe smudges off of it?" Jeannie asked.

"Sure, Jeannie," Danny replied as he handed her the cloth.

Gently she placed it on the piece of black material that appeared to be silk.

She tilted it to look at the engraving on the inside band. With her mouth gaping in awe, her questions rushed out. "What's this writing on the inside? The initials next to your name are not yours!"

She looked up at him and continued her quest for answers. "I don't know any of your relatives who have the initials SGV. Who gave you this ring?" Not waiting for his answers, she made a bold statement. "The only being with the initials of SGV I know is the supreme god Viracocha." Her mind filled with the most amazing thought. *My God, his ring has to have come from the finger of Viracocha!*

Their eyes met with the lingering questions that neither had ever had answered. She reached to touch his hand. She felt Danny relax a bit. It was her statement that grabbed his attention. In his mind, he asked the question, *Did she just reveal the source? I don't know.*

His voice was now tender, without a hint of harshness. For the first time in his life, he was going to disobey a warning. Drawn by the power of the love he had for Jeannie, he decided it was worth the chance he was about to take. Although he hoped he was meeting the requirement, he was ready to take the chance. "Jeannie, you can't laugh at me. I love you, and I don't want you to think less of me. I'm not a kook or a monster!"

His voice was now barely audible. Standing only inches from her, he competed with the breeze as he said, "I have supernatural strength. I have no idea where it comes from. At first, I thought I was a vampire or a werewolf."

At that moment, he paused and choked up. He looked into her eyes. Swallowing the lump in his throat, he continued. "Jeannie, I would never hurt you. I don't think I'm a monster. I take things seriously and don't get tangled up believing in the supernatural...or any of that weird stuff!"

She was ready to listen. She knew it would be good, but she had no idea how good. "Oh, my Danny...I do love you! I need to know about the ring, and I promise—I will always love you and be here for you!"

Their eyes remained locked as he told a strange story. "Jeannie, my parents told me that on their wedding night something very strange happened. They were poor, eighteen years old, and adventurous. They drove to the Boar's Tusk for their honeymoon. They spent their first night together under the stars in the Scarlet Desert. In the morning, they found the emerald ring next to them. There was a note lying beside it."

"What did the note say, my love?"

At this point, he couldn't get the words out fast enough. He had held the secret locked up inside of him his entire life. He had only talked briefly on one occasion with his parents about it. They only did what the note had asked. He had no idea what condemnation would befall him, but he could no longer live with the burden of carrying a mystery deep within him that haunted him every day, not knowing who he was.

"This is just crazy, Jeannie. Oh well, here goes. The note wasn't written on paper. It was engraved on a very thin sheet of gold. My mother had kept it for me for years, and now I have it and keep it as one of my treasures." For a moment, he stopped and just looked at her eyes. Then his hand reached out. "Jeannie, can I have your pad of paper?" Before she could hand it to him, he dropped his arm and said, "Ah...better yet, a piece of yellow paper that looks like gold!"

She put her pad of paper down and took a few moments to dig through her bag in search for a piece of yellow paper. She found it.

"Sure...here, Danny."

It wasn't hard for Danny to replicate the note. An image of it was etched in his mind. Taking a few minutes, he sketched out the note as it was engraved on the gold sheet. His intent was to capture the appearance of the gold note and any hidden significance in the writing style itself. He lifted the paper so she could clearly see it. Reading the incredible message, her heart leaped with joy just waiting for his explanation.

"This is what is engraved on that sheet of gold," he said, showing her the message:

Gifts from the Gods

❖ The boy will have emerald–green eyes and sun–
   colored yellow hair. He shall be called Danny,
   and endless time shall be his gift.

❖ The emerald ring he must have with him always
   and guard it with his life.

❖ The golden watch holds a secret. Reveal the
   secret to no one until they reveal the source.

❖ Disobey any: condemnation will fall upon him.

❖ Obey all: he inherits supreme power as TRPOV in
   union with TRPON.

SGV

At first, her stare concentrated on the two words of his note: *TRPOV* and *TRPON*. She was lost for words as her mind burst into thought. *He's connected to our legends. He's TRPOV. My God, I had no idea! I've fallen in love with the emissary of Viracocha.*

His face was set in unfamiliar lines of mystery that told her he was no normal human being. Yet there was something about his bearing that revealed his character was anything but devious. Speechless, she was mesmerized as he told his story.

"It was signed by someone with the initials SGV!"

She interrupted. "Those initials are also on your emerald ring. They have to stand for supreme god Viracocha."

Not listening to all of her words, he was focused on his own interest, wanting to get the full story off his chest. He broke in. "My parents had no idea who put the gold note and emerald ring on their blanket that warm summer night under the stars at the base of the Boar's Tusk. They were concerned that on their wedding night someone had been spying on them. Actually, they were quite upset about the whole situation. They thought someone was playing a prank on them!"

His breathing increased, and his story flowed on. "Nine months later, I was born. I had a full head of hair and the exact features that the gold note described. This really rattled my parents. No one in our family has ever had sun-colored yellow hair or brilliant emerald-green eyes. They were scared not to follow the instructions. They had no idea what 'condemnation would fall,' so they named me Danny and put the ring on a gold chain on my neck. I've worn it ever since."

Never in a hundred million years would she have suspected who he was. The excitement in Jeannie exploded in triumph. She had fallen in love with a gift from the gods. He was tied to her in some way yet to be determined. Now her face was drawn into unfamiliar lines of extravagant joy—joy she'd never experienced in her entire life, joy that all the money in the world couldn't buy. "My God, Danny! You are special! I knew it! Oh, my love, we are more than just a couple of kids raised in a coal camp! *Much more!*"

He had one more secret. "Jeannie, there is something else. I told you guys my golden watch was given to my father on his sixteenth birthday and that then it came to me. Well, that's not true!"

"What are you telling me, Danny?"

"The watch, chain, and fob were also on my parents' blanket. Like the emerald ring, it has my name engraved on it. It is weird! The damned thing never needs to be wound! It just keeps going on its own! That's why I made up the story about my dad's grandmother giving it to him on his sixteenth birthday. I've never told anybody because it is just too weird!"

Pulling on the gold chain, he took his watch from its hiding place in the small pocket of his Levi's. "Jeannie, look at this," he said as he opened the back cover of the watch, exposing the secret it held. "Engraved on the back of my watch are the exact mirror-image symbols that are on your golden key. Above each symbol is engraved either a Roman numeral I or X."

I X I X I X I X I X I

At least for Jeannie, the puzzle fit together. "*Oh my God, Danny!* Do you know what that signifies?"

Unfortunately, Danny was not following her train of excitement. "*No! What?*"

Looking at Tony, she moved closer to Danny so as to have privacy in their conversation. She took him into her arms and whispered, "Yes, my love, you are special! Here's what I'm thinking and why. You're mentioned in our legends. You're TRPOV, and I'm TRPON. You and I together have something to do with the supreme god Viracocha and his wife, Neferdor."

Caught up in a web of legends beyond his comprehension, he was left shaking his head, looking for answers. "What do you mean? TRPOV and TRPON? What does that stand for? Who is TRPOV? And who is

TRPON?"

Unfortunately, at first, she had no reply other than "You and me." He looked at her face and waited for more explanation, but her answer was not enlightening. "Danny, I do not know what TRPOV and TRPON stand for." But then her mind recalled something from the Legend of Kashom. "All I know is that our legends state that the Kashome people are waiting for the supreme god Viracocha and his wife, the supreme goddess Neferdor, to reveal their emissaries, TRPOV and TRPON. TRPOV will be designated by Viracocha's gift of the golden watch. The Neferzul, who is in possession of the golden key of Neferdor at the time when TRPOV is gifted the golden watch of Viracocha, will become TRPON."

Her words flew over his head. Jeannie's slip of the tongue, disclosing her sacred name of Neferzul, never registered with him. It could not have been more confusing if she were speaking in a foreign language. Danny's face was blank. "Jeannie, I have no idea what you're talking about."

Although he was lost, she was not. Whispering ever so quietly, she stared at the boy she'd fallen in love with. "Viracocha gave the golden watch to you—through your parents—to let you know that you are special, that there is a grander scheme to the eternal existence of time, that you are part of his plan to govern eternal youth. He projects his powers to you through the emerald ring."

She gently held his face and pressed their lips together. Slowly, she slid her cheek over his and moved her head to whisper into his ear. "Danny, somehow you're connected to Viracocha."

It was no longer a mystery. There could be no doubt that she had just unraveled a piece of the puzzle that was on the gold note—a mystery that had haunted him his entire life. Even though she had revealed the source of the secret of his ring, that his supernatural power came from Viracocha, Danny was more confused than ever.

She paused a short few seconds and then continued. "There's a secret inside your golden watch that's tied to my golden key! The symbols on your watch are somehow connected to my medallion. Both the golden key and golden watch are mentioned in our legends."

Her mind was entirely focused on the recent revelation. Her words repeated her continuing thoughts. "But even more important, both of us are connected to the gods. You're TRPOV, and I'm TRPON. Soon we shall know what that means."

But that did not stop the joy that was building in her. Although she did not understand the details, she had been raised in the culture of the Kashome people and knew all too well the significance of the events that had just taken place. Her heart pounded as she said, "Oh Danny, this is just too neat!"

Because Danny was not raised in the culture of the Kashome people, he had lingering questions. "Who are these people, TRPOV and TRPON? What do they do? Why are they special?"

Jeannie's response was not what he was looking for. Her simple answer, "I don't know, Danny," was not good enough for him.

As they looked at each other, there was a long stretch of silence. Then she added, "The only thing I know for sure is what is in our legends, what I just told you."

Now she looked at him from a different point of view, one that made him uneasy as her facial expression suggested a remoteness far from normal comprehension. "Danny, I just said it's all from our legends." She paused momentarily, with her eyes fixed on his, as she said with conviction, "Let me make that clear. My legends are not just about me, but they are also about you. You are central to the fulfillment of the Legend of Kashom."

A quick glance at Tony, standing fifty feet away, told Danny that he was getting impatient. He raised three fingers signifying he needed a few more minutes alone with Jeannie.

"My God, Jeannie, you have lost me. I have no idea what's going on," he whispered to her.

She attempted an explanation. "Here is what our legend says: Viracocha told Kashom if he is to regain his royal status as the prince of Kopaz, as part of his purgatory, he must aid TRPOV and TRPON in the fulfillment of their missions and declare to them who they are."

Her explanation was far from clear. Jeannie's attempt to unravel the mystery was not based on the sound facts he was looking for. Danny wanted something clearer, not simply the recitation of a legend. His mind seized on the question, *Who are TRPOV and TRPON?*

With an unforced look of concern, he said, "I don't know, Jeannie, if you have all the answers." He rolled his head and stared at the rock door. It remained a silent monster, one that had nearly taken their lives. The breeze rustled long blades of prairie grass against his pants leg.

Not looking away from the east wall of the Tusk, he entwined his fingers with hers and said in a low voice filled with uncertainty, "For all we know, these goofy symbols could be the letters of an ancient civilization's language, like Egyptian hieroglyphics."

Staring at the closed door that he had leaped through just minutes earlier, he lifted his hand to his mouth with his fingers curled over his lips. He thought, *I've lived with the knowledge my entire life that I have superhuman strength and speed. The symbols on my golden watch that match those on her golden key do not reveal the mystery of who I am.*

Then it hit him like a rock falling from the top of the Tusk. He quickly turned his head to look into her eyes and said in a strong voice, "Jeannie, there is something behind that rock door."

This time Tony heard Danny's comment, and his face showed lines of growing impatience.

She gave a quick glace in Tony's direction, flashed him a wink, and then pulled Danny a bit closer. She sweetly smiled. "I know that, Danny. There are forces beyond our control that are bringing you and me together."

CHAPTER 18

Treasure Trapped in the Tusk

The shadows drawn across his high cheekbones by the sun sinking to the western horizon amplified Danny's expression of longing. No doubt he was disappointed. Why wouldn't he be? He didn't get it. Whatever was in the secret chamber of the Boar's Tusk was still there. Danny's lost moment of triumph was visible in his look.

The thought of a trapped mystery in the Boar's Tusk haunted him. It might explain who he was and why he had supernatural strength. But even more exciting to Danny, he wondered if there might be a priceless treasure trapped behind that massive rock door. These mysteries caused a twinge of sadness to sweep across him as he reflected on the thought that they might be lost forever.

That was not the case for Jeannie. She was content to wait for the right moment, when Danny was ripe for action. Patience was her game plan. "Danny, thank you for saving my life! That emerald ring you wear around your neck has to be your source of power and strength." She choked up. "It was not only the emerald ring that saved my life. It was also you! You could have let me fall into the bottomless pit and raced for the door to save your own skin. But you didn't! You risked your life for me."

She pulled him into her arms and sweetly whispered to him, "Danny, I love you more than you could ever know!"

As it was, the intimate details of Danny and Jeannie's discussion of his gifts were not shared with Tony. He didn't want to know, even thought he was keenly aware that something special had gone on. He accepted Danny for who he was—his best buddy who had saved him from the hand of death, and his heart told him that Danny would do it again. That was good enough for Tony. Right now, he had another agenda. "OK, you guys, I haven't the foggiest what you're doing or what you're talking about! We damn near got killed, green light or no green light!" Tony said as he listened to Danny and Jeannie talk about a ring. "I don't care about Danny's ring. I'm more concerned about the event that almost killed us!"

But like in Danny and Jeannie's minds, a lingering curiosity about what was trapped in the secret chamber stayed at the forefront of Tony's consciousness. Staring at the silent wall that moments earlier had echoed with a loud slam, Tony had no game plan, but that didn't stop him from getting the ball rolling. "Let's move on!"

Even greater than his curiosity about what was concealed behind the rock door was Danny's love for Jeannie, and that's what had his attention. "Are you OK, Jeannie?" Danny asked, ignoring Tony. "I couldn't go on living if something happened to you." He pointed to the rock tower directly in front of them and said with a shiver in his voice, "You almost died in there."

The rock tower appeared normal. Cracks and lichen made a picture of tranquility on the east wall. Nary a sign, not even an inkling of a doorway crack, showed its face, nothing that would draw suspicion or cause onlookers to wonder what was hidden in a secret chamber behind a closed rock door.

Knowing their love was much grander than the usual puppy love between two teenagers, Jeannie was trying to look at a bigger picture—a picture that she felt was being directed by the gods. To fully comprehend the picture, she needed what was in the chamber.

Her hand lifted to touch his hair, which was moving ever so slightly in the breeze. "I'm OK. This has just got me really upset! I'm bruised. That's all." Now with a look of intent concern, she said in a sullen voice, "I almost got you guys killed. I'm the one that is leading this adventure. I don't know if it's worth it! Maybe you're right, Danny. Maybe we ought to settle for what we've already found."

For a long moment, he looked at her, his eyes melancholy and filled with understanding. "Ah, shoot, Jeannie, we're all involved in this. It's not just you. Tony and I are as involved as you are. I'm just pissed!" Danny muttered.

This signal for her game plan to go into effect came even earlier than Jeannie had anticipated. "What's wrong, Danny?" she asked.

"We didn't get it. Damn," said Danny. "We didn't get the treasure! Now what?"

Now she had support. "Do you think it is lost forever?" asked Tony.

"What?" blurted out Jeannie, quickly following up on her question to Danny, his answer, and Tony's question.

Tony might not have realized what he was doing, but Jeannie did. He was the catalyst that would allow her to set her plan in motion. "Well, we did get the chamber door open, didn't we? I didn't imagine going into that scary chasm in the Boar's Tusk, did you?" asked Tony.

She waited for the right moment as she looked to Tony for him to continue. But it was Danny who set the stage for her plan to go into motion.

"No, Tony. This has been one hell of a day! You didn't imagine anything—we found a secret chamber in the Boar's Tusk, and we came close to getting trapped inside! I just wish that door had stayed open long enough for us to have gotten the treasure," said Danny.

Her moment had arrived. She held back her smile, itching to make its presence known. "Do you think there's still a chance?" Jeannie cleverly asked as she listened to Danny lament about not getting what was in the granite vault.

"Hell if I know!" said Danny. "All I know is that we almost died trying to get it!" Shaking his finger at the wall, he ground his teeth and said, "When that damn door opened, it reminded me of a monster's mouth! Just look at it! Yeah, you saw it! You heard it! Just look at the Tusk, and visualize a monster bellowing, creaking, and roaring as it opens its mouth. I know it is just a rock door into a chamber, but holy mother of Saint Andrew, that door scares me."

Tony's technical mind went into gear. "That rock door must be on a timer," said Tony. "We didn't do anything to close it!"

Jeannie's clever interjection was timed perfectly. "Danny, maybe there's still a chance. Tony may be on to something!"

"What do you mean, Jeannie?" asked Danny.

Now for the moment of truth—was her plan ready to start? Forcing the right expression to coincide with her next comment, she said, "Hmm, let's try it out."

The boys weren't on board yet. "Try what out?" Danny shouted. "My God, Jeannie! I'm not going back in there! No way! Are you nuts?"

Quick thinking by Jeannie was all that it took. "I'm not saying we go back in there. I'm saying we try it out. What I mean is that we open the rock door again and check to see if it's timed. We can do it a couple of times. If it is, we open it, make a mad dash to get the box, then get the heck out of Danny's so called 'monster's mouth.' One of us can stand outside just in case the door closes up. I think we'll be OK!"

Getting bitten by the same rattlesnake twice, figuratively speaking, was not on Danny's list of favorite activities. "I don't know, Jeannie! That damn thing is spooky-scary! It almost killed us! I sure don't want to get trapped in there. I can't imagine spending an eternity in a chasm in the middle of the Boar's Tusk!"

Cleverly, her words were crafted to get them all on board the ship of discovery. "Look, Danny—Tony and I will go in and get the box. You can stand outside and be the guard if the rock closes us in."

"I don't think so! Not me!" Tony chimed in.

That was the response she was waiting for. "OK, I'll do it myself. You wimps can just stay outside and make sure I get out if the rock door closes on me."

Letting a girl do a man's job was not the CoalVille way—at least not for Danny. "OK, LoneTree, we get the message. What do we do?" Danny asked.

"Like I said, we open it and check to see how long it stays open. We do it a bunch of times. We just make sure we can get it open from the outside whenever we want."

With her plan in motion, Jeannie was content to sit back and wait for the emergence of hidden secrets that had only had the company of darkness in their hiding place for centuries.

"Do you think we'll be OK, Jeannie? Do you think we can do it—get to the granite vault and get the box that is inside before we get closed in?" Tony queried.

This was his domain. Danny was not about to let Jeannie answer Tony's question. "Well, it depends on how heavy that thing is. If it is only sixty or seventy pounds, it will be a piece of cake to get in, get the box, and get out before the door closes," said Danny forcefully. "All right, Jeannie, you win. Let's do it," he said, shaking his finger at the Tusk.

For the next half hour, the kids conducted an experiment at the Boar's Tusk. They opened the rock door using the brass bow and arrow and timed how long it took to automatically close. Once opened, it closed three minutes later on the dot.

"OK, open it up. Tony and I will race in and get the box. Jeannie, you make sure to open this rock door if it shuts on Tony and me! Let's do it."

"It's open! Let's go!" Danny hollered. "Come on, Tony. Let's go get the box."

Venturing into a black hole that had nearly taken their lives less than an hour ago was, to say the least, considerably more spooky than the first time.

"Don't get near that hole," Tony said as he led the way using Danny's flashlight. "We don't want to end up like Jeannie did—dangling on the edge or falling into that bottomless pit."

The clock was ticking. The door was patiently waiting for its time to usher blackness into the chasm once more.

Fortunately, the vault next to the bottomless pit had been opened on the first trip around the mouth of a gaping monster that almost swallowed Jeannie. Kneeling with arms extended, Danny and Tony reached for the treasure box.

"Hurry, Tony! Help me get this thing out of the granite vault! All right! We've got it! Let's get out of here. I can't imagine being trapped in this godforsaken black chasm!" Danny shouted. "Let me go first, Tony. This thing is heavy. Stay right behind me, and shine the light on the ground—shine it just in front of me. I don't want to fall."

Her mission complete, Jeannie let herself smile freely as she said, "Good work, guys! *You got it!*" She squealed with glee as Danny and Tony emerged from the doorway. "We're on our way!"

She was content to let Danny have his moments of joy. "This is the treasure box! We just found whatever somebody buried in this secret chamber in the Scarlet Desert! You know it!" yelled Danny.

His train of thought had never raced harder as he held on to a box that had just emerged from its ancient hiding place. *I can't wait to get my hands on what's inside this box.* Putting his thoughts into words, he said, "Wow! This box is it! This thing weighs a ton! It's a heavy one. I bet it weighs seventy…or maybe even a hundred pounds. I had a tough time getting it out of that chamber before the door closed!" His mind was wandering in nonstop ecstasy. *The treasure is in this box! Wow!* "Do you know what, Jeannie and Tony?" Danny asked, bursting with excitement from every part of his being.

"What?" Jeannie and Tony said in unison.

He had no way to stop the rush of words that just kept tumbling from his mouth. "There has to be something of unbelievable value in this box. Someone went to a lot of trouble to make this chamber. They would not go to that kind of trouble to hide something worthless! Whatever's in this box is worth a fortune!" exclaimed Danny.

Jeannie smiled, clearly cheered, knowing the most valuable treasure in the world was in the box before her. Schooled in her legends, there was no doubt in her mind that whatever was in it had to be connected to the Pearl of Time—eternal youth—which her people had waited centuries for.

"You're right, Danny! There is something of value in this box!" said Jeannie. Her mind was echoing the words of Johnny Bill's latest pop song, "Danny's Sunday Morning Pain."

> Just walking down life's lonesome highway
> I'm holding back my tears from sight.
> Oh yeah! 'Cause I'm a dreamer searching
> For treasures throughout the night.
> On the road of time, I'm drifting—drifting in vain

Hoping for a chance to win life's treasure game;
Oh yeah! 'Cause in my mind, I see a star;
Oh, lord, I'll make myself a name.

Johnny Bill, you're wrong! You missed your boat. We just found a treasure—and you know what? I think we found our star! She could not take her eyes off of the box. *It's just like the drawing on the gold tablets. It has a groove for the brass bow and a keyhole for the arrow. Wow! It has ten combination wheels. How neat!*

The excitement was palpable. Danny was sure it wasn't pirate treasure. He didn't have the foggiest who'd hid it at the Boar's Tusk. He didn't care. Whatever was in the bronze box belonged to the three of them. They had found it. But Danny's sense of humor was far from dull. Pirates were his fascination, and they would remain such. It was a fun time in the Scarlet Desert, and he was having fun. Playing out a fantasy of finding pirate treasure was his way of releasing tension.

"We're about to see a box full of gems. It's what I told you guys all along—you think you know everything, but I got this one right. I told you guys—we're Pirates in the Desert! And we just found a stash of booty! Pirate booty!"

Jeannie looked at Danny and read his body language. *He knows pirates didn't stash this treasure out here. His problem is he doesn't know who put it here. I do. Soon we'll all know.*

She gazed at him, saying nothing, only daydreaming. *There's no substitute for success. I knew we'd find something that keys would open—the bow and arrow are keys to the bottomless pit.*

A cloud drifted from the face of the sun, and she let its rays warm her face. She looked up. *I'm sure that what's in the box is connected to the sun.* Her fingers gently slid into the front pocket of her Levi's cutoffs. Her fingers grasping the leather pouch, her mind drifted as gently as a cloud floating in the sky. *The ten symbols we got using my golden key must open the combination—yes, it will be something that could change our lives forever! And who knows, we may take a journey like Kashom did. We may have found a way to adventure on a highway that few have taken—a journey on the Highway of Time.*

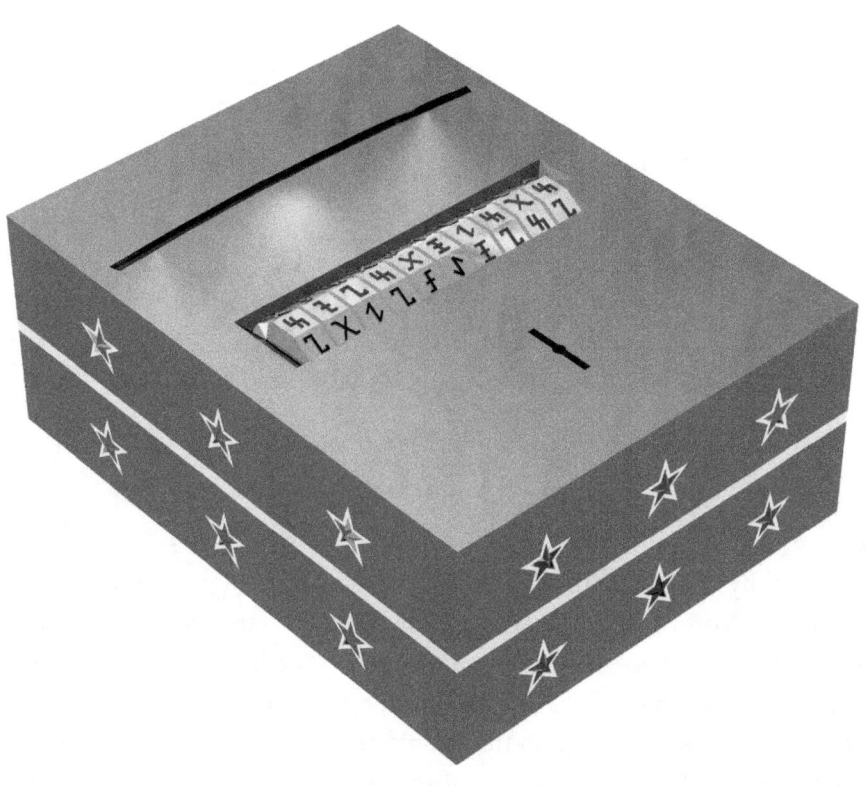

CHAPTER 19

An Emerald Star in a Golden Cradle

Lured by the glistening gold outlining star-shaped gemstones, Jeannie focused on resisting the urge to dive into the treasure box without a moment of caution. Aware of the enticement, she kept herself under control. That was Jeannie's way of navigating new territory. She had most of the keys, but not all. The item that would complete the set of keys—the answer to the riddle on the feathers of the brass arrow—remained a mystery. But therein lay the cleverness of the riddle. For even prior to the unveiling of its answer, the riddle by itself was a stark warning. Jeannie was not about to let hasty action ruin things or condone prying open the treasure box prematurely.

They studied the beautiful bronze box they had just retrieved from the granite vault hidden in a secret chamber inside the Boar's Tusk. They had no idea what they were staring at. Their thoughts were *What's inside it? How do we get into it?* In their entire lives, they had never seen such an ornate box. It surely had treasure in it. Their excitement level was climbing as high as the massive rock towers they were standing next to.

Gratitude formed the basis of Jeannie's culture. First and foremost was her gratitude to the sun as the giver of life on earth. But it did not end with that. "Thanks, guys, for getting the box. I know you didn't want to go back into that chamber. I don't blame you—whoa, scary! But now we have it. This thing has to have something pretty special in it to be locked in that secret chamber. Somebody went to a lot of effort to make sure it was safe!"

Anxiously waiting for action, Danny respected her leadership and trusted her judgment. His problem was that the box wasn't open.

Jeannie spotted the perfect workspace. A rock at the base of the east wall, not far from the doorway into the chamber, had tumbled from the side of the cliff eons ago. It had landed almost perfectly flat, leaving a level surface ready to be honed by Mother Nature. First she used her tools of wind, rain, sun, and blowing sand to polish and smooth it to a perfect surface. Then she had the lichen grow upon it to make a nice, soft surface—ready to have a priceless treasure rest on it or ready for comfortable seating.

Sitting next to her on the soft rock, cushioned by layers of lichen, Danny said, "Jeannie, look at those stars outlined by gold on the side of this box—they're precious gems—look at how they sparkle!" He was so excited—he couldn't wait to see what was inside. "We need to open this up. Let's go!"

Tony didn't have quite the respect for Jeannie's method of marching forward as Danny did. "Wow, this keyhole is the exact shape and size as the one on the box we found last week. This is where the arrow goes. There is also a slit for the bow. The bow and arrow are part of the keys to open this box. Can you believe the bow and arrow are used to open up all this stuff? They opened the bronze box we found at White Face Cliff; they opened the rock to the secret chamber in the Boar's Tusk. They also have riddles on them. I wonder what else they do?" Tony commented.

Now was the moment Tony had waited for. His many hours of finding a combination were ready to be put to the test. "I'm going to insert the bow in the slit and put the arrow into the keyhole—they're part of the keys to open this thing. I count ten symbols altogether—that means we need the symbols we derived for the word Intipraimi. They must be part of a mechanical lock that's used to keep the lid from being opened. Let me try something," Tony said as he reached to grab the box.

Then Tony got a taste of Jeannie's strong command and control. "*No! Tony, don't touch it!*" Jeannie screamed in a piercing, shrill voice. "Don't put the bow in the slit! Don't put the arrow in the keyhole! Don't touch the combination!"

He jerked his hand back away from the box as if it were a rattlesnake. Tony snapped, "*Lordy!* Jeannie, what's your problem?"

The next steps in her leadership were carried out more politely, with the aid of Danny. "Danny, would you hand me my canvas bag? It has the paper that has the code of symbols," she said.

Although Danny kept his questions about her leadership silent, his questions about her methods were not. "Jeannie, why are you snapping at Tony? He didn't do anything wrong, did he?" Danny looked at her with a puzzled expression as he handed her the canvas bag.

At that moment, she was Princess Jeannie. She exercised her role and sweetly made her comments. "Danny, if Tony put the wrong combination on the wheels, he might break or destroy what's in the box!" she said. "You know what the riddle says—eternal youth comes from 'the intact star'! I think there is something fragile in this box. I think the message on the brass arrow has a double meaning. The part about 'the intact star' is a warning. I think it's a warning for us not to use the wrong combination."

With a royal flair to her demeanor, she politely said, "The royal family of Kopaz would not be pleased if we destroyed the star, and that's not even counting the wrath that would be unleashed by the gods. We need the correct symbols, or we may destroy the star!"

Danny's concerns about her method of leadership were answered. Reacting swiftly to save the contents of the bronze box from destruction was understandable—even with harsh words, especially when they were followed by an apology. That's what she did.

"Sorry, Tony. I shouldn't have been so curt with you. Please forgive me," Jeannie said with a searching look.

"It's OK, Jeannie. I understand your concern. So what now, Jeannie?" Tony said as he and Danny placed the two bronze boxes they had found the previous week next to the one they had just retrieved from the chamber.

Things were well under control, and this was just the way she wanted it. Exercising even more diplomacy, she asked, "Tony, would you help me? I want to take the tablets out of the box and set them here."

"Sure, Jeannie. You grab that end, and I'll hold on to the other," Tony said as he helped Jeannie take them from the bronze box.

Jeannie flipped through the tablets until she found what she was looking for. "This is the one. This is the drawing that Danny pointed out last week. Look at this drawing," she said to Tony and Danny. "The drawing on the left side looks exactly like the top of the box we just found. It has a replica of the brass bow and arrow inlaid in the gold plaque."

Stopping for a brief moment, she pointed to the drawing that she was confident described the contents of the box. "This is fantastic. Now here's the interesting part. The right side depicts what I suspect is in this box—a star and five rainbow-colored orbs at the points of the star. I have no idea what the pink and green bars are or what those two round things might be."

They were looking at her as if they detected she was only guessing. She suspected they were wondering if her hunch would pay off once the box was open. To keep from being caught out by a wild guess, she added, "Heck, I have no idea what any of this means."

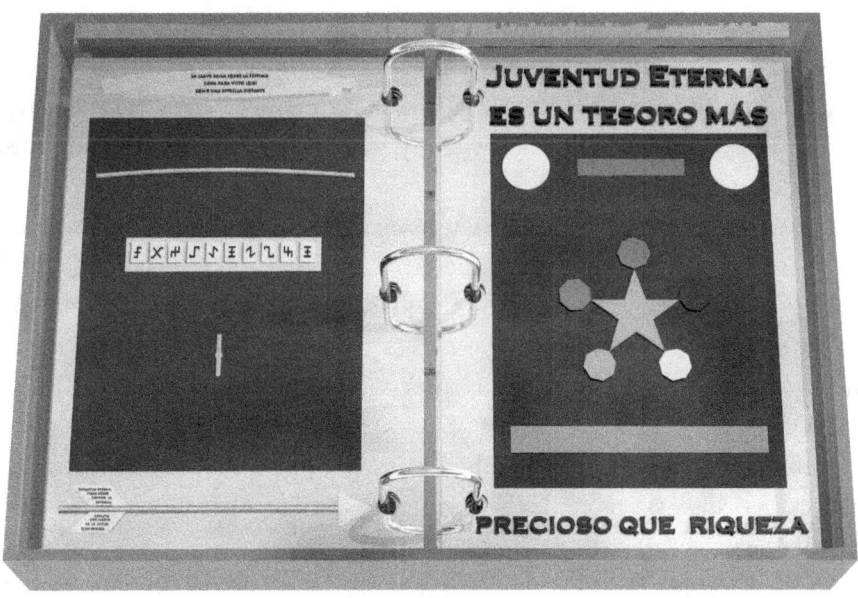

Danny's patience was waning. He thought, *She's guessing what's in this box. I just want it open.*

She detected his eagerness but had no choice but to reassert her control. "Danny, what are you looking at? I know what you're thinking. You just want the box open." *Yeah, he wants to dial those wheels and rush into opening this box—and I'm not going to let him.* "We are going to make sure the correct combination of symbols is dialed on these wheels. I do not want to break what's in this box."

A bit hesitant, but wanting her respect, Tony reached his arm to his side and pulled over her canvas bag. "Jeannie, here's your paper with those symbols," Tony said as he handed it to her. He gave her a glance and a little smile, and he said, "Let's be friends again, you guys!"

Her royal politeness continued. It was now time for her to let the boys charge on, knowing she had everything under control. "Thanks, Tony. Sorry for being snippy! I should have used more tact." Reaching for his face, she gently touched his cheek. "Yes, Tony, you're still my friend!"

She turned to face Danny and said, "Am I still *your* friend?" Jeannie batted her long, black eyelashes at him.

"Yes, Jeannie, you're my girl! Didn't I just pull you from the brink of a bottomless pit? You're not only my girl but also my best friend. You know I'd do anything for you!" He turned for a moment to Tony and repeated one of his favorite remarks. "Sorry, Tony, you can't be my best friend 'cause you ain't a girl."

They all laughed freely. But laughing was not getting them to where Danny wanted to be. Time continued to march on, and the box still wasn't open. It was now time. Danny had reached the end of his proverbial rope.

"OK, let's open it up! And, yes, Miss Jeannie, we will use the correct ones—we don't want to get any farther on your bad side than we already are," Danny said jokingly.

Tony made sure the bronze box was well positioned on the flat rock they were using as a table. Its bed of lichen was perfect to protect it from the rough surface of the old sandstone rock.

"OK, the bronze box is good and solid. It's level and we are good to go!" said Tony like an eager scientist in search of a new *discovery.*

"Good work, Tony!" Jeannie squealed with enthusiasm in her voice. "You're the captain. Danny's ready for orders."

She waved to Tony, motioning for him to have Danny lead. This was her way of directing. She had been waiting to give her love the chance to open a treasure box. She knew Tony was on board with that.

"Danny, you do the honors," Tony said to his best buddy, following Jeannie's cue and sensing his excitement.

Anxiously, he moved closer to the box. "Let me see the piece of paper with the combination code," said Danny.

"Guys, here's what we figured out at Danny's house," Jeannie said, as she turned and handed him her paper. "These symbols will open this box. Danny, it is all yours. Get 'er open!"

Danny dialed the ten wheels so that they showed the code of symbols they had derived from the word *Intipraimi*—the answer to the riddle on the brass bow. As they clicked into place, an intense feeling of excitement built.

"This is it! This is our treasure. *Wow!*" Danny said as he got ready to open the box.

Watching Danny, Jeannie giggled, knowing that in a few moments he would need her help again.

"It won't open," Danny commented. "What do you think the problem is, Tony?"

"I don't know, Danny. You didn't break it, *did you?*" Tony asked.

"You guys, I don't know what I'm going to do with you!" Jeannie said with a laugh. "If you guys had to figure out how to blow your own noses, your mothers would have been wiping them even today. I just know how guys are. Look, there's a keyhole on the lid of this box. So why don't you put the key in and turn it?"

"Oh yeah, the arrow! I got so excited I forgot it was the key," Danny blurted.

"Danny, don't forget the brass bow!" Jeannie reminded him the key was composed of both the arrow and bow.

"Thanks, Jeannie," said Danny. Danny placed the bow into its slot and the arrow into the keyhole and slowly turned the arrow clockwise. A clanking sound came from the inside of the box. "So far, so good," Danny said. "Do you think it's safe to lift the lid from the box?" Danny whispered to his friends, his body language showing building excitement.

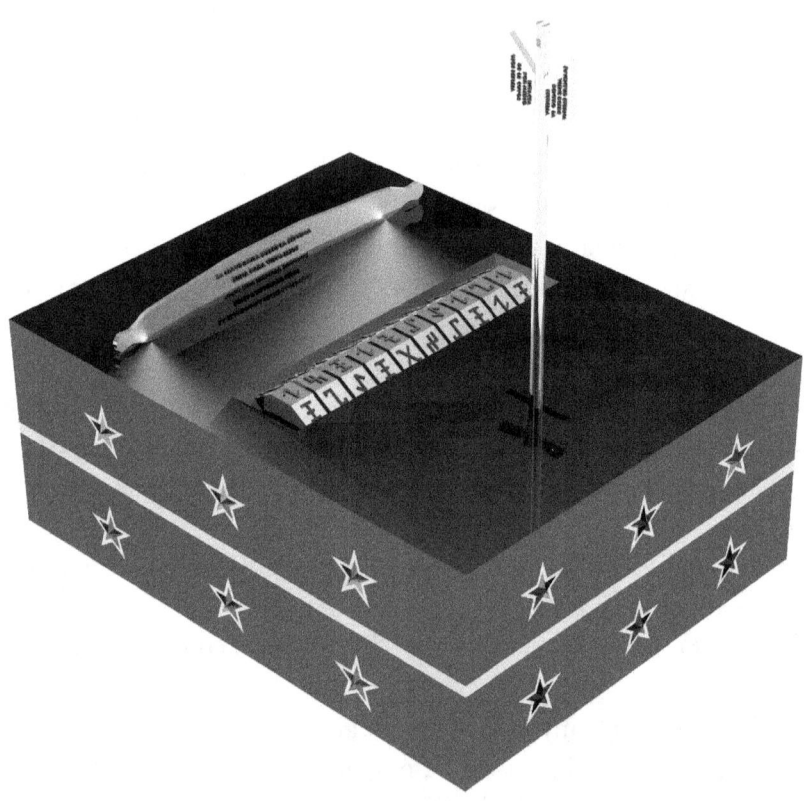

"Danny, why are you whispering?" Jeannie asked her question in jest, parroting what he had asked her when they went into the chamber a few minutes ago.

"Jeannie, this is treasure, and no loud noises allowed!" He smiled at her.

"You've got the honors, so get with it!" Jeannie hooted.

As Danny lifted the lid, all three crowded around to see what it would reveal. *What is hidden in this box? What does it have to do with eternal youth?*

"*Oh my God of mercy!*" yelled Danny. "Look at that!"

Now it was Jeannie who could hardly contain herself. "Yes, Danny. I'll say it again. God of mercy, it's the star of our legends! It's an emerald star."

Sitting before them, glistening in the bright sunlight, was the most beautiful sight Jeannie had ever seen. *It rests in a golden cradle. Wow! It's beautiful! It's the star of the gods!*

This was the moment he'd been waiting for. For almost seventeen years, Danny had wondered who he was and why he had supernatural strength and speed. He'd never dreamed that something hidden in the desert might reveal that secret. Now, thanks to the adventure that Jeannie had taken him on, he was 99 percent sure that whatever was hidden in the secret chamber of the Boar's Tusk would reveal the mystery to him. He looked at it in awe and wondered, *How does this treasure answer the mystery?*

CHAPTER 20

His Eyes Reflect the Star

I t was brilliant. A flawless emerald gemstone had been cut in the shape of a star at least eight inches across. It had to be two thousand carats and the most precious gemstone on the face of the earth. It rested in a cradle of pure gold. The sunlight was dancing on it, making it come alive, a fire of green flames that reached and beckoned her to search for answers—answers to the secrets it held.

But the secrets of the star weren't the only mystery on her mind. A set of keys was worthless if they weren't all there. There was no such thing as opening something with half a key when a full key was required.

It was a mystery. The answer to the riddle she sought was a source of frustration. The lack of an answer gnawed away at Jeannie. Staring at the star, she traveled into her consciousness, searching for answers.

When the missing key was an answer to a riddle, that was a problem. *What is it?* Jeannie pondered. *What does eternal youth have to do with this priceless treasure we just found? This green star…hmm. Eternal youth comes from within the intact star by him whose eyes it reflects! What's the answer to this riddle?*

In the excitement of it all, she turned to see the expression on Danny's face.

There was a smile on it. He pointed to the emerald star and said, "Look at that treasure…just look at it! Look how brilliantly green it is."

He turned and flashed his eyes at her. At that instant, her mind leaped. *Exactly like the gold note said—he has the most beautiful green eyes!*

"*My God! I've got it!* I just figured it out! Wow! Danny! Danny! *Thank you! Thank you!* Why didn't I see this before? It has been right in front of our faces," she screamed.

Stargazing and daydreaming ceased. Something else was happening. Danny didn't have a clue. For that matter, neither did Tony. He just wasn't as vocal as Danny.

Startled by her outburst, Danny's jaw dropped. He jerked his head from looking at the emerald star. He yelled, "My lord, Jeannie! What have you got? What on earth are you talking about?"

She giggled, watching the crazy wrinkled-up face he managed to put on as she thought, *Yeah, Danny, I knew you had the same features of Viracocha, but I didn't connect that to the riddle until I saw the color of the star.* "I've got the answer to the other riddle! I've got it! *Viracocha! Yes! Viracocha!*" She burst into laughter, and then, before he could say another word, she said, "Danny, let me ask you a question."

Whenever he felt like he was in way over his head, he never let the gap of misunderstanding be a source of frustration or confusion. He bridged the gap with humor. "What? Shoot! Go ahead with your question. You know I'm the Answer Man," he said with a grin on his face.

She had him right were she wanted him. Her mind swirling with thoughts—a strange little smile crept across her face as she shifted gears. *Danny, it's fun time. I just love it when I get you in this kind of a situation.*

He didn't have a clue what was going on, but he didn't care. He loved playing games with Jeannie, even though he hardly ever won, because she had a way of springing revelations on him and Tony that usually meant pay dirt.

"Here's the question. What color are your eyes, and what color is the star we just found?" Jeannie wore a knowing smile on her face.

"What color is the star we just found? Good grief. I thought you were on to something. You know exactly what color the star is—it's green. What color are my eyes? Green. They're both green. What's your point?"

"My point is, the riddle says eternal youth comes from someone with green eyes. You have green eyes, Danny."

This time, the revelation was more than he could handle. It did, however, plant a seed that would grow and in the near future mature to a tree of knowledge that would lead him to a startling discovery—who he really was. But for now, he remained puzzled. "*Me? No way!* You're not making a bit of sense!" Danny cut her off. "Eternal youth comes from me? That's a bit farfetched!"

"Danny, be patient. Just listen for a minute. The supreme god in the Kashome legends also has green eyes. The green gemstone and your green eyes triggered my mind." Calmly, she schooled Danny in a legend of her culture that she knew he was a part of. "According to the ancient ones of the Kashome, there is a supreme god. Legend tells us that he has sun-colored yellow hair and beautiful emerald-green eyes. His name is Viracocha."

She giggled, pointed at his eyes, and said, "Your eyes are the same color as Viracocha's. I don't believe anyone else on earth has the color of your eyes!"

CHAPTER 21

Endless Time—Eternal Youth

What is the bottomless pit referred to in our legends? That question had left her mind, but now it was back. She thought she had the answer. It had almost swallowed her up. *Is that the pit our legends talk about?* Jeannie wondered. She had her doubts.

The sun was climbing to its high point. Its warm rays put an extra measure of joy into what had been an extraordinary day. Jeannie took a break to watch cotton-white clouds form mysterious figures in one of those deep-blue Wyoming skies. She sat on the lichen-covered rock next to the treasure glistening in the noonday sun. *The only person who could have put this trail of treasure together is Kashom. Who else could it be?*

The hopes she'd talked to Danny about so many times were on her mind. She started thinking about a song that was making its way up the pop charts, Johnny Bill's "Danny's Sunday Morning Pain."

> On a lonesome Sunday morning, in a cold drizzling rain,
> I'm sifting through rubble of rejection and pain.
> Searching for a glimmer of hope, I'll make my spirit soar.
> Hope will drown the silent echoes of a sleeping city's roar
> And nothing short of madness will lift my soul from sorrow.
> In darkest clouds of sadness, lord, I'll find my fame

tomorrow.

Gazing at the emerald star had pulled Jeannie into a world of fantasy. Her mind filled with thoughts that contrasted the words of the latest pop song with her current state of happiness. *We don't have to look for our fame tomorrow. We found it today.*

Lost in her own little world, she didn't hear Tony ask a question. "Danny, isn't it time for lunch yet? It's past noon. I'm hungry."

Pulling his watch from his pocket, Danny realized he'd made a mistake—the mistake of telling a lie about his watch.

"I know I've never told you guys the real story about my golden watch. I told you I lied about my dad's grandmother giving it to him," Danny commented as he paused. "Do you guys want to hear the real story, what my dad told me about this watch?"

Hearing him talk about a gift from the gods, she stepped closer to him and concentrated on why he would ask that question.

"Go ahead and tell us the story," Jeannie said to Danny as she looked at Tony and gave him a wink of approval, letting him know it was OK for Danny to tell any story that he wanted about his watch. With her eyes focused on him, she asked, "What did your dad say about it, Danny?"

It was almost one o'clock, and they were perspiring lightly beneath their white T-shirts. He turned slightly to the left, and she smiled, clearly cheered, knowing he was someone out of the ordinary.

There was an honest look of concentration on his face, and his breathing was slow. "He didn't say much. What I remember is that he told me it was special and that if I guarded the watch and ring with my life, I'd never have to worry. I never did understand what that meant. He told me that it was a treasure, but he also said that there was a bigger treasure, which is the journey of life we all take during our earthly existence."

Pausing, his eyes not moving from his watch, he touched it with his finger. His eyelid twitched slightly, and Jeannie tried to grasp the bond he had had with his father—a friendship she had never had with hers. "My dad was a realist. He knew the dangers he faced each day in the coal mine. I guess he just wanted a better life for me and thought the ring and watch might be the means for me to get out of CoalVille. I don't know for sure what he had in mind. He was very private, but I know he did not want me to have to work in the coal mines. On many occasions, he told me the ring and watch would keep me safe from the coal-black pit." Danny sighed as he talked about his dad.

Jeannie watched Danny fiddle with the watch that his dad, Johnny, once considered a priceless gift, a magical treasure that would get his son out of CoalVille. Her eyes filled with sparkling moisture as she thought, *Here we just found a treasure of priceless value—but the truly priceless treasure of Danny having his father alive will never happen—or will it?*

She didn't expect it. Suddenly, out of the clear blue, Danny made a comment that took Jeannie by surprise. "Jeannie, do you think I'll ever see my dad again?" he asked, a tear running down his cheek.

It was something that had haunted her ever since she'd almost fallen into the bottomless pit. Even though she was caught off guard by his remark, she was well aware of the significance of their find hidden in a secret chamber in the Scarlet Desert.

"Oh, Danny, I do! Yes! I do think that you will see Johnny again." She took him in her arms and brushed his cheek with her hand, wiping away the tear running down it. Her train of thought did not stop. "My wonderful Danny, I can't explain how, but I think it will happen!" She held him closely, and then she kissed him. "You're so special, Danny. If anyone were to be graced by the gifts of the gods, it would be you! Yes, I do think you will see your best friend again, your beloved father, Johnny! We have so many priceless treasures in front of us: your emerald ring, your golden watch, my golden key, the emerald star and gemstones, the gold tablets. Could it be that they're all gifts from the gods? Who knows? And who knows where they will take us! Only the gods do!"

She looked at him, deep in thought. *I think I understand a little more about the meaning of the statement in our legends, that the keys unlock the bottomless pit by the star of the chamber. The star of our legends is the emerald star. I think there is a hidden meaning in that phrase. At first, I thought it only referred to keys opening the rock door to the secret chamber where the star was hidden. Hmm, I think it is telling us something much more profound!*

Now tears rolled down her cheeks as she pondered the meaning of her legends. *Yes, that phrase about the keys unlocking the bottomless pit by the emerald star of the chamber must be tied to the message on the arrow. I wonder if the bottomless pit is death and the emerald star somehow unlocks it! The message on the brass arrow seems to confirm that. It says that eternal youth comes from within the intact star by means of him whose eyes it reflects. The emerald star reflects the eyes of Viracocha. I wonder if Viracocha has given us the keys to unlock the bonds of death. I hope we can get to the bottom of these puzzles!*

Looking at her in intense thought, Danny said, "Jeannie, I believe you! You have filled my life with the most amazing adventure. It's like we're in a fairyland." He brushed at the tears rolling down her cheeks and gave her a wink. *I wonder what she's thinking? Could it be that we are about to embark on an adventure, even if we have no idea where it will take us? I hope we're making the right decisions.*

The afternoon sunlight on that Sunday in the Scarlet Desert of Wyoming could not have been more invigorating. The clouds had moved on, and that left the sun shedding its warmth on them. They sat together, just thinking of the magnitude of it all. It was a time to take a few minutes, have lunch, and relax. It was a time to just kick back and take five, a time to think about the events and discoveries of the last two weeks. It was a time to think about what all of it meant.

Danny's mind drifted to the thought of millions of dollars in precious gems. *Just look at all this beautiful stuff, all right before my very eyes. Isn't it gorgeous? I don't care what Tony thinks.*

Five minutes earlier, Danny had asked Tony what kind of gemstones they were looking at. Tony had been quick to respond. He said they might be glass because if they were gemstones they would be the most priceless gems on earth. Tony couldn't understand why anybody would leave that kind of a treasure in the desert.

Now Danny's mind leaped. *Hell, he's all wet. These sparkling, faceted rocks are not glass, as he thinks they are. Nope. They're rare gems worth millions. They're giant colored diamonds!*

Jeannie was lost in her own thoughts. The journey of the Chosen One had begun. She looked at the two towering pillars of rock. *Whoever put those petroglyphs high up on the side of the towering monument and made that secret hiding chamber inside them is tied to the legends of my people. Yes, and I'm the keeper of the golden key of time—the keeper whose sacred name is Neferzul.*

"Let's get going," Tony said, showing that he was getting impatient. "We've got stuff to study."

"Guys, what about the gold plaque that was with the star? We got so excited about the star and gemstones that we didn't look at it. Do we know what it says?" Danny cut into the conversation.

"Good suggestion, Danny," Jeannie piped up to give him some recognition. She sensed he felt left out of the hunt for answers. *I'm sure Kashom has included in his writings something that will give us a clue about the bottomless pit.*

"Can I see the gold plaque, Danny?" Jeannie said. "Again, the reference is in Spanish. It's an Reina-Valera reference: Isaías, chapter thirty, verse eight." Jeannie looked at the gold to make sure there was only the one reference. Then she looked it up in her Spanish-language Bible. "Here it is: *Ve pues ahora, y escribe esta visión en una tabla delante de ellos, y asiéntala en un libro, para que quede hasta el postrero día, para siempre por todos los siglos.*"

Jeannie wasn't about to let Tony outdo her in the pantomime department. "Here we go," she said, putting on a dramatic flair and standing in front of both Tony and Danny, her Reina-Valera in her outstretched arms, pretending she was in a school play, acting out a character who was reading seriously from a book. "Write it before them in a table...in a book...it may be for the time to come forever and ever."

Tony didn't pay a bit of attention to Jeannie's dramatic actions but just said, "That says a lot! In the first part, 'Write it before them in a table,' the word 'them' refers to us, I guess, and the word 'table' refers to a tablet or book. So someone is telling us something, and they have written it in a book or tablet. Then it goes on, 'It may be for the time to come for ever and ever.' Well, that's all I have. I don't know any more."

Tony's comment jangled Jeannie's memory. *The messages are connected,* she mused. "I have a thought. We have a lot to do and not a lot of time," Jeannie chimed in. "We just figured out the riddle on the brass arrow, and now we have this reference. I believe the answer to the riddle and this reference on this gold tablet are tied together."

At that, everyone realized it was time to get serious. Her comments changed the mood, and all recognized the day was drifting by. It was now two thirty. They all knew that in three hours they had to be back at their homes in CoalVille.

"Danny, would you hand me the brass arrow?" Jeannie politely asked him.

"Sure, Jeannie." Danny reached over and picked up the arrow and handed it to Jeannie.

"The Kashome people believe the gods govern the existence of eternal youth, which is being forever young!" she said, holding the arrow up. "I think this riddle gives us the answer of how to access eternal youth. Our job is to figure it out. I think the reference to the golden tablets we just read is a clue that tells us how to access it. This may be the clue to the bottomless pit."

She got Danny's attention. "What did you just say? Bottomless pit? Access it?" Danny asked, startled.

"Yes! There is more to learn. Somehow we can access eternal youth and open the bonds of death. How to do that is hidden in the pages of the gold tablets," she answered.

She didn't answer him the way he wanted her to. She stared as if she weren't looking at him but right through him. He had no idea what she was talking about. "Jeannie, this is crazy! Where are you getting all this stuff from? My God, Jeannie, you're not making a bit of sense. I know it's not pirate treasure, but I don't think any of us know what the hell this is all about." Danny sighed. Momentarily, he was silent. Then he asked a series of pointed questions. "Where is your proof? How do you know this business about eternal youth and the bottomless pit being death? How do you know our treasure unlocks death? Where is all this coming from?"

She said nothing, ignoring his questions. Jeannie knew even before he'd made his comments that Danny was no longer thinking about pirate treasure. She gazed at him as she drifted in thought. *I don't believe he fully comprehends the significance of what we have found and what we are involved with, but I do. I know what is going on. Kashom is revealing to me the role of the Chosen One. Zanzee is navigating the path. Danny and I are TRPOV and TRPON. We're locked together on a mission we have yet to fully discover.*

Danny didn't move. He was waiting for her answers. He wanted to get to the bottom of the bottomless-pit business. It wasn't happening.

She continued to stare at him and mused, *I wonder how Danny fits into this mystery? He is more than a tall, handsome boy from a coal camp. I know he plays a role in the mystery we are unraveling.*

It was time to react. Danny's intense look at her continued as he asked, "Why are you looking at me like that?"

Not taking her eyes off him, she answered, "I was just thinking! Our lives will never be the same again!"

It dawned on him. Events beyond his control had taken place. Jeannie was obviously involved in this wild adventure. But what struck him most was the possibility he was also involved. "You're right, Jeannie! They won't! I agree! We have stumbled on to something much bigger than we could ever have imagined. I'm puzzled!"

There was a moment of concentration, yet the shape of her lips was slowly changing with each twinkle of her eye. Her face broke into a huge smile. "Do you think the name of my medallion—Key of Time—has something to do with the messages and the supreme god Viracocha? 'Write it before them in a table…and note it in a book…that it may be for time to come for ever and ever.' Could it be that my golden key and your golden watch are the keys to eternal youth? Do we need to find something else that they will open together? Yes, I know from our legends that that is the case. It has to be that the mirror-image symbols on my golden key and your golden watch associate with Viracocha! What else is it?"

"I don't know, Jeannie! This is way beyond me! I thought it was all about pirate treasure, but it sure the hell isn't! I don't know what my ring is about. I don't know what my golden watch is about. I have no idea what is going on."

She turned and grabbed his hand, her smile replaced with her most serious look. She made her bold statement again. "I think we've stumbled on to something that unlocks the bottomless pit of death."

CHAPTER 22
Secrets Gold Tablets Reveal

She wasn't exactly sure what to look for. She was trying to solve a mystery. But as the Chosen One, studying the tablets to find the answers to a centuries-old mystery was her only option. She knew what her role was. She didn't know how to accomplish it. Gazing at the Tusk and then at the stack of golden pages, she had Danny's attention.

"The answers are in there," he heard Jeannie mutter.

Danny wasn't sure whether she was honestly confused or not. He put his index finger on his temple with a folded middle finger on his cheek. The furrows between his eyes grew. Then he muttered, "What answers?"

There came no answer from her. He had no idea what she was thinking or talking about.

Although she did not speak, her mind wasn't still. *What's the purpose of the gold tablets? They must be Kashom's journal! Yes, who but Kashom would have written them? So what is the purpose?* Then Jeannie answered her own question. *To reveal something about the author or reveal something the author wants someone else to know.*

Pointing at the gold tablets with her left hand and motioning to Tony and Danny with the other, she said, "Guys, we have a job."

They walked to where she was standing. "OK, what's next, Jeannie?" Tony asked.

The connection that Jeannie and Tony were making between time, legends, and her medallion was like linking dots on a paper. When the right dots were connected, there emerged a picture. Unfortunately, the picture was incomplete, as all the dots had not been connected—or even discovered.

Tony had a plan. The afternoon sun was low in the sky, telling him time was not on their side. "First, we need to make a decision what to do with this treasure. I think we should put it just inside the secret chamber of the Boar's Tusk. That would be the safest thing to do. If it's just on the other side of the rock door, we won't worry about getting it stuck in there. And if we all agree," said Tony, "let's call it a plan. The nice thing about this desert sandy soil is that no one will have any idea we've been out here. Even if they did, they have no idea that there is a secret chamber inside the Boar's Tusk."

"I agree with Tony," Danny replied. "We should keep all of the stuff here at the Boar's Tusk. So what's next?"

"Let's look at the tablets. That's what Kashom told us to do with his last Reina-Valera reference," Jeannie broke in. "We haven't spent any time looking at what they're about. This flat rock they're on is a perfect table." Motioning to Tony, she said, "Slide them over here."

"Help me, Danny. Let's lift 'em. They're heavy," Tony said with his hand held out.

Tony and Danny grabbed opposite ends of the red metal box containing the gold and carefully slid it to a spot where all three could see them.

"Did you guys ever in your wildest imaginations think we would be sitting here at the Boar's Tusk looking at solid gold tablets with ancient writing on them?" asked Tony.

No one answered him.

"Someplace in this journal are instructions on what Kashom wants me to do as the Chosen One," blurted Jeanie.

That blew Danny's mind. "What are you talking about? Hell, Jeannie, you don't know that Kashom wrote all this stuff on this gold!"

Grasping for words, not knowing quite how to answer him, she said, "Kashom absolutely did write it, and you will get the surprise of your life when you have to deal with him!"

Tony rolled his eyes beneath his bushy eyebrows, and his meaning was clear. Jeannie caught his glance, knowing what he was thinking. *He wants to move on. So do I. He's right. This nonproductive discussion about Kashom is wasting time.*

Tony started flipping through the pages of the tablets. He'd found something he wanted to share. "Look at this drawing," Tony said. "It's really fascinating. Look at the stick men—the mountains. *Wow!* What is this?" He pointed at the object on the drawing with his finger. "This is a clue! Someone is telling us something! But what?"

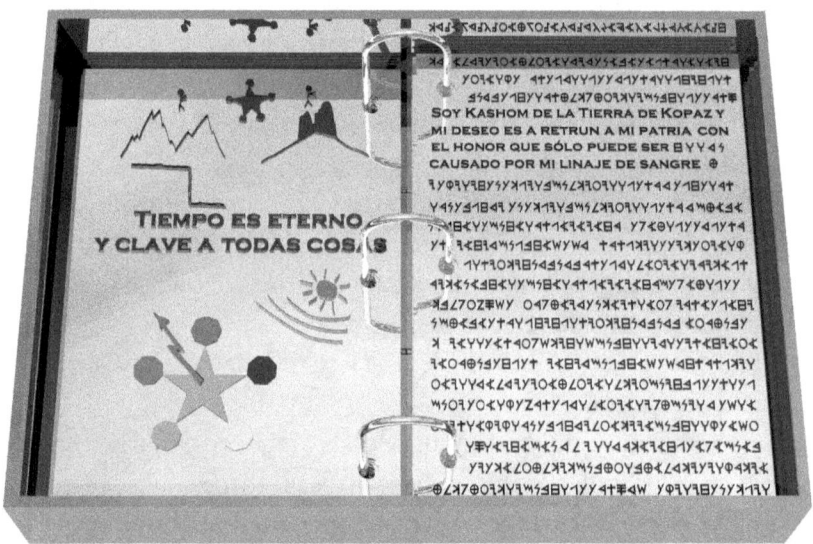

He studied the gold tablet closer. He held his hand out and asked Jeannie for her pad of paper. He took a moment to sketch out two drawings. "OK, I've got them done. Do you see this little stick figure man by these mountains and something that looks like a river?" Tony asked.

No one answered, so his finger traced across his drawing, and he added, "OK, there is also a stick man next to Boar's Tusk."

There could be no stopping him now. He had no intention of waiting for answers. He gulped air quickly and charged on. "Jeannie, the emerald star with the five rainbow-colored gemstone orbs at the star points we just found looks like this object between the two stick men on the drawing,"

He grabbed his other piece of paper and placed it in front of him, saying, "Look at this sketch. I also copied it."

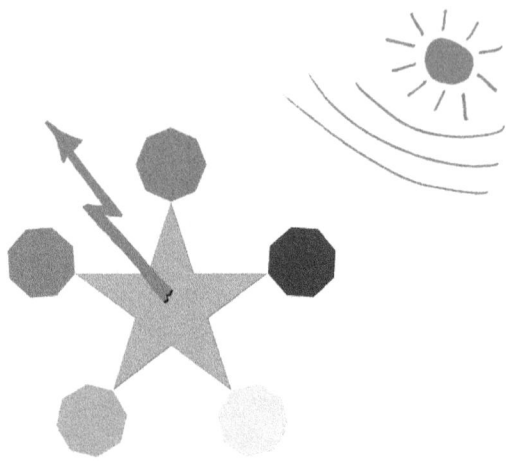

His heart was racing as he pointed. "There's the emerald star and the five orbs at the points of the star. I've included the sun shining on it."

His finger rested on his drawing—the red bolt of light coming from the center of the star. His mind was in high gear, thinking of how precious gemstones refract and reflect sunlight. He was puzzled but on his way to a fascinating discovery.

Knowing he had found something of importance, he yelled, "You see… what's this? Is it a red lightning bolt coming out of the middle of the star?"

Tony's excitement and his observation that connected the Boar's Tusk, the mountain, and the river sent Jeannie's mind into orbit. *That's in our legend! It has to be! Yes! It must be a depiction of the great falls that Princess Aerapondes plunged over! God, this is freaky!*

Her face was a sure giveaway. At first, it was seriously tense. Then Danny watched her smile emerge and wondered what was on her mind.

Her thoughts churned over the ancient legends of the sun that had stumped her people for centuries. She was starting to see the connection. She saw how the sun was central to the promise in the legends—the promise of the Pearl of Time—eternal youth. *Holy mackerel.*

Reaching into her mind, she searched for clues. *Kashom is at the bottom of this. Why else would my people have the Legend of the Boar's Tusk? Why would it show up on these gold tablets? Why would my medallion be a part of the sundial key?*

"Where do you think these mountains are?" Jeannie asked, as she pointed her finger at something that caught her eye. "Look at this thing under the mountains. If that's a river, it has one hellacious waterfall!"

"Boy, Jeannie, I don't know. If it's a drawing of a river, you could be right about the waterfall. Wow, I would not want to tumble over those falls—scaaaary! Why would somebody include this river thing in this drawing? We have nothing like this anywhere around here!" Tony muttered in a low tone of voice.

Jeannie listened intently. Her mind shifted into high gear. *Is there something about the emerald star that lets them travel? Yeah, travel through space and time?*

Her thoughts turned into words. "I wonder if that star has something to do with getting the stick man from the mountains to the Boar's Tusk! All of this must have something to do with the Legend of Kashom!" Jeannie said quietly, half to herself, not paying attention to the boys.

Astute to her comments, Danny's silence ended. "Jeannie, please!" His quick glance caught her glaring at him. It didn't stop him. "That doesn't make sense! Where'd you come up with that? Come on! What does this have to do with the legend?"

It was lesson time for Danny. "Danny, this is the legend: Kashom was a royal prince. He lost his honor and his position as heir to the royal throne of Kopaz. Somehow, he ended up in the Scarlet Desert—right here at the Boar's Tusk!"

He was amused but not convinced. "I see. You think this drawing depicts him being transported somehow from Kopaz to the Boar's Tusk here in the Scarlet Desert."

She was sure. "Yes, I do! I've already told you the Legend of Kashom, but I don't think you really comprehended what I said. Remember that the royal prince—Kashom—came from a land far away—Kopaz—in a time long ago. He was dishonored and had to leave his homeland because

Gorom Mochcom killed his sister and lied about it. The evil gorom tore the golden key—the very golden key that I have—from Princess Aerapondes's neck. He then drowned her in a river, and Kashom, standing on the river's bank, witnessed her body plunging over a giant waterfall."

She took a deep breath and jumped back in before Danny could grab center stage. "Evidently, Kashom got blamed for the murder, so he left Kopaz and ended up in the Scarlet Desert. He wants to go back to Kopaz and once again be the royal prince—he wants his honor back!"

She shivered at these thoughts. His smirk was growing. She was getting upset. "The first time I told you this legend, you laughed at me and made fun of my people's sacred beliefs. But the bottom line is that *it's true!* Could all of these treasures somehow be used to transport him from Kopaz to the Scarlet Desert and back to Kopaz?"

Danny had his own ideas. "Jeannie, here is the dilemma I see with your story. I don't mean to offend you, but if this is what he needs to go home— why doesn't he just do it?"

She didn't have a comeback. It was time to punt. "I don't know, Danny. I just don't know."

Danny waited for her to finish and came back with a zinging question. "OK, Jeannie, how do you know this guy that you call Kashom even exists?"

She didn't like his question. Her glare intensified.

Jeannie, this is way too complicated for me. I have no idea what's going on, thought Danny, and he sighed.

Tony had a game plan. He needed to change the discussion. He wanted confirmation from Danny, so he looked past Jeannie at his friend. What he saw he didn't understand.

Danny was squirming. His face was wearing a look of bewilderment. Tony was about to laugh, but he held it in. Then Danny did it again, but he squirmed so hard he bumped into Jeannie's side. She immediately turned her head to say something to him. His face was blank, and she didn't see anything unusual. He was sitting next to her with his legs hanging off the edge of the rock.

Danny's hand lifted high in the air, and he was about to swat at something when Tony hollered, "Wait!"

Danny jumped, and Zanzee leaped from beneath the edge of the rock. He had been concealed from view, close to where Danny's legs had been dangling over the edge.

Jeannie screamed, "Zanzee, what do you have for us?"

He bounded onto the rock and then onto her lap. She started petting him. A smile as big as the sun above lit up her face. She started laughing so hard that it was hard for her to speak. Between bursts of laughter, she said, "What do you make of Danny, Zanzee? It seems he has a fidgeting problem. What do you think, Zanzee?"

Tony could not stop his own laughter. Danny's face muscles were unable to contain his smile. He scratched Zanzee's ear and said, "I knew it was him all along."

Jeannie shook her finger at him and said, "You know, Danny, you go to hell for lying!"

After that comment, there was no containing any laughter for all three. The sounds that filled the air around the Boar's Tusk were like resonating joy, the sound of a party for a royal prince on his accession to the throne.

While Danny and Jeannie were still caught up in laughter, Tony kept his eye on Zanzee. He jumped from Jeannie's lap and stuck his paw on the golden page. Then Tony saw it. A Spanish phrase among the Phoenician letters. Smack in the middle of that phrase was the word "Kashom." It was clear as a bell.

With a burst of excitement, he yelled, "Look at that, Jeannie!"

Her and Danny's laughter came to a screeching halt. Tony pointed at Zanzee and then to the Spanish phrase.

Jeannie smiled and politely thanked Zanzee. She turned and looked at Danny. She was going to ring somebody's bell. "It says: '*Soy Kashom de la tierra de Kopaz y mi deseo es a retrun a mi patria con el honor y que sólo puede ser causado por mi linaje de sangre.*'" With grace and charm, she continued in English. "Now let me translate: 'I am Kashom of the world of Kopaz, and my desire is to return to my homeland with honor, and that can be caused only by my blood lineage.'"

She didn't have to say another word. Silence fell on the group. He had no doubt. His foot was in his mouth again. Now Danny realized there was validity to Jeannie's legends.

She grabbed center stage, along with Zanzee in her arms. "This is *neat! Really neat!*" Jeannie squealed with excitement. "Until now, my people only knew Kashom came from Kopaz. Now we know something about his homeland. There are mountains and a river there. It must be beautiful," said Jeannie, beaming at Tony and Danny. There was no stopping her. "Here's the neat part," Jeannie continued. "I now know that Kashom has a heart. He's lonesome and wants to go home. He has a soul! And do you know what's really cool? We can help him! He can only get home through me!"

All that Danny could do was nod his head and listen. *There she goes again. Damn, my foot gets bigger, and my mouth shrinks. When the hell am I going to learn!* Danny watched Jeannie explain Kashom's message and admired Zanzee. *I've got to hand it to him. He's one hell of a cat!*

Her eyes were watching Danny. As the smile on his face took shape, so did hers. *Her smile lights up the world! Yes, Jeannie, you are a royal princess—a beautiful royal princess!*

It wasn't just Danny staring at her. Tony had learned a lesson also—never underestimate a beautiful girl with a mystical cat who navigates for her.

"Why are you guys staring at me?" Jeannie asked Danny and Tony.

"Because you said Kashom can only get home through you," Danny answered. "I know your legend says that you're his great-great-great-great-granddaughter, but what do you mean? Why you, and what do you have to do?"

She couldn't think of a sound response. Her smile dropped, and the expression that replaced it clearly showed her longing for more answers. She spoke in a low monotone. "Yes! I'm from his bloodline, and I believe I can help him go home with honor. I don't know how. Maybe we'll soon find out."

Her mind at the same time was searching for answers also. *He's from a land far away in a time long ago. How can I help a prince I know so little about? He's from another place, and I have no idea where that is or how long ago he lived there.*

Her pause was momentary but not without concentration as she looked to the changing sky. "Let's continue." Her voice dropped to a whisper. "Soon old Mr. Sun will get tired and take his light from us when he goes to bed. He'll not wait for us but will just keep on dropping in the sky until blackness covers the earth. And speaking of blackness—those dark rain clouds are getting mighty close. We may have to wrap it up early and hightail it out of here."

Tony was well ahead of Danny and Jeannie. He'd already flipped to the next one. "We looked at this before. Remember when we found them at White Face Cliff? Look at the detail. Do you have your piece of paper that connects our English alphabet to the twenty-two Phoenician letters?" Tony asked Jeannie.

"Yeah, Tony. Here it is," she replied and handed him her paper.

For the next three minutes, no one said a word. Jeannie and Danny watched Tony, who was busy writing something on Jeannie's pad of paper.

"I've got it!" Tony was grinning from ear to ear as he pointed to the symbols. "Kashom is the author of these gold tablets. Check this out!"

KASHOM

PRINCE →

OF

KOPAZ

"*Wow!* Tony, that's just too cool! *Good work!*" said Jeannie.

"Yeah, Jeannie. Now we know Kashom was royalty. Do you know what that means?" Tony beamed with excitement.

"What?" blurted out Jeannie with anticipation.

"Jeannie, you're a princess, the great-great-great-great-granddaughter of Kashom."

"That's neat. I've been calling you a princess for a long time, but you really are!" Danny laughed to himself, listening to Tony. His lips curled, and his eyes squinted as he thought, *Tony, you're just a bit slow. I knew Jeannie was a royal princess when she translated Kashom's message a few minutes ago.*

She gently touched the side of his face and said in an unusually sweet voice, "Danny, do you understand now why we can't spend the treasure? These tablets are Kashom's journal! He's telling us about a treasure more precious than all the money in the world. We are discovering a priceless treasure that only Kashom can help us understand, and it's my heritage, Zanzee's help, and Kashom's guidance that are helping me to solve this mystery."

CHAPTER 23

Unleashing the Power of the Sun

Could this challenge have a more far-reaching impact than even the United States winning the space race? If anyone could figure it out, Tony could. There was no doubt that Tony had a deep and analytical intellect. His dream was to be a rocket scientist for his country, dedicated to the most important challenge facing the United States—winning the space race. The USSR had thrown the world into a conflict, the Cold War. So far, the Soviets were winning the space race, leading with their launch of Sputnik a few months earlier.

"Look at this, you guys!" Tony pointed to a drawing on the tablet. He had Jeannie's attention. Tony was a key player, and she knew it.

"I can see by the expression on Tony's face that he has some more goodies to share with us. Tony, you've got the floor. Charge on!" said Jeannie.

"Thanks, Jeannie. What do you guys think these Phoenician letters on this gold tablet mean?"

It was late in the day and not game time for Danny. "Not a clue, Tony. Beats me! There ya go again," Danny shot back.

Tony had no problem playing games despite it being late in the afternoon. "Well, we just heard from Danny. How about you, Jeannie? Do you know what they mean?" Tony asked in a voice that demonstrated his pride in his observation.

She knew he was up to something. She had no idea what it was. "Just like Danny. Not a clue, Tony!" She parroted the words of her love. *He has figured something out. He thinks he's smart. Well, maybe he does have something.*

Tony put the piece of paper that he'd been writing on in front of Danny and Jeannie. He made sure it lay flat on the rock so the writing was visible. "OK, look at these Phoenician letters." Tony proudly displayed his handiwork.

WYꟙ ꓱꟙꓱꓵꟈY

ꓕꓵꗟꟙWYOꓷWꓱꓵ

Danny was in no mood for Tony showing off his IQ. "Tony, what are you up to? Come on! We don't have time to look at your pigeon scratches. If you've something to say, just say it. Don't keep dancing around the subject." Danny snatched the paper and stared at it. "I can see you just copied the Phoenician letters from the gold tablet."

"Danny, just hold on for a minute! We're on to something that will blow your socks off," Tony said.

Before Tony could get another word in, Danny popped off. "Be my guest. Just blow my socks off, Tony!"

That was all it took. Tony dropped his bombshell. "OK, here ya go. Hold on to your socks." Tony put another piece of paper on the rock in front of them. "What do you make of this?"

SUN ENERGY TRANSFORMER

The thunder of Tony's explosive revelation brought Jeannie around very fast. "Tony, what are you saying? My lord, are you sure?" Jeannie had obviously comprehended what Tony just said.

Oh my God, Jeannie thought. *Our legends say, "The golden key unlocks the Highway of Time through the power of the sun and endows the travelers with the Pearl of Time—eternal youth." Could my key have something to do with the Sun Energy Transformer? We haven't discovered what the answer to the second riddle is for.*

The set of keys was almost complete. So far, they were Jeannie's golden key and the brass bow and arrow. They had been used to open a bronze box and a secret chamber in the Boar's Tusk. But the set of keys were also the answers to the riddles Intipraimi and Viracocha. These words were translated to strings of symbols using Jeannie's golden key acting as a Rosetta Stone. The symbols were combination codes for locks. The first set opened the cradle of the emerald star.

The missing piece to the puzzle was the object opened by using the combination code of mirror-image symbols derived from the word Viracocha. What was missing?

Saying nothing, she took her key from its pouch. She stared at it. *We used it as a Rosetta Stone to obtain the combination to unlock the cradle of the star. My God. We need to use it again. A combination to unlock the power of the sun? Oh my lord. This is way cool!*

"Yes, Jeannie, it's true," Tony said, putting his finger on the Phoenician symbols. "This drawing on the gold tablet represents a Sun Energy Transformer." Reflecting his deep concentration, his eyes twitched slightly. Slowly, Tony made his next comment. "Somehow it does something with the energy from the sun!" Tony looked at the puzzled expression on Danny's face. "Danny, just be patient. We don't have all the details, but this is *big*—I mean, really big! The transformer does something with the sun's energy, but what? I have no idea! We just need to keep unraveling the mystery."

It was time for Jeannie to have fun with Danny. "Danny, Tony just said these words would blow your socks off!" Jeannie started smiling at him. "Well, Danny, they did get blown away, didn't they? And oh, by the way, how did you end up in outer space?"

Danny ignored Jeannie, knowing she was trying to get a little rise out of him, but he wasn't going to let her. He looked at Tony. *It seems*, he mused, *that Tony has discovered something neat. I hope I can understand it. Does it mean that the sun's energy is being transformed for some purpose? What purpose?*

His thoughts popped into words. "Tony, what's the purpose of transforming the sun's energy?" Danny queried. But before Tony could answer, Danny decided to have a bit more fun. "Tony, Sun Energy Transformer is a mouthful. Why the hell don't you just call it the SET?"

"OK, Danny. We'll call it Danny's SET, or just SET. And the answer to your question is I don't know!" Tony blurted. "It's transforming the sun's energy for some purpose." Smiling at Danny, he giggled as he continued. "I don't have the foggiest notion what that purpose is. I haven't reached wizard status yet—but I'm working on it."

Maybe it was a coincidence. Maybe it was fate. Who knew? For whatever reason, Tony looked out at the distant western landscape where a thunderstorm was moving across hills of golden grass and scarlet paintbrush. He could see something forming on the horizon. The clouds moved. The sun peeked out from its hiding place with brilliant rays, and there it was—a double rainbow!

Wow, thought Tony. *That is a gift from the gods. We all know that. Wow! It is a double rainbow. I can't believe how the gods in their own way shed a little of their benevolence on us.*

The sun was not only shedding its rays on the distant horizon, but it was shining on Tony, Danny, and Jeannie as well.

Then, out of the corner of his eye, Tony caught a glance of something in the sand—a little flicker of light. His head snapped around to see what it was. Protruding partway out of the dirt was the jagged bottom of a bottle that someone had used for target practice. Standing straight up, it looked as if someone had poked a lens from a giant pair of eyeglasses halfway into the sand, partly hidden by a small clump of grass at the edge of a large sandstone rock. A sliver of light from the sun made its way to the round piece of jagged glass.

Tony's eyes flew open as he gazed intently at the broken bottle. An array of rainbow colors was laid out on the ground. He stared at them as if looking at a tiny, multicolored rainbow ending at a pot of gold.

Instantly, a revelation smacked him squarely in the middle of his mind. "Yikes!" he screamed. "*I've got it!*"

Danny opened his mouth and gazed intently at Tony. "Good lord, Tony, what's your problem?"

For just a moment, Tony laughed at Danny's reaction. Then his giggling stopped. His smile vanished. He was serious. Questions started tumbling from his mouth. "Do you know what? I have a theory! Do you guys know what a prism is?" asked Tony.

Jeannie had been watching the action and was hanging on to his words. She was ready with her answer. "Yeah, Tony. It separates light," she answered. "Do you think we slept through Mr. Bono's science class?"

His smile returned. Quickly snatching Jeannie's pad of paper, he went to work. They waited patiently for Tony to complete whatever he was drawing. There was a long moment before he responded. Then he added, "Yep! You're right, Jeannie! Look at this drawing."

Tony put his sketch of rainbow-colored light, which he had drawn with Jeannie's colored pencils, flat on the rock so all could see.

She was puzzled. Danny had no comprehension what was going on.

"What does that have to do with Danny's SET?" she asked.

Even though Danny was lost, he was curious. "Are you just guessing, Tony?" he asked.

"*Nope*, I'm not!" Tony shot back.

"Yeah, are you sure you have connected the dots, or are you just, as I said before, *guessing*?" asked Danny a second time.

"*No!* Just hang on for a minute! I think I may have something."

"Tony, you don't know what you are talking about. You are drawing a bunch of colored lines on a paper. What's that about?" snorted Danny.

"Give me a piece of clean paper, Danny," yelped Tony.

"What?" queried Danny.

"You heard me," snapped Tony.

It was Jeannie who stepped in. She could see the boys were getting carried away. "Tony, I have a piece of clean paper. It is not white but a light grey. Is that OK?" asked Jeannie in her cute little girlish voice. She suspected Tony was on to something.

"Sure," replied Tony. "That will do just fine."

It took Tony a few minutes to set up a field experiment. He wanted to let Danny know that he was on to something big. "OK, here is what we have," said Tony as he positioned the piece of paper on a flat section of ground. It had been an old mud puddle when the rainstorms came through, but now it was just a level piece of dirt with cracks in it from the water drying up.

Once he had the paper just so, he reached and picked up the broken bottle. It had probably been used for target practice by some would-be hunters who could not find game to shoot.

Tony carefully placed the end of the broken bottle on the paper. He aligned it perfectly to catch the suns rays that were doing their thing. "OK, guys...*hurrah. Here it is!*" Tony stood and took a bow.

"Holy shit, Tony, maybe you do know what you are talking about!" said Danny with a somewhat sheepish grin growing on his face.

Tony walked to Danny and threw his hand in the air, palm open and fingers and thumb outstretched. It was Danny's turn to give Tony, his best buddy, a high five, his outstretched hand slapping Tony's.

Now the budding scientist was ready to make his debut. "Well, I think there's something in front of us that does just the opposite of what the prism does," explained Tony. He had their attention—even Danny's. "I think there's something right here that combines light." Tony pointed to the emerald star sparkling in the afternoon sun, resting in a gold cradle. "I think it's more than just the star. I think the five gemstones have something to do with it also. You see, this broken bottle is a prism. It is doing exactly what a prism does, separating light into the basic colors of the rainbow."

Both Danny and Jeannie were nodding. Tony pointed to the display of colored light on the paper, created by light passing through the thick curved glass of the bottle's bottom. "Look at the colors that the prism separates light into—red, blue, yellow, green, and purple. They're the colors of the rainbow."

Tony then lifted his arm, pointed to the distant rainbow, and said, "That rainbow is a gift from the gods. What are the colors of the rainbow but a gift from the gods? What are the colors of these round gemstones—also a gift from the gods?"

Now he had Jeannie's undivided attention. He didn't wait for an answer. "They're red, blue, yellow, green, and purple—they're also the colors of the rainbow."

Tony basked in the spotlight of his friends' attention. He'd taken it away from Jeannie. This was his turf, and she knew it. He charged on with enthusiastic determination. "Here's the way I think it works to combine the sun's light energy. The sun's rays are captured by the faceted gemstones, Danny's giant diamonds, at the end points of the star. The angle and point where the rays enter the gemstone determines the length of time they bounce around inside—until they exit and travel down the arms of the star. The sun's energy from each arm of the star combines and comes out of its middle as a lighting bolt—a bolt of transformed light energy."

He positioned the treasure of gemstones so all could see. Taking a deep breath, he said, "The giant colored diamonds at the end of the star points have something to do with light. I haven't got it all figured out yet, but I'm getting there."

Tony smiled confidently, as he knew his center-stage performance as the budding scientist was stealing the limelight from Jeannie, and he loved it. He reached and grabbed the drawing he'd made earlier. "Look guys, this is what this picture is all about. Here's the lightning bolt of combined light energy."

He pointed to the drawing and then to the treasure of gems in plain sight.

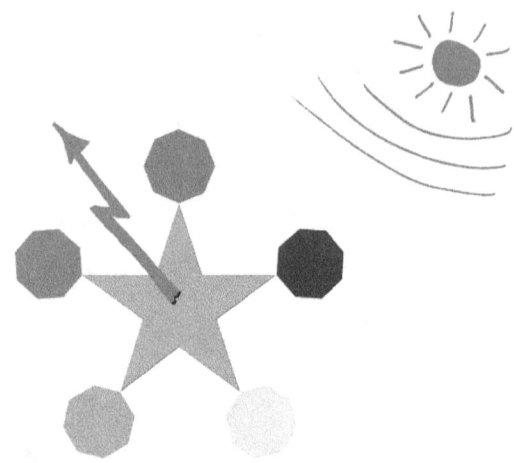

"Here is what I think," said Tony as he summarized his theory to his friends. "Do you get it? The *prism separates light energy!* This thing does just the opposite! *It combines light energy!*"

He stopped. Despite the blank looks on their faces, their eyes were on him. There was silence. Their mouths gaped. Then it happened.

"Do you know what, guys?" Tony screamed even louder. He jumped to his feet from the flat rock he'd been sitting on.

"Yikes," yelled Jeannie and Danny, again.

"What now, Tony? Do you know what you're doing?" asked Jeannie in a shaky voice. "I sure don't!"

"Sorry to startle you guys, but I just had an epiphany," Tony shouted with excitement. "Here's what's going on. The Sun Energy Transformer." He stopped, chuckled a bit, and then started again. "I mean, Danny's SET transports us from one point in time and space to another point in time and space. You see, it can take us to a faraway place in a faraway time."

Danny laughed. "Hey Tony, you can say that mouthful of words if you want. Hell, either one: Sun Energy Transformer...or just SET!"

Ignoring Danny, Tony picked up the other drawing he'd sketched out. "Remember this?" he said seriously.

Danny wasn't bashful. He had no problem admitting his ignorance. "You've lost me again, Tony. I don't know what an epiphany is, and I don't have the foggiest what you're saying—but please go on. Hopefully, I'll get my brain working along the same line yours is and make sense of what you're saying," Danny interjected.

Tony was gracious. He knew the role Jeannie was playing. He suspected Danny's role would soon be front and center. But this was his moment. This was his role, and he played it well.

"For every point in time and space, light is different. Danny's SET is able to identify those differences at each point in time and at each location." He took a huge gulp of air and looked to the sky, watching the sun. "I have no idea how the transformer identifies those differences, but I'm almost positive that is what's happening."

Again, he stopped momentarily, tapping his finger on the emerald star. He added, "Somehow, you can program it to go to a specific point in time and a specific location because it identifies the differences. It programs the colors of light needed to do that."

There were many blank looks from Danny and Jeannie, and then understanding dawned.

"I think I understand what you're saying! Are you sure?" Danny asked.

"Me too," Jeannie echoed Danny. "Where are you getting all this from? Are you sure you know what you're doing? This is way too important for you to be winging it!"

Tony wanted no more questions. "Guys, the damn thing works! Just trust me! It can take us to a faraway land at a time long ago or to a time yet to come. *That's it. Just trust me!*"

"If you say so, Tony! My God, you really have reached wizard status by figuring out that mystery of crap!" Danny hooted.

CHAPTER 24

A Priceless Treasure

What's the worth of a priceless gemstone? No doubt, it was an interesting question that had been rolling around Danny's mind ever since he could remember. As a boy, the colored gemstones in the window of Paul's Confectionary Store on Main Street in Granite Springs seemed priceless. He wanted them but didn't own 'em, so to him they were priceless. Now he owned some real gemstones, but he had no idea what they were worth. Their worth, he would soon find, would be mind-boggling.

"Good lord, Danny. So you know what these gemstones are worth?" Tony screamed.

Caught by surprise, Danny jumped and spun around to see what Tony was up to. "Yeah! What? Now what's going on? Are you changing your tune? What are they worth? You didn't have a clue a few minutes ago. You even said they might be glass!" Danny shot back.

Not only was he a budding scientist, but Tony also had some serious knowledge of precious gemstones. "Danny, do you know what the Hope Diamond is?" Tony asked excitedly.

The corners of Danny's eyebrows pulled down around his eyes. "Nope! Not a clue! What are you talking about?" Danny answered with a puzzled look. "A Hope Diamond! What the hell is that?"

Tony put just a bit of a smart look on his face, but not too much. He didn't overdo it, but he curled his lip a little and nodded. "Danny, the Hope

Diamond is in the Smithsonian Museum. It's the most famous diamond in the world! It's forty-five and a half carats. It's roughly one inch by one inch in size. It's the same color blue as this round gemstone," Tony said, pointing to the blue gem he was talking about. He stopped and stared into Danny's eyes. "Can you guess what the Hope Diamond is worth?"

Danny was not into a guessing game. "No! What?" snapped Danny.

"Danny, the Hope Diamond is priceless." Putting his finger on the round, blue gem in the golden cradle, Tony said, "This thing is beyond priceless! This blue-colored gemstone is a blue diamond that is at least fifteen hundred carats in weight! That is THIRTY-THREE TIMES LARGER than the Hope Diamond!"

He picked it up. Jeannie gave him a dirty look. He paid no attention to her. He had the floor. "We have five of these colored diamonds: blue, red, purple, green, and yellow. They're all fifteen hundred carats."

Tony's voice grew louder in his excitement. His energy level was on the rise. Pointing to the others, he said, "Together, they're worth over a hundred and fifty times what the Hope Diamond is!"

His eyes were as wide as the moon hubcaps on Danny's truck. "Do you get the picture?"

Danny had had it with Tony's question-answer game. "Holy shit. Tony, what are you talking about? This carat, that carat, fifteen hundred carats, a hundred and fifty times something. I don't have a clue what you're talking about!" Danny snorted.

Tony had the floor, and he wasn't about to relinquish it. "These gemstones are obviously not glass. They are diamonds. I don't know about the star—it's probably an emerald. I also think the pink and green hexagonal gemstones are diamonds. These gemstones have to be the most precious in the world," shouted Tony.

He had Danny's attention, but Tony had waffled not too long ago, saying they might be glass, so Danny wasn't going to buy everything without question. "How do you know that, Tony? Are you guessing?"

Tony grabbed his drawings and flapped them in the air. "NO!" snapped Tony. "To make this whole transformation of the sun's rays with the round gemstones and the emerald star work, they must be very precious gems.

They have to be *very precious* gems to have the light-refracting and light-reflecting qualities needed to transform the sun's rays."

Danny had no more comebacks. He calmly said, "If you say so!"

"Well, they are, Danny! And I do say so!" Tony's eyes never left Danny's. He saw a glimmer of a smile starting to emerge and thought, *Danny has seen the light!*

The big picture was emerging for Danny, and there were more questions just bursting to pop out of his mouth. "I don't have a clue what you're talking about, but it's music to my ears. When you say very precious—just how precious do you mean?" yelled Danny with excitement.

Now it was Tony's prime time. He was ready to make a startling revelation to Danny. "My God, Danny! There is nothing in the world more precious or worth more money than what is sitting in front of us!" shouted Tony.

Danny's mouth dropped open. Jeannie just looked on. "*Holy crap!* Are you sure?" Danny hooted.

With a slap on his knee, Tony was pleased to answer. "Yep! No doubt in my mind!" Finally, Tony saw the big smile come across Danny's face. "I know what you're thinking, Danny," Tony said. "You're calculating the value of these gemstones, aren't you?"

"Yeah, Tony, I am. These gems sitting before us must be worth countless millions!"

"Danny, what about trillions?" Tony squealed.

Danny's mind was not working. He squinted at Tony, pulling his jaw down slightly. "Tony, what did you just say? What's a trillion? How much is it?"

"A literal mountain of money! You get the picture! *A pile of money as big as White Mountain!*" screamed Tony, pointing to the western horizon stretching for miles along the top of White Mountain.

Mentally counting a sum of money as big as a mountain was not a commonplace activity in CoalVille.

"Oh my lord in heaven, are you sure?" Danny was trying to comprehend the full significance of possessing the most priceless treasure in the world. He hesitated, and then the questions kept coming. "Are you absolutely sure?"

"Yes! Absolutely! That's it! They're priceless!" shouted Tony.

Jeannie was content to watch the boys discuss the sun's rays and how they could be transformed by the most precious gemstones in the world. She was well aware of the gems' monetary value, but she also fully comprehended their real value, which had nothing to do with money and everything to do with being forever young. *I don't care what those things are worth. They're not going to be spent! And furthermore, I don't fully understand what Tony is talking about, but what the heck. As long as it works!*

"What else, Tony?" Jeannie chimed in, knowing that time was not on their side. She noticed the sun touching the distant horizon.

Tony continued. "I made another drawing of what's on this gold tablet." He took a few minutes to complete his drawing.

"Everything makes more sense now. It looks like people are holding hands and objects. Well, what I think is going on is that the sun's light rays are transformed by the emerald star and round gemstones—Danny's giant colored diamonds. That transformed energy comes out of the middle of the star and enters the person who is holding on to the green handle connected to the Sun Energy Transformer, or, if you like, Danny's SET. That energy passes through all the people holding hands and all the objects they're holding in their hands. Then the energy coming from the transformer transports all those who are energized to a new point in time and a new point in space."

Tony looked at Danny and Jeannie to see if they had any questions. *Obviously, they don't have questions. Jeepers, I don't think they fully understand.*

Jeannie took Danny by the hand and spoke softly to him. "My love, these gemstones are priceless. Somehow they are connected to the gift of eternal youth, so there is nothing on earth more valuable! If by chance we experience that most precious gift from the gods, you will appreciate why we can never sell this priceless treasure."

CHAPTER 25
A Phantom Wins

Terry stomped his foot on his shovel. It dug into the soft white sand. He dropped his hands from the handle. It stayed there, standing erect. His drooping head lifted, and he snapped, "Eddie, I've had it! I'm through! I'm out of here! It's three o'clock, and I am not hunting for any more buried boxes. Hell, I don't even know if there's a buried box out here. We just might be chasing a fart in the shape of a box!" Terry threw his shovel down.

Eddie was stubborn. He was in charge and wasn't about to give up. "Come on, Terry. You saw Danny and Tony carry that heavy box around the back side of Rabbit Ears. It has to be buried out here. We've got a few more minutes before we have to leave. Let's not give up now," Eddie snorted.

Terry was out of there come hell or high water. "Well, I don't know about you, but I'm leaving with or without you! I'll walk back to CoalVille if I have to. I've just had it! See ya!" Terry took off.

Mochcom's shovel was erect and gently quivering, held in his shaking hand. Moving his head slightly, his eyes rolled into position. The brim of his large hat moved slowly around the edge of the sage bush. He was able to capture the view he wanted.

"Looks like one is leaving. Are they giving up? Don't give up, my little lambs," Mochcom mumbled, observing the activities at the Rabbit Ears sandstone formation. "You need to help me find the gifts of Viracocha—the emerald star and five worox stones. Neferzul buried them down there. I know she did."

Eddie had a plan. "OK! Terry, you win! We'll leave early! But only on one condition."

Terry was curious. He stopped. "What's that, Eddie?"

Eddie smiled. He wasn't ready to leave yet and was sure his friend would oblige him. He had to be on Terry's terms, but that was fine with him. "Come on back, and I'll tell you. Come on. Let's be friends."

Terry started walking again. "No! I'm going to the truck."

Eddie ran to catch him. They walked together until they got to the truck. Eddie opened the door on the driver's side and jumped in. He reached across the seat, opened the passenger door, and said, "Hop in, Terry." Terry did.

Eddie knew Terry's weak point—cruising Main in Granite Springs. "Tomorrow morning, early, we go to LeRoy's house and snoop around. I think that Danny, Jeannie, and Tony have something going on up there. We caught them up there once. I have a sneaking suspicion they're up to something at that crazy old fool's house. I'll pick you up at a quarter to seven, OK? We snoop around at the crazy man's house and then beeline it back out here to find the treasure."

Staring out the window, Terry slapped his knee. A cloud of dust flew from it and floated over the front seat of Eddie's truck. He shook his head and rolled down the window for some air.

Eddie slapped the steering wheel. His eyes were getting a fiery red. He slowly ground his teeth.

Terry didn't want to stay another moment. He'd had it. He wasn't sure if he'd even come back to dig, let along go snooping at a crazy man's house. He looked disgustedly at Eddie's snarling face, opened the door, and jumped out. He slammed the passenger door with a bang. "I don't know about that idea. You know what the outside of his house looks like—a run-down shack. I'll bet the inside is also a filthy rathole! That crazy old bastard scares the hell out of me, and I don't want to go up there! I'm afraid of him! He killed Danny's mom, and I think he's still around here. He's a lunatic, and just because the cops said he's gone…well, we don't know what he'd do if he caught us snooping around," Terry said, talking through the open passenger-side window.

Eddie worked to get a smile on his face but not successfully. Only a half smirk emerged. "Look, Terry. We don't have school tomorrow. Besides, Crazy LeRoy is out of here. He won't catch us—I promise you. Let's skip going to see my grandmother in Winton. Come on. We'll only spend a half hour up there," Eddie commented.

Then something caught Eddie's attention. His finger pointed toward the windshield at a strange bird in the sky. It was large and black, but it did not hold his attention for long. Eddie dropped his hand, rested it on the metal dashboard, and started tapping his fingers. "Terry, I'll make a deal with you."

The bird was of little concern to Terry as well. He was listening to Eddie. Turning slightly and leaning against the door, Terry raised his arm and rested his hand on the open window. He looked through it at Eddie and asked, "What deal?"

Eddie's hand came off the dashboard. He put it on the seat and slid it to the front. He let his fingers tighten around the top edge of the Naugahyde-covered seat.

"If you go to LeRoy's house with me in the morning, as I said, we'll only spend a half hour up there. Snooping around! Then we'll bug out, dig out here for an hour, and head for Granite Springs. We'll spend all afternoon cruising Main and trying to pick up girls. Who knows? We may get lucky! Is it a deal?" Eddie asked Terry as he gestured to him to get in his truck.

Terry took the bait. He opened the door, hopped back in, and said, "Yeah, that's OK. I'll do it." Eddie put his 1942 blue Dodge truck in gear, and they headed back to CoalVille.

LeRoy stood up and stretched his legs. "How interesting—they left. Oh, that's OK. I'll come back tomorrow. They showed me where I don't have to dig. Yes, they spent six hours out here digging. I'll not have to dig where they found nothing." Mochcom smiled as he pivoted to start his walk back to his palace.

He watched his faithful servant circle the old Dodge truck heading back to CoalVille. He motioned to the bird, his hand waving in the late afternoon breeze. Vulture saw his master's signal and changed his flight pattern.

"Tomorrow, I'll bring Vulture with me," he muttered as he looked to the ground. He focused on the spot where he had been sitting and while nodding his head he said, "He'll help me find where Neferzul buried the gifts of Viracocha. The two little sacrificial lambs didn't find them, so they're still buried out here in the desert. Vulture and I will search for the emerald star and five worox stones tomorrow. Everyone thinks that I've gone—left the scene of the crime—but No! I'm still here and I'll be searching for precious treasures at Rabbit Ears. Vulture will help me—he always does."

His makeshift seat was still lying on the sand. He picked his filthy coat up, flung it over his shoulder, and yelled up at Vulture in the sky, "Let's go!"

CHAPTER 26

Death to Neferzul

Death was his trademark. He had used it for centuries to get what he wanted. Lord Mochcom, the Prince of Darkness, knew no boundaries in his quest to control eternal youth. He would kill again. His eye was on Neferzul.

Like Mochcom using his trademark skills to get what he wanted, Mother Nature used her trademark skills to get what she wanted. She was constantly sculpting the landscape with wind, rain, lightning, and scorching sunlight. She used flash floods rushing through sand to carve new lines on the faces of the surrounding hills with torrents of storm water seeking lower elevations. Her goal was to redecorate her mansion, the Scarlet Desert. On that beautiful day in 1958, things were changing fast. Lord Mochcom had his eye on redecorating a filthy hiding place used to carry out rituals of horror.

Raised in the desert, the three teenagers were keenly aware of when things were changing. If there was anything certain about Wyoming, it wasn't the weather. The sleepy Sunday had started with a cold, drizzling rain, but then the dark clouds at the Boar's Tusk had given way to clear blue skies and the radiant warmth of the sun. Not far from the Boar's Tusk, however, thunder rumbled over White Mountain, and the dark clouds gathering reminded Jeannie that nothing is caught motionless in time. All things change.

Their lives were changing too. Danny's dreams of finding treasure in the Scarlet Desert were no longer dreams. Unaware that the treasure he had found could be a curse as well as a blessing, he did not suspect the approaching danger. An unassuming man who hid behind a façade of retardation and poverty was crafting a plot of horror. Little did Danny know that someone more crafty than his appearance would suggest was seeking the same treasure but for a very different reason than leaving poverty behind.

Tony noticed the long shadows caused by the sun sinking on the western horizon were stretching across the golden journal of Kashom. For him, time was of the essence. Not wanting to be caught in a springtime storm that he could see in the black clouds gathering over White Mountain, he elected to move the heavy tablets to a new spot.

"If we are to make any progress before it's time to go, we need to get these tablets out of the shadows and into the sunlight," he said.

He spotted a sunlit area. Eight hours of baking in the sun made it a warm work area—ideal for the task of studying the ancient writings. Mother Nature's decorating left the edges jagged, but that didn't distract from the smooth surface honed over eons of time.

"Jeannie, would you help me?" he asked. "I want to move them."

"Sure, Tony, you grab that end, and I'll grab the other," Jeannie replied, her hands already moving to grab her end of the heavy box.

Standing with his legs pressing against the rock edge, he leaned forward and reached to pick the metal box containing the gold tablets.

As they started picking it up, Tony felt like a bolt of alternating current had shot through him, convulsing his muscles in uncontrollable jerks. He dropped his end.

Jeannie's hand was caught between the rock and the heavy box of gold, and the bottom edge cut through the flesh of her fingers like a razor. Blood snaked out from under the box in a tiny stream.

"Lordy! Lordy! *Ouch!*" Jeannie screamed. "Tony, you just smashed my fingers." She gave him a startled look. "Why did you do that?"

Danny jumped to his feet. She saw his right hand yanking something from his back pocket. "Jeannie, here's my handkerchief. It's clean. Wrap it around your fingers to stop the bleeding." He looked at Tony and asked, "Why did you do that? You hurt Jeannie!"

Tony didn't answer Danny's question. He stared at the shimmering plates of gold reflecting their surroundings like priceless mirrors. Tony was shaking. His voice was quivering.

Danny shifted his attention to Jeannie. "Are you OK?" he asked.

"Yeah, the cut was only surface. I have a tendency to bleed a lot with even a small scratch. Thanks, Danny, for the handkerchief," she said looking at him.

Tony couldn't move. His strength was sapped. Grabbing the rock edge with both hands, he found the support he needed to keep from tumbling.

"What's with you, Tony? You haven't said a word since you dropped that heavy box on Jeannie's hand. What were you thinking?" Danny snapped, returning his attention to his friend.

Jeannie's eagle eye detected Tony's unsteadiness. She said, "You look like you just saw a ghost! What's going on?" Her focus was on Tony. His actions and behavior were uncharacteristic.

Struggling for composure, he looked at her. "Forgive me, Jeannie. I'm so sorry." He turned his head in the direction of the red metal box, to the gold tablets. Staring at the gold tablet, he gasped, "I just saw an image of Crazy LeRoy Nabal."

That scared her. She dropped her bloody handkerchief. "What? How could you? He's not here. Is he?"

Tony was sure he'd seen him. He didn't look up.

What the hell is going on? thought Danny. He walked to the edge of the rock, put his hands on it, and leaned forward. He gawked at the gold. "I don't see Crazy LeRoy—only the reflection of the Boar's Tusk. Tony, you're hallucinating!"

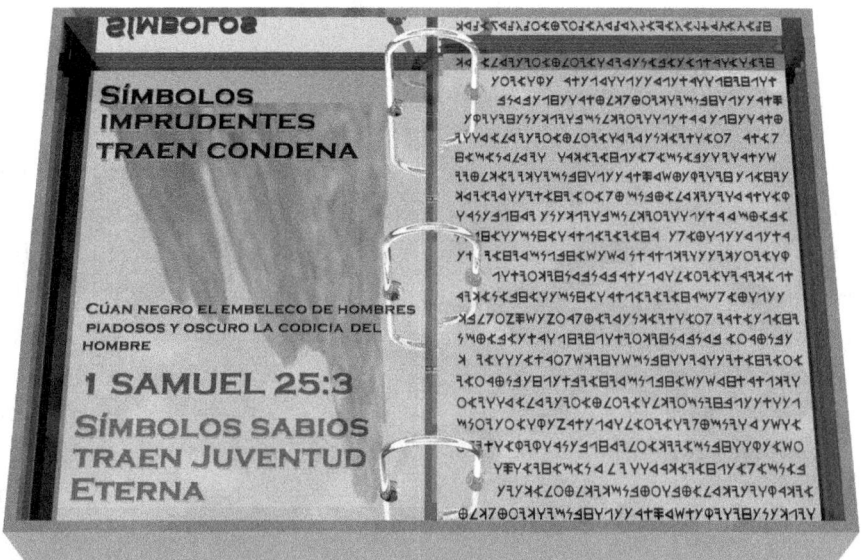

Somberly, Tony's attention went back to Jeannie. "Forgive me for dropping this thing on your fingers. Are you OK?" he asked for the second time, his voice full of remorse.

She nodded, but he didn't seem relieved. His eyes went blank as he stared into nowhere. Danny and Jeannie were concerned. With no words exchanged, they moved closer to him.

Both of his hands slowly slid along the edge of the rock. Taking a tiny step in the sand, he moved to a spot and turned, and leaning his weight on his left hand, he managed to get to a sitting position.

He looked up at Danny and Jeannie. Their mouths were gaping, and they wore expressions of shock. Misreading their concerned looks, he thought, *They're looking at me in a strange way.* He immediately jumped to defend himself. "Look, you guys. I'm not crazy—the image of Crazy LeRoy seemed so real. Maybe I did imagine it, Danny. I know I was preoccupied, and I had just recalled being in his house. My mind must have played a trick on me. Maybe that's why I thought I saw his reflection on the gold."

"It's OK, Tony, I understand. I have some pretty weird feelings about this place too. It gives me the willies," whispered Jeannie as she put her hand on his shoulder, assuring him he had her support.

Her fingers felt his quivering. His mind, not idle, was drifting. He shuddered at the memory of the image he just saw. *I don't understand, but I'm sure I saw an image of that crazy idiot.*

The sun hadn't yet moved to its evening resting place. It was still shedding its warmth, but Tony was chilled. "Jeannie…Danny, a cold chill has come over my entire body. This episode has sapped my energy. It… I've run out of gas. Jeannie, there's some Spanish on these tablets. While I catch my breath and calm down, would you translate them for us?" he said, shivering all over.

"Tony, I would be pleased to," she said as she thought, *I wonder what triggered his hallucination.* "OK, here is the first. '*Símbolos imprudentes traen condena.*' Translated, it means, 'Imprudent symbols bring condemnation.' The next one is similar, so maybe we should talk about them together. OK, the next one says, '*Símbolos sabios traen juventud eterna.*' This is the translation: 'Wise symbols bring eternal youth.'"

Jeannie thought for a moment—she wanted to be clear about what the verses meant. "These two messages are tied together. The first is a warning, and the next one is a promise. Basically, Kashom is telling us to use the correct mirror-image symbols to unlock or energize the Sun Energy Transformer. He says condemnation will befall us if we use the wrong ones! We need to proceed with caution."

Danny was not moving. He hung on to every word she was saying. "Jeannie, where do you think the Sun Energy Transformer is? We don't have it!"

At that question, she paused a moment. Her face was blank. "I don't know, Danny! I guess we have another mystery to solve." Looking again at the gold tablets, she stared intently. "The second one is a glorious promise! I don't have to expound on it."

Suddenly, her eyes caught it—a reference inscribed on the tablet. Theirs didn't. Jeannie looked at the sun reflecting from the gold with a weird expression on her face. She grabbed her Reina-Valera and started flipped pages in a wild manner, which was not her style.

Danny knew something was up. Things were changing dramatically fast. "Jeannie, what's the problem?" he yelled. The volume of his voice increased with each word. "What's going on? I know you! Something is up!" Danny screamed louder as he watched Jeannie start to shake.

Her composure was fractured by uncontrolled twitching. Her attention was not on either Danny or Tony. Her focus was on a verse she'd already translated mentally. "This is crazy." She stared at her Reina-Valera, mumbling to herself as she read the verse—1 Samuel 25:3—in Spanish. She choked up. "*El nombre de aquel varón era Nabal, y el nombre de su mujer, Abigail. Y era aquella mujer de buen entendimiento y de buena gracia; mas el hombre era duro y de malos hechos; y era del linaje de Caleb.*"

Jeannie didn't even realize she was speaking Spanish. She couldn't stop the words.

His eyes wide open, his voice continued to elevate. "What's going on?" Danny yelled. "Speak English!" His mind was ramping up, elevating his thoughts of terror. *She's already translated the Spanish, and I can see by the anguish on her face something is dreadfully wrong.*

Jeannie's voice was barley audible. She was struggling. She stammered, "O-oh...m-my God! Guys, here's part of the translation: 'The name of the man was Nabal...he was evil.'"

"Oh lord!" screamed Tony. He found a jolt of strength and jumped to his feet. "I knew that simple-minded bugger was an evil man," he screamed.

Tony and Danny were shocked by what they just heard. Tony was unable to contain his emotions. His hands were shaking. He started stuttering as well. "Th-this all t-ties together. It's why I-I hallucinated Crazy LeRoy."

As he talked, Tony's mind dredged up his memory of a scene of horror. He had locked it away in a hidden corner and wanted to keep it there. But like the jester of a royal court bringing out a thorny crown, something fetched the scene of horror from its hiding place, and there it was, right at the forefront of his consciousness.

"Jeannie and Danny, I didn't tell you guys everything that happened when we went up to LeRoy Nabal's house to snoop. Well, it...was...oh, it was just evil!" Tony stopped in the middle of his sentence.

"What's wrong, Tony?" yelled Danny.

"The day we went to LeRoy's house, while I was snooping around in his bedroom, I found...you won't believe it! It was...oh, my heavens, I saw the most wretched things in the world—including a human skull."

Danny cut in. He wanted the real issue that Tony was dealing with. He knew it was more than the skull. "Tony, I do remember. You did tell us about the skull. I just thought the old bastard was a crazy lunatic and had dug it up at the cemetery," Danny added. "Get to your point!"

Tony started rambling—talking in generalities. He stammered and repeated his words. He struggled for composure. "LeRoy Nabal is...is a very...very bad man. H-he's involved in the d-dark side of life. He's the d-devil himself."

Then his ramblings focused on something specific. In his mind's eye, he again saw the image of a painting. The paintings on LeRoy's wall were painted on Tony's mind, every detail as vivid as if he were looking at the oil paintings on the walls of the Louvre. "H-h-he's got paintings on his walls," muttered Tony.

"You already mentioned something about a painting! *Get to the point, Tony!*" shouted Danny.

"Oh my lord, he...he has a-a painting of Jeannie on his wall," said Tony.

Danny jumped in again. "What? *Oh my God, what did you say, Tony? What the hell are you saying?*"

"Jeannie is one painting, and he's in the other. H-he's in the painting. H-he's the one!" rambled Tony.

They all looked at each other in shocked silence.

Jeannie shook, wondering why she was in a painting hanging on the wall of a crazy man's palace.

Then Tony's face changed. It was as if he had just walked into LeRoy's dungeon of death and was again witnessing scenes of horror unfold before his eyes. His mouth and eyes flew open. The words rushed out. There was no further need to search. The citadel in Tony's mind where the vulture had been hiding flew open. The bird in the painting that Tony had stumbled upon was no longer a mystery.

"Oh my God!" Tony screamed. "H-he's real! H-he's the black bird of death!" His hand rushed to his mouth. His eyes burst open, and his body was at the point of convulsing. Looking at Danny, his trembling hands reaching for his lips, Tony stammered, "Danny, his helper is that black vulture. We're in a race for our lives!"

Danny's hands dropped. His face grew troubled. "Holy crap," he answered. "I knew it. That bird has been haunting me also. He first showed up at my dad's funeral."

Now Tony had to sit as he continued his tale of horror. "In the painting, LeRoy has a human heart in h-h-his hand. There's a black vulture sitting next to him. My God, there was blood dripping from the bird's mouth."

Tony's breath was gone. He forced himself to take a deep breath and waited for strength. His eyes grew blank as he looked into space. His tale continued. Struggling for words, words that could only stutter out of his mouth, he said, "I-I tried to forget about it. I locked it away in my mind and thought it was g-gone. N-now I can't get rid of those horrible images." Tony's breathing increased with each word. "M-m-my God Almighty—oh, it's nasty and sick! J-J-Jeannie...it's the most beautiful picture of Jeannie, but it has a really sick message on it. At the top of the painting, it says 'Death to Neferzul by *Caopachocha.*'"

Instantly, screams of horror cracked through the air like the booms of thunder moving fast in their direction.

"*No! No!*" Jeannie screamed. "My lord in heaven, no! *No!* What are you saying, Tony? My God, we're in terrible danger. I'm scared! I'm really scared!" She dropped to her knees, digging her fingers into the sand next the warm rock. Jeannie broke out in a cold sweat. Her entire body started shaking. She stuttered, "I'm...I'm...the...the...third Nefer...Nefer... Neferzul. Gorom Mochcom wants to cut my heart out!"

Her ramblings were meaningless to Danny. He gaped at her while trying to comprehend. Every inch of her body was trembling. Jeannie was at the point of collapsing. She fumbled for a place to sit on the rock next to her.

Danny raced to her. He picked her up like a small baby and pulled her body next to his. "Jeannie, what's going on?" he whispered into her ear, cradling her in his arms.

"Danny," she whimpered, "he has committed murder in the past. He killed the first Neferzul, a twelve-year-old princess, Aerapondes, for the golden key." She choked up for a moment and then added, "He killed your mom. He will kill me to get this key. He will kill you to get to me. What are we going to do?"

"Jeannie, who is Neferzul? I don't understand what you're saying. You don't make any sense! I don't understand! Who is Gorom Mochcom? What's going on?" Danny shouted.

"Danny, I'm Neferzul! Gorom Mochcom is Crazy LeRoy!" she cried.

"Neferzul? Crazy LeRoy? Gorom Mochcom? Holy shit! What a nightmare!"

Danny gently helped her to her feet, supporting her. His hands softly slid around her waist as he pulled her close to him. He rocked her sweetly from side to side, squeezing her tightly to his body.

"It will be OK. Jeannie, I'll protect you. You know that!" he said, grasping her face with his hands and slowly moving her face next to his. His lips touched hers in a sweet embrace.

"Danny, you were right." Jeannie regained some composure and moved her head so she could look into his eyes. "Crazy LeRoy is hiding who he is. Do you remember the day we were going to snoop at his house and passed him on our way? You said, 'I'm more concerned that he may be hiding who he really is.' You pointed out that goofy answer he always gives about how he is Crazy LeRoy. Then you asked us, 'Don't you think he may be acting or pretending to be someone he isn't?' Do you remember that, Danny?" Jeannie asked in a somber voice.

"I do, Jeannie. I've always felt that he was concealing his identity. Previously it was just a gut feeling, but this confirms it," he said, wiping a tear from her cheek.

"Danny," she said, looking into his eyes, "that is why he lives in a palace. My God, do you remember the initials on his table and chairs?"

A mental picture appeared in Danny's mind.

"Yeah, Jeannie…what are you saying?" Danny asked.

"Those initials, Danny and Tony, well, they mean Head High Priest, Gorom Mochcom."

The happy, joyful mood that had defined the events of the day turned to one of fright and bewilderment. Three weeks ago, Danny, Jeannie, and Tony had started on an adventure to bring happiness to their bleak existence. They found adventure, but much more than adventure, they found a priceless treasure and a royal destiny. Now their lives were in grave danger.

CHAPTER 27

A Somber Ride With a Mystical Friend

Their day started with hope and excitement only to end with impending doom. They were now facing the oppressive specter of death. On their way from the Boar's Tusk to CoalVille, Danny, Jeannie, and Tony had one thing on their minds: Mochcom had killed already to get the golden key—he would kill again.

The beads on her leather pouch rolled under her fingers. Pulling her golden key from its case, she fidgeted with it nervously. Jeannie held it tightly between her two hands, her outstretched fingers together as if she were clapping. Her forearms rested on her thighs. She slid her hands and the key between her knees and pressed them tightly together, finding warmth.

Her role was clear. Jeannie was the Chosen One whose sacred name was Neferzul. She must redeem the honor of a fallen prince.

"What if LeRoy tries to kill me?" Jeannie asked Danny. "What do I do? Danny, I'm scared—really scared."

The fingers of his left hand tightened around the steering wheel. He slid his right hand over her leg, bumping into her arm. Tenderly he moved his hand down her leg until he found her hands between her knees. He gently placed his hand over hers. She watched him out of the corner of her eye. Her heart pounded, knowing he would risk his life for her.

Danny's role as something more than human was evident—or was it? Was he a human, a god, or part god and part human? He understood he had power no other human had. He had mysteries yet to solve. Who was he? And where did his powers come from? Neither he nor Jeannie understood his supernatural capabilities. But Jeannie suspected they were a gift from the supreme god Viracocha.

"Jeannie, it will be OK. I'll protect you. You know I have superhuman strength, my love. I'll rip his head off if he comes near you. We will figure this out," Danny said as he moved his fingers between her legs and touched her key, his other hand on the steering wheel.

Tony's role was to figure out the details. "Do we go to the cops? Do we tell my mother or Jeannie's mother? What do we do?"

Danny listened to Tony's questions, knowing his superhuman powers were not mysteries to him. "Tony, I don't know for sure. When we're out, the one thing I do know is that we'll always have to be together. I have power that he is unaware of, and that could keep us safe. If he comes near us, I'll kill him!"

Jeannie wanted the subject changed. "Tony, did you make any notes of the messages we were studying on the gold tablets?" she asked to get her mind off the oppressive thoughts of death.

His answer was not consoling. "I did Jeannie," Tony said in a sullen voice. "Here's the Spanish phrase I wrote down: *cuán negro el embeleco de hombres piadosos y oscuro la codicia del hombre.*"

"Whoa, this confirms another part of the mystery about LeRoy Nabal." Jeannie choked up, searching for the strength to speak as she translated the Spanish phrase. "How black the con of pious men and dark the greed of man."

She stumbled for words—words she'd heard her mother speak when they talked of Kashome legends. "The Legend of Kashom tells that Mochcom conned the royal family of Kopaz. I suspect he also conned Kashom, so they both—that is, he and Gorom Mochcom—ended up in the Scarlet Desert."

Tony, Jeannie, and Danny looked at each other. They didn't need words to know what was on each of their minds. Their challenge was to be as normal as possible so as not to bring attention to what they had found. Their vow of secrecy was now paramount—their lives were in danger!

Then there was Zanzee. His role was defined. Zanzee was the navigator and protector of the Chosen One.

"Meow. Meow."

"Oh, Zanzee, you know when I need you the most." Jeannie started petting her cat, which was just climbing into her lap. "Zanzee, I'm scared! I'm so glad you're here! I wondered where you went today. You showed us how to open the secret chamber. You showed us where the emerald star was. You saved our lives, and then you took off. I was worried about you! I knew you wouldn't stay away long. You know just how to find me when I need you the most."

Danny had a shared role with Zanzee. Both were protectors of Neferzul. "My lord, Jeannie, how did he get into this moving truck? The doors are closed, and we are going forty-five miles per hour. It's impossible for him to be here! Whoa—now I know for sure, everything you said about Zanzee is for real," said Danny.

He reached over to Jeannie's lap and scratched Zanzee behind his ear. "You and I have our work cut out for us. We are the protectors of this beautiful girl who has captured my heart. What do you say, Zanzee?"

"Merowwwwwwww, merowwwwwww."

"Good boy. You stay close by, and we'll keep Jeannie safe from that crazy old bastard." Danny laughed to lift the mood.

Tony's ability to spot the unusual was a gift. He was observant and had recognized something quite unique about Zanzee.

"Somehow," said Tony, looking at Jeannie, "Zanzee has his own transformer. He's able to move to any location at any point in time."

Tony's observation and comment about Zanzee brought to mind another observation that presented a deathly challenge. His brow furrowed as he said, "And speaking of the transformer, I saw it in the hole in Crazy LeRoy Nabal's floor."

Jeannie's eyes popped open wide. Words rushed out of her mouth. "My God, Tony! *What now?* What did you just say about the transformer?"

Jeannie squealed.

"Oh my lord, Tony, you saw it? Where? What do we do?" blurted out Danny.

Before the boys could continue, Jeannie jumped in. "We have no choice but to go to his house and get the transformer under his bedroom floor. That is the power he has. We need to take it from him. We need to get the power."

"What power are you talking about?" asked Danny.

"Danny, we know from our legends that the gifts from the gods have very special powers. We have part of the gifts, but LeRoy also has part of them. He has the transformer. Evidently, as Tony figured out and explained to us, it opens the Highway of Time and allows travelers to venture to other points in time long ago or points in time yet to come. Those who take the journey somehow inherit eternal youth—they do not age!"

Jeannie paused and looked down at Zanzee, shocked by her realizations. "Do you know what that means, Danny?" She did not wait for his answer, rushing on. "Danny, if we have all the gifts from the gods, we will control the most sought-after power on earth. You know from our history books that Ponce de León spent his life looking for the Fountain of Youth. This is something that humans have wanted from the dawn of time."

She paused. The only sounds they heard were the purring of Zanzee and Danny's truck engine. "It could very well be that we will have this power! Yes, the power to travel in time and to control eternal youth." She put her left hand behind his back and scooted as close to him as she could get.

"Whoa! Are you sure, Jeannie?" Danny said in a quiet voice.

She touched his arm with her right hand. Her fingers rubbed through the hair on his forearm. She looked at him. He glanced at her from the corner of his eye. His attention was also on the road ahead as the storm had arrived, and rainwater was starting to gather in puddles.

"Yes! I'm positive! Do you understand the significance of what we're dealing with? I have no idea how it works. This is the mystery we must find!"

For the first time in quite some time, a smile graced her face. Danny smiled too. He felt her spirit lifting. As hers lifted, his soared to a new height, knowing that they could share a magical life together forever.

"Jeannie, my God, this is unreal! I...I...I don't know what to say." He was struggling with his emotions.

"Danny, it's OK!" said Jeannie. She wrapped her arm around him and gently touched his face with her other hand. "My wonderful Danny, wouldn't this be a dream come true? We would be forever young!" Her voice was choked with emotion. "Danny, we would no longer be poor kids living in a coal camp."

For a moment, there was silence. Theirs was no longer an impossible dream. The journey had started, and the missing piece was in a hole under the bedroom floor of a monster that thrived on death.

"Danny, as long as Mochcom has part of the transformer, we cannot escape from him. He will stop at nothing to get the other part—the emerald star and Danny's giant colored diamonds. He will kill us to get them."

She brushed his cheek with her fingers. "Our only choice, Danny, is to get the part of the transformer that he has. The only way we will be able to escape his evil reign of death is by using all the gifts the gods gave to the royal family of Kopaz."

Zanzee's tail twitched. He put his paw on Jeannie's cheek. She smiled down at him and said, "Zanzee, you, Danny, and I will have a long time together. What do you think of that?"

"Meow, meow, MEOW!" he said, each meow getting louder.

"We must put our trust in Kashom. We must know why Kashom said, 'Time is eternal and the key to all things'! We must heed his warning—'that very dark is the greed of bad men'—because I think Kashom is guiding us. We must not fall into the trap that Crazy LeRoy did."

He put his hand on her knee and tightened his fingers. "What trap is that, Jeannie?" Danny asked her in a quiet voice.

"Danny, the gods are not pleased with Gorom Mochcom for killing a little girl whom the goddess Neferdor considered her special human doll. Gorom Mochcom was greedy and wanted the golden key, the golden watch, the emerald star, the colored diamonds, and the Sun Energy Transformer, your SET, to control the powers of the sun. He wanted to have supreme control over eternal youth. I believe Kashom was careless and was conned by Gorom Mochcom."

For the first time, she was about to reveal something to Danny that she had long kept secret. Watching him stare out the windshield, she said, "Kashom once owned the golden watch you have. Maybe that's why he has spent centuries in the Scarlet Desert. Maybe he is doing penance for not being obedient and for not protecting his sister and thus losing the precious gifts from the gods."

There was a moment of silence. Riveted, their attention fixed on her, Danny and Tony waited for Jeannie to continue.

"I know from our legends that Viracocha took the golden watch back from Kashom. Danny, I don't know the answers to all of these mysteries. I can only speculate. Maybe we will soon find them ourselves."

Jeannie turned her face to look directly at him as she continued. "Viracocha gave the watch to you. He put it on the blanket next to your parents the night of their honeymoon at the Boar's Tusk." Her hand rested on his. "We're involved in something way beyond our control."

She had no concrete answers, but his fingers remained tense, gripping her knee. A quick glance at Jeannie told him her mind was searching, searching for answers to a mystery that her people had sought for centuries. "What answers are you talking about, Jeannie?" Still trying to comprehend what she'd just said, he thought, *I believe you, Jeannie. Kashom lost possession of the golden watch. I will not fall into a trap and be careless. I can't let that happen. I won't!*

The storm had caught up with them and was in full rage. Quickly turning his head away from Jeannie, Danny focused his attention on the road ahead. Lightning streaking from the sky flashed in front of them, striking a scrub cedar tree. Jeannie shuddered and looked at it in amazement as it smoldered and burst into flames. The loud crack of thunder caused Zanzee to growl. Jeannie snuggled him close to her. The clouds broke open and dumped their water on the road ahead.

Danny lifted his hand from Jeannie's knee and reached for the knob. The *flap, flap, flap* of the wipers going back and forth on the windshield added a new tempo to the rhythm of the falling rain. A dangling piece of rubber from a wiper long in need of replacement smeared the pelting water.

Since both of Danny's hands were now on the wheel, Jeannie's fingers stroked his arm. Searching for the words that she knew her love was yearning for, she said, "Danny, that's why they're questions. We don't have all the answers, but I believe the answers are worth more than all the riches we found hidden in the secret chamber at the Boar's Tusk."

Tony was plotting. Little did he know that the diversion Jeannie had put in place to trick Eddie and Terry had also diverted Mochcom—buying them time. Tony had no idea that Mochcom was even tricked, let alone how long it would be until the gorom discovered the deception. All he knew was that the sooner they got the missing piece from LeRoy, the better their chance of escape.

"Danny, Jeannie is right. We need to get the transformer from Nabal's house because it may help us answer some of the questions," said Tony. "Tomorrow is the ideal day. We don't have school because they gave us a free day for winning the game Friday and getting ready for the state tournament."

He stopped, and the sound of the pouring rain took over. Tony thought about what to say next. Grasping for comfort, he said, "I'm sure he won't go near his house. The police have roped it off with crime tape. I'm sure they have set up alarms to catch him if he came back."

Now he uncovered a problem, but he ventured a solution. "Ah, ah, hell. We need to break the window and get into his house. Who cares if the alarm goes off! We'll get the transformer and get the hell out of there before the police have a clue what's going on. Shit, they'll think it's LeRoy who is breaking into his own house."

Tony laughed. "Terry told me that he and Eddie were going to spend this Sunday evening and Monday with Eddie's grandmother in Winton. We won't have to worry about them. I suggest we go to LeRoy's house around eight thirty, get Danny's SET, and get the hell out of there."

Nodding his head, he indicated he supported Tony and Jeannie as he said, "That's a plan. Let's meet at six out in front of Jeannie's house. I'll do the driving."

The beliefs ingrained by the culture of the Kashome people in the Scarlet Desert over the centuries were a powerful driving force. A young girl with shiny black hair and deep-blue eyes sat with her mystical friend on her lap, a cat whose features were the oddly similar to hers. She knew they must get the transformer from Gorom Mochcom. She knew it would lead to the Pearl of Time—eternal youth—the essence of the Legend of Kashom. She snuggled next to her love and wondered who he was. She knew the legend was not a myth. She and Danny were not only young lovers but partners the gods had brought together in a most fascinating way. They understood the role her gift from the gods played and how it was connected to the Legend of Kashom.

The impulse to protect the one you love from perilous danger was an equally powerful driving force. A young man with supernatural powers, sun-colored yellow hair, and deep-green eyes, a boy whose features were the same as those of the supreme god Viracocha, sat next to his love. He wondered who he was. He now realized he got his superhuman strength from a ring—supernatural strength that had saved both his of friends' lives. He knew the Legend of Kashom was not a myth. He suspected he was also connected to the legend. His days of dreaming of pirate treasure were over. He was a partner with the most beautiful girl on earth, and they had been brought together by the gods. He knew his golden watch was connected to the legend of Kashom, but he still wondered how. He suspected his ring had once been worn on the hand of the supreme god Viracocha.

CHAPTER 28

Evil Lurks

Jeannie shuddered and woke in a cold sweat. The vision of a hand covering the mouth of a beautiful twelve-year-old girl terrified her. In her mind, she reviewed the nightmare that had awakened her. *Aerapondes tried to scream as Mochcom's fierce yank tore the golden key from her neck.* She clutched at her pillow. Jeannie's entire body was shaking. She trembled as she tried to regain composure, but she couldn't. Her mind was consumed with thoughts of horror. *I can't go to the police. They won't believe me. They'll think I'm the crazy one.*

Reaching for anything of comfort, she gripped her blankets with trembling hands. Her heart sank. *I have no place to hide. He's going to kill me!* She couldn't keep the thoughts of horror out of her mind. *He continues his reign of death—the human skull that Tony found was from one of his victims! My God, what shall I do?*

"Zanzee. Zanzee, where are you?" Jeannie whimpered. She reached for her kitty but in vain. Her heart sank further.

Her eyes searched for him. She found him standing on the windowsill, the full moon behind him. His outline in the pale moonlight made an awesome silhouette that brought a glimmer of hope to Jeannie.

The moon at five in the morning was high in the sky, its light shining through Jeannie's bedroom window. Bright moonlight lit up her room.

"Zanzee, come here!"

He leaped from the windowsill and jumped onto her bed, snuggling next to her. "Zanzee, don't let Mochcom cut my heart out! He's the devil. He wants to kill me!" she whimpered. She touched his pink nose, and he put his paw on her hand. "You must not go near him. Zanzee, he'll hurt you. He's a bad man! Zanzee, what shall we do?"

These thoughts of horror and evil were not limited to Jeannie. Danny clutched his pillow in a cold sweat. *I've got to save Jeannie from a madman! My lord, what have we gotten ourselves into? I can't forget my knife. I'll have to carry it with me. I have no choice but to protect my love. I'll kill that bastard if I have to.* He shuddered at the thought that just entered his mind. *My ring protects me.* But then his mind filled with a shadowy realization. *He has a ring also. My God, who is this crazy old devil? I hope that purple light from his ring is not his protection.*

Noise coming from the kitchen startled Danny. *I wonder why Rose is up rustling around at five thirty. She didn't tell us she had to work today, but maybe she does. I hope she's OK.*

There was no reason to turn his light on. The haloed moon was shedding its pale light in the dark hours of the predawn. It streamed through Danny's window and had the desert coyotes yelping. A pack of them chased a helpless rabbit under the moon's bright radiance. Their yipping songs intensified with the kill and flooded the early morning air with haunting sounds that sent a chill down Danny's spine. Then all was quiet, and for a few moments, silence fell in the early dawn.

He pulled his pillow tightly to his chest, hugging it with both arms. He lay on top of the covers, searching for answers as the sun began to come up, marking the dawning of a new day. There was a lone coyote howl right outside his window and a yelp or two. He was ready to get up. He rolled and jumped off his bed. He looked at his watch. It was five fifteen. He thought, *I have time to get my clothes together. I'll put an extra change in my canvas bag.* He concentrated. *Let's see…what else do I need?* He grabbed his Pirate Log and tossed it in the bag.

Danny opened his door and darted across the kitchen on his way to the bathroom. He had the clothes he would wear—his shirt, pants and boxers—in his hands. His consciousness was rushing with rage. There was no stopping the anger that filled every cavern and crevasse of his mind. *I'm stronger than he is. If that crazy old bastard comes near Jeannie, I'll rip his head off.*

His cold-water face splash, sponge bath over his chest, arms and legs, and quick brush of his teeth and hair were all done in haste. He stepped out of the bathroom and was startled to find Rose crying.

"What's the matter, Rose?" Danny asked as he walked to the table where she was crying. Her body jerked when he put his hand on her shoulder. Her mind had been visiting a not-so-distant past when her lover would banter with her in love play before he went off to the mine.

"Oh—I—I—well…nothing. I was just having a sleepless night," she said, trying to hold back the tears.

Her longing look sent a feeling of helplessness through Danny. He had no words for the situation. He struggled to find any words of comfort, not wanting to see Tony's mom in pain.

"Oh, Mrs. Lopez, don't worry. You'll see Jack again. I hope and dream that someday, somehow, we'll all have our loved ones back. I can't tell you why I feel this, but I know there's something grander and more glorious than we could ever imagine that controls our destiny. We think we have the answers, but we don't!"

A small smile was all that she could muster. "Danny, that's sweet of you to say. I know you have a good spirit. I also know that wherever your mom and dad are they are very proud of you." Her eyes dried as she looked at him. "Tony, you, and I, we'll make it. Somehow, we'll make it." Rose's smile grew larger.

The old black Bakelite phone rang. It hung on the wall next to the doorway between the kitchen and Danny's room. Quickly, she got up from the chair at the table and hustled across the room. Wrapping her slender fingers wrapped around the large receiver, she answered the phone. "Oh, hi, Pastor Duncan."

Danny turned quickly, overhearing her conversation. His mind stumbled. *Why is Pastor Duncan calling Mrs. Lopez at six in the morning?*

The pastor's voice was so loud that Danny could hear every word. "Mrs. Lopez, good to hear your voice. It has been a few weeks since I saw you, and I was just wondering how you are doing." He didn't wait for an answer but charged on. "How is Danny doing?"

Her tears were replaced with a smile. "Oh, he's doing just fine. He's a blessing to both Tony and me. We just love having him in our home. He's my second son!"

"Oh, how wonderful!" There was a brief moment of silence broken only by the electronic *hmmmmm* of the phone line. Rose waited, and then he said, "I was thinking that we might have dinner some evening. I know you work at the hospital and get off around five."

This time there was a long silence. Danny listened intently, and Mrs. Lopez stared out the window with the receiver held to her ear. Then she said, "Yes, that would be nice."

And again the pastor said, "Oh, how wonderful. I'll call and set up a day and time. I would love to have a meal with you. You know, Rose, I'm here for you."

Danny's surprise caused him to stiffen a bit, wondering how often the preacher had been calling Rose. Realizing something was upsetting Danny, she sweetly said, "I'll let you know," and hung the receiver back on its hook.

Now her attention was on Danny, and she wondered about his concerned look. "Is there something wrong, Danny?"

"Oh no, Rose. Ah...er. I...I...ah...I like Pastor Duncan," stammered Danny as he watched her face tighten. Quickly, Danny put a forced smile on his face and continued. "Rose, you will have a good dinner. I know you're lonely. Ah, maybe Tony and I'll take you out some night also." He hesitated and then added, "Would you like that?"

The sound of bustling came from the room adjoining the kitchen. Tony opened his bedroom door and said, "Hi, Mom. Sounds like you and Danny are up to something. I heard the phone ring! What's up?"

She laughed. "Danny was just setting up a dinner date for all of us!"

It was Tony who picked up on the lateness of the hour. He nonchalantly pointed to Danny and then at his wristwatch.

Danny looked at the soot-covered clock on the wall and realized it was late. He turned to Tony's mother and said, "Rose, there's no school today. They gave us a free day for winning the game on Friday. Tony and

I are going to pick up Jeannie in five minutes. We have a day's adventure planned."

Rose blurted, "Tony, you didn't tell me!"

Not answering her, Tony turned quickly and ran back to his bedroom. He was out of sight for only a minute, and then he emerged with his knapsack. "We're going to grab a sandwich someplace. See ya later, Mom!"

There was a moment of intense anguish as she stared at him, her face not necessarily displaying anger but concern. Before he could take another step toward the back door, she said, "Tony, you haven't had your breakfast. You're leaving awful early! What are you doing today?"

Stammering for words, he replied, "Oh…ah…well, we…we're going to—"

Not waiting for him to search on for meaningless words, she broke in. "What are you up to? I know something is going on. What is it?"

He had no answer. "Mom, we've got to go." Reading her expression of concern, he looked at her and added, "We're just snooping around. You know…we have a free day, so we're just horsing around in the desert."

Her mind immediately focused on his strange behavior. *Tony has never acted this way. He's always told me his plans!* Throwing her hand in the air as if to say stop, she asked again, "What are you guys doing today?"

It was Danny who answered. "Rose, Tony, Jeannie, and I need to take care of some business." And at that moment, a little white lie drifted out of his mouth. "We're going to search for something we think LeRoy hid. We think it may help solve the murder."

Tony's mother froze. She blurted out, "Danny, you're scaring me. What are you saying? What's going on in your life? Are you, Jeannie, and Tony doing something that I should know about? For God's sake, you're not in danger are you? I could not go on if I lost either Tony or you."

Tony turned and gave his mom a wave. "I love you. We're fine. Don't worry about us. We'll be back this afternoon."

Then Danny and Tony turned and raced for the door. Rose called after them, "Be careful. Please don't go near Mr. Nabal's house. The police have fenced it off as a crime scene."

Tony and Danny were in such a hurry to beeline it out of his house that they didn't hear Rose's words of concern.

Danny had one thing on his mind. *Damn. I hope everything goes well. I sure hope we don't get tangled up in a horror episode!*

As he walked down the porch stairs, he clenched his fist around the canvas bag holding his Pirate Log and change of clothes.

His truck radio was silent. Today it was not blaring out rock 'n' roll music, waking the late risers of CoalVille. His mind, however, was not silent—the echoing sounds of Elvis Presley's song "Heartbreak Hotel" haunted him:

> Well, since my baby left me,
> I found a new place to dwell.
> It's down at the end of Lonely Street
> At Heartbreak Hotel.

Standing at their rendezvous spot, Jeannie could see Danny and Tony through the front windshield. Danny was not his old self, slapping the steering wheel to keep time with the music. His look was somber, and he made no movement to keep rhythm with the music.

Jeannie cringed as her mind swirled with thoughts of terror. She clutched her golden key. She had it in its leather pouch in her pocket. *He has to be thinking the same dreadful thoughts that I am. Gorom Mochcom is a murderer, and he won't stop his killing. Mochcom has killed for this key. He wants it and will do anything to get it.*

Danny was not looking at Jeannie or Tony. He was stargazing and listening to Elvis's song rumble through his mind.

> Hey now, if your baby leaves you,
> I get so lonely,
> I get so lonely I could die.

Then it hit him like a thousand ton of bricks. *God! What if something did happen to us and we never saw Tony's mom again? I don't think she could take it. She would get so lonely, she would die.* That piercing thought gripped his mind and made his entire body tremble.

Then an even more foreboding thought seized him. *Mom, I'm so sorry for not protecting you from Crazy LeRoy. God, I going to kill that bastard. If it's the last thing I do, I'll find him and send him straight to hell!*

He slammed on the brakes, and his truck came to an abrupt stop.

Standing next to his open window, Jeannie sensed his anguish, and she desperately wanted to comfort him. But down deep inside, she knew that until they got the transformer from LeRoy, no words of comfort were possible. Still, her only choice was to try. "Danny, are you OK?" Jeannie asked, watching his arm quiver.

There was no answer, only a look from him.

She walked around the front of the truck and opened the passenger door. "Are you ready for today?" Jeannie asked the boys as Tony jumped out, and she took her place in the middle, between Danny and Tony.

Danny's silence rolled on, and her concern rose. "Do you think we'll be OK?" It was an attempt at conversation, even though she was well aware they were all in the same boat. There was no hiding it. She knew as well as Danny did the danger they were in. If they sailed, they sailed on together. If they sank, well, she had that clear in her mind also.

Finally, she heard his voice. "Jeannie, I hope this day goes well. I've got a lot on my mind. This is one tangled-up mess we could end up in if all does not go well!" Danny said, glancing at her.

Now it was Jeannie taking the role of the comforter. He needed consoling, and she knew it. "Danny, everything will be OK. Remember what I told you about hope. Danny, hope is a good thing. Hope is the defining factor between having a good life and having a bad life."

He was a man and knew all too well that danger did not diminish with a few words of hope. "Well, what I hope is that crazy old bastard doesn't try to kill us," Danny replied.

He didn't want to raise the alarm level higher than it already was. His plan was to let Jeannie lay out her plan. He was well aware of her comfort zone, and being the leader made her happy. "What's the plan, Jeannie?"

She jumped on it. If there ever was a time to wiffle-waffle, it wasn't now. "Here's the plan. We drive down to the CoalVille junction then over to the base of White Mountain. If anyone is watching us, they'll think that something is going on at the mountain. That should take twenty-five to thirty minutes. After fiddling around at White Mountain for half an hour, we turn around and head back to CoalVille."

Her fingers kept going back and forth across her leather pouch, rolling over each bead. She was quiet for a long moment, breathed heavily two or three times, and then finished explaining her plan. "That should take us a total of forty-five minutes—so it will be around eight. We'll take the side road and drive to Middle Camp—that will put us behind the CoalVille Company Store. From that point, we have a perfect spot to watch the coal miners go past old man Nabal's house. When the last of them have gone to work, we beeline it to his house. Then it will be safe for us to go inside his palace and get the transformer. And if we have to smash windows to get in, well, so be it!"

But then she paused and asked, "Tony did you throw the ladder in the back of the truck?"

"Yep!" was his quick answer.

"OK, let's do it," Danny said, agreeing with Jeannie's plan.

CHAPTER 29

The Dark Side of Crazy LeRoy

Avast expanse of sage-covered dunes stretched from CoalVille to the base of White Mountain, outlining the western horizon. Long as it was, the horizon on White Mountain was a silver line. Now it was painted by the golden threads of light penetrating the clouds on the eastern horizon as the sun climbed over the hill behind CoalVille.

Although Tony gazed at the tiny little whirlwinds that danced through the brush picking up dirt, his mind never focused on them. Those brown columns of dirt whirling in circles, reaching into the sky were the furthest things from his mind.

Jeannie, Danny, and Tony left CoalVille early on that Monday morning in the spring of 1958 searching for hope. They were searching for a way to escape the deadly clutches of an evil madman. They had no idea if they were grasping at straws in search of answers—answers that would save them from death, answers that would give them hope.

"So what do we do once we get the box at LeRoy's house?" Tony asked with a bewildered look on his face.

Jeannie touched his arm as she answered softly, "As I said earlier, and as you explained, I believe the box LeRoy has can harness the power of the sun. I have no idea how the box does it. Our job is to find out. Here's what I think."

She paused momentarily, considering her next statement. Looking at

Danny, who was deep in thought, staring out the windshield, she laid out her next plan. "Once we get the transformer from LeRoy's bedroom, we head back to the Boar's Tusk. We should be there around ten thirty."

Jeannie's face was thoughtful, no longer serious as she asked her next question. "We all brought a lunch for today, right? If not, I have two dollars, so we can stop at Sam's Bungalow and pick up a loaf of bread, Pepsi, some Planter's Peanuts for our pop, and lunchmeat. Is that OK?"

Excited to move on, she did not wait for a response to her question. "Once we get our lunch stuff, we head out to the Boar's Tusk. We'll get the treasure from the secret chamber in the Boar's Tusk. That should take a half hour—so it may be a little early—but we'll eat at eleven. I thought we could look at the gold tablets while we were eating. Kashom must have left clues in his journals about how the transformer—" She stopped and laughed. "I mean, Danny's SET, uses the sun's energy."

Danny listened to Jeannie, but he was not paying attention to her words. His mind was still drifting, and he was thinking about his mom. *Jeepers, I wish I could have given one of those giant gems to my mom. That would have fixed everything. She wouldn't have been sad anymore.*

Like Danny's mind, Tony's was also racing. *If we get caught at Crazy LeRoy's house, he will kill us. What would my mom do? There isn't enough money in the entire world to get her through the grief of losing both her husband and her only son.*

It must have been instinctive because Jeannie could tell when Danny was drifting into a never-never place, a place in his mind that pulled him into despair. She knew what was going on. She looked at his face and understood his deep feeling of anxiety.

Softly, she slid her hand down his forearm, feeling every golden hair being warmed by the sun shining through the windshield.

"Danny, we're here!" she said in a pleasant voice. "We don't have a lot of time. Let's just mess around for twenty minutes."

Danny opened his door first. He held her arm as she scooted under the steering wheel and hopped out. Grabbing his arm with both hands, her eyes looked up at him with a feeling of security. "Danny, we have each other! I'll always be here for you, my love," she said, wrapping her arm around his as they walked toward the base of the mountain. "I have a good feeling. I believe that things will turn out OK."

But deep in her heart, she knew otherwise. She looked at the love of her life and thought, *Danny is not stupid. He knows the danger we are in and that we are dealing with a madman who puts no value on life! I hope things turn out OK.*

Small, fossilized sea animals were everywhere. It was no mystery that the Scarlet Desert was once the bottom of a sea. When that sea had dried up millions of years ago, the sea creatures turned to stone. Jeannie and Danny walked hand in hand, picking up and inspecting the strange-looking shellfish frozen in time as rocks. Jeannie spotted a large snail fossil six inches long. It had become pink agate with a hint of gray moss threaded through it.

"Look, Danny, this is a neat one."

"Yeah, Jeannie, that's a keeper. Do you want me to carry it for you?"

She nodded. He pointed to his watch and then the truck. They headed back.

Twenty minutes was but a flash against the eternal perspective of never-ending time. As the sun continued its morning climb, that flash of twenty minutes was gone before Danny, Jeannie, or Tony could walk one hundred yards from the truck and return.

"Time to head back," Danny said to Tony, who was standing fifty feet from his truck.

When they arrived behind the CPC store at the bottom of Middle Camp, Danny found the perfect place to park his truck. From that spot, they had a clear view of the path that coal miners drove or walked along to get to the mine shaft. They also had a clear view of the hill between Granite Springs and CoalVille.

Tony stuck his arm out the window. "Check that out. There's that gray truck again," Tony said, pointing to the hillside about a half mile from where Danny's truck was parked.

Now Jeannie got into the act, watching something strange going on. "Look!" Jeannie pointed. "Someone just got out. He's limping. Is that Crazy LeRoy?"

"Who the hell knows?" said Danny as he started his truck and spun the wheels. "Let's go! He's gone!" Danny said. "Let's not dillydally. I hate that house, and I don't give a shit if it is a palace. The sooner we get the box and get the *hell* out of there, well, that will not be soon enough for me."

The high priest of the royal court of Kopaz had an innate ability to detect danger. He watched Black Vulture fly ahead of him. No sooner had Crazy LeRoy started down the back side of the hill than Vulture started screaming, letting him know that something was amiss.

"I watched those kids head out to White Mountain early this morning. I thought they would go to Rabbit Ears, and when they didn't, I let my guard down. How foolish of me. I should have known. I was going to walk today to keep up my disguise. They can't con me. I'm a lot wiser than they'll ever know. They're up to something. I've got to get back quickly," he mumbled, "for they are sure to discover my little lamb."

Now LeRoy's face was full of concern as he thought, *The boy they call Eddie is still making lots of noise, so I must hasten back.*

Driving into Crazy LeRoy's yard was a bit scary for Danny. But even spookier was going to the back door. It was locked and had yellow crime-scene tape plastered all over it.

"Damn! This is spooky, scary shit. And to top it off, I feel like a common criminal," Tony said as he and his friends carried the ladder to a window on the north side of the house.

"All right, guys. Let's make this quick. I don't want to stick around here any longer than necessary." Danny was the first to climb up and smash the window. "We're good to go," he said as he jumped through it.

Tony was next, and he helped Jeannie get through the opening. A yank on the window tapestry let the sunlight in, filling the bedroom with morning light. Tony saw his best buddy staring at Jeannie's picture.

Tony said, "I'm with you, Danny. We'll be common thieves today, get what we came for and, just like you said, get the heck out of here."

Jeannie was not listening to the conversation between Danny and Tony. No, her eyes were fixed on something that tore at her very being and was almost enough to make her upchuck her breakfast. She gulped.

Danny heard a strange sound coming from her. He wheeled around and shouted, "What's happening?" And then even louder he yelled, "Jeannie, what's the matter?"

"I'm OK, Danny," Jeannie whimpered, standing in front of the painting of LeRoy holding a human heart, and by his side was that terrible bird, the black vulture they'd all seen.

Running to her side, he grabbed her and turned her with his strong arms. "Don't look at that painting!" Gazing into her eyes, he said, "Jeannie, do me a favor!" He held her arms. "Don't look at that evil stuff!"

Jeannie was shaking in panic. Her trembling was affecting Danny even though he held her tightly. "Look, Jeannie, I want to get out of here as soon as we can. We're in a world of buzzard shit—you know it! I want to flee this place posthaste. Come on now, settle down. Everything is going to be OK. I'll protect you."

Then there was a noise. A rumbling grind came from the floor.

"Tony, where are you?" Jeannie called in a somewhat quieter voice. "What's happening?"

A faint voice from the far wall of the bedroom said, "I'm here. I opened up the vault."

Danny had retrieved the ladder by pulling it through the window. He held it and asked, "What now, Tony?"

"Into the hole, best buddy," answered Tony, pointing to the vault opening on the floor.

Bang went the ladder as Danny shoved it into the hidden chamber.

"Whoa…there are two boxes!" yelled Tony as his flashlight lit up the objects on the vault floor.

"Two boxes?" said Jeannie in a voice of sweet surprise.

By this time, Tony was already down the ladder and in the hole, and so his voice echoed in the chamber as he answered her. "Yep! Two boxes!"

"Tony, what can we do to help?" asked Danny.

"Jump in, and help me carry them out," yelled Tony.

It was only a matter of seconds before Danny was at Tony's side. But then they heard it. The timed door was closing much sooner than Tony had calculated.

Grind, grind came the deathly sounds that meant the vault doors were closing, creating a tomb for two unsuspecting teenagers stealing something of value from a crazy man's palace.

"NO!" screamed Jeannie.

Instantly, Danny grabbed Tony and threw him at the opening. He flew out on the floor and rolled to Jeannie's feet.

With the door well on its way to trapping Danny, he grabbed the boxes faster than lightning and leaped upward. His shoe snagged in the closing door, and Danny yanked his foot from it. The door, even with an old leather shoe in its jaws, slammed shut with a thundering *boom.*

"Oh, *man!*" yelled Danny. "That thing ate my shoe!"

Jennie had no time to talk about shoes. "Oh, thank the gods, you're safe!" She raced to his side, placed her hands on either side of his face, and kissed him. Then she smiled and said, "OK, time for shoes. Danny, I saw your basketball tennies in your truck. You also have your engineers' boots with them. I think you ought to take your boots. They match mine, and something is special about my boots. My uncle Tom, my mother's brother, made a special hiding place in the heal for my golden key. We will be fine with them."

Danny's laughter filled the palace. It was a strange sound that caused them all to stand quiet and still. As the walls ceased their echoing, he whispered, "You're right, Jeannie, I hardly ever wear my boots, as I want to keep them in good shape. I'll take my boots and my tennies, as they are much better than these duds with holes in the soles!"

Tony was still lying on the floor, staring at something. "Holy Mother of Jesus, get me out of here! That old bastard has another skull down here. Let's get out of here! Hurry, you guys!"

"Tony, quit sniffing, and just give me your hand," said Danny as he reached out and pulled Tony to his feet.

They had got what they came for from Crazy LeRoy's palace. Now it was time to skedaddle before the police or anyone else showed up.

Then it happened—something they never suspected. A terrible howling filled their ears. Danny, Jeannie, and Tony froze, motionless. Tony dropped his flashlight. He watched it roll under the bed. "Oh no, where did it go?" Quickly he turned to Jeannie and whispered, "Take this tin box. It's light. I want to get my flashlight."

Without hesitation, Danny went into high gear, orchestrating their getaway. "Tony." Danny grabbed his friend. "Don't worry about your flashlight. I'll buy you another one. We've got bigger problems than a flashlight in a stink hole. Let's get out of here."

The only sound was the eerie howling, and it was coming through the open window. It suddenly stopped. For a moment, there was silence—then the silence was broken again as the howling started up, louder than before.

At this point, even Danny was unsure what to do next. His high-gear orchestration of their getaway turned to caution.

"What in the name of hell?" Danny whispered.

"It sounds like the howling of a wolf at bay, doesn't it?" Tony whispered.

"What is it? It's coming from outside by the woodshed!" Danny mumbled.

Tony started to shake. His hand gripped his mouth. His eyes were as big as the bright moon that glowed in the early morning sky. "I have no idea," said Tony. Then the howling intensified. "It sounds like two wolves."

Danny, Tony, and Jeannie darted downstairs and ran through the kitchen. They bolted to the door, unlocked it, and raced outside. They were startled by what they saw.

"Good heavens! Look! Those giant dogs are howling at the woodshed," Jeannie squealed.

The woodshed was one hundred feet from the back door of LeRoy Nabal's house, where the three kids were standing.

"Look, you scared them," Danny said to Jeannie as he pointed at three dogs running up the hill behind the woodshed.

"There must be something in the woodshed," Tony said with a startled look.

"Who cares? Let's get out of here. We got what we came for," Jeannie said in a quivering voice.

"Wait, we need to check this out," Tony whispered, his voice muffled.

There was no stopping him, but Danny wanted out of there. "Be my guest, Tony, but Jeannie and I are out of here, with or without you," Danny shot back as he gripped the bronze object they had retrieved from the secret vault in the bedroom of Mochcom's palace. "Jeannie, you still have the small tin box, don't you?" He looked at Jeannie who was staring at the woodshed door.

"Yeah, Danny, I have the small tin box."

Danny was on his way out of a hellhole, or at least that's what he thought. "OK, let's get out of here—with or without Tony."

Tony darted to the woodshed. *I've got to know what's in here.* He flung the door wide open. "*Help! Help! My Lord in heaven! My God in heaven! Come here, you guys! I need your help!*" Tony screamed. "*Get over here! Hurry!*"

What they saw on that Monday morning in 1958, they'd never forget. Horror gripped them as they stared at the back wall of the woodshed.

My God, Jeannie thought. *How black the con of pious men and dark the greed of man.*

CHAPTER 30
Horror in a Woodshed

Jeannie had started the day in the wee hours of the morning, wakened by dreams of horror, her body trembling in a cold sweat. Zanzee had snuggled next to her, bringing her a moment of comfort, but comfort was fleeting. Her mind envisioned terrors waiting to occur. Even then, she never dreamed, looking at the silhouette of Zanzee in the pale, early morning moonlight, that her day would lead to the horror she was witnessing in Crazy LeRoy's woodshed. Through the open woodshed door, she viewed a scene more horrifying than a painting could ever be. Her entire body trembled as a cold chill of fear engulfed her being.

Her mind raced. *Capacocha is the darkest of evils—human sacrifice—my God, the sacrifice of little kids.*

Eddie's arms and legs were outstretched. He was tied in an X position to four round iron rings on the back wall of LeRoy's woodshed. He was exhausted from trying to shift his weight from his legs to his arms and then back to his legs. His bloody shirt dangled from his waist, exposing a deep, heart-shaped cut on his bare chest.

Jeannie and Danny lifted his limp body, relieving the tension on the ropes that held him to the back wall of the woodshed. Tony used his knife to cut the ropes that bound Eddie's hands and feet.

"Be careful now. I think he's free," Danny said in a quiet voice.

They gently removed him from the back wall. Eddie was barely conscious. They laid his limp body on the floor of the woodshed. Jeannie, Danny, and Tony knelt over him, trying to make him as comfortable as possible.

Jeannie's canker of hatred that she'd harbored in her heart for Eddie vanished. Her back-alley encounter with him was the furthest thing from her mind. She now was a beacon of compassion, helping a young boy who was the victim of a madman.

"This is horrible. Why would the gods let something like this happen? My lord, look at that cut on the left side of his chest," Jeannie said as she took a handkerchief from her pocket and wiped the blood that was oozing from it.

"He's starting to breathe a little more normally. His eyes are starting to open," said Danny. Touching his face, Danny felt the boy regain some strength. "Eddie, can you hear us?" Danny asked. "Do you want some water?"

Jeannie was alarmed and desperately sensed Eddie's need for care. "We've got to call an ambulance! We need to get the cops! Let's do something!" screamed Jeannie.

Danny's clear thinking gave him a better idea. "We can put him in my pickup," exclaimed Danny.

"I think he's regaining consciousness," Tony remarked. "Let's try to talk to him. He's coming around."

Eddie gave Jeannie a gentle smile. He tried to touch her hand but lacked the strength.

"What happened to you, Eddie? Who did this to you?" Jeannie said as she wiped Eddie's brow with a handkerchief that Tony handed her.

It was a few more minutes before Eddie could talk.

"I think he's doing a little better," Jeannie asserted. "Eddie, can you hear me?" she asked. "What happened?"

His words could hardly make their way out of his mouth. "We…w-we came…we spent five hours digging around Rabbit Ears, looking for what you guys buried there. We didn't…w-we didn't find anything. I told Terry that you guys would probably be snooping…around up here today. We were going to go to Winton to spend the night with Terry's grandmother.

W-we didn't. We came up here at seven this morning. T-Terry...yeah... Terry and me."

His eyes rolled back and forth as if he were in a trance. His words just kept pouring forth. "We wanted to beat you guys to whatever you were planning to do. We were going to wait until you arrived and spoil whatever you were up to. We...we...wanted to crash your party. Crazy LeRoy. He... he spotted us...he came running out of his house, and we took off running as fast as we could. I think Terry got away...but I...I tripped on a board... Crazy LeRoy grabbed me," Eddie said, panting and struggling for each breath as he told his tale of horror.

He stopped and rolled his head back and forth in a circular motion. His face was blank. He rested for a minute and then started stuttering and rambling on again. "That crazy man locked me in this woodshed. He... he...was gone for forty-five minutes. He came back and tried to cut my heart out. H-he...he...t-tied me to the back wall of the woodshed and started dancing...d-dancing...and ch-chanting. He kept chanting some weird word that sounded like 'capochaa.' That evil monster kept chanting the word over and over...capochaa...capochaa. Then he took a knife and started cutting. H-he cut me open."

Danny's mind filled with anger as he listened to Eddie. *It was that son of a bitch we saw over the hill this morning. I'm gonna kill him if it's the last thing I do!*

Jeannie moved to Eddie's side. He rolled his head, looked into her eyes, and said, "Thank you, Jeannie. Please forgive me!" He reached and touched her hand.

A tear rolled from her eye, and she said, "Oh, Eddie, how terrible. We'll get you to a doctor." She wiped the blood that was still oozing from his chest.

Danny stepped to Jeannie's side. "What happened then?" Danny said in a sincere voice.

"Somebody pulled into his driveway. Th-they...starting honking their horn. I think it was Terry's...yeah...Terry's dad. I think Mr. Zumford was looking for Terry. Crazy LeRoy ran out. I don't know what happened after that. I-I couldn't hear the conversation. Then I...I...I screamed. I think Mr.

Zumford...I think...he...had already left. I hurt so badly...I kept trying to shift my weight around so I wouldn't hurt so much. It was awful. The next thing I remember is seeing you guys."

Eddie was shaking, talking with a quivering voice. His entire chest was covered with blood from the deep, heart-shaped cut on his left side. The top of his pants was bright red from blood oozing out of the cut and running down his stomach.

Eddie stared into space. Then he started yelling, "He's nuts! He tried to kill me! I'm going home...I...I...am...and tell my mother to call the cops. He's a crazy, evil man. He's a murderer. I know...he...was trying to cut my heart out."

Without explanation, Eddie got up from the floor of the woodshed and staggered down the driveway.

"Eddie!" Danny hollered. "Let us give you a ride home! I'll rip that bastard's head off if he comes near any of us again!"

"No!" Eddie yelled back. "I'm...getting...I'm out of here. I'm going home. I'm calling...th-the cops!"

At that instant, Danny, Jeannie, and Tony didn't know what to do.

"Eddie, we need to get you to a hospital!" shouted Tony.

"I'm going...I want my mom!" Eddie whimpered as he staggered off toward the back alley, not more than two blocks from LeRoy's house.

His home was less than a block away from the alley entrance.

Jeannie was horrified. She grabbed Danny's hand and started pulling at it. "Oh no! He needs our help. What should we do? Should we try to catch him?" squealed Jeannie.

Danny turned quickly and put both hands on Jeannie's shoulders. His heart was sinking fast, but his face wore a look of urgency.

"He'll be at his home before we get to him. He'll be there in two or three minutes. We need to get out of here! Let's not dillydally!" said Danny.

He held her steady and looked squarely in her eyes, letting her know the dire situation they were in. They had to leave immediately. "Let's get to the truck and go! That crazy bastard Nabal is probably around here. We have to get out of here...*now!*"

She got it. The urgency to get out of there closed in on her like dense fog on a dark night. Jeannie grabbed Danny's arm. "Let's run. He's around here someplace." Her mind visualized LeRoy jumping out of a dark corner to get her. "Hurry, let's go. We've got to get out of here fast!"

They ran to Danny's truck and jumped in. The seriousness of their situation was causing Jeannie's feelings of impending doom to escalate.

"Put the truck in gear and go! He's going to jump out of a hiding place and get us!" squealed Jeannie.

"Oh my lord in heaven, how can this get any worse?" Danny rasped as he floored the gas pedal, spinning the tires and making a cloud of dust, rocks, and dirt fly into the air.

CHAPTER 31

Vulture Watches
Terror Unfold

Skulking in the shadowy back alley of CoalVille on that early Monday morning of March 1958, Crazy LeRoy spotted someone.

Woooooop, woooooop, woooooop. Vulture fluttered his wings, sitting on top of a wooden fence, howling and screaming. "*Rawaarrrr! Rarrrarreeee,*" he screeched as he watched his master, Lord Mochcom.

Caught in a state of panic, the sound made Eddie freeze. His eyes focused on a ghastly figure draped in a long black coat, a piece of rope dangling from its pocket. Leaping from the shadows, Gorom Mochcom grabbed the teenage boy.

"How did you get away, my little sacrificial lamb? Who untied you?" LeRoy growled in a coarse voice as he grabbed Eddie.

At first, Eddie was dazed and did not know what was happening. He cringed from the horrifying sounds coming from the dark shadows of the alley just to his left.

With each second that ticked by, Vulture grew more vocal with his screeching howls. His fancy foot movements on the top of the old gray fence were not unlike those of a jester in a movie providing a vocal, deathly serenade as the main actor carried out a human sacrifice.

Eddie felt the tight grip of a long-fingered hand clutching him. He lunged in an effort to get away, but he couldn't. He saw the long, black, outstretched wings of Vulture and felt gusts of air from his fluttering on the fence. He had no idea what was going on and was not ready for a scuffle during the early hours of that fateful Monday morning.

The sharp fingernails on Mochcom's gripping hand dug deeply into Eddie's flesh. Crimson blood oozed from around each nail and made tiny red rivers flow down Eddie's arm.

Swinging his head away from of Vulture, he never dreamed whose face was just inches from his.

"*M-my God! It's y-you!*" Eddie screamed. He wrenched his gaze from Black Vulture to focus on the steely blue eyes of LeRoy. The man was so close that Eddie could smell the sour-milk breath coming from him. The pain in Eddie's arm was growing with each jolt of Mochcom's fingers as he rocked them back and forth, digging them deeper into the boy's flesh. Eddie was slowly drifting into shock.

"Tell me who untied you, my little lamb?" he rasped, his hot breath striking Eddie's face.

"T-Terry did, you d-dummy!" Eddie's eyes blinked as he tried to focus on the face of a devil a few inches away.

"Oh no. That scrawny runt didn't let you go. He ran for the hills. The look of terror on his face when I grabbed you told me he'd never show his face in my woodshed again."

The ends of Mochcom's handlebar mustache lifted slightly, signaling the smile of pleasure erupting on his face as he stared into Eddie's eyes. "For all you know, I have your friend's heart."

The pain on Eddie's chest was unbearable. His heart sank as if into a hole and fluttered as terror gripped his soul and sent rippling twinges racing around his body.

LeRoy cackled and smiled more vigorously. "Who knows? My collection of skulls may soon grow. Yes, in just a short time, I could have other skulls to place by KeeLord's."

He reached and stroked his long bony fingers through Eddie's sandy-blond hair. Mochcom moved his face closer to Eddie's. His hot breath, now just an inch away, was blowing on Eddie's face with each word. "Do you have other friends? Who are they? You better tell Crazy LeRoy. I will hurt you—unless you help me. It will be our little secret, my little lamb! Oh, was it the pretty little girl with shiny black hair and blue eyes? Her name is Neferzul. You didn't know that—of course not," Crazy LeRoy said as he drew his words out, mumbling in an eerie singsong tone of voice.

Eddie's heart was ready to stop. He had only a tiny amount of strength left. "You…y-you…will you…let me go…if…if I tell you?" Eddie stuttered in a quavering voice. "Just let me go. It was Jeannie, Danny, and Tony—now let me go!"

LeRoy moved one hand toward the inner pocket of his filthy jacket. Eddie noticed the outline of a knife as LeRoy leered. "Let me touch the cut on your chest! I started the Capacocha ceremony with the marking. Let me finish the heart removal!"

"You…y-you…bastard. Did you hurt Terry?" Eddie yelled. He took a deep breath and waited for the right moment. Lunging forward violently with all the strength he could muster, he freed himself from the one-handed grip LeRoy had on him.

He screamed into the still air. "Danny will—will rip your head off, y-you bastard!"

Eddie's mind was engulfed with thoughts of horror. *Oh my God! Oh my God, I hope he didn't hurt Terry!* He staggered and hobbled as fast as he could. *Why did I want to go snooping at that crazy bastard's house? It's my fault! Why did I insist that we go up there?* His right hand pressed on the cut over his heart. *I need help to get this cut fixed—I've got to get home.* His eyes filled with tears as he raced for safer ground and thought of his best friend, Terry. *I have to tell my mom. We have to find Terry's dad. We have to get the cops!*

Crazy LeRoy remained standing, a chunk of a tattered, bloody shirt in his hand. "Damn, that little bugger got away. Now I'll have to find another place and a new disguise. Shoot, I should have finished him off…and his friend too—damn, I screwed up." Crazy LeRoy smiled.

His thoughts of Eddie and Terry drifted away as he mumbled, "I'm the greatest gorom of all! I'm Mochcom—I bring death to Neferzul! I have before and will again. Her heart belongs to me!"

Eddie stumbled on to his back porch. He collapsed from loss of blood and rolled backward onto the stairs. The rips in his bloody T-shirt exposed the heart-shaped wound on his chest.

Eddie's mother heard the ruckus and raced to the door. She found her son lying helpless and barely conscious—exhausted from an ordeal with a monster, his head turned skyward, and his eyes wide open.

CHAPTER 32
Their Final Ride to the Tusk

Her mind was trapped in a nightmare. There was no escaping the image of a quivering body, blood oozing from the heart-shaped cut on its chest. A haunting feeling of death gripped the very core of Jeannie's being. She screamed, "*No!*"

Slamming on the brakes, Danny's truck veered sideways on the road, coming to a screeching halt. "My God, Jeannie, what's wrong?" he yelled.

"Oh, I'm so sorry, Danny. I'm scared. Hold me, Danny," she cried.

It was not an ordinary situation. A pickup truck parked sideways in the middle of the dirt road leading to the Boar's Tusk was starkly out of place on an early Monday morning. Three kids were caught in an episode of terror that was ripping at the very core of their souls.

He held her body next to his. His fingers caressed her face. "Jeannie, I'll protect you," said Danny, reminding her that he had superhuman powers. Her body relaxed a bit. Feeling the tenseness start to leave her, he asked, "Do we go to the Tusk?"

"I'm sorry, Danny. Forgive me for being upset." She looked into his eyes and wiped a tear that rolled down his cheek. Knowing the effect she was having on him, in a stronger voice she said, "Let's go to the Tusk. We have no choice except to try to figure out the mystery."

She paused. Saying nothing, he looked into her eyes. She continued, "If we don't, LeRoy will kill us. He'll kill us all. I think he can even kill you!"

Danny started his truck. He put it in gear, and they were on their way once more. The graveness of the situation they were in was heavy on their minds. Silence took over.

For Tony, their problem was real. There was no escaping the fact the mystery was not solved. Keen on cutting to the heart of the matter, he was all too aware that danger was looming greater without the final details of the mystery in place. His only option was to press on in search of the answers that would give them the power to use the secrets of the sun.

Danny's job was to protect Jeannie and Tony from a madman who would stop at nothing to get what he wanted. There was no doubt that the last piece of the puzzle was sitting on Jeannie's lap. The problem he faced was that none of them knew how to use it. They didn't even really know what it could do or how long it would take to solve the last part of this mystery. Time was not on their side, and he knew it.

There was no stopping the marathon her mind was running. She couldn't stop the endless swirling of thought. Jeannie was torn between thoughts of horror and hope for the future. She raced from one thought and then to another. *I don't blame him. What's there to talk about? What's there to say to Danny and Tony? How do you talk about horror?* Her consciousness kept echoing the chorus of Johnny Bill's song "Danny's Sunday Morning Pain" as they raced along the dirt road.

> I can't hear the music playing or see the stars of fame,
> 'Cause I'm listening to the silence of a sleeping city's shame.
> On a gloomy Sunday morning, on a sidewalk all alone,
> Makes a body wonder, why I ever left my home.

And then her mind would shift gears. First one thought and then another would drift in and settle on her. *What are we doing? Are we tangled up in a horror episode? Are we going to end up like Eddie or, even worse, like Danny's mother? What is it that we're doing—searching for the Pearl of Time, the Kashome legend of eternal youth? Are we searching to find something that's beyond our reach?*

Her soft white fingers explored the Sun Energy Transformer sitting on her lap. She gripped a little gold knob and turned it slightly. A golden shutter with a small square hole in it moved. Watching it, her mind raced on. *What's the last part of that song? I know it says something about hope. What is it? Oh yeah, it says, "Through the darkest clouds of sadness, Lord I'll find my fame tomorrow." Will we find the Pearl of Time today?*

After ten minutes of intense gloominess, it was Jeannie who finally spoke. "Poor Eddie. I can't believe what he went through. Can you imagine hanging like that for an hour? He went through hell! I hate that crazy man!"

She heard nothing. She looked at Tony and asked, "Why aren't you guys answering me? Oh well. It's just awful. I hate that evil creature."

Then Jeannie looked at Danny. "What do you think?"

Turning his head slightly, taking his eyes from the road for an instant, Danny answered her. "Jeannie, he's a mean, evil bastard. I just hope he doesn't figure out that we took the stuff from his house. I hope he doesn't figure out we are headed to the Boar's Tusk...but you know what? I'll bet he does!"

Her fingers grabbed the tablet of paper under the transformer. She pulled it out for study. Nervously, she fiddled with the edges of the dirty old sheets of paper she'd been dragging around the desert for the last several weeks.

For what seemed like an eternity, there was silence again. Then Danny added, "I hope he rots in hell! Jeannie, I just don't want to talk about it. Let's change the subject."

She put her left arm around him and her right hand on his—the one he was clutching the steering wheel with.

"We're going to be OK! I just know we're going to be OK. We're a team, and we need to stick together," she said with upbeat courage.

Then she started digging though her notes in the papers on her lap. Danny's '55 Chevy bounced over the rocks and holes in the ruts on the dirt road leading to the Boar's Tusk as they traveled on.

Where's that Reina-Valera verse, she thought, *the one that says something about saving me from violence? What did I do with it? Oh, there it is!* Jeannie spotted what she was looking for in her pile of notes and started reading. "The god of the rock and high tower is our shield and saves us from violence."

That put a big question in her mind. *Who is the god of the high towers at the Boar's Tusk? If we put our trust in him, will that being be our shield and save us from Mochcom? Is that what this verse means?*

With the truck bouncing up and down, her notepad of papers started slipping off her lap. Grabbing it before it fell to the rubber mat on the dirty floor, her eyes focused on the bronze object that they had just stolen. It immediately sent new thoughts to the forefront of her mind.

Why are the gemstones cut in the shape of stars? They're in the same pattern that's on the bronze boxes we found at the Boar's Tusk and White Face Cliff. Why would Crazy LeRoy have this thing? Did he steal it from Kashom?

Not knowing what she was looking at, she decided to hold that subject for a moment and switch back to another as she said, "My lord in heaven—I hate that crazy old man."

"What did you just say?" Danny asked. He had heard Jeannie mumbling something in a low voice, but his focus was on the road ahead and the Boar's Tusk coming into view.

"I was just trying to make sense out of one of the Reina-Valera verses." She looked at his face staring at the road ahead. "Danny, do you think we'll be safe? Do you think Crazy LeRoy will come after us?"

Their thoughts were traveling along parallel paths. Danny could tell that Jeannie was concerned about what Crazy LeRoy might do to them. His problem was that they were dealing with a reality—the reality of LeRoy discovering what they were up to and what they had stolen from him.

"Jeannie, I have to be honest with you. I think we're in grave danger! We know what that evil bastard is capable of. We just have to hope that he doesn't connect us with stealing this transformer and that other tin box from his house."

He took his eyes briefly from the road ahead and glanced at her. There was no way to hide it. His words of concern tumbled out without hesitation. "Jeannie, the reality is that my shoe is caught in the vault door, and there's a flashlight shining on his bedroom floor—from under his bed. He'll find it! I think we have big problems!"

At that very moment, Crazy LeRoy kicked open the door leading into his mansion.

"They've been here! How did they know? What were they after in my palace?"

He rushed to his bedroom. In the dark void, he immediately saw the beam of light coming from under his bed.

He howled in rage. "They got my money, my treasure, and my Sun Energy Transformer! Damn! I have to get them! I can't let them get away! I have to hurry. Vulture will help me get them before they figure how to use the power of the sun to transport them to Kopaz."

He stormed out of his marble palace and screamed at Black Vulture sitting on the roof of the woodshed of horror. "Vulture, help me! We must find them! Lead me! Take me to them! We can't let them get away!"

Once more, Tony, Danny, and Jeannie sat quietly as Danny's truck raced through the Scarlet Desert. Jeannie clutched the object on her lap. *I don't care if Danny has a lead foot. I don't care if he races through the desert. We just want to get to the Boar's Tusk. We just want to find refuge. Danny is right. Crazy LeRoy will kill us the first chance he gets. He's the most evil person I've ever known!*

Tony had been the first person to see Eddie hanging on the back wall of LeRoy Nabal's woodshed, and now he was desperately trying to get that image out of his mind. *Our adventures have turned to horror—our hopes and dreams have become nightmares!*

Tony's heart jumped as he stared through the windshield. A glimmer of hope crossed his mind as Danny pulled his truck onto a flat area at the base of the hill the Tusk jutted out of.

Oh, thank God we're here! Maybe getting busy doing stuff out here at the Boar's Tusk will take our minds off Eddie, Crazy LeRoy, and all the evil we found.

"It's ten o'clock, guys, and we're here—what do we do now?" Danny asked, breaking the silence.

A pang shot through him as a sobering thought entered his mind. *Is this our final ride in my truck to the Tusk?*

CHAPTER 33
Vulture Takes Orders

I t towered in front of them, reaching to the sky as if to touch the lone cloud drifting quietly above.

Staring at the rock formation, Jeannie's mind was captured by foreboding thoughts of viewing the Boar's Tusk for the final time. Goose bumps rippled over her body. There was no question left in Jeannie's mind about what could happen. *Mochcom will figure out that we have stolen his transformer. My God, he'll kill us to get it back. We have to figure out how it works. Without the final piece of the puzzle, we're doomed.*

In every direction as far as the eye could see, the desert was an expansive vista of gentle rolling hills covered with purple sage. The only significant change in the landscape surrounding them was the rock towers she was standing by. There was no escaping into the desert if for some reason someone spotted them at the Tusk. There was no place to hide and no place to go.

Her mind froze. *We're like little rubber ducks sitting in a pail of water at a carnival, just waiting for the first guy to give the attendant a dime for a shot at the prize—a shot that could win him a teddy bear if he hits one of us.*

Then she cringed. *My God, LeRoy would have us trapped here like fish in a barrel. His prize would be my golden key.*

Tony noticed her body quivering slightly. He suspected what was going on in her mind, knowing the race they were in was for real. They had to find an answer to the final piece of the puzzle—a puzzle that had remained a mystery for centuries, and yet now time was running out.

"Let's take Danny's SET and the tin box we got from Crazy LeRoy's house and put them on the flat rock at the base of the Tusk. We'll open up the secret chamber and get the other treasures," Tony said, wanting to get their minds off thoughts of death.

Looking at Jeannie, he asked, "Do you have your key? We may need it. Who knows what we will unravel today? Things are a bit crazy."

"Yeah, Tony, I do, and things are not just a bit crazy. We are in a race for our lives."

It was not only Tony who knew what they were dealing with but also Danny. "Jeannie, we just have to get our minds off Crazy LeRoy. Let's just get busy and forget about how evil he is. Look, we have each other—there are three of us—we'll be OK!" Danny said in an effort to calm Jeannie's fears. "Jeannie, did you remember to put the brass bow and arrow in your canvas bag?"

"I did. Here they are. You can have the honor of opening the rock door." She handed them to him. "I know you like to open the secret chamber of the Boar's Tusk."

He smiled and said, "You figured me out!"

Danny inserted the brass bow and arrow into their slits. He turned the arrow. The screeching and squealing noises of the massive rock moving to its open position filled the air. The eerie sounds caused Jeannie to cringe.

Standing back from the giant moving rock, Danny gazed at it with amazement. "My hell, that's a freaky sight! Don't you guys think this doorway looks like a monster's mouth on the Tusk?"

"It does, Danny. It scares me! I'm glad that noise is finished," said Jeannie.

Danny grabbed Tony's arm and motioned to him. "Let's hurry, Tony. We have to get in and get the boxes before that rock door closes."

Releasing Tony's arm, he bolted for the doorway and said, "I'm glad we decided to set the treasures just inside the opening. We don't have to walk around the edge of that bottomless pit and mess with the granite vault."

Within seconds, Danny and Tony were standing over the treasure.

"You grab the two bronze boxes, and I'll get the one containing the emerald star," said Danny.

"OK, we got them. Let's get out of here," Tony yelled.

It took Danny and Tony less than a minute to get all of the treasures from inside the chamber.

For the first time on that fateful day, Jeannie's face broke into a huge smile.

"*Good work, guys!* We're ready to go," squealed Jeannie as Danny and Tony emerged from the chamber.

"We'll put them next to the stuff we just took from the crazy man's house," Danny said as he pointed his finger to the flat, lichen-covered rock where Jeannie was standing.

Although she had just expressed a few words of joy, her stance was a sure giveaway to Danny. She did usually need to hold herself steady with one hand on the rock.

Now Danny explained the plan. He gave Tony the first assignment, knowing he was ready to solve the final puzzle. "Tony, do you think you know how to make this stuff work?" asked Danny as he helped Tony set their treasures on the rock.

Tony was ready. "Yes, Danny, I do. I'm positive that the SET we got from LeRoy is another lid for the emerald star box. Look at the star patterns on the sides of the boxes. They match the original lid."

Tony carefully set the Sun Energy Transformer next to the emerald star. "And yes, Danny's SET is a top that fits! It's another lid for the cradle of the emerald star."

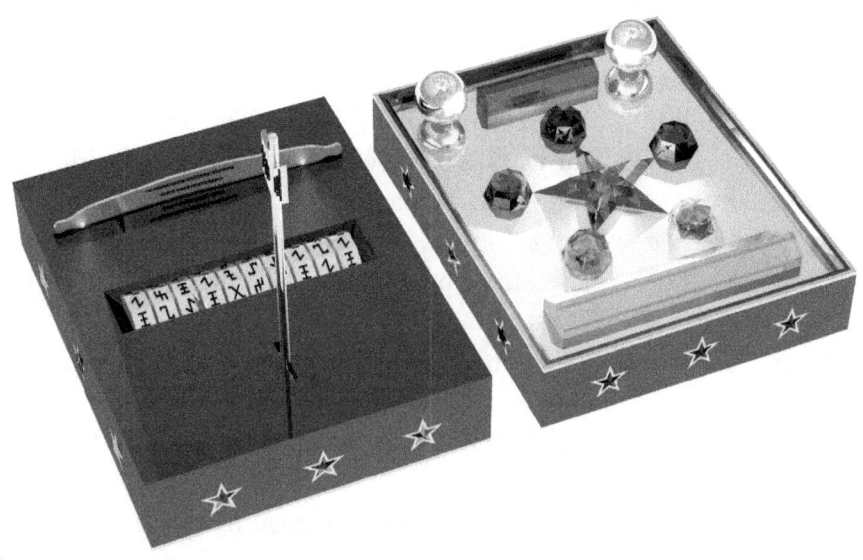

Leaning close to Danny, Tony spoke in a low voice so Jeannie couldn't hear. "You and Jeannie take five. She needs some reassurance, Danny. I'll have this SET figured out in no time."

In ten steps, Danny was by Jeannie's side. Pointing to his truck not more than a hundred fifty feet down the hill, he said, "Jeannie, let's take a hike. Tony has this under control."

Her face lit up. "Thanks Danny. That'll be fun. You and I will have a few moments alone in your truck. I need some downtime alone with you."

Before strolling down the hill, she paused and looked into Tony's face, knowing the puzzle was not complete. "We just need to keep figuring out how it works. Those answers must be in Kashom's journal. So far, he has guided us correctly!"

Giving her a thumbs-up, Tony answered, "I know that, Jeannie. No worries. I'll search through the tablets and find the answers."

He gave her a quick wink as he said, "You and Danny have fun for a few minutes."

Tony threw his hand in the air, and she slapped it, giving him a high five. She spun around, grabbed Danny's hand, and started swinging his arm as they walked off toward the truck.

Time marched on. Danny, Jeannie, and Tony were in a race to find answers to questions they knew so little about. They searched for ancient secrets—secrets that would unlock the power of the sun through gifts from the gods. They were in a race against time.

Mochcom raced through the desert, following Vulture. *Woooop, woooop, woooop.* Black Vulture's great wings propelled him through the air. He flew low in the sky, just in front of LeRoy's green 1948 Ford truck.

"Where have they taken it?" Mochcom's mind raced for answers as he mumbled to himself. "Where are they? Worst case, they're at the Boar's Tusk. Since Kashom and I were transported from Kopaz to the Boar's Tusk, the only way they can leave is from the Boar's Tusk. I've got to get them before they leave," growled LeRoy angrily.

As Mochcom raced through the desert, other races were underway. An ambulance raced through the streets of CoalVille carrying Eddie, with his mother next to him, to the Granite Springs Hospital—a race to save his life. Shattered, an emotionally distraught father raced to the police station with a story of horror, the story of a crazy man stalking his son.

Unexpectedly, Mochcom slammed on his brakes. The cloud of dust that had been traveling behind the truck engulfed the parked vehicle. LeRoy jumped out and screamed, *"Vulture, go! Find them now!"*

His faithful servant had his flight orders and obeyed, flying into the sun as he headed for the Boar's Tusk.

Yes, time marched on. The race to find answers to ancient secrets was in full swing.

CHAPTER 34

A Puzzle is Complete

I t was a glorious day. Sitting next to each other on the seat of his truck, Danny and Jeannie were lost in a few moments of joy they were sharing as young lovers, dreaming of what might be. Searching for hope, they could only imagine what lay ahead.

Jeannie was so right, thought Danny. *We've started a journey. I think the transformer and gems could be exactly what Jeannie believes—the means to a magical life far from CoalVille.*

On that warm spring day at the Boar's Tusk, Danny's watch glittered in the morning sun as he dangled it in front of Jeannie.

She giggled and said, "Danny, do you remember the day we went snooping and you held me in your arms for the first time?" Her smiling eyes found his, and she grabbed his arms as he swung his watch between them once more.

He said nothing. His arms circled her small body and gently pulled her closer. With their bodies pressed tightly together and a golden watch between them, their mouths met, and they closed their eyes, enjoying the sweetness of their embrace.

As he gently put his hands on either side of her face, he noticed her tear-filled eyes sparkled like gems. He studied every minute detail of her beautiful face.

"Jeannie, do you think we will solve this mystery?" There was a moment of silence before Danny himself offered an answer to his question. "Oh Jeannie, I hope so. I really do."

His deep baritone voice was soft as his fingers stroked her hair. He let his thumbs extend to her soft white cheeks. "Do you think we will venture on the Highway of Time...the highway you always talk about?" Now his voice was even lower as he continued. "Do you think we will find our fountain of youth? Do you think we will find a magical way to leave CoalVille?"

Her smiling eyes never left his as she said, "Yes, Danny! I think we will!"

She followed his eye movements. His mind now was far from thinking of pirate treasure. *She's always right. Right before our eyes, we're solving a mystery.*

From the corner of his eye, he caught a glimpse of something that made him jerk. He wasn't sure what it was. Whatever he thought he saw was high in the sky, directly in front of the sun. Throwing the worst thought away—that it was a black vulture—his mind sought comfort. *It was probably just a golden eagle.*

Then his mind returned to the mystery. *Yeah! But what is the mystery?*

Suddenly, he lurched. His stare was blank as he reached to his face. His fingers curled over his lips. His mind took off. *My God in heaven, what did Tony's mom say to us this morning?*

His body tensed, his mind recalling every detail of the conversation he had with Tony's mother. *"For God's sake, son—you're not in danger are you? I could not go on if I lost you and Danny.*

Jeannie blinked, watching Danny move into a weird emotional state. "Danny, what's going on with you?" She turned and held him by both hands. "What are you thinking, my love? I know you so well. I know something is bothering you. What is it?" Jeannie said, her soft, sweet voice full of concern.

"Oh, Jeannie," he said with a sigh, squeezing her hands as he looked into her eyes. "I was just thinking about my mom and dad, and Tony's mom, and all the stuff that's going on. I wanted to say something to Rose, but knew I couldn't. She isn't dumb. She sensed that we're up to something."

His eyes grew shiny as he took a breath of air and continued. "Tony's mom is very concerned about our safety. The last thing she said before we left this morning was, 'Danny and Tony, I worry. Don't go near LeRoy Nabal's house. Be careful. Crazy LeRoy is an evil man.'"

His thoughts were racing all over the place, shooting in every direction. He blurted out, "I hope LeRoy doesn't try to get us. I hope he doesn't try to get Tony's mom."

Jeannie knew exactly what he was racing through his mind. *He's thinking about LeRoy murdering his mom.*

Then Danny's mind shot back to his dad's funeral. He shuddered at the thought of that preacher touching Tony's mom. "I hope Pastor Duncan has good intentions," Danny said. "He called Tony's mom and asked her to go out with him."

Her reaction was instant. "Danny, Danny, Danny, settle down. You're getting carried away." She pulled his body next to hers and embraced him. "You're letting your imagination run wild. Just settle down. Nothing is going to happen," she whispered in his ear.

His response sent a wave of joy through her as his body relaxed.

"Tony's mom will be fine. Nothing is going to happen to her. Crazy LeRoy isn't going to hurt her. Pastor Duncan will look out for her—she'll be fine." Jeannie moved her hands to his face. Gently, she slid her fingers into his long yellow hair and pulled his face to hers. Her mouth touched his, and she kissed him. She softly held his face in her hands as she looked into his eyes. She smiled. She tenderly brushed his cheeks with her fingers.

Danny's heart pounded. *She's great. I just love her!*

But that was a fleeting moment of joy. The next sighting of a black object flying in front of the sun proved it was not a golden eagle.

"My God, he's here," screamed Danny.

Her eyes searched the sky where Danny was staring, and she saw it. "*Danny, we need to run. Quick! We need to get back to Tony. Hurry!*"

The two teenagers scurrying out of a parked pickup truck alerted Vulture. He diverted his flight pattern and circled behind the Boar's Tusk. Out of sight, the Tusk shielding his activities, he spotted a clump of scrub cedar trees and swooped to them. In moments, he was safely hidden.

Sprinting to the top of the hill, Jeannie was the first to scream. "Tony, did you see the vulture? Danny and I think he's out here!"

Tony's face went blank. He snapped his head around to look even before Jeannie had finished her words. He searched the barren sky but found nothing. "I don't think he's here. I don't think he could fly so fast that we would lose sight of him. Maybe you didn't see him."

Shaking, Jeannie was not convinced. "I know he's here! Tony, we need to hurry. Mochcom will jump out and get us!"

Before Tony could respond, she grabbed his hand and pulled on it freely. Her voice was wrought with concern as she continued. "Mochcom is hiding out here. He wants to cut my heart out. His vulture helps him."

At that moment, it was Tony who took command. He gently put his arms around Jeannie and gave her a bear hug. Looking over her shoulder at Danny standing behind them, Tony said, "Jeannie, Danny has the power to kill the vulture and Mochcom. I don't think that vulture is out here. I don't think Mochcom is here. Let's not worry."

"OK," she whimpered. "What have you discovered?"

Sensing she was anxious to find the answers to ancient secrets, he took the lead. "All right. Look at this drawing. It's identical to the transformer.

Excited, Tony charged on. He looked at the drawing and placed his finger on it to show Jeannie where to look. "Look at the drawing on the left." Pointing to the pink and green hexagonal gemstones and the two white-gold balls, he said, "That means that those objects need to be transferred."

And with the excitement of a young boy in a candy shop, he took the precious objects from the golden cradle and placed them on the lid of the transformer.

Tony looked at his watch.

Strategically positioned behind the cover of a bush, Vulture was now where he wanted to be.

The sun came out from behind a lone cloud, and it was if its rays set the green handle on fire. Its brilliance was unmistakable. Vulture's instructions were clear in his mind. He moved his head so that his beady eyes could get a better view.

"Let's keep going," said Tony with a hint of concern.

Jeannie sensed that Danny had settled down. She held his face in her soft hands for another moment as she thought, *I'm sure glad I have my friends. I guess we just have to put our trust in Kashom. He hasn't led us astray so far.*

"Tony, what do you think has to happen?" Danny asked.

"I think this stuff is going to work! I'm excited!" answered Tony.

Jeannie felt a sense of accomplishment. *We were diligent and followed what Kashom wanted us to do. We have been placed in a state of danger, but Kashom has said to put his trust in him. Could it be that the trust he's talking about is this transformer, this device that's capturing the sun's rays and sparkles like a treasure whose value is incalculable yet cannot be spent?*

"Our job is to figure out how it works," she commented with a sigh.

Something puzzled Tony. "Jeannie, what do we do with the three combination wheels at the top right corner of the transformer?" asked Tony.

Jeannie's face has a curious look if there ever was one, Danny thought. He could see the questions written all over her sad look. "Don't worry, Jeannie. Tony will figure it out. He always does! Get figuring, Tony! Jeannie and I are counting on you, so don't just sit there."

"You're right, Danny. Fortunately, Kashom always helps us out. Hopefully he'll continue." Tony paused and looked at Jeannie. "Jeannie, what does this mean?" he asked as he pointed to the marking at the top of the drawing.

"Let me see what you're talking about, Tony. Oh…yes. It says, '*Aguja en disco de llave del sol*,'" said Jeannie, and she giggled—trying to get a more jovial mood underway. "Oh, I'm sorrrrrrrrrry. I forgot you guys are Spanish ignorant." She laughed and then continued. "It means, 'Needle on disc of key of the sun.'"

Danny listened. Then it hit him. *The only objects with Roman numerals on them are my watch and the sundial key.*

For a moment, he looked to the sky. Then he looked at Jeannie, thinking, *If that is true, to operate the Sun Energy Transformer, both Jeannie's golden key and my gold watch are needed. My watch is needed to identify the arrowhead pointer on the sundial key. Then Jeannie's golden key translates the code. Wow!*

She was watching him look at her intently. *What's he thinking?*

Without warning, a strange, fickle smile streaked across Danny's face. Normally, it was not his territory, but it dawned on him that he had the answer.

He paused, curled his lower lip under his front teeth, and took his watch out of his pocket. With his eyes sparkling, he said, "Look at the symbols," tilting it so Tony could also see.

I X I X I X I X I X I X I

⅄ᕼⱿX⅂ᴲ⌠X⅁ᖲ⅄

Pointing to the three combination wheels on the transformer, Danny yelled out, "Look at these three symbols." Tony and Jeannie gawked at the

symbols **ⱿX⅂** and then back at Danny.

His excitement building with every breath he took, Danny charged on. "Now look at the Roman numerals above the three mirror-image symbols on my golden watch. Put them together, and what do you have?" he asked rhetorically. Walking to the rock, he took a piece of paper from the tablet, wrote on it, and pointed. "And voilá! You see, we have an XXI."

Tony could wait no longer. "Oh my God, Danny, you've done it. It's clear." Tony pointed to the eight arrowhead points on the sundial key. "Danny's watch tells us how to align Jeannie's key on the dial so we can translate the code of symbols. Can I see the paper, Danny? I'll draw it out. Here it is."

ⱿX⅂ ➤ XXI

Tony could not stop the rush of words that flew from his mouth. "Danny, you've just solved the last piece of the puzzle. We know now how to get the code of symbols that unlock the transformer! We know how to unlock the power of the sun."

Vulture waited for the opportunity he needed. It wasn't quite yet.

It took Tony all of ten minutes to figure out the code of symbols—

symbols that corresponded to Viracocha.

"All right, guys! I've got it figured out." Tony was obviously pleased with his accomplishment. *I knew I could do it*, he thought happily. "Here's the code of nine mirror-image symbols that unlocks Danny's SET," he said.

Deliberately smug, he asked, "Well, guys, I got the code dialed in, so now what?"

CHAPTER 35
Deathly Strike

A gangly neck supported the featherless head adorned with bright-red, wrinkled skin. His bobbing beak moved with each careful step. Now the time was at hand. With the moment of surprise approaching, Black Vulture fluttered his wings uncontrollably.

From the corner of his eye, Tony caught a glimpse of red moving behind the nearby bush. His head jerked to look. "My God, what is it?" screamed Tony.

Vulture jumped onto the large rock at the side of the bush. He then leaped from his vantage point and instantly raked the air to set his flight in motion. His first maneuver was a circular climb to gain altitude. It was perfectly executed.

Now he was where he wanted to be—above and behind Danny—hiding his location from the wrath of the superhuman. With his wings tucked tightly against his body and his outstretched talons perfectly positioned, he began to dive. Like the torpedo from a German U-Boat striking the blind side of a British warship, Vulture's attack was perfect. His forty pounds of muscle traveling sixty miles per hour struck Danny's back like the deathblow of an iron ball from a pirate's cannon.

It was perfect. Vulture blinked. Danny fell to the ground, his head striking a rock. A gaping wound on the side of his face sent a shock of pain through him. His yellow hair turned crimson red, and he lay motionless in a pool of bloody sand.

Chaos ensued. Vulture's plan was working flawlessly.

Jeannie screamed, "*Danny! Danny!*"

His wings fully outstretched, Vulture maneuvered in Tony's direction. His razor-sharp talons were the perfect knives to cut deep into Tony's forearm. The boy screamed with pain as blood gushed from the wounds.

Jeannie threw her body over the unconscious Danny. Her hand furiously slapped his face. His head was still. His eyes remained closed. She screamed louder. "*Danny! Danny! Wake up!*"

Then she was no longer screaming. She was crying. With shaking fingers, she touched his blood-soaked hair. Barely audible, she whimpered, "He's going to kill us. We're going to die."

The time was now. Vulture seized the opportunity in the middle of the mayhem to snatch what he wanted. He wrapped his talons around the green handle of the transformer. His wings batted the air, lifting him almost vertically.

Tony's heart sank as he watched the bird take flight. *My God, we're doomed! That creature stole the handle. We're helpless without it.*

His mind collapsing in utter desperation, his eyes focused on his canteen of water. It was only two feet in front of him on the rock. Snatching it, he whirled around and ripped its lid off. Standing over Danny, he shook it, covering Danny's bleeding head with cold water.

It worked. Danny rolled over.

"*Your ring! Use it! Stop Vulture!*" screamed Tony.

With the precise execution of a god in training, Danny grabbed the chain around his neck and yanked his ring from under his T-shirt.

With the rays of the sun perfectly placed, he captured them with the emerald stone and focused a beam of green light on the fleeing bird high in the sky. His aim was right on target.

Shrieking in pain, Vulture released the green handle, which had turned white hot from the beam of light penetrating it.

Following every movement of Danny and Vulture, Jeannie watched the handle fall to the ground. She screamed in sheer panic, "*Oh no! The handle is going to break!*"

Tony took off running toward where he thought it had landed. While he ran, he ripped his T-shirt off and wrapped it around his arm to stop the bleeding.

Although dazed and a bit confused, Danny was on his feet. At his side, Jeannie clung to his left arm. There was no comfort in her eyes, knowing a smashed handle was useless. They watched Tony and waited. As they stood watching Tony, Danny fumbled with his chain and the ring that he was holding. To keep them safe, Danny put his ring on the chain and secured it around his neck.

It was only a matter of moments before a loud cry pierced the still air. *"It landed on a red-ant hill…it's fine!"*

Tony raced back to Jeannie and Danny, handle in hand. He was shaking as he said, "We're OK!"

Danny and Jeannie nodded their heads mutely. But then Tony who screeched, *"We've got to get the hell out of here now!"*

Staring at Tony, Danny and Jeannie at first said nothing. They watched his face go blank as his body stiffened. Danny reached to grab his friend's shaking hand. He asked, "What's wrong Tony?"

Something else was on Tony's mind. Although his composure was not the greatest, he clasped Danny's hand with a strong grip and said in shaky voice, "Danny, KateLynn told me it was the right time of the month…what if she is carrying my child? What shall I do? What if I die out here?"

That was something he had never expected, and Danny was at a loss for words. His mind erupted with strange thoughts. *My God, Tony. I don't have the answers. I don't know what is happening. It's like a whirlwind nightmare!*

Jeannie dropped Danny's hand and slowly walked to the lichen-covered rock where the tablets were. She had no thoughts. She had no idea what to do. She started flipping through the pages of gold without really focusing on what she was doing. One by one, she flipped them over the silver rings of the binder.

The conversation between Danny and Tony was guarded. They were mumbling words she could not make out. She glanced at the page she had flipped to. Then her eyes focused on the words *"TRPOV y TRPON muestran el camino."* Her face was puzzled as she translated it to herself.

"TRPOV and TRPON show the way."

Then her mind went back to a time when she had sat with her mother in their living room, being schooled in the legends of her people. Repeating every word in her mind, her revelation was almost more than she could handle. *This is the fulfillment of the last part of the Legend of Kashom. Viracocha told Kashom that if he is to regain his royal status, as part of his purgatory, he must aid TRPOV and TRPON in the fulfillment of their missions and declare to them who they are.*

No longer was she listening to Danny and Tony's private conversation. Her mind was not on KateLynn and what Tony had just said. Now she was staring at the last page of Kashom's journal. There it was. Her mind not stopping, her eyes raced on, looking at each Spanish word as she read them to herself, translating as she went:

> *The royal prince of Viracocha is TRPOV and the royal princess of Neferdor is TRPON. TRPOV and TRPON must fulfill the following conditions:*
>
> (1)   *They must kill all of the goroms in Kopaz and throw their bodies not yet ashes into the fiery depths of Vulcan—the gateway to hell guarded by CrystalFlame—so their eternity is destined to be everlasting embers in the belly of the outer reaches of darkness.*
>
> (2)   *They must kill Mochcom and wrap his ashes in the Ancient Shroud of Goroms and throw them into the fiery depths of Vulcan so his eternity is destined to be everlasting anguish in the belly of the outer reaches of darkness.*
>
> *Then, and only then, shall the TRPOV and TRPON sit on thrones of pure gold alongside the gods at their council table of red worox stone and control the gift of eternal youth for all humans throughout the universe.*
>
> *Beware that the bodies of the goroms of Kopaz remain not outside the gateway to hell past the evening of the high moon, for if they do, all is lost.*
>
> *And to the TRPOV, his beast, Yellzor, shall devour imposters and throw them into the fiery mouth of CrystalFlame.*

Hit with that affirmation, she was speechless. Although she did not fully comprehend the references to the CrystalFlame or the beast, Yellzor, there could be no denying the emotion that surged through Jeannie's body. Her mind erupted in the most unbelievable revelation. *My God! My God! Danny and I are destined to be part of the family of the gods! He's the royal prince of Viracocha, and I'm the royal princess of Neferdor, TRPOV and TRPON.*

She continued translating silently as she read to herself the last entry in Kashom's golden journal. *To the Chosen One: may the gods speed your journey as you embark on your new conquest with the royal prince of Viracocha. I have done all I can to open the Highway of Time. I ask you, as the last Neferzul, to give my regards to my parents when you stand before them in the royal court of Kopaz. Tell my mother, the royal queen of Kopaz, there is still a red ribbon tied around my heart. She will know what that means.*

A tear spilled from her eye, and great joy overtook her heart. Out of the clear blue, she turned to Danny and asked, "What now?"

He was caught by surprise. First Tony's revelation with the possibility of KateLynn getting pregnant had put a new spin on the situation, and now Jeannie was asking him "What now?" with a grin on her face.

Danny's only comeback was another question. "What's going on?"

Tony's eyes were as large as two full moons. "I will tell you guys what's going on!" he screamed as loudly as he could. "*There's a vehicle racing up the dirt road to the Boar's Tusk!*"

CHAPTER 36
A Race With Death

Bloodstained fingernails tapped the Bakelite steering wheel of a 1948 Ford truck in rhythm with the thoughts of grandeur racing through Mochcom's consciousness. "I just love to transmogrify my body," Mochcom said as he smiled and watched Black Vulture through the windshield. The bird fanned the air with his wings to propel his flight. Mochcom's ability to transmogrify his body, or change it in appearance or form, especially strangely or grotesquely, was his gift from Zuron, and he loved it.

"I've enjoyed masquerading under the disguises of innocent people over my centuries in the Scarlet Desert, but now I'll be Lord Mochcom once more and rule as the gorom of Kopaz." LeRoy's spirit soared when he spotted the 1955 red Chevy pickup at the base of the hill leading to the Boar's Tusk.

"I was right! They've figured out enough to come here! I'll get them!" *Woooop, woooop, woooop.* LeRoy heard the pleasant sound of his servant's wings as Vulture led him to his prize. "Good work, Vulture! You found them!"

Mochcom, his left hand on the steering wheel, reached into the pocket of his grimy pants with his right hand. With grating teeth, the disciple of Zuron snarled, "A traitor in Viracocha's midst is helping us, most honorable Zuron."

Clutching the object, his face turned to the sky, he looked through the windshield as he howled, "I have half of the symbol medallion with one of the two code words that you need to control Lenszar, and I will find a way to get the other half and complete my mission, most noble Zuron!"

And to the rhythm of the truck bouncing over potholes, Mochcom's howls turned to laughter as he held his hand in the air, half a golden medallion glinting in the light. He rasped, "For you, Zuron, I will have not only both pieces of the symbol medallion but also Neferzul's golden key. Without it, she will not be able to unlock GAMMAZEL, and Viracocha will lose the war! I can't wait! *Ahhh!* The keys that unlock the power to the universe. And her heart will no longer beat in her chest but in my hands! *Haaaa! Haaaaaaaaa!*"

Spinning around, Danny flinched uncontrollably. "*Oh my God! What do we do now?*" Danny screamed. "*That has to be Crazy Leroy!*"

Her hands flew from her side to her face. Jeannie placed her fingers over her mouth, pulling them slowly down her lips as if to hold back her screams, but she could not. "*It's him! It's him! Gorom Mochcom!* He's in that old '48 Ford pickup that was parked in Crazy LeRoy's shed!" Jeannie squealed.

Panic was setting in. They were trapped, and Tony was without options other than the Sun Energy Transformer.

"*What do we do?* There's no place to go or hide. These two rock towers at the top of this small hill have us isolated with no place to run!" screamed Tony.

Jeannie shook as she stared at the east wall of the Tusk, wondering if its sanctuary was their only escape from a horrible death.

"Let's go into the secret chamber of the Boar's Tusk!" hollered Jeannie.

Danny's mind was churning. Any notions of cutting up, any thoughts of humor had left him. His thoughts and decisions had to be sound and firm if there could be even a sliver of hope of escaping their impending death. "Jeannie, we can't! We'd die in there! There is no way to open it from the inside! We'd be stuck!" yelled Danny.

Tony saw the cloud of dust engulfing the truck. He yelled, "It's slowing down! I can almost see the driver!" Grabbing his binoculars and staring at the approaching vehicle, which was still a mile from them, he screamed, *"It's not Crazy Leroy! It's Pastor Duncan! We're OK!"* Relieved, he said in a calmer tone of voice, "Why would Pastor Duncan come here? To see us?"

Then Jeannie saw it. There were no clouds in the sky. The sun beating down on the desert and its inhabitants made it happen. The memory of a beam of purple light grabbed her mind. Ignoring Danny, her thoughts filled with panic as details of the ancient legend again flashed across her consciousness. *After Gorom Mochcom killed Princess Aerapondes, he conned Kashom into using the golden key and golden watch to venture onto the Highway of Time. They both ended up in the Scarlet Desert at the Boar's Tusk.*

And as far as the Kashome people know, Mochcom still lives in the Scarlet Desert. He is the emissary of the dark god, Zuron. It was Zuron who personally gave Mochcom the black ring that protects him. The energy from the ring is a beam of purple light. That is why Kashom was unable to kill him.

The gods were furious with the royal family of Kopaz because they failed to protect Aerapondes from the goroms and the precious gifts that open the Highway of Time.

She screamed, *"Leroy is Mochcom, and Duncan is Mochcom! My God! He's been masquerading as two people!"*

She was going to pieces, losing her composure entirely. Her mind was on death—a death coming to them in a truck racing down a dirt road at full speed.

"*No! Now what do we do? He'll kill us! He's a madman!*" Jeannie screamed, horror written all over her face. Biting her lips, her eyes never blinked. Her only response to her impending death was vocal. "*It's Mochcom! What do we do?*" shrieked Jeannie.

Her reasoning was gone. Her hopes and dreams of a glorious life with Danny forever and ever were slipping away.

As for Danny, the image of his mother's body draped over the steering wheel of their 1953 Buick Special appeared in his mind as if he were staring at it. He roared with anger. "*That bastard killed my mom, and I befriended him. I'm going to kill him if it's the last thing I do on earth!*"

But the gravity of their situation far outweighed the cancer of hate that was clouding Danny's judgment. His hands gesticulating wildly, Danny waved at Tony, pointing to the transformer.

Jeannie could not hide her uncontrolled fear. Watching Danny point to Tony and the transformer, she nodded, terror ruling her expression. Her hands pressed against the sides of her cheeks. She screamed through fingers curled over her mouth, her shrill voice piercing the air. "Do you have it figured out, Tony? *My God, get it figured out! We're doomed! Oh my God!*" She was grasping at anything—anything that would give them hope in the face of sure death.

Danny's mind was not idle as he considered all possibilities. He had no plan. However, he understood that his physical strength and his strength of character were vital to their hopes of escape.

"It looks as if he just stopped the truck and got out," Danny shouted and intently watched the activities happening at the truck.

Mochcom had stopped at least a half mile away. Knowing his ring was only a protection and not a lethal weapon, to get the gifts he had to kill the teenagers using his 30-06 rifle, modified for semiautomatic action. He rested it on the hood of his truck and gently started squeezing the trigger of the high-powered rifle.

Bang! Bang! Bang! Bang! Bang!

"*Oh shit!* He just shot at us—that was bullets! I can see him with the rifle in his hands!" screamed Danny.

Danny waved for Jeannie and Tony to take cover. The problem was—

there was no cover. They were sitting ducks.

"*Oh my lord! What do we do now?* That crazy bastard is back in the pickup and heading our way again!" shouted Danny.

Tony's role was and would always be a technical one. Unfortunately, figuring out complex technical solutions took time and patience. He had neither. "Let's be calm," Tony said, trying to get control of the situation. He ran to the flat rock where Kashom's golden journal lay open. "I think we do what the drawing says. It's our only hope."

Pointing his finger right in Tony's face, Danny roared in anger. "For crying out loud, Tony—*do what?* You're not making a bit of sense. *Come on, guy!* Do something that makes sense, or we're all dead!"

His keen sense of judgment was not rattled by Danny's sudden loss of composure. "Danny, just listen! We're going to do what this drawing says to do. We're going to hold hands and hold on to the bronze boxes and their contents. Then one of us will grasp the handle of the transformer. Jeannie will put the arrow into the keyhole and turn it."

With his hand trembling, Tony shouted, "If it works, we will vanish!"

Danny gritted his teeth as he answered his friend, still panicking because he did not comprehend Tony's brilliance. "You're loony! What the *hell* is that supposed to accomplish?" Danny shot back frantically. "We don't have—" Danny hesitated. "That crazy old bastard is almost to the Boar's Tusk. We have about three minutes to do something, or we *die!*"

Danny didn't understand, but Jeannie did. She grabbed his arm and pulled him to the treasures sitting on the rock at the base of the Boar's Tusk on that beautiful sunny afternoon. "Danny, you must listen to Tony. It's our only hope. Please! For me—just do it!" she said with conviction.

Not convinced, Danny stepped back, pulling his arm away from her. He didn't know what to believe. He screamed at Tony, "Tony, you're nuts! What do you mean—we'll vanish? You've been reading way too many comic books," shouted Danny, "Get that damn thing figured out. Come on! Get the lead out!"

Tony took charge. If Danny didn't have the wherewithal, he did. "Do you have a better idea? That old bastard tried to cut Eddie's heart out! He'll do much worse to us! You get the answer, Mr. Answer Man!" Tony ripped at Danny. "We have two minutes to somehow leave here or be shot by that crazy son of a bitch."

Danny saw Jeannie crying, her hands covering her face. They were doomed if he didn't fall in line. His judgment and strength took hold again.

Tony picked up on the change coming over Danny. With a smile of excitement he said, "I think the transformer will make us invisible!" Tony screamed. His thoughts drifted to the Reina-Valera verse that they discovered at the Boar's Tusk the day before. *That reference had something about us putting trust in someone to save us from violence. What did it say?* Tony's mind raced from one thing then to another.

Jeannie stopped crying and waved at Tony. She had to be strong for Danny. She was Neferzul, and the fulfillment of her mission was paramount.

She took charge and gave orders. "Tony, quick! Put the lid on! I told you to do that already! What are you waiting for?" she screamed.

She had never failed him. He responded to her orders. "OK! Here it is! Now what?" Tony yelled.

Danny's watchful eye was monitoring the approaching truck of death. "He's got his rifle out his window again. *He's shooting!*" yelled Danny.

Her excitement was building exponentially, almost overtaking her fear. Jeannie's mind was darting to-and-fro. *I have to think. I can't let my emotions control my decisions. I must use logic and common sense.* Her thoughts came to a screeching halt as she listened intently.

Tinkle, tinkle. Her spirit soared to a new height as she heard the familiar sound. She knew exactly what came next. "Meow, meow."

"Oh, Zanzee! You're here! Oh, my kitty! Oh, Zanzee, don't let LeRoy hurt you! You must save us!" shouted Jeannie. "*Help us!* I know you can. LeRoy is evil. He is going to kill us!" She watched Zanzee as he jumped onto the rock where Tony was.

Zanzee did not go to Jeannie. He jumped next to Tony and made his statement clear with a loud "Merowwwooooww!"

"Jeannie, come here! I need your help!" Tony yelled at the top of his lungs, trying to be heard over the sound of the gunshots. "Zanzee is pawing at this diagram on this gold page! *Hurry, Jeannie!* LeRoy is getting closer. He is going to kill us. *My God, hurry!*" screamed Tony.

Wizz binng! Wizz binng! Wizz binng!

Danny ducked. Bullets flew over his head. "*He's shooting at us!* Those are bullets ricocheting off the rocks! We need to do something fast! We have less than a minute!" Danny screamed with terror!

Jeannie raced toward Tony.

"*Merrrrooowwww! Merrrrooowwww!*" growled Zanzee.

"*Let me see what he's pawing at!*" she yelled as she ran to him.

Wizz binng! Wizz binng!

She didn't make it to Zanzee. She stumbled and fell helpless to the ground.

Tony hadn't noticed. He was concentrating on the gold tablet Zanzee was telling him about. "Jeannie, what do we do? Zanzee is warning us!"

His head snapped around to find Jeannie. "*Good lord, Jeannie…Get up! What are you doing? I need you!*" Tony screamed even louder.

Jeannie managed to stand up and slowly took a step toward Tony. "Where is it Tony? What's Zanzee pawing at?" she said in a barely audible voice.

Tony pointed at the spot on the gold tablet. "Look at this drawing, Jeannie. Zanzee wants us to look at it. There's a bunch of Spanish on it. We need to figure it out!"

Tony lifted his head to see where LeRoy was. Tony saw him in his truck, not more than five hundred yards from them. Mochcom stopped and got out of his truck. He wanted to make his shots count. LeRoy's nervous hands rested his rifle on the hood again to steady it. He took aim at Danny. Danny was jumping and dodging like the best basketball player of all time—not giving Crazy LeRoy a stationary target.

Tony's heart sank. His best friend was trying desperately to stay out of harm's way, but Mochcom had his eye on Danny, and Tony sensed it. He had no choice but to continue figuring out the mystery as fast as he could. Danny was on his own.

Tony reeled around to look at Jeannie standing next to him. "Jeannie, we have to hurry. LeRoy will be here in a second! He's going to kill us— hurry! What does this Spanish say?"

Tony didn't know what to say or what to do. He was terrified and grasping for straws. "Watch out, Zanzee!" he screamed as he grabbed the tablets and pulled them next to him so Jeannie could get a better look at the drawing. "Here it is, Jeannie! Here it is! Look at what it says, and hurry! LeRoy is going to shoot us! *He's crazy! He's going to kill us!*" Tony kept shouting over and over.

Tony's eyes said it all. He looked at Jeannie and saw that she was pale, almost fainting. She was holding her beloved cat. Her shirt was covered with blood.

"Tony, I'm bleeding. *I've been shot!*" Jeannie cried.

"*My God in heaven, Jeannie!*" he screamed.

Mochcom pulled his rifle back into his truck. He put it in gear and raced the engine. He knew time was not on his side. He suspected the kids might know how to use the gifts from the gods.

His foot slammed on the accelerator, gunning the engine. His eyes were on Tony. His mind exploded. *Damn! They're trying to get the transformer to work. Is it the black-haired boy who is the brains? I'll kill him!*

Danny took advantage of the break once Duncan was in his truck again. He heard Jeannie moaning, and he knew exactly what had happened. He raced to her side. He saw her bloody T-shirt. His heart dropped as if into a bottomless pit.

"Oh no! Jeannie, give me your hand! Let me help you!" Danny grabbed her with his strong grip—her blood splashed onto the gold. "Hold on to me, Jeannie."

She pointed to where Tony was standing. In a whimpering voice, she said, "Danny, I have to help Tony. Hold me tight so I don't fall. I need to look at something. Help me get over to him."

She looked at the Spanish phrase on Kashom's golden tablets, *Mayo dioses estar con usted*, as her mind was engulfed the thought. *I hope Danny and I are TRPOV and TRPON. Oh, I hope the gods are with us!*

"Tony," she whispered faintly. "The Spanish, '*El reloj de oro encuentra la aguja para la llave de oro*,' means 'The golden watch finds the needle for the golden key.' You've already figured this out. It's on your piece of paper... remember. Zanzee is pointing out what Kashom wants us to do. Kashom is telling us to use the settings for the dials that you wrote out on your tablet. It's on the piece of paper you put in your pocket, remember? Do you see what to do?" she moaned.

Tony put his hand on her wound. She was trembling. He saw she was bleeding to death, and time was not on their side. He answered, "Yes, Jeannie."

Danny reeled in horror as Tony took his bloody hand from Jeannie's side. He shrieked in fright. "Tony, do you have the dials set? If you don't get the lead out of your pants and get those things set, we won't be the Pirates in the Desert anymore. Crazy LeRoy's lead will make us all cadavers in the desert."

She sensed the boys were concentrating on her and not on the transformer. "Danny and Tony, I'll be OK. You guys figure out what has to happen," she said in the sweetest voice she could muster. "Tony?" Jeannie reached and touched his hand. "Don't forget to put the brass arrow into the keyhole and turn it. That's part of what needs to happen," she whimpered, her voice growing ever fainter. She watched Tony while at the same time watching Crazy LeRoy getting closer and closer, his rifle hanging out the window. His truck was almost to the base of the hill from which the Boar's Tusk rose. She touched Tony again. "Check the combination code."

The paper in his fingers containing the code of symbols was quivering in rhythm with his trembling hand. In spite of his body shaking uncontrollably, he forced himself to focus. He had to get the code of symbols on the wheels set absolutely perfectly. Carefully, Tony looked at each wheel on the combination lock and made sure the code that unlocked the Sun Energy Transformer was set correctly.

⚡ᚺᚊᚺᚠ✕ᛊ✕ᛌᚠ

"OK, the combination is good," said Tony, using every fiber of his being to concentrate and maintain control.

He then set the five dials that controlled the little shutters over the star points to the exact same positions as indicated on the gold tablet drawing. He put the arrow into the keyhole and turned it. His eyes said it all. They lit up like the giant crystal ball in Times Square on New Year's Eve.

"Look! The little mirror in the middle of this thing just flipped up! Look at this thing! What's going on? Can...can you believe it? Now, what do we do?"

Danny and Jeannie stared in amazement. The handle on the Sun Energy Transformer was glowing as if it were surrounded by the aurora borealis.

"What's going on, Tony?" Danny screamed as they watched Tony. A huge glimmer of hope raced thought Danny's consciousness. His hopes and dreams were still alive. "Look at the brilliant light coming from the middle of the star. It's underneath this mirror that just flipped up," yelled Danny.

Brilliant, bright light, like a bolt of lightning, was shooting out of the middle of the emerald star under the mirror.

"My God, look at that! The light from the star is bouncing off the mirror and going into the end of the purple guide. It's going down the guide and into the green handle," screeched Tony.

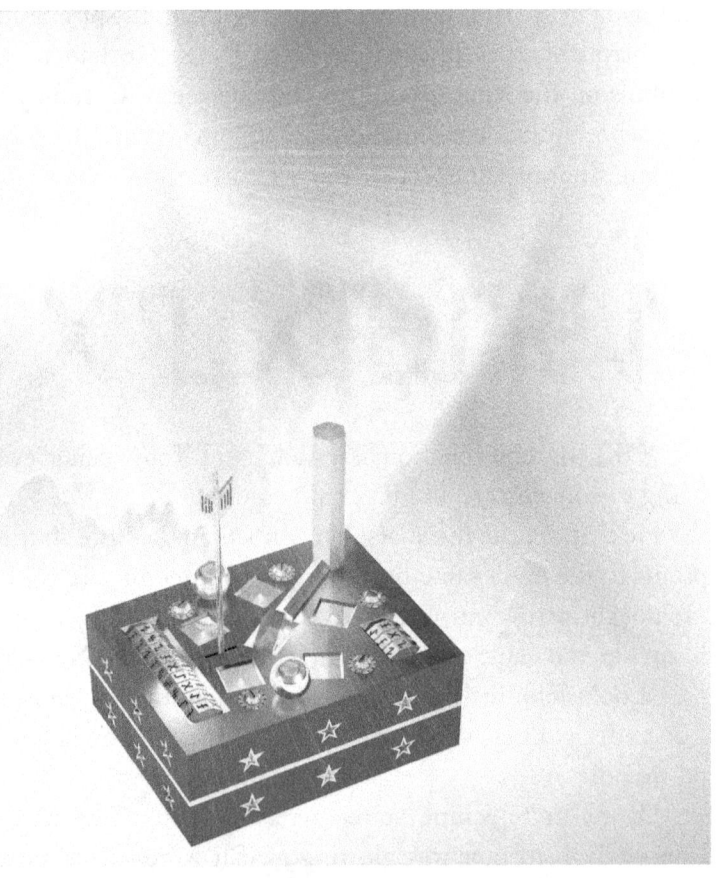

Zanzee's paw lifted and gently touched her face with his soft, fur-lined footpads. He then jumped from Jeannie's arms. He raced to a large sagebrush thirty feet from her.

Her heart sank. "*No! Run, Zanzee!* LeRoy will kill you! *Run and hide!* His vulture will hurt you! Run fast, Zanzee! Run away as fast as you can!"

Jeannie watched her beloved cat run. The anguish in her heart was almost more than she could bear. No one had to tell her the horror and evil that Crazy LeRoy was capable of inflicting. *He's gone. I hope he's safe.* "Good-bye, Zanzee! I love you!" whimpered Jeannie.

Mochcom's truck was fast approaching the base of the Boar's Tusk hill. His watchful eye caught something. "*Damn!* Kashom's cat is here! That damn bird lied to me. He didn't kill Kashom's cat. That black devil is helping them. I'll kill him. I hate that cat!" LeRoy bellowed, watching Zanzee race into the desert.

Tony was shaking. His eyes could not open wider. They reflected the brilliance of the handle. "Guys, look at it! The green handle is glowing. We have no choice but to do what the drawing says to do. Come on, Danny. We need to grab all the boxes and hold on to them. We're going to go on a trip into time."

Danny gently held Jeannie and helped her sit next to Tony. "Jeannie, stay here for a minute. Tony and I will grab the boxes."

Pressing her hand to her wound to slow the bleeding, Jeannie sat motionless on the rock. She was getting weaker by the second. She was overcome with emotion as she watched the emerald-green handle of the transformer glow as if surrounded by all the stars of the Milky Way. *It's a gift from Viracocha!* Her thoughts took her to a new dimension. *We need to follow Kashom's advice. We need to travel the Highway of Time. Where will it take us? Will I get to see Kashom's sister, the one killed by the evil Gorom Mochcom?*

Boxes in hand, Danny and Tony raced back to where Jeannie was sitting next to the transformer. She was alive but still bleeding and losing strength.

"We've got the boxes. Everything else needs to be picked up—grab our canvas bags, everything on the flat rock!" Danny yelled.

Silence fell on the Boar's Tusk. *Oh my God!* Danny thought.

The roaring motor of the 1948 Ford truck went silent. Danny watched Crazy LeRoy Nabal jump out, his gun in hand. He was less than a football field's length from where the teens were standing.

His hand flew up. He motioned to Black Vulture flying overhead. Vulture dipped in flight. He swooped to his master. "*Help me!*" he yelled. Mochcom's arm waved for his disciple to dive. "*Kill her!*" he screamed louder.

He lifted his rifle to his shoulder and aimed the barrel at Danny. "Oh, my little, yellow-haired boy," he mumbled, a contorted grin on his face. "You've been so loudly telling your friends you'll rip my head off. No, no. You'll rip no one's head off—certainly not mine! Mochcom is far wiser than you know. *Now you die*, and I'll have Neferzul all to myself!" he growled as he squeezed the trigger.

Kaboom. The sound engulfed the air at the Boar's Tusk. Danny collapsed to the ground next to his friends.

He felt a burning pain pierce his stomach. Danny grabbed his shirt and felt the hole made by the bullet. His heart jumped. *That crazy old bastard just shot me!*

Jeannie screamed, "*No! No!*" Her entire body was hard as a rock. Her mouth could open no wider as choking sounds tried to make their way out. Her strength was sapped. She had barely had the energy to sit on the sandstone formation. Her eyes reflected the light of the sun, glittering with tears. First they were on Danny, who was lying on the ground, bleeding to death, and then on the approaching crazy man. Horror overcame her. Everything went into slow motion. She could not move. She froze in time. Her mind was engulfed with terror. *What do I do? Danny's dead! We're going to die!*

For a moment, the sun lit her face as the white billowing clouds drifted by. She looked at Tony. Her eyes rolled from LeRoy to the Boar's Tusk. Her thoughts were shooting all over the place. *In the face of sure death, we have no choice except to follow the path set before us by Kashom. We're like the ship on a stormy sea whose course is determined by the violent waters. We must put trust in the builders of the vessel as we travel to an unknown destination. Like the passengers on the ship in a violent storm, our only choice is to have trust in the builders of the ship, that it will bring us to a land of hope. We must navigate through this horror. Will we go to a land of hope?*

Suddenly, she saw it. A brilliant green light was coming from Danny's chest. A glimmer of hope emerged.

Spiraling around Danny in an amazing display, the green light from his ring encircled his body like a coil of fire. Danny's eyes moved away from LeRoy and focused on his shirt. *Why don't I see any blood? Why has the pain gone away? What's going on? I'm not dead, or am I?* Like a phoenix rising from its own ashes, he rose and ran to Jeannie and Tony.

Tony watched Danny. His sprit soared to the height of the sun. *Oh, my great lord in heaven—Danny is on his feet.*

Vulture's dive was like the flight of a deadly homing missile, zeroing in on its target. His black silhouette streaked through the air as he dropped from the sky, wings tightly held against his body. As he neared his prey, his legs moved into attack position. His razor-sharp talons were spread wide, ready for the kill. His target was in sight. He was going for her jugular.

Jeannie turned her face to the sky. Her face was contorted with terror. She watched the black devil of death closing on her, his claws reaching for the kill. "Help me, Danny!" she cried in a faint voice.

His keen ear heard her cries. He leaped in front of her. With his free hand, he grabbed his binoculars, which were hanging from a strap around his neck. His arm swung them like a slingshot. They were on target, and with the force of a rocket, they ripped the bird's head off. Danny's binoculars hit the ground, the lenses smattered with blood.

The twitching body of the headless bird seized Mochcom's attention. Mochcom dropped his rifle to his side and stared in amazement at Danny. *I just shot him. I just shot that yellow-haired, green-eyed boy, and he's not bleeding—he's not dead. How can this be? What's going on? Where did that brilliant green light come from? Who is this kid with the sun-colored yellow hair and emerald-green eyes? Has Viracocha intervened? Could it be? Is he the royal prince of Viracocha? It must be! Who else would it be?*

He railed in fury. "I should have recognized him!" Mochcom hobbled painfully to his bird's bloody body in the sand. He snatched some feathers from it and put them in the side pocket of his filthy coat.

Fear gripped Tony as he watched the crazy man orchestrating his next move. In sheer panic, he screamed, "My God, Danny, do something!"

Mochcom pointed a shaking finger at Jeannie. Erupting again, his voice exploded in anger. "*I'm going to kill you, Neferzul!*"

The ability of the high priest of the royal court of Kopaz to focus and concentrate in moments of panic had served him well over the centuries. His mind shifted into high gear. Mochcom's hand pointed at Tony. One arm outstretched, he lifted his gun with his other hand. Panic jangled through Tony's body. Instantly, Tony dropped to the ground. Looking upward, he caught sight of movement. Danny raced to position himself between Tony and Mochcom. With the security of Danny in front of him, Tony jumped back to his feet. He monitored Mochcom's every move. Tony's mind swirled with questions. *Why has he stopped shooting?*

"It's the black-haired boy I must stop. I can't kill the prince of Viracocha, but I can kill his friend. He's the brains. I must stop him!" Mochcom muttered. "I have two shots left. I'll use them wisely!"

Tony was jumping up and down in panic. "You're alive—thank the god of the rock! Come on, guys. We need the boxes. Grab the boxes, and I'll grab the handle," screamed Tony. "I've got one box. Grab the others."

But at that point, panic also gripped Danny. To grab the boxes, he had to move. If he moved, he couldn't shield both Tony and Jeannie at the same time. The question—*my God, what should I do?*—ripped through Danny's mind.

In a split-second judgment, Danny stared at the Tusk. His mind filled with the image of light flashing through the sky as an atomic explosion spiraled around the Boar's Tusk with rings of fire. The image in his mind was now gloriously brilliant in every detail. To him it was real. The glowing scarlet Tusk was blinding to look at. From the tower of brilliance in his mind, Danny was sure he heard a sharp voice bellowing, "*Use your ring!*"

Ripping his ring from under his shirt, Danny yelled, "Jeannie, can you hold the tin box? It's real light! Take my ring."

"Yes, give it to me," she whimpered in a barely audible voice.

Jeannie held the tin box they had stolen from LeRoy's house—her canvas bag was tied to her waist, her personal items in it. A ring of blazing green light encircled her.

Furious with Danny, Mochcom screamed, "*You'll pay for this. You killed*

Vulture! Your friend is going to die."

The last words Danny had heard Tony's mother say as they ran out the back door—just a few hours ago—echoed through his mind. *Tony and Danny, you're scaring me. For God's sake, son, you're not in danger, are you? I could not go on if I lost you.*

Then Danny's thoughts drifted to his own mom. His heart was pounding. "Mom, I'm so sorry! Forgive me!" he whimpered.

A loud crack of thunder ripped through the air. Tony fell to the ground at Danny's feet. His head rolled in a pool of blood to look at Danny for the last time. With his dying words, he whispered instructions to his best friend. "Grab the green handle. Grab Jeannie's hand." His strength was almost gone. His eyes closed. In the softest of whispers, his last words faded. "Stand on all the boxes of treasures you want to take." Then he was lying lifeless on the ground, and he said nothing more.

Danny's canvas bag with his Pirate Log and a change of clothes hung from his shoulder.

Danny grabbed Jeannie's trembling body firmly. His mind swirled with so many thoughts: thoughts of his mom, thoughts of his dad, thoughts of his true love. *I love you, Mom. Dad, you were right—I'm a dreamer! I've always had my dreams—dreams of finding treasure in the Scarlet Desert!*

His eyes filled with tears. *Will Jeannie, my real treasure, and I die in each other's arms?*

Jeannie watched in horror as the crazy man lifted his rifle to his shoulder and aimed down its barrel. His eyes glared at Jeannie as a smile erupted on his face, lifting the ends of his mustache. The rounded dome of his hat tilted back with the motion of his head as he supported his rifle with one hand, the other on the trigger, ready for the kill.

"You're bleeding to death, my little Neferzul. Your green-eyed friend will not have you long—I will." He chuckled freely. "Yes, my bullet has already found its mark in the heart of the black-haired boy!" And with a howl, he raged on, pointing his finger at Jeannie. "You're next!"

Danny grabbed the green handle. The transformed sun's energy emanating from it traveled down his arm and into Jeannie.

She could not scream any more. Scarlet red blood soaked the T-shirt stretched tightly around her small breasts. She cringed with fright. Her precious life was slowly drifting away, oozing from her body with every drop of blood. She closed her eyes so she could no longer see Mochcom's face. Her mind was no longer on his evil acts. She was preparing herself for death—yet there was a faint glimmer of hope.

My God, are we all going to die—or are we going to Kopaz? Is there hope? Will Kashom find his honor? Will Danny see his dad? Oh, my wonderful Danny, are these our last moments together?

Danny felt her body go limp in his arms. Riveted by the fear of losing Jeannie forever, his heart sank into a bottomless pit of hopeless desperation.

The exuberance on Mochcom's face was almost beyond the brightness of the sun as he squeezed the trigger.

The final sound they heard was the loud crack of a rifle, like the explosion of a cannon in the evening quiet. Then they were gone.

"Damn!" bellowed LeRoy, squinting and staring at the spot where two kids had stood holding hands just seconds earlier. Tony's dead body lay lifeless in a pool of blood on the desert sands. "They have the emerald star and five worox stones—*damn!*" he howled.

It was a gorgeous day, but Mochcom was not impressed by the weather. His eyes were red with unabated violence. He fumed in a fit of explosive anger, "I should have killed the black-haired boy sooner. His freckled, red-headed cheerleader will pay for this!" He rambled on to himself. "I need a new plan—a new disguise. I'll trap her. Someday that yellow-haired boy will come back. I know he will. He'll want revenge."

On that fateful Monday afternoon in the Scarlet Desert, all was quiet at the Boar's Tusk—except for the howling screams of another, younger Black Vulture and the ravings of a crazy man.

As the ranting Mochcom kicked at the headless body of his former servant, feathers flew. He glared at a speck circling above him in the sky. Black Vulture had a son that he had been training, but that training had now been cut short by his dad's death. Despite the timing, it was now time for Black Vulture's offspring to step onto the stage of evil and take the place of his father. "That miserable little bird! Vulture's son is a little monster. Now I have to train the next Black Vulture, that little offspring flying around and howling like a crazed idiot!"

Holding Jeannie tightly in one arm and grasping the green handle with his other hand, Danny felt the bolt of energy from the sun lift them onto a plane of existence he'd never imagined. They were on a journey to the faraway land of Kopaz at a time long ago. For now, they had escaped the deadly hand of Mochcom, but their mystical journey had just begun. Danny's dream had finally turned into a reality. He was leaving CoalVille with his true love, but he wondered what would be waiting for them when they reached their new home. He was now faced with a deathly challenge—keeping Jeannie from drifting down the River Styx to the Land of the Dead.

There could be no denying the gravity of the situation. Jeannie was drifting to the Land of the Dead. She had just completed one mystical journey to the Land of Kopaz, but her journey continued. Mochcom's bullet had found its mark. Danny was helpless. If there were a glimmer of hope, he could not grasp it.

The sun shone brightly on two teenagers who had landed on the banks of the Yellshome River. Its tranquil waters glistened like silver strings on a guitar, just waiting for the artist's hand to make lively music, but they were in a foreign land, and there were no musicians—the only sound was Mother Nature's gentle music.

The priceless treasure of gemstones was no longer transforming the sun's energy, and it rested next to them, its mission complete. Their travels through space and time had ended.

The tall grass was as soft as a bed for the gods, and it was just waiting for visitors from the faraway Scarlet Desert. Danny crouched over Jeannie. It was an emerald-green meadow filled with colorful, long-stemmed flowers. The breeze blowing over the ground sent waves of motion rippling through the flowers. And like the waves on the ocean making their way to sandy beaches, the waves traveling across the grass and flowers ended at the river's bank.

Gurgling sounds coming from the gentle flow of water over the boulders in the river filled the air with a sense of security. The serenading waters were calling Jeannie's spirit to board the boat and travel down the

Styx to the houses of the dead.

In his mind, Danny was certain that he could hear Tony. It was as if his best friend stood next to him screaming, *"Do something, Danny. Jeannie is dying!"* Then, like a figment of his imagination, he heard Tony scream even louder. *"Hurry! Do something!"*

Touching her motionless face with trembling fingers, Danny felt his utter hopelessness hang over him like an oppressive fog in a deathly hollow. His mood was stark and grim. A deafening silence filled the air as Danny looked into Jeannie's eyes. They stared into nowhere with the blank gaze of death. Kneeling over her, he dropped his arms to her sides. His heart pounded, and his intensely strong hands held her with loving tenderness. Her blood-soaked T-shirt stretched around her lifeless body. With a somber expression, he lifted his hand once more to her face and gently touched her cheek in what he imagined was his last gesture of love to her.

Was his mind playing tricks on him? Danny's eyes locked with those of a ghostly image who looked like Tony. It was as clear as if his best buddy were standing there. Fear and panic descending on him, Danny was nevertheless sure he heard Tony's voice rushing from the shadowy figure's mouth. *"Danny, you have the power. Just do it!"*

Although he heard the words, Danny did not comprehend the command echoing through his mind. He screamed in reply, "What? What can I do? Tony, help me!"

Now was not the time for idle chatter. Now was the time for the young god to exercise his power. A thundering voice pierced the very core of his soul. "My prince, use your ring!"

Her body was growing cold. Her color was fading. Her breath was all but gone. It hit him. Danny's judgment was no longer impaired by his desperation. A baseball bat striking his head could not have captured his attention more starkly. Who he was hit him like a lightning bolt. He was a god. He and he alone had the power and the will to save the only treasure in his life that meant anything to him.

Danny's hands tugged on Jeannie's T-shirt, pulling it out of her cutoffs. Gently, he lifted it, exposing her soft white body to the rays of the sun, which sweetly kissed her skin. Crimson-red blood covered her breasts. His concentration was not disrupted by the beauty of her naked body. His mind was focused on saving her from the journey she was about to embark upon, on snatching her from the angel of death that was dragging her to the Styx, where the boatman of the underworld was waiting for her soul to jump aboard.

His hand reached for his ring. For as long as he had worn it around his neck on its gold chain, he had never commanded its powers. In the past, at those special times when its powers had saved the lives of both Tony and Jeannie, Danny had not asked for its help. It had come as a gift. But now, his knowledge of who he was changed his actions, made them more purposeful.

The bullet wound in Jeannie's side was a gaping hole from which her blood still gushed. Time was running out. There could be no uncertainty in his mind. Realizing it was the voice of Viracocha thundering in his mind, Danny wailed, "It is I who must do this alone."

He raised his ring, exposing it to the sun. Looking to the sky, he gave a powerful cry, calling to the supreme god Viracocha. "I'm your royal prince. Before you is the royal princess of Neferdor. My gift from you is the source of power and life that will save her from the grasp of the angel of death. The goddess Neferdor must not relinquish another Neferzul."

His voice bellowing like the roar of a fiery volcano, Danny unleashed his final words. "Let the power of Viracocha save the life of Neferzul! Almighty supreme God, let your power come forth through your royal prince!"

The power of the gods was displayed once more through the might of sun energy. Like the Greek god Zeus holding a lightning bolt, Danny wielded a sword of brilliant green light that came from his ring. It found its mark and penetrated the wound in Jeannie's side.

Her eyes no longer stared into nowhere. They found her treasure—her royal prince. Although, at that moment, she grasped her role as the royal princess of Neferdor in union with the royal price of Viracocha who was standing over her, she could never resist her girlish desire to have fun with Danny. Now, her eyes sparkling with tears of joy, she giggled and said,

"Danny, I didn't tell you it was time to peek!"

Still holding on to the T-shirt that he had lifted from her body, Danny first gave her a quick glance, briefly locking his eyes with hers, and then he looked downward, staring pointedly at her soft white breasts.

She followed his eyes, but before she could say another word, he pulled her shirt down to cover her exposed body. "Jeannie, what am I going to do with you? You scared the living hell out of me!"

That was all she needed. Jeannie seized the opportunity for more fun. "I didn't think they were that scary!" She giggled again. "Danny, how old are we?"

"Seventeen," he replied.

"Well…maybe!" Jeannie shot back.

What? The question raced through Danny's mind. He definitely was not following her conversation.

"Danny, we've traveled the Highway of Time, and guess what?" asked Jeannie with a grin. Danny said nothing, so Jeannie added, still trying to make her point, "We are on the gods' time now, which means that we will be forever seventeen! Do you know what that means, Danny?"

"Nope!" replied Danny. He was obviously lost, but he knew that Jeannie was about to surprise him.

"It is time! Yep, we are going to have some fun!" Her words did not need translating.

Danny's spirit lifted. For the first time is a long while, a smile emerged on his face. He gently picked her up and pulled her warm, soft body next to his. His lips found her ear as he whispered, "My God, Jeannie, I did take a peek! You have the most beautiful body!"

She moved her head to see his face. The mood defined by the few moments of fun now drew to a serious moment.

Although she had a plan in mind—to experience those first treasured moments of first intimate love—she wanted to enjoy the moment and cherish the reality of what had just happened to her and Danny.

At least for Jeannie, the mystery of dying that had gripped the human race with a cloud of secrecy was gone. Her words were waiting to rush out. There could be no more mystiques in the battle against time. Danny and

Jeannie were but two of the myriad of souls that had walked the earth with the fear of the ravages of time slowly tearing away at their bodies.

Looking into the eyes of her partner as a god, Jeannie's mind filled with one thought. *Those simple fears—the fear of death and the fear of what follows death—have forged the dictates of religious zealots on mankind for tens of thousands of years. But for us, those fears have just been blown away. Our journey is leading us to sit at the table with the family of gods that rule the universe.*

He studied her face intently, knowing her mind was exploring the most profound of thoughts.

Like ten thousand years of emotions locked up in the human soul, Jeannie could wait no longer with the words that defined her triumphant victory in the battle against time. "Oh, Danny, it's happened! We're no longer poor kids struggling for an existence in a coal camp. Our battle with time is over." And in the sweetest voice that she could find, she said, "We've found our fountain of youth! Oh, my wonderful Danny, we'll share our lives together…forever young!" Then it dawned on her. There was silence. She looked around. "Danny, is Tony gone?" she whispered.

Danny could not stop his tears. "Jeannie, a monster took my best friend from me." The tears rolling down his cheeks and over his mouth were the outward expression of the devastating feelings that were wrenching his soul. Slowly, he said, "I couldn't save both you and Tony from that monster." Stumbling over his words, he added, "I chose you."

Now with a river of tears flowing from her eyes, her hand gently reached to touch his cheek. She said in a trembling voice, "I'm so sorry, Danny. You did love Tony. He was special in so many ways. Yes, he was a friend to both of us…like no other."

She couldn't stop her fingers from shaking. Searching for consoling words, she sweetly wiped away a tear that had spilled from his eye. "Danny, maybe the gods will step in and help us find our friend in the vast expanse of time."

With a longing look of sadness, he said, "I hope so."

Watch for the next adventure in the Kopaz series:

—Young Gods of Kopaz—

Secrets of the Sun

Dale Groutage

Dale Groutage was born and raised in Reliance, Wyoming, a poverty-stricken coal camp in the state's southwestern desert. His childhood reading

inspired him to pursue a better life, leading to BS, MS, and PhD degrees from the University of Wyoming.

Groutage served as a senior scientist for the US Navy, developing missile guidance and submarine silencing technology. He was inducted into the University of Wyoming Engineering Hall of Fame for his service to his country and honored as one of the top ten engineers in federal government by the National Society of Professional Engineers.

Now retired, Groutage is married with three kids. The former adjunct professor for the University of California and the University of Washington lives in Neenah, Wisconsin.